CW01211126

THE DANCER AND THE MASKS

BOOK ONE - THEIR OBSESSION

BEA PAIGE

Poppy
The Masks love you!
Bea Paige

Copyright ©: Kelly Stock writing as Bea Paige

First Published: 30th August 2021

Publisher: Kelly Stock
Cover by: Moonstruck Cover Designs
Photography by: Talk Nerdy 2 Me
Formatted by: The Nutty Formatter

Kelly Stock writing as Bea Paige to be identified as author of this work has been asserted by her in accordance with sections 77 and 78 of the Copyright, Designs and Patents Act 1988.

All rights reserved. No part of this publication may be reproduced, stored in a retrieval system, copied in any form or by any means, electronic, mechanical, photocopying, recording or otherwise transmitted without written permission from the publisher. You must not circulate this book in any format.

This book is licensed for your personal enjoyment only. This ebook may not be resold or given away to other people. If you would like to share this book with another person, please purchase an additional copy for each recipient. Thank you for respecting the hard work of this author.

FOREWORD

Dear Reader,

This book is dark. If you've read my Finding Their Muse series, I would classify that as grey. Not this book. This book is my darkest romance yet. Leon, Konrad and Jakub are twisted men with a warped view of the world. They're dangerous, cruel, twisted.
They're damaged.
Christy, however, is the definition of strong. She is made of pure steel.
Together they are explosive.
Their story is unlike anything I've written before. It's depraved, perverted and filled with scenes that you may find uncomfortable to read.
Here's a quote that I think sums up the story perfectly:

"Redemption is not just about the survival of our soul. It's about the revival of a soul that was once dead."
~ Rebekah Hallberg.

FOREWORD

Ultimately, this is a love story, but like all my books it will be hard won. You've got to trust me that they will get there. I promise, I won't let you down.

TRIGGER WARNING:

This book contains graphic abuse, dub and non-con, blood and knife play, forced orgasms, and other uncomfortable situations. Please read at your own discretion.

PLAYLIST

If you love a Spotify playlist then you can find The Dancer and The Masks here.

https://open.spotify.com/playlist/0HPqoINcGSVurDI4ck0HaW

"If I am the phantom, it is because man's hatred has made me so. If I am to be saved it is because your love redeems me."
— **Gaston Leroux, The Phantom of the Opera**

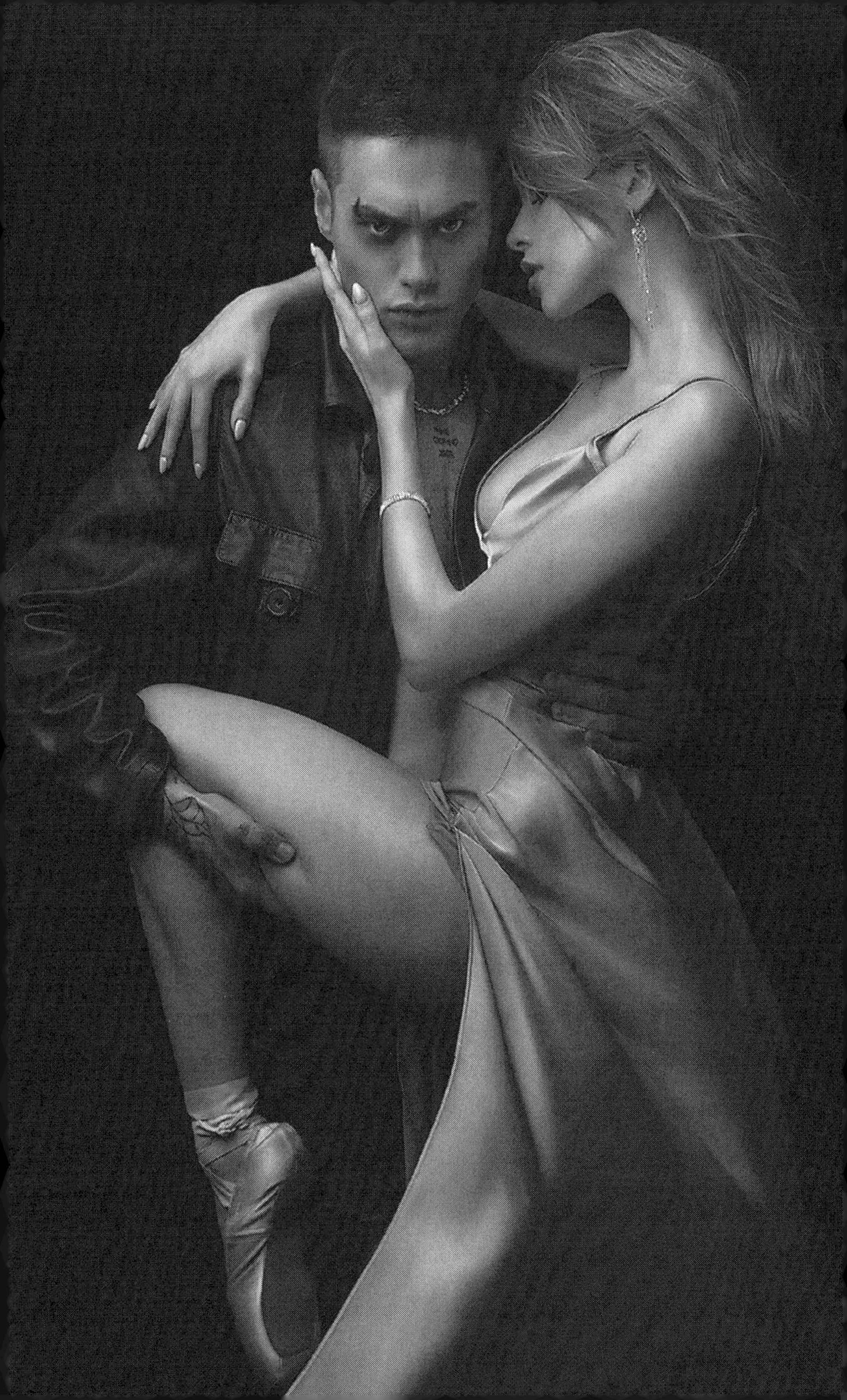

PROLOGUE

JAKUB

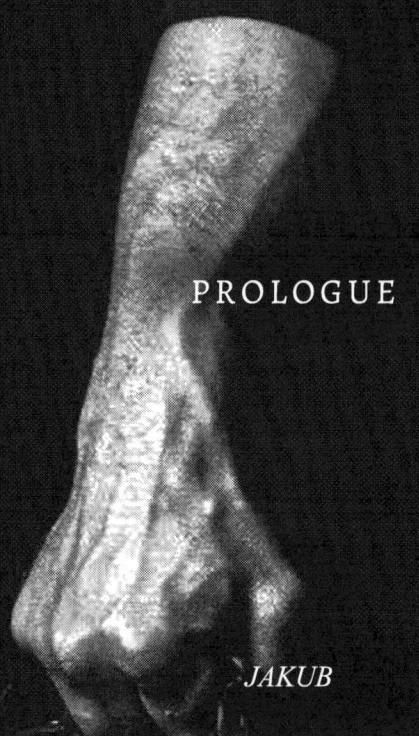

My brother and I watch as Konrad shackles our newest acquisition to the stone wall with chains. Manacles secure her wrists and ankles, spreading her feet and arms wide apart and showing off her perfectly proportioned figure. She's naked and cast in an orange glow from the flaming torches attached to the wall. Yet, despite her ample breasts, small waist, bare pussy, curvaceous hips and long, dark hair, I feel nothing but apathy.

Even her screams bore me.

"Your efforts are a waste of energy, *Twelve*, no one will hear your screams," Konrad reminds her, his middle finger swiping at the tears that cascade from her dark brown eyes and slide over her smooth olive skin. He places the jewelled teardrop in his mouth, tasting her fear.

"Fuck you, *hijo de puta*! My name is Carmen. Car-men! I am not a number!" she screams, yanking at the chains and darkening the bruises around her wrists and ankles further.

"Hush now. Don't make this any harder for yourself," he whispers, his voice a warm caress as he slides his fingers over her collarbone and down the centre of her chest all the way to her bellybutton which he circles lazily with his finger. "Allow yourself to feel the pleasure."

"Touch me again and I'll...!" she warns, hissing between gritted teeth.

"And you'll do what, *Twelve*?" he taunts, baring his teeth in a slow smile and showing a glimpse of the man he could be if pushed too far. He wears his mask with pride, just like Leon and I do. It covers the majority of his face, leaving his mouth, chin, and left eye free. We wear these masks not because we wish to hide our identity at this point, but because they instill a level of fear in our acquisitions. No one leaves the castle once inside of it, no one, but nevertheless the masks we wear remain on our faces. The only time we remove them is in the sanctity of our private rooms.

"Please," she whispers, her instincts kicking in. Her anger subsides, replaced instead with fear and the innate need to please the one man who she believes has the power to free her. Whilst that might be true, and Konrad could very well let her go, he won't, because the man with the ultimate power is *The Collector*, our father, and he wields that over the three of us like an iron fist.

"Giving up so soon?" Konrad taunts.

"You don't have to do this..." Twelve continues, her fire tempered.

She glances at me hoping that I'll step in and stop what's happening. Instead, I watch with detachment. She's just like all the rest, breakable, malleable, and ultimately submissive, though not in a way that gives her power, but in a way that relinquishes it. Eventually all of our acquisitions come to accept their life here, and are comfortable, even. Once they accept their fate, we treat them well. No harm will come to our Numbers from any of the clients we entertain. The last person who tried to fulfil his fantasy on Eight without her permission is now a rotting corpse in the catacombs beneath our home. Leon's wrath that night was exquisite to behold. We protect what belongs to us. Always have. Always will.

"Keep any marks to the bare minimum," I warn Konrad.

Leon smirks. "Let him have his fun. Besides, this one likes it."

Of the three of us, Leon is by far the most dangerous. I've seen what happens when he lets go, and it's not pretty. He may be beautiful, with thick black hair and deep set, pale green eyes but there's nothing *pretty* about him. Like Konrad and me, Leon thrives in the darkness. The masks we wear are more our true faces than the ones we were born with.

"I know the rules, Brother..." Konrad's voice trails off as he strokes the flat of his hand over Twelve's stomach and hips, caressing her gently. She flinches away from his touch, the shackles rattling. "She's exquisite, no?"

"Yes. She'll draw the attention of many of our clients," I agree, adjusting my mask.

"Such a fine specimen," Konrad growls, the low rumble of his voice intoxicating to many.

Yet her appearance, however beautiful, isn't why our father acquired her. No. This woman—who from now on will only be referred to as Twelve—is a soprano. Her voice is enchanting, beautiful, and the real reason why she's here now. Ten women, and one man have come before her. Aside from their beauty, they have one thing in common, they're all artists and they will live the rest of their days in this castle to serve one purpose: to entertain our clients.

"I am *not* a whore!" Twelve screams, visibly shaking as Konrad cups her pussy, telling her without words, that we own her. *All* of her.

She'll be a whore if we ask her to, and she *will* enjoy it.

Eventually.

Her screams die down to whimpers as he coaxes her with his talented hands. Leon and I watch with mild interest as he gently fingers her. For someone with so much brutality inside of him, he certainly knows how to keep it under control when required.

"You're wet," Konrad muses, his thumb slowly circling her clit as he runs the tip of his tongue against her jaw.

"And you're *sick*!"

"Your body doesn't seem to think so," he chuckles, bringing his glistening fingers to his mouth and sucking on them. Twelve's nostrils flare and her cheeks flush as he reaches back between her legs and rubs her clit once again. She hates him, there's no doubt about that.

Regardless, her body reacts to the pleasure he brings her, twisting her up inside, fucking with her head, just like he intended. That's the idea, break them down until they crack, then build them back up with a mixture of fear and pleasure. We train them to respond to both. They've all learnt to heel, craving the attention we give them. Good or bad. So long as they behave, accept their lives here, we give them what they want, what they really, *truly* want.

For Twelve, that's passion, the high of an orgasm, being owned and taken without her permission, punished with a whip or a paddle. She may not like to admit it, but it's the truth nevertheless. It's why Konrad is the perfect man for the job. He studied her for weeks before she arrived, watched her social media posts, delved into her private chats that our hacker, Charles, managed to get hold of. He knows her better than she knows herself. Ultimately, he's giving her what her soul craves. That's the key to what we do.

It's different for each of the Numbers, and the three of us are masters at delving into the deepest parts of their psyches to draw out what makes them tick. To give them their ultimate sin.

We do it with ease, whilst never truly indulging our own wants or desires.

"My father will *kill* you for this!" she hushes out, still fighting, though with less rage and more passion now. The kind she thrives on.

Next to me Leon chuckles darkly. "Should we tell her that it was her father who betrayed her?"

"No. Let Konrad have his fun first. We'll douse the rest of her rage later with that knowledge," I reply.

"She'll be screaming his name and coming before long," Leon remarks, focusing on her peaked nipples. Like pretty little buds, puckered and desperate to be licked.

"No doubt. It's why he's the best man for the job. He knows what she wants. Can sense it. All that emotion has to have an outlet, yes?" I reply, pushing off from the wall. "Come on, our guests will be here in a few hours and with Father away there is much to do."

"I hope she's worth all the trouble," Leon says, referring to the latest girl our father has become obsessed with. It's why he's still in London, instead of entertaining our clients this evening.

"She must be. I haven't seen him this excited since he brought home Six. He thinks this girl will draw in clients from across the world. He even named her."

"He did?" Leon asks, his voice giving away his surprise.

"Yes, he did. *Stopy Płomieniach*."

"Feet of Flames? Fuck, he has got it bad."

"Indeed…"

"What?" Leon asks, resting his hand on my arm and stopping me in my tracks. On the other side of the room Konrad is currently too preoccupied with Twelve to be concerned with our hushed conversation. "Are you worried because he's named her?"

"No," I reply, shaking my head. "She'll become a Number the moment she steps inside these walls, just like all the rest. That's not the issue."

"Then what?"

"Grim has already claimed her. She's not for sale."

"*Grim*? Doesn't she own that fight club, Tales, in London?"

"Yes, she does."

"That's problematic."

"It is. This girl, Penelope Scott, means something to her."

"We both know that won't stop Father from collecting what he wants."

"Precisely. If she's held in such high esteem by someone of Grim's calibre then he'll only want her more. That's part of the excitement for him, he always wants what he can't have. It makes the acquisition all the more sweet once he's able to secure it by whatever means possible."

Leon nods. "So we might have trouble coming our way?"

"Without a doubt."

"Then we'll prepare for the worst, just like we always do," he reassures me.

"Fuck sake!" Konrad growls. "I'm trying to do a job here. Either be quiet and enjoy the show, or fucking leave." He levels his gaze on us both, his hand lazily rubbing between Twelve's legs, his fingers pinching and twisting her nipple, darkening her skin with bruises.

"Konrad. You know the rules. Keep within them," I warn. Again.

Despite the lingering hate in Twelve's eyes, her body reacts to Konrad's skilled fingers. He knows how to play the most difficult of instruments, and it's a skill that we use to our advantage. Sometimes, however, my brothers need to be reminded that the Numbers aren't ours. Never will be. There's only so far we can go with them. He knows it, as do Leon and I.

"What? She likes it," he retorts as her hips grind against his hand, the slickness of her pussy glistening in the firelight. "See?"

"Fuck you!" she bites out, but it has less venom now. More acceptance.

"Regardless. Remember why she's here. She isn't yours."

Konrad smirks, catching my eye before dropping to his knees in front of her glistening cunt. Her hips buck as he presses a gentle kiss against her bare mound, then winks at me. "Stay, you might enjoy it." I shake my head. "You know me better than that."

"I do. Maybe we could keep this one to ourselves," he suggests. "You could do what you want to her without fear of Father's wrath."

"No." The truth is, I don't *want* any of the Numbers. Perfection turns me off. Beauty lies. It hides ugliness beneath a pretty shell. The three of us are the perfect example of such a truth. We three are handsome beneath these masks, but have twisted, black hearts. I don't deny that fact. Never have.

"Leon, are you staying?"

He shakes his head. "Not today, Brother."

"Suit yourself." Konrad shrugs before replacing his fingers with his lips and tongue and eats Twelve out.

She jerks against his face, a cry of pleasure ripping from her mouth, followed by broken sobs that wrack her body. She hates herself for reacting the way she does. Society has conditioned her to believe what she truly wants, *needs*, is wrong. She believes that her body is betraying her spirit, her soul. It isn't. It's showing her the truth.

When she realises that, she'll understand, and she'll never try to leave here. Our castle may have brick walls, and iron bars. It may have an ancient forest surrounding the castle that's so dense, escape is impossible, but contrary to popular belief, it is not a prison. At least not a traditional one. The Numbers stay of their own free will. Well, perhaps with a little coercion in the beginning. A few more weeks of this and she'll be under our spell completely. I already see her fracturing apart. Every orgasm she gives up, another chink in her carefully constructed armor. Eventually it will crumble, and like an addict she will look to Konrad for her next fix. She will chase the high. He will make her believe that he is the only one who can give it to her, and *that* is why she'll stay.

Reaching for the heavy, iron door, I release the latch and pull it towards me. I have no intention of spending any more time in this cold, dark chamber, preferring the darkness to be found in the forest than these cool dungeons Konrad thrives in, or the cold underground lake Leon prefers. Stepping out into the hallway, Leon following close behind, I come face to face with Renard, our elderly butler.

"Sir…" His face is pale, not because of what's happening inside the dungeon behind us—he's immune to such things now—but because something else appears to be troubling him.

"Renard, why are you down here?" My voice is sharp, reacting instinctively to the tension he holds.

"I have some news," he begins, the wrinkles around his eyes deepening as he frowns.

"What is it?" I demand. His gaze flicks to the girl and Konrad before returning back to me. "Speak!"

He swallows hard then nods. "It's your father. He's dead."

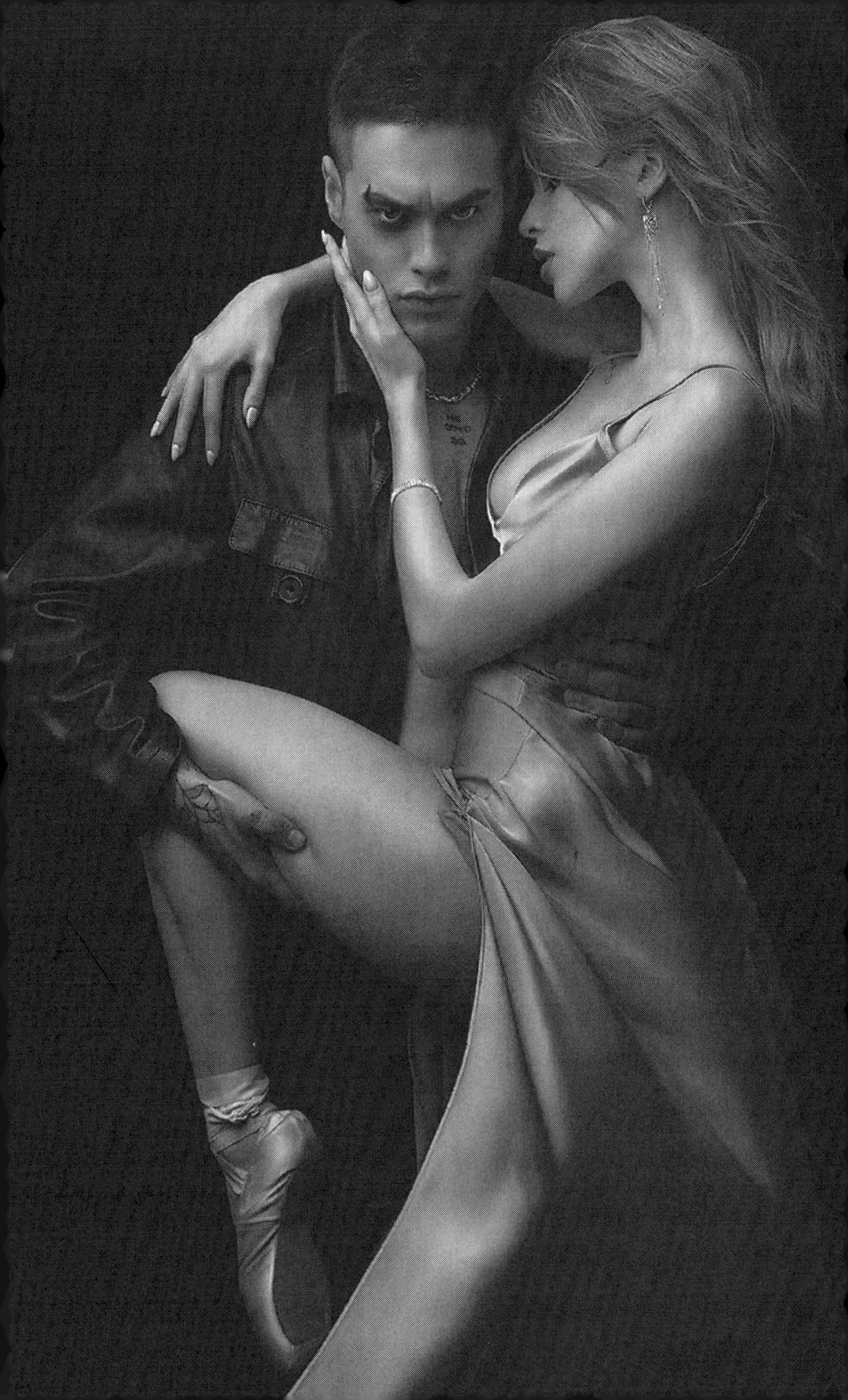

CHAPTER 1

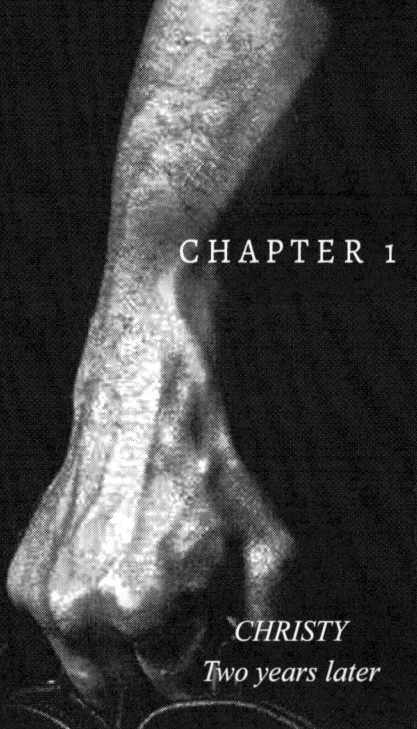

CHRISTY
Two years later

"We don't hide behind the masks. We are The Masks, and we're coming for you..."

Sitting bolt upright in bed, I swipe at the bead of sweat rolling over my cheek that's stained a deep pink by a large port-wine birthmark. My heart thunders violently, my pulse racing as my mind tries to make sense of the vision. I rarely dream. I don't even have nightmares. I *see* things, things that haven't happened yet. Things that will come true. It's both a gift and a curse.

Gritting my jaw against the feeling of dread that's trying its best to incapacitate me, I force my fingers to relax and let go of the duvet. Over the years I've learnt how to control my fear, embrace it even. So that's what I do now. I embrace it. Fear only ever has power if you let it. I refuse. I'm stronger than that. I've had to be.

"Just breathe, Christy. You can't change what's to come, but you can prepare yourself for it," I say, repeating the mantra that I've often told myself over the years. Goosebumps rise on my arms as I force myself to look into the dark corners of my room and calmly assess whether I'm alone or not.

I am.

Tonight isn't the night they'll come for me, but it will be soon. I'm as certain of that as I am of my next breath.

These faceless men, *The Masks*, have visited my dreams on and off for almost two years. I haven't had any visions of them for months and I've managed to lull myself into a false sense of security because of it, convincing myself that they weren't real, that our fates aren't intertwined.

I was wrong.

These men aren't the kind of monsters that live in books and movies, nightmares even. These men are as *real* as I am. Without ever having met them, I already know that they're twisted, perverted, and *dangerous* in ways I don't wish to look too closely at right now.

Blowing out a breath to calm my racing heart, I lean over and reach for my bedside lamp, switching it on. My warmly decorated bedroom is illuminated with a soft white glow, chasing away the darkness and the visions, at least temporarily. For now at least I can function, even if the familiar, yet disturbing voices of the three masked men still linger.

"Who are you?" I whisper as I pull back my sweat-soaked duvet and climb out of bed, my bare feet sinking into the thick, plush carpet. "What do you want from me?"

I don't get an answer. Instead, the ticking of my wall clock fills the silence. It's barely five am. Knowing that sleep will be impossible now, I grab my phone, clothes, and makeup bag and head into my ensuite to shower and change. Stripping, I set the water temperature to cool and step under the spray. Tipping my head back, I allow the water to cascade over my skin, humming gratefully at the feeling. I can't stand any kind of heat on my scarred back. Doctors have said that I've become sensitive to heat, a lingering psychological effect from the burns I endured as a child when my house caught fire and my mother was killed, swallowed up by the licking flames. I may have grown a thick skin on my back, but it's sensitive to the touch. Aside from cool water that eases the phantom pain, the slightest pressure reminds me of everything I've lost.

When I step out of the shower and wrap a towel around myself, I can't help but grit my teeth at the sensation of the soft cotton sliding over my scarred skin. Forcing myself to keep still, I grip the side of the vanity unit and focus on my breathing. With every inhale and exhale of breath I take my mind elsewhere briefly, unhinging myself from sensation, from reality, until the pain disperses. It's a skill I've learnt over the years and enables me to function day-to-day.

Once I'm tethered back in the here and now, I dry myself off, pull on my knickers and get dressed in a pair of faded blue jeans and a grey sweater. I don't own a bra, and have never worn one. The tightness of the straps is one step too far in my ability to ignore the pain successfully.

Brushing a comb through my long, wet hair, I study my reflection. The deep red birthmark covers the majority of my right cheek, my eyelid, and part of my forehead above my eyebrow. Lifting my hand I place it over my birthmark and stare at the unblemished side of my face. Objectively, I can see that side is pretty. In the past, I've felt the attention from others when they've looked at me from this side, only to reel back in horror when I've turned to face them fully. It's why I now choose to cover it up with makeup, not for my own vanity but for everyone else's peace of mind. When I slide my hand across my face to study my birthmark, a familiar feeling of being *different* washes over me.

I have two faces. The one I see when I wake up in the morning, and the one everyone else sees when I wear makeup. One is disfigured, the other… a lie.

The only people who've ever seen the real me are my aunt and uncle who I live with, my half-sister, Kate, and her partner, Roger. Whilst my sister and I share the same father, we couldn't be any more different if we tried. I'm my mother's daughter with flaming red hair and heterochromia. Another abnormality that marks me as different. I have two different coloured eyes. My left eye is a bright blue, my right eye a brown so dark it verges on black.

Kate, however, is raven-haired, unblemished, perfect.

I hadn't even known I'd had a sister until the night I'd dreamt of her when I was twelve. Two weeks later we met at the reading of my father's will, a man I never knew or had even met. Not in real life and not in my dreams, though by all accounts he had known who I was and had kept a close eye on me. I've often wondered why he never came to claim me when my mother had died in the fire when I was eight. It's a question I've never been able to get an answer to. Not even Kate can tell me that.

As my fingertips glide over my birthmark, my palm pressing against the splotch of colour marking half of my face, I feel nothing but abstract acceptance. I've long since distanced myself from my reflection. It's easier that way.

"*Beauty is in the eye of the beholder,*" I say, repeating my mother's words.

She used to say that to me all the time growing up. I'd come home from school heartbroken from the verbal abuse of cruel kids and she would tell me that one day someone would love me for all that I am. I never believed her as a child, and I don't buy into that crap now.

Beauty isn't everything, it fades with time, but there's no denying that it's a currency that has meaning in the world, and something that I've never been rich with. I'm deformed, marked, disfigured, repulsive. I've been called all of those words and more, and whilst they no longer have the power to hurt me, they *have* scarred me. Hating my reflection was something the child I had once been indulged in. I don't hate what I see anymore, after all, it's who I am, but it isn't all of me, just the surface.

Like I said, I've grown a thick skin, both metaphorically and physically, and the very same skin on my back suddenly begins to prickle with *knowing*. I can't describe it any other way. It's another gift, not as powerful as my visions, but a part of me nonetheless. Call it intuition, gut instinct, whatever you like, but I know that any second now my phone is about to ring.

Half a beat later, it does.

Picking up my phone, I press the connect button to answer the video call. "Hey, how's Iris?" I ask as a familiar face appears on the screen. It's not my sister, but her partner Roger, or should I say *Beast*. He's long since dropped his given name, just like my sister did many years ago.

"What the fuck, Christy? Are you doing that witchy shit again? The phone barely even rang," he responds with a chuckle.

I roll my eyes, refusing to acknowledge that he's right, and knowing that despite his teasing, he's wary of my gift. The unexplainable scares most people, including this man who's afraid of very little. "What's up? Where's Kate?"

"Nothing's up, Grim just wanted a chat but Iris isn't settling so she's asked me to call whilst she deals with our little princess first."

"But it's six o'clock in the morning. Isn't that when babies *should* be waking up?" I point out.

"You think?" he says, shaking his head. "Not Iris. We've been up with her all night. None of us have gotten a wink of sleep."

I laugh. "She's going to be so much trouble. You'd better get used to sleepless nights, Roger."

"That's Beast to you, *witch*," he replies with a chuckle, swiping a tattooed hand over his face before grinning at me. "And don't let Grim hear you call her Kate, either. You know she hates it."

"She hates it when *you* call her Kate. Maybe she just doesn't love you as much as you think she does, huh?"

"Now I know you're a fraud. That woman loves me more than life itself."

"Correction, she loves *Iris* more than life itself... She just tolerates you," I retort, laughter in my voice.

"You and I both know that Grim doesn't tolerate anyone," he points out.

"Wait, you're right," I say, tapping my chin thoughtfully. "Didn't she shoot you once?"

Beast grins, his white teeth straight and even. "Yeah, alright. I might have overstepped the mark a little on that occasion..."

"She never did tell me what you did," I muse, narrowing my eyes at him.

His smile fades and he shifts uncomfortably in his seat. "Then it ain't my place to tell. I may just end up dead this time."

"Fair enough. I don't want your death on my conscience."

"Anyway, how're you doing?" he asks me, changing the subject with a wink and a dazzling smile.

Beast might be a huge tattooed man with violent tendencies and a darkness that should never be underestimated, but beneath all of that is a man who is fiercely protective and loving to those he extends his warmth to. He's a good man. I don't need to know what happened between my sister and him to know that. In fact, I was the one who'd convinced Kate to give him a chance after seeing him in one of my visions. When we first met, she hated him. Or at least that's what she'd convinced herself. I knew better.

"I'm fine, but by the looks of it Iris is running rings around you."

"You've no idea," Grim says, joining the conversation as she peers over Beast's shoulder. "Hey, Christy."

"Hey, Kate. Everything okay?" She might look perpetually tired these days, but I see the happiness in her eyes. Motherhood was never in her plan, but she's amazing at it.

"Everything's great," Grim replies, sitting on Beast's lap. She winds her arm around his neck and he folds his thick, tattooed arms around her waist, pulling her closer against his broad chest.

"Yeah, so great that you threatened to cut off my balls if I didn't call Christy even though it's the arse crack of dawn and no one with any sense is awake at this time in the morning," Beast says, yawning.

"*I'm* awake," I point out.

Beast winks. "Exactly. No sense."

"I just had the urge to call my little sister. What's wrong with that?" Grim protests with a shrug of her shoulders, but I see the concern in her eyes. Grim has incredible intuition, which she refuses to acknowledge. I'm pretty sure her intuition has saved her countless times over the years, especially in her line of work. As one of the most respected gangsters in all of London, she's had to trust her intuition, or gut instinct, as she prefers to call it.

"That's called *worry*. Grim wants to mother everyone these days," Beast explains.

She clicks her tongue, lifting off of Beast's lap and grabbing the phone, moving away from him. "Why don't you go and make yourself useful, Beast, and put on some coffee, I'm barely hanging on here," she says over her shoulder.

"Fine, fine, I know when I'm not wanted. Catch you later, *witch*," Beast says, appearing back on the screen. He gives me a small wave before planting a kiss on Grim's cheek.

"Don't mind him. He's cranky lately. No sex for a week can do that to you," Grim says with a wry grin as he leaves the room.

"He's cranky because he hasn't had sex in a *week*?" I laugh at that. "How about never having sex. You're talking to the oldest virgin on Earth right now."

"Twenty-three is hardly old."

"Maybe so, but it's not as if I'm going to be getting any. Have you seen my face?"

Grim scowls. "Don't do that. Don't put yourself down. You're perfectly you, Christy."

I snort. "I wasn't putting myself down, just stating a fact. It is what it is. I'll just have to marry my vibrator."

"Want to know what I think?" she asks, looking at me intently through the screen.

"Sure, why not? But if you're about to say *beauty is in the eye of the beholder* to try and make me feel better, I might hang up."

"I wasn't going to. We both know that beauty holds value in this fucked-up world we live in. There's no getting away from that fact. But do you know what else has value? Strength. Courage. A sense of self-worth. The ability to dance as beautifully as you do. Not to mention the ability to see into the future. You're the real deal, Christy. The *whole package*, even if you can't see that right now."

The sudden sound of Iris crying filters through the screen, followed by Beast shouting that he's going to handle it. "Teething..." she explains with a sigh.

"That bad, huh?" I ask, glad of the change in subject. I start applying foundation to my skin as we talk. Slowly my birthmark disappears beneath the creamy liquid, and before me, the person that I truly am disappears. I become acceptable to look at even if it is a falsity.

"I'm telling you, gangsters haven't got shit on a thirteen month-old baby. Most days I can barely function. She's a menace."

"That's why you love her though, right?"

"I love her so much it scares me," Grim responds with a smile in her voice and love in her eyes, but there's fear too. She might be able to hide that from most people, but not me.

"That little girl will live a long, happy life. I can *promise* you that," I say, knowing it to be true.

"Christy," Grim warns. "You know how I feel about this."

"I get it. You don't want to know if I see any of you in my visions. It's just…" Sighing, I blow out a breath. "It's just, you're always so worried about Iris and something terrible happening to her that you're making yourself ill. You might be able to put up a front for those who don't know you well enough. But I see you, Kate."

"Doesn't every mother do the same thing: worry? That's what we do, right?"

"Yes, they do. But not every mother is a gangster with as many enemies as she has friends. I get it."

"Still…" she hesitates, but despite her reservations I know she needs to hear me say the words.

"Iris will have her personal battles like the rest of us, but I've only ever seen *good* things for her."

"Just because you haven't seen bad things doesn't mean that they won't happen though," she counters.

"I agree, and as much as you might wish it to be true for Iris, no one goes through life without pain and hardship. We both know that better than anyone."

"I'm not sure I feel any better. I don't want her to go through *anything* painful. Not ever."

"She has you and Beast, Kate. She also has an extended family that loves her and will protect her just as fiercely. There was a reason why

Pen and the Breakers came into your life. They're not just friends, but I don't need to tell you that because you know it already, right?"

"They're family," she adds thoughtfully. "I'm sorry you haven't had a chance to meet them yet. I've been meaning to bring you down to London for some time now. It would be good for you to get out of Wales for a bit. You'd get on really well. Like you, Pen is a gifted dancer and her guys aren't too bad either."

"Sure, that'd be nice," I reply, the tone of my voice noncommittal. My voice trails off as I'm reminded of my vision. It's not that I don't want to meet Pen and the Breakers, it's just that I know they're not in my immediate future. I see nothing but The Masks, and even though I don't see much else, I do know that it is just *them*. We have an undefinable future together. Right now, I have no idea about my part in it, but I am in it.

"They're good people. I want you to be friends. Besides, I don't fancy another four hour journey with Iris screaming her head off and Beast driving like a maniac. I swear, I almost shoved him off the Prince of Wales Bridge when we visited you last, he pissed me off that much."

I laugh. "You two are so in love it's ridiculous."

"Yeah, he'll do." Her cheeks tinge pink and I catch a glimpse of the girl she must've been before she was thrown into a lifestyle that has made her toughen up. For a while, Grim is silent on the other end of the line. She watches me as I continue to apply makeup. I slick on some lip gloss and mascara, and wait.

"Christy, I'm calling because…" She frowns, chewing on her lip. "Have you…"

I know what she's about to ask, but after her initial reaction to me telling her about my visions of The Masks, I've never brought the subject up again. The last time we spoke about them was just before Iris was born. She flipped out when I described the men, so I know she's hiding something big from me. I believe she knows them and isn't saying how or why to protect me. It doesn't matter either way, she can't change what's going to happen any more than I can. So, I lie.

I lie to ease her worries, and to hide from my own.

"No, I haven't. Everything's good here. Sometimes I get things wrong."

"Yeah and I'm the Queen of England," she retorts with a snort. "You don't need to protect me."

"I know that, and I'm not."

"Okay," she says after a while, scrutinising my face. "But if you're lying to me, Christy..." Her voice darkens and I hear the formidable woman that she is in those few words. Motherhood hasn't softened her in the least, if anything it's made her stronger, *more* fierce.

"Yeah, I know. I love you, Kate."

"I love you too, Christy, but please call me Grim."

"You'll always be Kate to me, *Grim*," I reply, a smile in my voice.

"And you'll always be my little sister. I protect the ones I love, no matter what. Do you hear me?"

"I hear you."

"Good. I'll call back soon, arrange some dates for you to come visit, okay?"

"Okay," I agree.

With that she hangs up, and I'm left with a feeling of foreboding that scares me far more than my visions ever have.

CHAPTER 2

CHRISTY

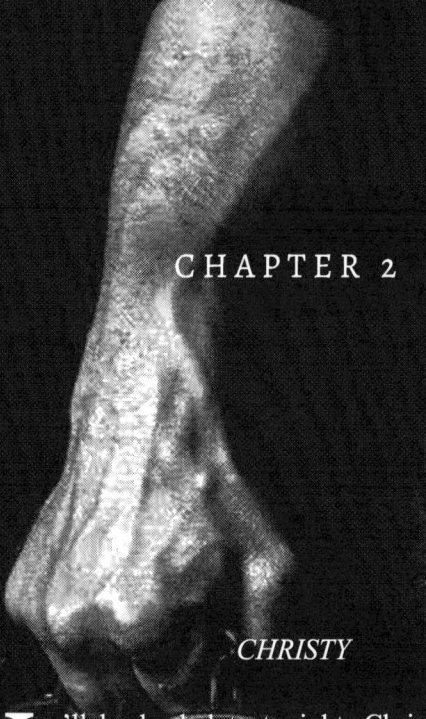

"We'll be back late tonight, Christy. Don't wait up," my aunt says a few days later as I sit at the kitchen table. She wraps her arms around me and presses a kiss to my cheek, her signature scent of Coco Chanel washing over me. "You look pretty, are you going out too?"

I shake my head, unravelling from her hold and avoiding eye contact with her, as I grab my empty dishes from the table and place them in the sink. I'm afraid if she looks too closely she'll see the truth I'm trying to hide, that I won't be here when they get home. "No, I was just experimenting with some new makeup. This foundation has better coverage. I'm actually planning on having an early night."

"You should go out more often. Be social, make friends. A wonderful woman like you shouldn't hide themself away."

"I'm not hiding. I go to work," I reply, plastering a smile on my face before turning back around to face her.

"That's true, and whilst it's wonderful you've found a great job at the hospice, that isn't what I meant. You need to be around people your own age instead of us old timers and those poor people waiting to die."

"I dance. I read. I'm happy, Sandy. Honestly."

"You dance in the studio Frank built you at the bottom of the garden rather than go to the one in town where you could meet like-minded people. You live vicariously through those books you read. You spend your days with the sick and dying, forming relationships with people who have little time left in this world. You're avoiding *life*."

"No, I'm not. I'm happy, and I just haven't found anyone I click with all that well."

She frowns, worry creasing her brow. "You won't find anyone to click with if you don't actually socialise more. You need to get out there, Christy."

"I *do* leave the house. I'm going to work every day."

"Christy—"

She's about to push the point further, but I shake my head. "Let's not get into a discussion about this tonight. I want you to stop worrying about me. Whatever happens to me in the future is my concern. I love that you care, I really do, but things are different for me. You know that as well as I do..."

My voice trails off as I reel myself in. I'm not just talking about my birthmark and the scars on my back, I'm talking about my ability to see into the future. All day long I've been debating whether to say something to her, knowing that tonight is the night The Masks will come for me, and every time I come close I shut the thought down because I know, like Grim, she would somehow try to change the course of fate and put herself in danger.

"Okay, I'll back off, but I do believe that there is someone out there for you, Christy. How could there not be?"

I give her a smile, hiding my feelings beneath the mask I wear daily. "Actually, I have it on good authority that Henry Cavill is going to be my future husband," I joke, trying to lighten the mood.

My aunt claps her hands together, her face lighting up with glee. "Oh, really? How wonderful! Do I know him? I don't recognise the name."

"Oh my God. I was joking, Henry Cavill is a *movie* star."

Sandy chuckles. "Don't joke, you know I'm getting old and my poor heart can't take it."

"I'm sorry," I reply, meaning it. I'm sorry for lying to her, for what's about to happen and all the worry it will cause.

"Frank and I have been looking forward to this evening for such a long time," she continues on, waving away my apology, oblivious to the internal war raging within me.

"You and Frank deserve a night out," I say, feeling a rush of love for this woman who's been like a mother to me ever since she took me in after the fire, nursing me back to health both physically and emotionally.

"Thank you, darling. Now, tell me the truth. Do you *really* think I look okay? It's been a while since I've worn a dress this short. I could change." She smooths her hands over her purple chiffon dress that floats gently around her knees.

"Seriously, you look beautiful. You'll have all the men at Frank's golf club wanting a dance with you."

"Not a chance," Uncle Frank says, stepping into the kitchen in his black suit and shiny black shoes. At sixty-five, he's a handsome man with salt and pepper hair and bright blue eyes that twinkle with mischief. He winks at me, straightening his tie as he enters. "I'm not sharing Sandy with any-damn-one. She's *my* lady."

"Stop it, Frank. You're making me blush," my aunt replies, her cheeks pinking up as he strides over to her and pulls her in for a hug. They hold onto one another, their love warm and affectionate. Since I came to live with them I don't think I've ever heard them argue, not once, and as I watch them hug, the ache in my heart grows with every passing second. By the time they pull apart, I've got my emotions under control enough to say goodbye.

"Have a wonderful time tonight," I say, hugging Frank a little tighter than normal and planting a kiss on his smoothly shaven cheek.

"We will, Christy," he replies, before stepping aside so Sandy can give me a hug too. I wrap my arms around her slim frame, breathing in her familiar scent and committing it to memory.

"I love you," I whisper.

Sandy pulls back, her hands cupping my upper arms as she stares at me. "Christy, is everything okay?" she questions. "We don't have to go tonight."

I shake my head, refusing to crumble. "I'm absolutely fine, nothing that a Netflix binge and a bag of popcorn won't fix..." My voice trails off as she stares at me, hesitating. "I'm on my period," I lie, needing to give her something to explain my behaviour. Fortunately for us both, she believes me.

"Ah, I see. Then you'll be wanting that extra special bar of chocolate that I keep for such occasions, yes?" she asks, lowering her voice conspiratorially.

Frank's eyes light up. "Did you just say chocolate?"

"No, Frank. No, I didn't."

He narrows his eyes at her, then flicks his gaze to me. I just shrug, knowing all too well he has a chocolate addiction to rival all others. "Hmm..."

"Come on, old man. Let's get going," Sandy says, taking his hand and pulling him towards the back door, before stepping out into the night.

"I'm going to miss you," I say, watching them leave, my words snatched by the breeze and dispersed before even reaching their ears.

∾

THE CLOCK in my bedroom strikes midnight, and I can't help but shake my head at the irony. This isn't the start of a fairy tale, at least not the romantic ones Grim liked to read to me as a kid. Since she found out about me, she would call me at bedtime from her home in London and read me all her favourite fairy tales. I think, for her, they were a way to escape the environment she lived in. Those stories gave her respite and they helped our bond grow into something strong and unbreakable.

The thing is, whilst Grim's very own fairy tale may have worked out in the end, I'm not so hopeful about mine. I don't see love and happiness in my future, just darkness.

Just *them*.

Drawing my legs up, I wrap my arms around my shins, hugging myself. The skin on my back prickles uncomfortably.

They're close.

Minutes tick by, time stretching on endlessly as I wait for The Masks to break into my home. I flinch at every sound, on edge. Waiting.

It's agonising knowing your own fate. With every passing second, my courage wanes and my need to run from my future begins to take hold. Fight or flight is a natural instinct, and neither was an option I believed I had until right this second. I've always assumed that everyone's future is written, and for some reason I just happen to be one of those people who's able to read what no one else could. But what if I was given this ability so that I *can* change the course of my future? What if I've misunderstood my gift all this time?

I *could* still run.

I may only have a few minutes, but that might be all I need. I have a car. I can drive away from here. Spurned into action, I leap off my bed and pull on my trainers, momentarily rocked by a sudden wave of dizziness that almost brings me to my knees. Grabbing hold of my chest-of-drawers, I blink back the black spots dotting my vision and breathe in heavily through my nose. *Weird.* I've never suffered from fainting spells or anything like that before. Perhaps it's the stress and sudden rush of adrenaline at my decision. Regardless, the second my dizzy spell passes I grab my mobile phone, car keys and wallet, and stuff them into the pocket of my hoodie, grateful that I chose to remain fully dressed. I didn't even remove my makeup. Subconsciously or not, I didn't want them to see me at my most vulnerable. Besides, there was no way I was going to be half naked when they took me.

With adrenaline pumping in my veins I pull open my bedroom door and step into the darkened hallway. My heart thumps wildly in my chest as I creep towards the kitchen and my car parked in the driveway beyond. I try to make as little noise as possible, already fearful that they're in the house.

With every step I take towards escape, the skin on my back tightens, the painful memory of the night I nearly lost my life to the fire, returning. Ignoring the memory and the sense of foreboding, I focus on pushing open the door only to come to a complete standstill the second I step into the kitchen.

No. This isn't happening.

I look at my aunt and uncle sitting at the table with abject terror. They can't be here. They *shouldn't* be here.

"What are you doing home?" I ask, the words tumbling out the moment my shock subsides.

"Interesting..." my aunt says, cocking her head to the side as she regards me with a cold, absent gaze.

"Interesting?" I question, my throat tightening. "What do you mean by that?"

"You'll find out soon enough," she answers, avoiding my question altogether.

There isn't any warmth in her voice, and none of the love that usually emanates from her. Swallowing hard, I look from my aunt to my uncle sitting opposite. His attention is drawn towards the back door that's flung open. He ignores me, completely oblivious to my presence. Outside rain lashes down, and a rumble of thunder cracks overhead, making me jump.

"Sandy...? Frank...?" My voice cracks, the skin on my back prickles. Something isn't right. This feels *wrong*. Yet, despite every instinct telling me to turn around and run, my feet have a mind of their own and I step further into the kitchen.

"You're not what I was expecting," my aunt continues, her gaze trailing over me. She looks at me as though I'm a stranger, as though we haven't spent the last fifteen years living together, that she hasn't held me when I've cried, or made me laugh until my stomach hurt.

"Sandy, what's going on...?"

She cocks her head to the side, scrutinising me in a way that makes the hair on the back of my neck stand up. She doesn't answer. Instead, a slow smile pulls up her lips, contorting her face, twisting it into something else, into *someone* else. Her brown eyes turn green. Her body stretches and pulls into someone much taller, broader, until she becomes...

A man in a black mask.

The Masks, they're *here*.

My stomach bottoms out, sickness rolling through me. Stumbling, my eyes slam shut as I reach for the counter, but all I feel is air as I fall sideways. Gritting my teeth, I wait for the impact, my arms suddenly useless. Instead, I'm supported by the man whose eyes are green like crisp, frosted grass in winter.

Sharp, cold, unemotional.

He pushes against my shoulders, forcing me flat on my back as my surroundings morph, the kitchen cabinets melting just like the clock face in Salvador Dali's painting, becoming a puddle of colour that turns murky, black. I blink back the fog, fighting the heaviness I feel in my limbs as a small white light floats above his head, helping me to see what truly is in front of me.

"You can't escape us," he says, his lips plump, surrounded by a dark stubble. The mask he wears covers the top half of his face, revealing his mouth and chin, giving me a glimpse of the man beneath. Drawing back, he moves away and my vision blurs, fading in and out.

"No!" I groan, understanding now that it wasn't my aunt or uncle that I saw, but a mirage, something I'd conjured up between dream and reality to help me to cope with the trauma.

I've been drugged.

I was too late to run.

I'm already theirs.

"Yes," the man counters, laughing now.

My uncle joins in with him. Only it isn't my uncle's face I see anymore but another black mask, two cool blue eyes staring back at me. "You're *here*," I say, trying and failing to move my body. I can barely lift my head, but that doesn't stop me from trying.

"If by here you mean in your home, I can tell you that we are a long way from there now."

"Please," I beg, uncertain of what I'm begging for, but unable to help myself. All thoughts of accepting my fate are replaced with the stark reality of my situation. I knew this day would come, yet now that it's here I can't help but feel afraid.

"She's becoming more lucid," the man, who's no longer my uncle, states. His voice is thick and syrupy like molasses. "You're stronger than you seem."

One minute he's sitting over me, the next kneeling by my side. My heart beats in my throat as I read his intention. "Don't," I warn, knowing I'm nothing but a lamb ready to be offered up for slaughter.

His glacier eyes glitter dangerously. "Is that a challenge?"

"We're almost there, Konrad. Give her another dose. It will tide her over until we're home. *Then* you can indulge," another voice, different from the other two, says. There's a melodious note to his voice, and a foreign edge, making it difficult to place his accent. I can only hear him. He's nearby, but not close enough for me to see.

"Stay away from me!" I grind out, panic sliding like acid through my veins. But the man I now know as Konrad ignores me, and reaches for something tucked inside his jacket pocket. It doesn't take a genius to work out what he's reaching for, and what he intends to do, *again*.

"I'm afraid we can't do that, *Zero*," he says, leaning closer.

Zero? He says that as though it's my name. Maybe I misheard, maybe this is all part of the strange in-between place I'm in right now, my mind conjuring up realities to help me to cope with this living nightmare.

"You don't like your new name? I thought it was apt," he says, noting the confusion in my eyes and choosing to add insult to injury. He pulls his hand back from his pocket, deciding that he'd rather torture me with words than knock me out again.

"My name is Christy, my sister is *Grim*. Do you know who you're fucking with?" I ask, pouring as much strength into my trembling voice as possible. I've never, not once, used my sister's name to warn people off me. I've always fought my own battles, never claiming power from a family line, until now. With his hand cupping my cheek and the pad of his thumb brushing over my bottom lip, he slowly lowers his face towards mine.

"We know exactly who your sister is. Unfortunately for you, we also know how much you mean to her. She hid you well. Just not well enough."

THE DANCER AND THE MASKS

"She'll *kill* you all," I say, knowing it to be true, my heart breaking because of it. She has enough blood on her hands. Too much. She pretends like that doesn't matter to her, but I *know* it does.

"She'll *die* trying," he counters, saying out loud what I've known all along. It's why I never told her about my visions after that first time. I knew how Kate would react. What she'd try to do. What she'll *still* try to do. The second she finds out I'm gone, she'll drop everything to hunt these men down.

"No! Leave her out of this. I won't fight you. I'll do what you want."

"It doesn't matter whether you come willingly or not. You were always going to be ours the moment she ordered Beast to kill our father over that girl," a detached voice, belonging to the third Mask I've yet to be introduced to, says.

"What girl? Why would Beast kill your father?" My questions tumble out of my mouth in a stream of badly strung-together sounds as I try to look behind me.

"The details aren't important. What's important is that from this moment on you will pay for your sister's actions," Konrad says, drawing my attention back to him.

"They *will* come for me..." I say.

"We're not afraid of your sister or her lover. Let them come," the Mask with the green eyes retorts with a smirk.

"W—we can work something out," I say, trying a different approach.

"There will be no negotiations. You're *ours* now. Get used to it," Konrad retorts, swiping his tongue over his lower lip in a way that tells me exactly what being *theirs* means.

"I know that. I've known that for some time," I mutter, managing to lift my arm a few inches, only for it to drop back down.

Konrad looks at me then back to green eyes. "Did you hear that, Leon?"

"It's the drug. She was calling me Sandy a moment ago. Give her another dose. We've still got a couple of hours to go."

"No!" I blurt out, knowing I'd rather be awake than asleep right now.

"But she's entertaining..." Konrad muses, watching me closely.

Words fail to form, fear nips at my ability to remain calm. I *need* to remain calm. Pressing my palms against the floor, I feel cool metal. It grounds me somehow. The sensation anchors me in the moment, enabling me to focus on reality. I look past Konrad, focusing on the wall and ceiling behind and above him. I soon realise that it isn't a wall, but more metal. My drugged-up brain tries to make sense of where I am, as slowly more sounds filter in. Familiar sounds.

We're in a vehicle. *Moving.*

It's a van, judging by the size, and it jerks suddenly, lifting my body off the floor an inch before slamming me back down. I vaguely wonder why I'm not screaming in pain, then I remember I've been drugged. I'm numb, and the phantom pain I live with every second of every day is not affecting me right now. Small mercies, I guess.

Leon bashes his fist against the wall. "Slow the fuck down, Jakub. The last thing we need is the police pulling us over."

"Talk to me like that again, *Brother,* and I'll make sure that you never get to unleash yourself on her," he retorts.

Jakub.

So that's his name, the one who's driving.

"Do you hear me, Leon? Never," Jakub repeats, his voice menacing in a way that makes my heart leap in fear and my throat constrict, not because of what he's just said but because I realise that it's *his* voice I recognise. The voice that I've always heard in my visions. *Jakub* is The Mask who always spoke to me. The other two remained mute, until now.

"*Never?*" Leon barks out a dismissive laugh, but there's a flicker of something in his gaze as he glances at me. Something I can't untangle. Could it be regret for speaking out of turn or anger for being called out for it? I'm not sure, I'm too bound up in my own fear to care. Right now, I don't want to know about how they fit together or the hierarchy of their twisted trio. My short term goal is to stay conscious.

Digging deep, I focus on my surroundings, concentrating on the here and now, refusing to fall back into that weird dream state where nothing is real and bad people are camouflaged by good people. The more lucid I become, the more I should be able to move my body. Forcing all fear out of my mind, I look at the two men as they talk in hushed words beside me. I grit my teeth, and with every passing second my motor functions return. With superhuman effort, I manage to lift my arm and grasp Konrad's ankle, squeezing tight.

"What the fu—"

His head snaps back around as he looks at my hand clutching his ankle. Leaning over, he unhooks my fingers, plucking them free like petals from a flower. His penetrating blue eyes cut through my precarious bravery, and every second he holds my gaze I feel it waning.

"Don't touch me. There are *rules*," he warns, shifting his position so that he's back to kneeling beside me once more.

"Rules?" I shake my head, my body spasming as sensation returns. My body doesn't feel like my own, and I try desperately to regain control over it.

"Yes, rules that you *will* obey," he continues.

"Never," I snap.

Behind Konrad, Leon scoffs. "Your fight is admirable, but it won't save you, it will only make this all the more delicious."

His full, plump lips part, a slow smile dragging across his face. I watch him, unable to tear my eyes away. He seems feral somehow, like there's an animal lurking just beneath the thin surface of his composure.

"Indeed, Brother," Konrad agrees, cocking his head to the side.

He rests his hand against my stomach, watching me. I feel the warmth from his palm despite the lack of any kind of empathy in his gaze. Trapped in the sheer dominance of his actions, I remain mute, the word *obey* rattling around my mind like a pinball in an arcade game. Time slows as his hand lowers, his fingers brushing over my hip bone, edging towards the place touched by no man before him.

"No!" I shout, feeling a sudden rush of anger, of disbelief. *This* is what they have in mind for me. "Don't!"

My kidnapper's hand stills, his fingertip resting lightly against the seam of my jeans that runs between my legs. "Don't?" He licks his bottom lip as he adds more pressure against my clit, a crooked smile growing across his face. I don't need to see all his features to know he's beautiful beneath that mask, externally at least.

"You have no right," I add, forcing myself to sound strong when everything else feels weak. He rubs me slowly, gently, *expertly*. His touch should have me screaming with disgust, and yet I remain impassive, shocked into submission.

"I have every right to do whatever the hell I want to you, Zero, same as my brothers. I can touch you, taste you, fuck you, *punish* you. You. Are. Ours. You belong to The Masks."

I flinch internally at every word, at the ferocity of his belief. The ownership.

I'm theirs. I belong to them. Something flares inside my chest. Something that makes no sense given the circumstances.

It *shocks* me.

Everything about this situation is wrong, and yet... Even though Konrad's touch is unwanted, uninvited, something disquieting happens as he adds more pressure. My clit *pulses*. It comes alive. For the briefest of moments, pleasure teases my senses. The feeling is fleeting, short-lived, but it cuts deeper than I ever expected it could. It *hurts*. Enjoyment has no place in this situation. None.

"No!" I shout, more to myself and the feeling that his surprisingly gentle touch invokes. It forces more tears to the surface but I blink them away, rationalising that my reaction to his touch is an unwanted effect of the drug they've immobilised me with and nothing more.

"I'm not a fan of that word, Zero. It upsets me, and you really don't want to see me upset."

I swallow hard, my gaze flicking to Leon. Is he okay with this too? Can he truly allow this to happen?

"You're seeking help from *me*?" he asks, amusement in his tone whilst shaking his head.

"You're beyond help now. Take what we give, and you'll survive.

Fight it, and you'll perish..." Konrad says, pressing his finger harder against my clit, adding pressure to the throb that's building.

"Perishing sounds delicious. *Fight* us. Do it!" Leon goads.

His taunt slashes at the tantalizing pleasure my body refuses to ignore and hurtles me into despair. These men are kidnappers, monsters, deviants. Yet my body acts instinctively, confused by the drug, this new sensation, and being touched so intimately. Konrad increases the pressure all the while watching me, drinking in my reaction, my turmoil. Getting off on it.

Stop!

The command remains trapped in my head as I war with myself. Turning my face away, I refuse to look at him. He doesn't stop. He continues to rub me over my jeans, another finger adding to the first, the seam of my jeans tight between my crotch. With his other hand he grasps my chin, forcing me to look at him. He's trying to read me, trying to see into my thoughts, to peel back the layers. But I'm not so easily read. Years of hiding who I really am protects me from such intrusion.

"So beautiful. Your hair is like flaming torches," he murmurs, eyes laced with lust. "Your eyes are unusual too. I've never seen it before. One is as blue as a meadow filled with cornflowers, the other rivalling the darkness of the dungeons beneath the castle we live in. I wonder, do they reflect who you are?"

I might have been mildly impressed with his almost poetic words had it not been for the description of his home. Dungeons and castles, flaming torches. It all sounds so... medieval. Panic rises, and as I blink back the terror, I notice my reflection in the widened pupils of his eyes. Fear is the first thing I see, followed by the mask I'm still wearing. At that moment something fundamental dawns on me. He *can't* see my true face.

I never removed my makeup before I fell asleep. It remains intact, hiding the reality of who I am. Right now these men see the lie, and for the first time in my life that thought gives me *strength*, not abstract sadness. I can be someone else too. I can find strength beneath my own mask. I can be whoever I need to be to survive. So long as they never truly see who I am, they can never have power over me. I can be a force to be reckoned with, just like my sister.

"Get your motherfucking hands off of me!" I growl, funneling Kate's spirit. No, funnelling *Grim's* spirit. The sound is so feral that I don't even recognise my own voice. Konrad raises a brow then grins widely, showing me perfectly straight, white teeth.

"I love your fight, Zero. Let's see how long it will last, hmm?"

"Fuck you, arsehole!"

"She's strong," Leon says absently, a pique of interest in his voice.

My attention snaps to the green-eyed Mask as he assesses me like he might an animal, with vague interest and a desire to see what would happen if he poked me with something sharp. The frost in his gaze makes my teeth clack and my skin cover in goosebumps, but I remain determined.

"You have no idea," I reply, kicking out, my anger overriding the heaviness in my limbs, enabling me to fight back, even if, ultimately, it's useless to do so right now.

"Shh, this doesn't have to be a struggle," Konrad says, sliding his hand upwards and resting it against the centre of my chest, over the frantic beat of my heart. Leaning closer, he pins me to the van floor, his minty breath whispering against my lips. "Easy now."

Although his words are soothing on the surface, they're laced with a promise of darker things if I disobey. Words form on my tongue, angry, confused, rage-filled words that Grim would be proud of, but every single one dissolves the moment he jabs a needle into the side of my neck. The cool liquid enters my bloodstream in a rush, the effects immediate and debilitating.

I lose consciousness once more.

CHAPTER 3

CHRISTY

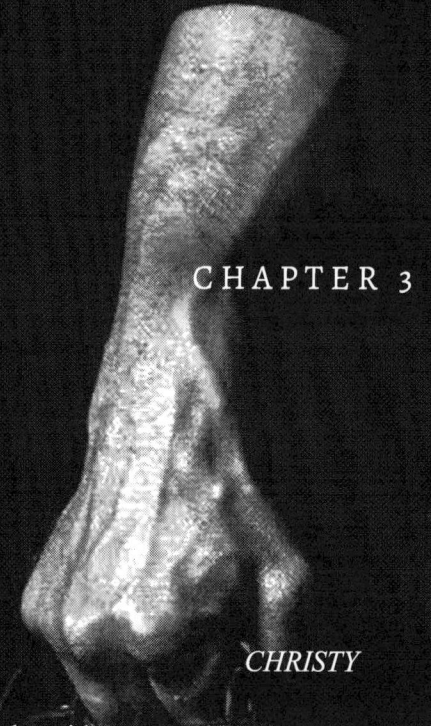

I awake with a start. Shivers wrack my body as I blink through the heavy fog of sleep and my eyes try to find a source of light in what otherwise seems like the pitch black of night. Drawing on all my senses, I notice three things at once.

It's cold.
There's a lingering smell of dampness and mildew.
And I'm chained to a wall.
Chained.
To.
A.
Wall.

"No! No! NO!" I shout, everything coming back to me in a rush as I remember what happened.

I've been kidnapped. Captured. *Stolen.*

They took me from the people I love. They drugged me. They've chained me up.

"NO!" My voice is hoarse. My throat is dry. My tongue, swollen and heavy. A thumping, pounding headache takes a hold of me and I groan. Lifting a shaking hand, I rub the pad of my fingers over my temple to try and ease the pain. Even that movement takes immense effort, given the manacles attached to both of my wrists and the chink, chink, chink of the heavy metal chain crashing like thunderclaps inside my head.

Dropping my hand, I give up on trying to rub away the pain. A tear slides down my cheek and my tongue automatically seeks it out as I desperately try to quench my thirst.

I'm so thirsty. How long have I been here? I remember nothing after Konrad injected me.

Crying is the last thing I want to do, and even though I might've already known my fate, had forewarning, that doesn't change the fact that I'm scared. Knowing what's coming and living it are two very different things.

A scream builds in my throat, but I swallow it down, forcing myself to breathe, to concentrate on what I know right here in this moment. Blinking back more tears threatening to fall, I draw in several calming breaths. The lingering lightheadedness from the drug The Masks had given me begins to ease as I regulate my jittering pulse. It still thumps, but loses its erratic beat the more I force precious oxygen into my lungs.

It's imperative that I stay calm. I *know* this. So, just like I've trained myself to do after every vision, I ground myself in the moment. It doesn't matter if this moment is one filled with uncertainties, with dread and anxiety. All that matters is my need to calm the well of fear inside, and not let it take hold.

"Just breathe," I tell myself.

Pressing my back against the cold, damp wall, I draw my bare feet up, the heavy chains I'm wearing scraping across the concrete floor, chinking as I move. The sound is harsh and obtrusive in this otherwise silent room. *Room*? Who am I trying to kid? This is a *prison*, I see that now as the tiniest amount of light penetrates beneath what looks to be an iron door. I stare at that strip of light, focusing on it and what it reveals.

A stone cell. No bigger than ten feet square.

This is my fate.

This room.

These men.

The Masks.

Konrad. Leon. Jakub.

I've looked into the eyes of two of them, and heard the voice of the third, and I'm no better off knowing who they are, apart from the fact they believe Roger killed their father on Kate's orders or rather their alter egos did. Beast and Grim are feared and respected in equal measure by many.

Except by these men.

Taking me is their revenge.

They came for me. They drugged me. They stole me away.

Now I'm imprisoned in their home with no idea what they intend to do to me...

That's a lie. You know exactly *what they want from you.*

I do. I do know.

"You're ours now, Zero," Konrad had said.

Ours.

Theirs.

I'm theirs.

Konrad had shown me a glimpse of what being theirs meant. He'd touched me intimately. He did it without any thought or care, without remorse or guilt, without empathy. He stole a first of mine and tainted it. How many more firsts will he steal? Will *they* steal? Am I to become their plaything? Is this what my future holds? I'm to be used and abused for revenge?

Yes.

Yes, that's exactly what they'll do to you.

My fingers curl around the cold metal wrapped around my ankles as I try in vain to free myself. It's a futile act, but I persist nevertheless. I'd known that The Masks were dangerous, dark, twisted men. My visions had revealed that to me, but I'd accepted that without fully understanding what it meant. I'd convinced myself that Fate knew what she was doing. That she had a plan for me, for them, for us. That she'd brought us together for a reason. A small part of me had romanticised what Fate had in store, had trusted that I'd paid the highest price already. I'd already lost my mum to Fate's whims, and had been scarred by her capriciousness.

I believed I'd paid my due, and with that belief I'd allowed a sliver of optimism to take seed and silently grew it into hope. Whilst doing that, I'd done the one thing I vowed never to do; I had numbed myself to Fate's cruelty, to the wickedness she could dole out when the mood took her. I had forgotten just what Fate is capable of. She had shown me as a child the extent of her savagery, and I've lived with the consequences of it my whole life. Fate is a wily bitch. She wears her crown of stars with pride, sprinkling love and happiness on those she feels are deserving. But like me, like The Masks, Fate has two faces, and for some reason she's only ever shown me the barbaric one.

Pain. Anguish. Heartache. Cruelty. *Death*.

I've lived through all of it and have suffered the consequences.

Maybe Fate has chosen this path for me because, unlike everyone else, I can see my destiny and the destiny of others. Maybe it's because I see her *true* face. Maybe I'm being punished for my gift that is ultimately my curse.

Maybe... Maybe... Maybe...

My shoulders drop, and I stop yanking at the shackles around my ankles. It's futile. Even if I were strong enough to break these chains, to escape the prison cell, to find my way out of this place, away from The Masks, I know that I won't be able to run forever.

There's no running from Fate. No hiding.

Our fate, The Masks and mine, has been written, not in the stars—because only happy futures reside there—but sealed in death, blood and murder. She has made her decree and now I have to suffer the consequences of it. Only what Fate forgets and what The Masks have no understanding of is this: I've been here before. I've suffered before, but more importantly, I've survived.

"Wake up. I've brought you food and water," a gentle, feminine voice says.

My eyes snap open, then slam shut almost immediately as a beam of light blazes in my face, stinging my eyes. My fingers press against my closed eyelids and I let out a groan as black spots dance behind my eyelids.

"I'm so sorry!" the voice quickly replies, swinging the light away. "I forget how dark it is down here."

Blinking rapidly, I push upright. The uneven stone of the wall digs into my back as I move. Wincing, I suck in a pained breath.

"Are you hurt?" the young girl before me asks. She can't be more than fifteen or sixteen years old.

Of course I'm hurt. I'm shackled to a damn wall!

That rage-filled thought slices through my mind, but I don't voice it. Only one word comes out in its place. "Water," I croak. The need to quench my thirst overrides everything else.

The girl nods, resting the torch on the floor by her feet. I don't ask her who she is. I don't even look at her for that long. Instead, my eyes focus on what she holds in her hands. I'm so, so thirsty.

"Yes, of course, here." She places a plastic bottle in my outstretched hand. "I removed the cuffs from around your wrists whilst you slept. Drinking and eating whilst wearing them would be too difficult."

Peeking between my slitted eyelids, I ignore every single question running through my head and concentrate on the very immediate need to slake my thirst as I press the cool lip of the bottle against my dry and cracked lips. I drink greedily, not caring that ribbons of water slide down my chin and neck.

"Easy. You'll make yourself sick," the girl advises. "Take slow sips. Let the water soothe you, not choke you." Her delicate fingers press against the back of my hand, urging me to slow down. Something tells me to listen, to trust her. I sip at the water, meeting her hazel gaze warily.

"How long have I been down here?" I eventually ask.

"Almost a day. Konrad brought you down here yesterday morning."

"I don't remember..."

"No. You were out cold," she says softly. There's sympathy in her gaze. I latch onto it, desperate to understand why I'm here in this cell, who she is and why she's brought me water and food.

"What do they mean to do to me?"

The girl chews on her lip. Indecision crossing her features. "I— I don't know."

She's lying. The way her eyes flick away, avoiding my gaze, tells me as much. She knows exactly what's going to happen to me. "Please..." I whisper.

She shakes her head, removing the bottle of water from my hand and handing me a thickly sliced sandwich filled with ham and salad. The delicious smell of bread and honey-cured meat hits my nose. "You should eat."

"Who are you?" I ask, ignoring the rumble of hunger in my stomach and the saliva pooling in my mouth. The sandwich is pressed between my fingers, but I refuse to take a bite until she answers me. She gnaws on her bottom lip, looking over her shoulder briefly before turning back to face me. Her eyes tell me what her words can't. We're not alone. I swallow hard, framing the question differently. "What's your name?"

She relaxes a little, some of the tension leaving her shoulders. "My name is Nala."

"Nala?" I ask, my eyes trailing over her face. She's pretty. With rosy cheeks, wide hazel eyes and long blonde hair that's tied back off her face in a low ponytail. She's wearing a black dress with a white pinafore. A maid's uniform.

"That's an unusual name..."

"It is," she agrees with a gentle nod.

"I'm Christy," I whisper. "Will you help me?"

"I am helping you," she replies, cupping my hand that's holding onto the sandwich and urging me to take a bite. "*Please*, eat."

My eyes flick to the sandwich and the sudden, overwhelming urge to fill my empty stomach takes over my need to escape; after all, I won't get very far if I don't have the energy to move. Taking a bite, I chew gratefully, trying and failing to hide the sounds of my appreciation. She watches me eat half the sandwich before speaking again.

"That's better."

"Will you unlock my ankles?" I ask.

"I can't do that. I'm so sorry."

"Why? You don't look like you're happy about me being here."

"You can't leave. No one leaves."

"I was *kidnapped*. Please, I just want to go home. You'll help me, won't you?"

Her eyes widen and my need to question her reaction dissolves on my lips as she shakes her head. "Finish the sandwich. You'll need your strength."

"My strength?" They way she says it is layered with meaning. "What do you mean by that?"

"Konrad will come for you soon."

"Nala!" An older male voice snaps.

She stiffens, and we both look over her shoulder at the man standing in the open doorway, an old-fashioned gas lamp held aloft in front of him. It casts his features in shadows and light, the lines and wrinkles on his face distorted, making him look ancient, decrepit. When he lowers the gas lamp, the shadows recede to reveal a man that looks to be in his early seventies. Thinning, white hair covers his balding head, and liver spots dot the skin of his hands and face. He has a white goatee beard and, surprisingly kind, watery blue eyes.

"Who are you?" I snap, unable to reel in my temper. The girl before me is a child. He's an elderly man who should know better.

"I'm Renard, the butler here at Ardelby Castle. This is my granddaughter, Nala," he explains, turning his attention back to the girl before me.

"Ardelby Castle? That's not in Wales."

"Wales? No. We're in the Scottish Highlands," Nala says.

"I'm in *Scotland*?"

She nods her head. "Yes. It's very remote here."

"Nala enough." Renard warns. "We need to go."

"I know." She looks at me apologetically. "I'm sorry, Christy."

"Don't call her by her name. You know the rules," he admonishes, reaching for a gold fob watch hanging from his black waistcoat pocket.

"What's that supposed to mean? Don't call me by my name? What rules?" With sustenance comes anger. It's fiery and alive and I grasp hold of it, determined not to be weak.

"He'll be back soon. We need to leave. If Konrad finds us down here..." she says, her voice trailing off as she glances at her grandfather.

He sighs, and the kindness in his eyes is tempered with a sad kind of acceptance. "I shall tell you what I told the other Numbers—"

I cut him off. "There are more people imprisoned here?"

"There's no escape," he continues, refusing to answer my question. "Even if you managed to leave the castle grounds you would lose yourself in the forest surrounding it, swallowed up by ancient trees and devoured by the wild animals that roam there. The sooner you accept your position here, the easier it will be for you."

"The other Numbers...? My position?" I look from Reynard back to Nala, who is reattaching the manacles to my left wrist. I don't even bother to fight her, too shocked to do much else but ask questions. "Are you a Number?"

"No. I'm a staff member here at the castle, just like my grandfather. The Numbers are... *more*," she says.

I watch in horror as she turns the key with a resounding click, repeating the action until both wrists are secure. "No, please. Let me go." I beg, dropping the uneaten half of the sandwich to the stone floor, forgetting my hunger.

"I'm sorry, I have to go. Eat the sandwich. Make sure there's nothing left. They can't know we came. Promise me you won't tell them we were here."

"What will happen if I do?" I ask, hardening my heart against her fear. She's young, just a child, and my natural instincts are to trust her, protect her, but I force those feelings away in the moment. She just reattached the manacles, after all.

"They'll kill us."

Shock renders me speechless. The skin on my back prickles and I know that she's telling the truth. Grabbing the torch, Nala gets to her feet. With one last tight smile, she turns on her heel and walks past Renard standing in the doorway and out into the darkened corridor beyond. He sighs, tipping his head and lowering his gaze. It's a respectful gesture, surprising given the circumstances.

"Welcome to Ardelby Castle, Miss."

"Wait—"

He doesn't. The iron door slams shut, pitching me back into darkness once more.

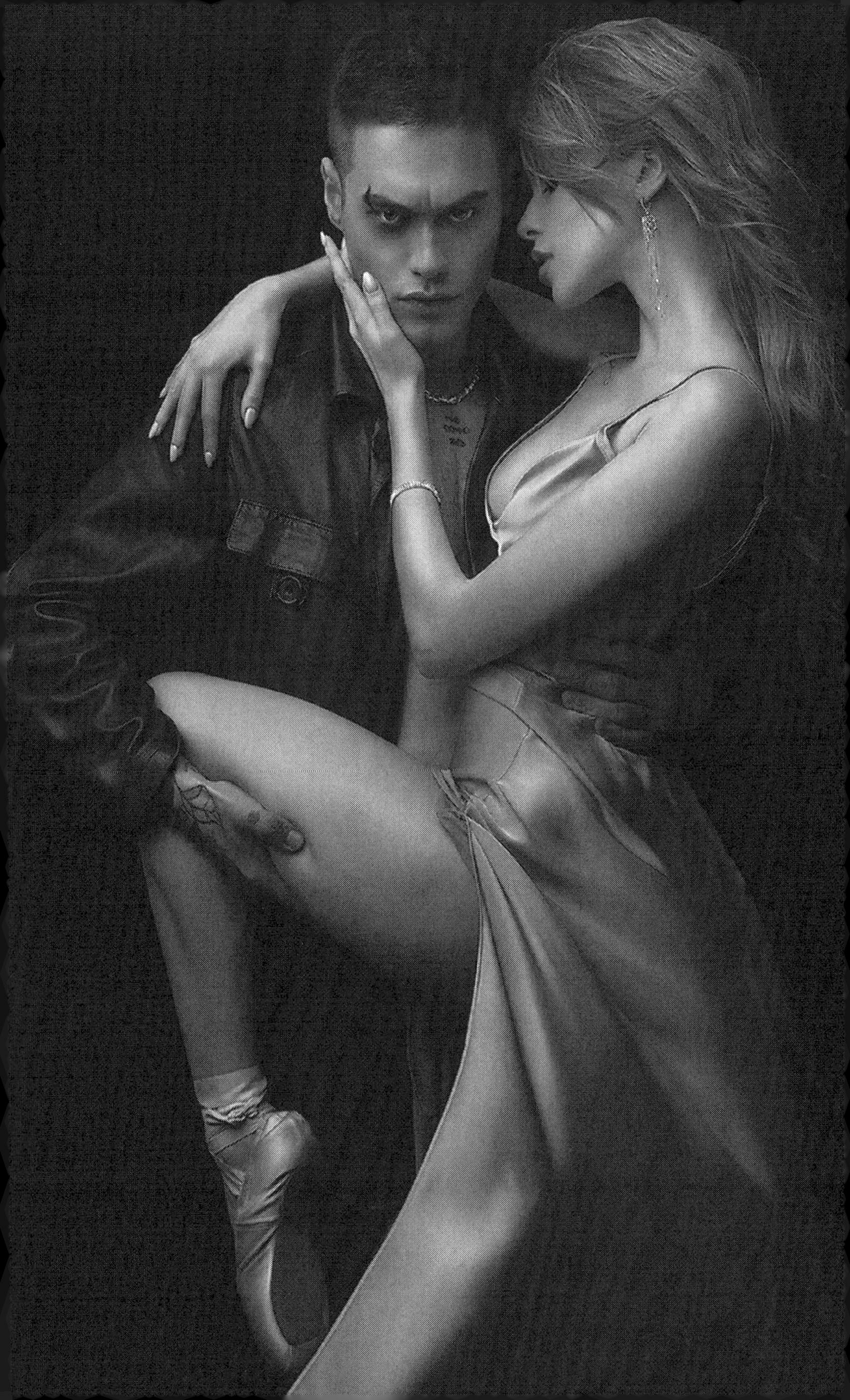

CHAPTER 4

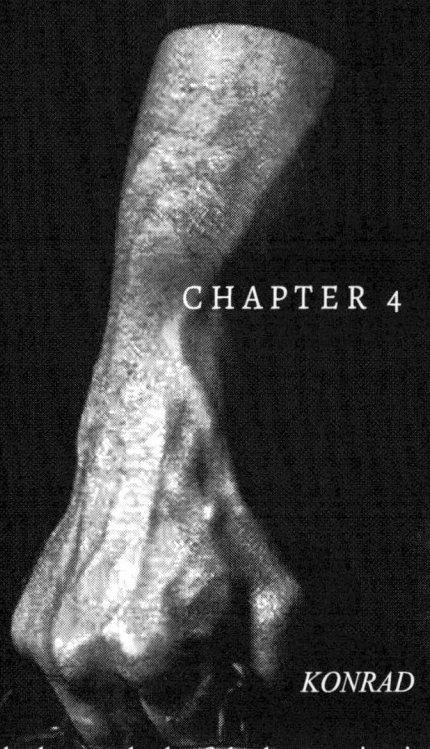

KONRAD

The heavy clunk of the key turning in the lock forces Zero out of her apathy. I can hear the sound of her teeth clacking as I push open the iron door and whilst, admittedly, the cell is cold, she's dressed warmly enough not to be in immediate danger. I know it's more likely fear that's causing her teeth to chatter and not hypothermia. My stomach tightens with twisted delight. Fear is a dish I like to indulge in regularly, and the thought of having Zero at my mercy instantly fuels my hunger.

I'm ravenous.

Stepping into the cell, I relish the fact that there's no one around but me. Leon is busy going over the arrangements with the Numbers for the next show, and Jakub has taken himself off to the forest doing fuck knows what, leaving me free to indulge in a little mindfuckery.

"Who's there?" she calls out, her voice tight, trembling.

I don't answer right away, instead I enjoy the rapid rise and fall of her breath and the chink of the chains as she shifts position. Leaning against the doorframe, I allow my eyes to adjust to the darkness, her form taking shape before me. My eyes are keener than most, and over the years have somehow adjusted to the low levels of light in the dungeons, though I suppose that's not all that surprising given the amount of time I spend down here.

"*Who's there?*" Zero repeats.

She's leaning against the wall, her side pressed against it, her knees drawn up, her arms wrapped tightly around them. She doesn't look at me, instead she presses her cheek against the cold stone as though hoping it will somehow draw her into its embrace.

"Which of you is it?" she asks, a sudden strength in her voice that surprises me. She showed her fight in the van, and now it's here once again. Fear might be something I enjoy immensely, but give me an acquisition that fights back, and well, I'm fucking hooked.

"This is *my* domain," I rumble. My voice is naturally low, gruff. I swallow hard, trying to temper the need within it.

She flinches, but remains resolute. "Konrad?"

"Yes, that's right. How did you know?"

"You have a distinctive voice. It's hard to forget."

"So I've been told."

She shifts her position, the low groan emanating from her lips as she moves, only adding to the intensity of my feelings. It's going to be hard to control myself around Zero knowing that she's *ours*, and that means sharing. My brothers and I made a pact and we won't break it no matter how strong our individual desires or needs might be. Growing up under the domineering presence of our father, and his very particular choice of discipline, made us form a tight bond. An unbreakable one. We trust each other above all else, and whilst we may all have needs that we wish to explore fully with Zero, sharing her means there is a line we cannot cross unless all three of us agree.

"What do you want from me?" she asks, the tremble in her voice fucking with my need to stay strong.

What do I want…? I want you naked, bound and whipped. I want to run my tongue over the red welts from the lashes that will redden your skin. I want your tears. I want your fear. I want your orgasms and your screams of lust. I want your pain. I want to cause it.

I want to heal *your wounds. Fuck, I want that so bad.*

I think about all those things, not voicing any of them. "Right now I want your cooperation."

"My cooperation?" A bitter laugh escapes her lips. "You chain me up in this room for hours with no water or food and you expect my cooperation?"

"I don't expect it. I *demand* it," I counter. "You do as I ask, when I ask, and you'll be free of this cell. You refuse, you stay. Either way makes no difference to me. This dungeon, these cells are where I thrive. Stay as long as you like, Zero."

"And the others? What do they want?"

"We're all in agreement that you need to earn the right to comfort through obedience," I say, telling her a little white lie.

The truth is, Leon and Jakub had argued against me bringing her down here, not because they felt any sympathy for her plight, but because their own selfish needs fought for precedence. Eventually my argument won out, that a few hours down here in the dungeon would reinforce her position as captive and slave. She might be *ours*, but she still needs to learn her place, first and foremost. Besides, the thought of her alone and afraid in my dungeon turned me on like nothing else. I've had a semi ever since I locked her up down here. A few hours had turned into twenty-four and I'm done waiting.

She snorts. "You want me to *obey* you?"

"Honestly, I'd rather you didn't. The longer you're down here, the more fun it is for me."

"You really are monsters," she whispers, as though she'd hoped otherwise, had thought that perhaps there was a chance we weren't everything we appear to be.

But we are. We *are* the monsters of her nightmares.

I grin in the darkness, stepping closer. "That all depends…"

"On what?"

Reaching for the lighter in my pocket, I unhook the oil lamp that hangs midway along the stone wall to my right. Lighting it, I rest it back on the hook then turn to face her. "On how you behave, Zero…"

My voice trails off, stunned momentarily by her thick, wavy hair. My fingers itch to stroke the strands. In the darkness the colour was dulled, but now I see it in all its glory—a crown of red tresses, highlighted with oranges and golds as it tumbles down her back—I imagine it wrapped around my fist, her lush mouth choking on my cock.

Fuck. Focus, Konrad.

"And if I don't behave?" she asks, surprising me with her forthright question.

She can't help but glance at me sideways beneath the curtain of her hair. Her eyes trail slowly upwards, taking in my appearance and widening at my choice of mask. It's different to the plain black one we wore to kidnap her in. This is a full face mask, with larger slits for the eyeholes and a gaping mouth with pointy gold teeth. Both it and the sharp cut of the suit I'm wearing now is another form of camouflage, designed to intimidate the type of clientele we entertain. Not that we really need to. Our reputation precedes us. When you're in our home, you obey our rules or end up a rotting corpse in the lower bowels of the castle. Everyone knows that. Stepping towards her, I tip my head to the side, fully aware of how menacing I look.

"We're men with very... *particular* desires. Fail to follow orders and you'll soon learn what it means to be *truly* owned by The Masks."

"I think I already have a good idea," she mutters sarcastically, turning her gaze away, her long red hair hiding her face from me once again. Her response isn't typical. There's normally tears, begging, anger and rage, but never sarcasm. Her will is strong. It impresses me.

"Whatever you think you know about us, think again. You can't even begin to understand who we are, Zero."

"Stop calling me that. My name is Christy. *Christy*," she repeats.

"No, it isn't. That person is gone. You'll do well to remember that."

"And what if I choose not to? What if I choose to remind you every day who I am? What if I choose to fight back?"

"Then the fun really begins. We're more than willing to play that game, but know this," I say, crouching before her. "The Masks *always* win."

Reaching out, I grab a strand of her hair, rubbing the silkiness between my thumb and finger, recalling the way it had spread out across her pillow as she'd slept peacefully in her home, unaware of the danger she'd been in. I swear to fuck, when we'd crept into her room and I laid eyes on her, she took my breath away. Her hair was a splash of red, stark against the white cotton. Her plump lips, so pink and full. Her long, dark lashes fluttered against her perfect porcelain skin as she slept. Leon had remained impassive as he injected her with the drug that kept her under the first time around, and Jakub appeared uninterested, unaffected by her beauty. But me? I'd been entranced.

Truth be told, for the few hours we've spent apart, I've been wondering whether the silky strands would burn me as much as a naked flame would. An abstract thought that has no basis in reality, but one in which I indulged nonetheless. In all honesty, her fight in the van, her beauty, and the strangeness of her eyes, has enraptured me more than I'd care to admit. It's not as if I haven't been around beautiful women before; every single Number my father had collected before that motherfucker, Beast, killed him, is stunning. It's just that there's something so… *alluring* about her that I can't put my finger on. Something I wish to explore further.

Reaching into my inside pocket I pull out my flick-knife. My fingers run over the ivory, smooth now from years of use. With a snap of my wrist the blade slides free, the sharp edge glinting in the firelight from the oil lamp. Zero stiffens, her fingers digging into her arms as her courage wanes. Without saying a word, I cut away a length of her hair, placing both it and the knife back in my pocket.

"Do you always take what isn't yours?" she asks, the shackles rattling as she reaches for the spot now missing six inches.

"Yes.".

"Next time you try and take something that doesn't belong to you, don't expect to keep your fingers."

I laugh. Her defiance is both amusing and tries my patience. "Keep turning me on like that and I might just forget the pact I made with my brothers and lock you up down here permanently."

She has the good sense to keep her response to herself, even though I can tell that's hard to do. Her whole body is strung tight, wired and ready to react, to fight, and whilst it would be so easy to indulge, to forget the promise I made to Leon and Jakub not hours before, I won't. That doesn't mean I can't have a little fun though. Reaching over, I press my fingers against her hand.

"You're cold," I observe, expecting her to flinch away from my touch. She doesn't.

"I've been locked in this cell for hours with no heat, no light, no blanket to keep me warm. Of course I'm cold," she snaps back. "If you wanted me dead, then you're going the right way about it."

I laugh, drawing my hand away, impressed by the disdain in her voice and the fight that comes out through her gritted teeth. It fires me up inside. She doesn't realise how fucking attractive it is. Taming the wild ones is my speciality after all.

"That can be rectified."

"How?"

"I could *fuck* you warm."

Her head snaps around and this time her gaze meets mine. For a moment I'm rendered speechless by the opposing colours of her eyes and the fire that burns within them.

"You could try!"

"I could. I *can*, but fucking you chained up like this isn't on the top of the list of things I wish to do to you right now."

"I don't believe that for a second," she spits, fury bathing her voice in fire. "Isn't that what you do down here in this place, abuse people whilst they're helpless?"

"Yes, when the mood takes me," I admit. "Though, if you *really* want to know what happens in these chambers, I'm happy to show you." I reach in my pocket for the knife once more, flicking it open, then I press the flat side of the blade beneath her chin, lifting her face. Her breath stills, her eyes widening. "Do you *want* me to show you, Zero?" I ask, licking my lips, my heart pounding, my fingers itching to nick her skin. Pushing her like this, testing her boundaries, enjoying her flush of fear, it turns me on.

"Do I have a choice? Aren't I already yours? Won't you act regardless of whether I want you to or not?"

"That's very true. You're learning fast," I say, drawing back the knife and tucking it back into my pocket. She looks away, refusing to meet my gaze. "Besides," I continue. "I'm getting the feeling that you like to hide from the things that haunt you. Fortunately for you, I *love* to unmask them so I'm happy to indulge you if we both get something out of it."

"Ha!" she laughs, shaking her head. "You don't know the first thing about me."

"I know plenty." *But not enough.*

Grim had hid her well. Zero, by all accounts, doesn't use social media. Keeps to herself. Is a recluse apart from when she goes to work at the hospice, an interesting choice of job if you ask me. Her older, half-sister might be Grim, fearless ruler of Tales, but she doesn't share any of the same history, or at least never met their father before he died. It was difficult to find out much about Zero's past before Grim came into her life, aside from the fact her mother died in a house fire and she'd somehow survived it.

"You'll never know the real me. Never!" she insists.

"I'll find out what makes you tick. I'll find your truth. I always do."

Laughter bursts free from her lips. "You're wrong, you won't be able to see past your own desires to unravel the truth of who I am. Monsters like you are selfish, greedy, self-centred."

"Is that a challenge, Zero?"

"It's an invitation. I'm *not* afraid of you," she replies, lifting her chin, her nostrils flaring just like the wild horses that roam the hills and valleys surrounding our remote castle. She reminds me of them, untamed in a way that is thrilling to witness.

"You should be afraid, but in a way I'm glad you're not. It will make this so much more enjoyable. Someone who's easily scared is also easily manipulated. You, however, are not, and *that* intrigues me." I grasp her chin, my fingers digging into bone and flesh, capturing strands of her long hair. She grits her teeth, I feel them grinding together beneath my touch. Leaning closer, my lips brushing against hers, I allow some of the truth of who I am to bleed into my voice. "My brothers and I find pleasure in many things. Passion, fight, *fear*.

They all turn us on, but hunting a worthy foe, that is something we crave above all else. Three against one, not very good odds, hmm?"

"Fuck you," she mutters.

"Such dirty words coming from such a pretty mouth. I wonder, Zero, are you *really* this brave or are you just like the other Numbers and full of bluster and bravado?"

Suddenly, my need to take what isn't freely given is overridden by my desire to tame the untamable without it breaking. Every single Number who lives in this castle has had their spirit crushed. They've become a weaker, duller version of themselves no matter how they might seem on the surface. I don't want that to happen to Zero, not because I feel any kind of empathy for her situation or remorse for kidnapping her, but because she'll be so much more enjoyable if she maintains this fire, her *fight*.

Long may it rage.

"You seem to think you know everything there is to know about me, what do you think?" she counters.

"If I sliced these clothes from your body, and fucked you until you couldn't feel your legs, would you still be as brave then?"

"Try me."

"I'd love nothing more than to test that theory right now—"

"So what are you waiting for? *Do it*. Do what you came here to do! Fuck me. Abuse me. *Rape* me. Take my body and use it! That's what you want, isn't it? Stop talking about it and do it! Or is it *you* who is full of bluster and bravado?" she snarls, throwing my words back at me.

"No."

"No?"

Her eyebrows pull together in a frown, her lips trembling. I find myself leaning back, my fingers freeing her chin and sliding over her cheek so I can cup her face. It's a tender gesture and throws her. I see the uncertainty, the flicker of hope in her gaze as I hold her captive in my stare. I watch in fascination as she studies me, her strange eyes both alluring in their own way.

"Ghost eyes," I mutter.

"What?" She flinches as though I've struck her.

"Tell me, can you see into Heaven and Earth at the same time?"

"I don't know what you're talking about.

"Your eyes. They're different."

"So I've been told," she responds sarcastically.

"Native Americans believe that people with different coloured eyes can see Heaven and Earth at the same time through each eye. So, can you?" I ask, curious as to why me bringing up what was meant to be an offhand comment, is so triggering for our newly acquired plaything.

She snorts. "Next you'll be asking if I can see into the future!"

I study her for a second, my thumb rubbing over her lips. She tells me nothing, closing down completely so I can't read her. What I do know is that her unusual eyes are somehow a trigger for her. *Interesting.* Tucking that piece of information away to unravel at a later date I smile slowly, languishing in her self-consciousness. She doesn't try to move her hair away from her face, instead she uses it like a shield, hiding behind it. Angry tears pool in her eyes, but she blinks them back refusing to allow them to fall, unlike the tears she had so freely allowed to escape previously given the trails of black mascara over her cheeks.

"Right now, Zero, I want nothing more than to set you free so I can *hunt*."

But that's not the entire truth. My desires are far more complicated than that. I want to hunt. Fuck. Heal. Then I want to do it over again.

She swallows hard, but unlike every other Number, she doesn't wither beneath my stare. This woman has courage. "So do it then. Set me free. *Hunt*."

Somewhere tucked inside the cavernous cage of my chest, my dark heart beats. It goddamn beats as though someone's stuck a fucking cattle prod in it.

Fuck.

I flinch, letting her go abruptly.

"Let's go. I'm taking you to our quarters. We can all get better acquainted there."

"Why not keep me here? Don't you want me chained up and at your mercy?"

"Eventually, yes, but my brothers are impatient to see you. So our quarters it is."

Her eyes narrow through the curtain of her hair. "Into the lion's den...?" she mutters.

I don't bother to deny it. On the surface my offer appears to be an olive branch, an act of kindness, but it's nothing more than manipulation. She knows it as well as I do. "You can get out of these filthy clothes, bathe, eat, drink, and rest in a bed."

For a moment she remains impassive, no doubt considering her choices. Eventually she nods, holding her hands out, her arms trembling from the weight of the chains. "Fine," she concedes. "Let's get this over with."

CHAPTER 5

CHRISTY

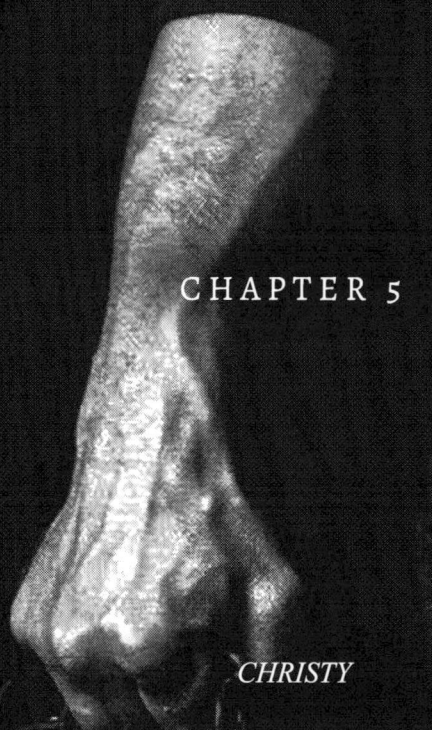

"I'll run you a bath, you can clean up. I'll ask Renard to bring you something to eat," Konrad says as he leads me into a large bathroom situated at the far end of a long, wood-paneled corridor. This is the only room Konrad has bothered to show me after unlocking the door into what I assume is The Masks private quarters.

"Who's Renard?" I ask, knowing full well who he is, and not buying Konrad's sudden kindness for one second.

"Our butler."

I nod, watching Konrad warily as he moves about the space gathering towels from a cabinet situated beside another door that leads to God knows where. He moves with confidence, not in the least bit bothered that I might try to attack him and run. Though, I'm not foolish enough to try. Aside from the fact that he stands at least half a foot taller than me, putting him at least six-three, he has wide shoulders, thick arms and thighs that fill out his suit. Konrad is built, *intimidating*. He'd overpower me in seconds.

"Don't you have maids who do this kind of thing?" I ask, swallowing hard and wondering how, in the twenty minutes it took us to walk here from the dungeons, I didn't see another living soul. Nala and Renard had mentioned the *'Numbers'* but who were they? Where were they? Surely a place as huge as this required staff to run it?

"We have staff, yes, but the majority are forbidden to enter our quarters, or this wing of the castle."

"Wing?" *How big is this place?*

"Our home is vast. You could easily get lost in it. There are many hiding places..." His voice trails off as he eyes me. I can't help but shiver at the implication of his words. He's already admitted he likes the chase. He *wants* me to run and hide. The man's a predator, that much is clear. Swallowing my nausea, I push down the fear I feel bubbling, refusing to give him that. "There are only two other people who are allowed up here. Renard, and Nala. You'll get to meet them soon enough."

"Nala?" I ask, feeling sick that a girl as young as her is forced to work for such men.

"Renard's granddaughter. She grew up here. This is her *home* as much as it is ours. I warn you though, both are loyal to The Masks. Understand?" I meet his gaze, and there's a flicker of challenge in them. Little does he know that I've already met both. Nala had brought me food and water, her grandfather had helped. Knowing that gives me strength. Perhaps I've found allies in them both. "Understand?" he repeats.

Nodding, I look away as he busies himself filling the clawfoot bathtub that sits in the centre of the room. The walls are thick stone, much like the dungeon we've just come from, except there's no mold or dampness in this room. In fact it's warm, heated by an open fire. There's a small, arched, leaded window that sits to the left of the room, allowing natural light into the space. I find myself wanting to peer out of it, to know that there's a world out there, a world where my family is waiting for me.

"The view is quite spectacular," Konrad says, noticing me staring. "But in case you were wondering about escaping through it, I will warn you that the drop is more than a hundred feet. Not even the moat that surrounds the castle will break your fall. At best you'd break your neck and be paralysed, at worst crack that pretty little head of yours wide open. Both would be a waste."

Snatching my eyes back to his face, I swallow hard. The thought hadn't even occurred to me. I have no intention of escaping, at least not today. First, I need to find a piece of paper and a pen so that I can write down all the directions I've memorised walking here from the dungeons. I have no idea whether they intend to lock me up in these rooms or allow me the freedom to roam, either way I need to be smart, and writing down everything I noticed on our walk here is the right thing to do.

"I'm not a fool," I blurt out, before slamming my mouth shut.

"We'll see," he replies, and even though I can't see his face, I know he's smirking beneath the Mask.

My throat tightens with anger, but I swallow down my sarcastic response. He can goad me all he wants. He can try to intimidate with bloated silence, but it won't work. I think he's expecting me to run. I think he expected it the moment he unchained me, but that's what he wants, and I won't give him that despite me goading him earlier. Instead, I meet his gaze, the cool blue of his eyes assessing me as he perches on the edge of the bath, waiting for it to fill.

I stare back, refusing to back down.

The silence between us allows me to go over the mental map that has formed in my head, and that's what I do as he tries to unravel me with his stare. I've memorised how the smell of damp and mold of the dungeons made way for the scent of dust and mothballs as we passed through some kind of cellar, the walls lined with bottles and bottles of alcohol. I recall the way the uneven cobblestone beneath my feet had turned into smooth wooden floorboards, as we stepped out of the cellar into a cavernous room that echoed with every step. My stomach grumbles, reminding me of the smell of bread baking in some distant part of the castle as we walked along a dimly lit corridor that was lined with wooden panels, periodically lit by ornate sconces. We passed door after door, most of which were closed, and those that were open were empty of people.

"I think that's deep enough," Konrad says, standing suddenly. He cocks his head to the side, waiting.

"Will you be expecting me to strip and bathe whilst you watch, or am I to have some privacy?" I ask.

Konrad's hand stills over the bottle he's picked up and is about to unscrew. Presumably it contains some kind of bubble bath, though there's no label that gives any indication to what the liquid is that's sloshing around inside. "When we strip you bare for the first time it will be all *three* of our gazes that drink you in, not just mine. There are rules we have agreed upon, that is one of them."

"How very noble of you all," I scoff. "I'm surprised you've got the wherewithal to hold back, given all your threats so far."

Turning my back to him, I grab a glass resting on the sink behind me and hold it under the tap, filling it halfway before lifting it to my lips. The water is cold, soothing, and instantly quenches my thirst. Nala and her grandfather, Renard, might have brought me food and water previously, but that only took the edge off my hunger and thirst. I'm ravenous. My stomach growls once again, reminding me that I have more pressing needs beyond the one to escape this place.

"How irresponsible of me. I never offered you any water. You've been in that cell for quite some time. Tell me, Zero, how come you haven't begged for it before now?" Konrad asks, his tone suspicious as I turn back around to face him.

Remembering Nala's request to keep her visit secret, I think on my feet. "The stone walls were damp. I didn't know how long you'd keep me there and I wasn't willing to die of dehydration. I did what I had to do."

"So you're a survivalist? Interesting," he remarks, uncapping the bottle and pouring the purple-coloured liquid into the water. The smell is heavenly and for some reason it makes my shoulders relax a little as the scent of lavender and bergamot rises in the air.

"You could say that," I reply, not giving anything away. It's true that I may know a little about surviving in extreme conditions, but it's not because I have any experience of it. I just have a healthy thirst for knowledge. It comes with the territory. Not having friends of my own

—unless you count the dying—means I have to fill my time with other things. Ballet and reading anything and everything helps me not to feel so lonely. "Besides, I don't beg," I add, unable to help myself.

"Is that so?" Konrad removes his suit jacket, chucking it onto a chair situated next to the window. I watch as he unbuttons his cuff, and rolls up his shirt sleeve showing off thick forearms with veins that protrude beneath his skin. He has beautiful arms. Powerful. *Lethal*.

"I *won't* beg."

"You really are very certain of yourself, aren't you?" he asks.

"Yes," I say.

No, I think.

He can't know I'm struggling to remain strong, to keep my mask in place. What he said earlier, about my *ghost eyes*... For a moment I'd stopped breathing. It was as though he'd looked right inside my soul and saw who I *truly* was. No one has ever, not once, looked at me that way and for the briefest of moments I'd felt not fear, but interest... In *him*. I don't want to look at him and see anything other than what he is. He *isn't* interesting. He isn't attractive.

He's a villain. A fiend. A monster.

He locked me up in a cell, for crying out loud.

He's my *enemy*.

I finish the last of the water and place it back on the sink behind me, refusing to turn back around. Nothing shows more strength or courage than turning your back on a predator. So I remain facing away from him, using the mirror before me to watch what he does next. His eyes undress me as his gaze wanders over my back, arse and legs. Despite being fully dressed, I feel utterly naked under his slow perusal.

"I wonder, Zero, how much courage will you have when I'm flogging your backside raw, hmm? Will you be as stubborn then?"

My heart ratchets up a notch at the threat and the lazy way he swirls the water. The dark hair on his forearm slicks against his olive skin and I wonder for the first time since waking up who the man is beneath the mask. I suspect he has a beautiful face. The most dangerous people usually do. Those thoughts dance in my head as he straightens up and steps around the bath towards me. My skin prickles as he approaches but I still refuse to turn around and face him.

"Answer me, Zero. Will you refuse to beg for mercy when I'm pushing you to your breaking point?" he insists, stepping up behind me. He's so tall that I feel dwarfed by him but I don't let my fear show. "Well?"

"I guess there's only one way to find out," I retort, gasping as he presses his chest against my back and grasps the sink on either side of my body, his thick fingers curling over the white porcelain. A waft of his scent washes over me, he smells of leather and metal, spice and musk.

"Oh, believe me. I'm going to enjoy every second of finding out what will make you crack," he replies, rocking his hips against my back, making certain I know just how turned on he is.

I whimper again, and I hear his soft chuckle. He thinks my reaction is through fear. It's not. Right now the skin on my back screams with phantom pain, nerve endings that shouldn't exist are brought to life by the sudden pressure and heat seeping from him into me. I grit my jaw and force myself to focus on my reflection in the mirror, to ground myself like I always do.

"So you keep saying," I bite out, refusing to give him even the tiniest insight into what I'm trying to hide. Instead, I focus on my appearance before me, the mirror reflecting my position trapped within his arms. For some reason, looking at myself as a reflection allows me to detach from the moment, from what's happening, from the pain. It's easier to control how I feel when the person staring back at me isn't who I truly am. My hair is messy, tangled, my eyes haunted, but it's my skin that tells the biggest lie. Despite streaks of black mascara covering my cheeks, my foundation is still relatively intact, my birthmark hidden. The slight blush of my cheek could be interpreted as a reaction to Konrad being close to me rather than the truth.

Thank God.

"You really are beautiful," Konrad says, his voice lowering to a rumble that I feel reverberating down my spine. "It was quite the surprise, honestly."

THE DANCER AND THE MASKS

For the briefest of moments I wonder about smashing the glass and using a shard to stab him with, then discard the thought. I'm not stupid, I'd be no match at the best of times, let alone weakened by hunger, thirst, and muscle-numbing fatigue.

"Beauty isn't everything," I say, my voice tight, disgusted that he's so enraptured by the lie.

"Says the beautiful woman…" His voice trails off as he steps back, and the breath I was holding releases in a puff. Not wanting to feel him against me again, I turn back around to face him.

"Beauty is in the eye of the beholder," I say firmly, steeling myself, finding comfort in my mother's words when normally all they do is irritate me.

He scoffs. "Bathe. I will lay out clothes for you on the bed in the room next door," he says, pointing to the door on the opposite side of the bathroom. "Put them on and wait for us there."

"Us?" I question, knowing full well who he's talking about.

"I've kept you to myself long enough. It's time."

"You're leaving me alone? Aren't you worried I'll try to escape?"

"There is no escape. Even if you were to find your way out of these rooms, through the castle, over the moat, and the forest beyond without being caught, we're miles away from any form of civilisation. Overnight you'd die of hypothermia before you even stumble across our nearest neighbour. The highlands are not a place for a woman such as yourself. This is your home, for however long we choose to keep you here. Get that through your pretty, little head."

My mouth opens and closes, uncertain how to take that last statement or even how to respond. What does he mean by saying *however long we choose to keep you here*? Do they intend on setting me free one day, or is he implying that I'll *never* be free, only in death?

"Besides," he continues, "Now that you've seen my face. You'll never be allowed to leave."

"But I haven't seen—"

He cocks his head to the side, then reaches up and unfastens the ties that keep his mask in position. Grasping the front of the mask with one hand, he pulls it free from his face. Showing me who he is beneath the mask.

It's not what I expected. Not at all.

"You're..." I begin, my words swallowed down by the tightness in my throat and the frantic beat of my heart pounding inside my chest.

"*Deformed,*" he spits, his eyes flaring with anger.

"Deformed?" I frown, my eyebrows pulling together as I drink in the sight of him. "That wasn't what I was going to say at all." Goosebumps rise across my skin and my stomach flips with both pity, empathy, and beneath it all, a glimmer of... *lust*. That reaction, most of all, sickens me. I force it away, lock it down. I will not be attracted to this man. No. Never.

"Then what were you about to say?" he asks, misreading my reaction. He thinks I'm disgusted by him. I'm not.

"I—"

"Be careful, Zero... Well?" he insists.

You're like me.

Those are the words that sit on my tongue as I stare at the thick, red scar that runs from just beneath his left eye, across his cheek and ends up beneath his ear. The skin is raised, puckered and pinched around the scar. In some parts it's lumpy where the scar tissue hasn't healed well. It's a prominent disfigurement, an obvious flaw on an otherwise beautiful face. The wound that caused it must've been horrific. What on earth happened to him, and more importantly, why do I even care?

"Someone hurt you," I find myself saying.

His eyes flash, the blue lighting up like lightning parting the rolling clouds of a stormy sky. "I don't need or want your pity."

"Is that why you wear a mask?" I press, unable to hide the compassion in my voice. He's younger than I thought, no more than his late twenties, and yet that scar and the way he's looking at me now makes him seem far older than his years.

"I wear a mask because I *like* it. Nothing more, nothing less."

"You're hiding," I whisper, and I don't mean his scar. I'm not talking about his predilections either, given he's so open about those, but something else, something deeper. My skin prickles, telling me I'm right.

For a moment he doesn't respond, instead we stare at one another as though trying to understand the true depths of the person standing before us. Then his nostrils flare, and before I even know what's happening, Konrad has my arms gripped in his large hands, his fingers pinching my skin through the hoodie I'm wearing.

"I'm *not* hiding," he spits. "You think I care about this scar, or the pity I see in your strange eyes. You think I'm weak for choosing to wear a mask to cover what people find unacceptable, disgusting?"

"N—no, that isn't what I think," I retort, flinching as his grip tightens and he lifts me off the floor. My fingers fly to his chest, grasping a hold of the lapels of his suit jacket to steady myself on my tiptoes.

"I don't hide behind the masks any more than my brothers do. We wear them because that's *who* we are."

"What does that even mean?" I find myself asking. "Who are you, really?"

Pushing me away so that I stumble back against the sink, he snarls at me, his top lip curling. "You don't get to question me. Get washed, you smell like cow shit."

With that, he snatches up his mask and walks out of the bathroom, leaving me panting, breathless, and utterly confused by the sudden overwhelming sympathy I feel for him and the desire to truly see the man beneath the mask.

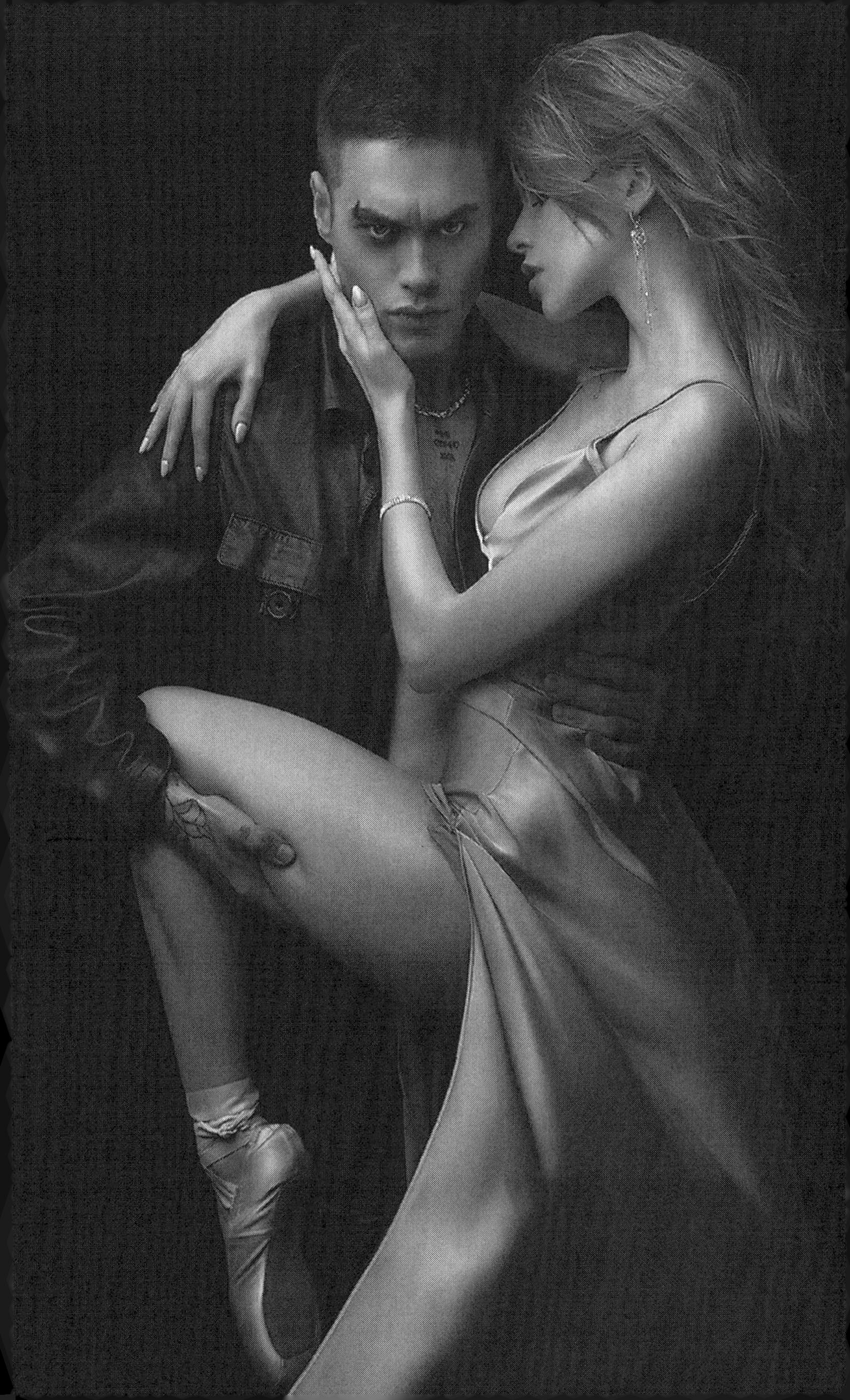

CHAPTER 6

CHRISTY

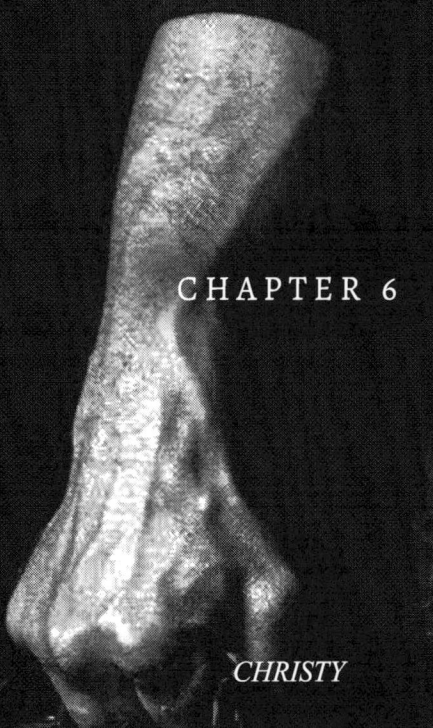

As soon as I think it's safe to do so, I ignore Konrad's demand for me to wash, step out of the bathroom and walk hesitantly into the bedroom. My bare feet pass from the cool stone of the bathroom onto warm floorboards that creak and groan as I walk into the centre of the room.

On the opposite side of the space, light spills in through a huge arched window, the glass divided up into small square panes by lead strips. Through it, I can see a vast forest, the dark, evergreen canopy a thick blanket that stretches on for miles and miles. Beyond the forest are mountains with snow capped peaks, the horizon pitted with heavy grey clouds. It might only be early autumn but I have a feeling that snow falls heavily and often here. Konrad was right. Even if I were able to escape the castle, and find my way through the forest, it would be all too easy to perish in the highlands beyond. My heart sinks. No wonder he felt so at ease leaving me here alone. The whole landscape is a prison.

Blowing out a shaky breath, I allow my gaze to drift around the room. The walls are painted cream and are framed with intricate gold cornicing, giving it an opulent feel. In the centre of the room is a large four-poster bed made of a light-coloured wood, maybe oak or maple. Dark gold, damask curtains hang from the posts and are pulled back to reveal a cream bedspread with matching pillows. A beige throw edged with golden thread is folded across the bottom of the bed, and there's a plain, white cotton nightdress and matching robe lain across the top of it. I eye the clothing Konrad has left for me to wear, and snort. There isn't a chance in hell I'm putting that on. I'd rather pay the price of disobedience than wear an outfit that makes me feel that vulnerable.

Striding past the offending items, I walk towards the vanity table situated to the left of the imposing bed. It has an ornate gold mirror sitting on top of it and an antique hairbrush and comb set resting on the surface. My fingers absently run over the handle of the brush, it looks and feels like elephant ivory, though my knowledge is limited to books, not actual expertise, so I can't be certain. Regardless, my heart spikes with sadness imagining what such a creature must have suffered in order for man to benefit from something so beautiful.

Isn't that always the way? Aren't things of beauty always coveted? The ivory of an elephant, the pelt of a tiger, the fur of a fox. Some are more expensive than others, but all have value. Is it the rarity of such things that make them so alluring or the fact that they are simply beautiful? The skin on my back prickles with knowing, my thoughts close to a truth I'm yet to fully understand. What had Nala mentioned in the dungeons? Something about the *Numbers* being *more*. She had referred to herself as staff, but the Numbers were something else. I know nothing of The Masks, what I do know is that they've kidnapped me. Isn't it possible they've done the same to others? Are the Numbers victims of kidnap? How many are there? Is their purpose to entertain The Masks too? Are they their slaves, trapped in sexual servitude?

Drawing my hand back from the handle of the brush, I force those thoughts away and focus on the task at hand, too overwhelmed with the knowledge that I may be right. What I need right now is a pen and some paper. A quick glance around the room tells me neither item is obviously available, that doesn't stop me from looking though. I open the drawer to the vanity unit, finding it empty, then move quickly on to the chest-of-drawers situated beneath the window. Each drawer is filled with the same white cotton dress that has been laid out on the bed, and nothing else. No underwear, no socks, no jumpers or t-shirts, jeans or trousers.

My heart sinks, and my throat squeezes but I refuse to let fear creep back in. Moving on to the bedside cabinet, I pull open the drawer and am relieved to find a leatherbound copy of the Bible, not because I'm religious and will find peace in the pages, but because I can use it to write upon.

"Now I just need a pen," I mumble, snatching up the bible and pulling the drawer open further.

Nothing.

Feeling frustrated, I scan the room one last time then remember the jacket Konrad left behind in the bathroom. Half of me hopes to find my lock of hair and his knife tucked inside one of the pockets, but of course he's taken those with him. I do, however, find a fountain pen.

I practically scream in joy. It feels like a victory, however small.

Clutching both items in my hand, I settle myself on the stool tucked beneath the vanity table and write down everything I observed on my walk to these quarters with Konrad and what I've gleaned from Nala and her Grandfather. A huge part of me feels guilt at defacing such a sacred item, but for the next five minutes, I do exactly that. I'm so engrossed in what I'm doing that I don't notice someone entering the room until it's too late.

"Why aren't you changed?" a familiar voice asks, shocking me out of my concentration.

I jump, looking over my shoulder as Nala steps into the room from a door that seems to have magically appeared out of the stretch of wall opposite. She's holding a tray, on it is a silver dome covering what I presume is a plate of food. Next to it is a pot of tea and a cup and saucer. Sliding the fountain pen between the pages of the Bible, I carefully close it then cross my chest, hoping that she buys the lie.

"Praying," I reply, tucking the Bible into the drawer of the vanity unit and turning to face her.

"You'll be praying to the *Lord Almighty* for mercy when Konrad finds out you've not followed his orders," she scoffs with a shake of her head and roll of her eyes.

"Is that for me?" I ask, ignoring her sarcasm as she settles the tray on top of the chest-of-drawers. She seems different, less sympathetic than when we first met.

"You're supposed to be washed and changed into those clothes," she says, pointing to the cotton dress laid out across the bed. "They'll be here within the hour. You don't want to disappoint them... And, yes, this is for you."

"What will happen if I disappoint them?" I can't help but ask.

She bites on her lip, sighing. "You'll end up like the others."

"Others?"

"Yes, the other Numbers. Better to be owned by The Masks than loaned out to the men and women who come here."

"What do you mean, *loaned out*—"

"I mean it's not all bad," she interrupts quickly. "The show is *great*, magnificent actually. The Numbers are truly gifted. It's just the other stuff..." her voice trails off and her cheeks tinge pink.

"What show? What is this place exactly? Who comes here? What *other* stuff?"

Squaring her shoulders, she shakes her head and strides across the room towards me. "I've said too much."

"You've barely said anything. Please, Nala, tell me what's happening here."

She shakes her head, her small hands wringing in front of her. "They will tell you everything so long as you behave. You will behave, won't you?"

"By *behave*, do you mean allow them to keep me prisoner? You think I should let them hurt me?"

"I mean, being what they need."

"What they need?" I question, reminded of what Konrad had threatened. What they appear to need is someone to torture, to command, to hunt, to be their sex slave. They want me to *obey*. "You can't be serious?"

"Just be what they need and everything will be okay. I promise."

My fingers curl into my hands and I shake my head. "You're young, so maybe you don't understand how things work, but I will never willingly give them what they want. It isn't right! You *must* see that."

Her lips press into a thin line, her eyes hardening. "Come on. You must bathe. Change," she urges, reaching for my hand and pulling me to my feet. "You need to prepare yourself for Leon and Jakub. Make a good impression."

"I've already met Konrad, and I don't like him," I snap, forcing away the feeling of sympathy I'd felt for him and concentrating on his true ugliness instead. "Why should I bother to make a good impression on the other two?"

"Konrad is the kindest of the three," she murmurs, looking up at me from beneath thick eyelashes. "He cares for the Numbers. They adore him."

"*He's* the kindest," I say with disbelief.

"Yes." Squeezing my hand, Nala pulls me back into the bathroom. "Better him that you met first than Leon or Jakub. If you'd given them this much sass they'd have made you pay for it."

"Fantastic," I mutter, yanking my hand out of her hold and refusing to follow her further into the bathroom. "If Konrad's the kindest, there really is no hope for me."

"You must wash. It will be worse if you don't. Please. If not for you, then for me."

"For you? What difference would me washing or putting on that cotton nightdress make to you?"

"I am to be your personal maid. If you don't do it, it reflects badly on me. I don't want to upset them."

"Because they will punish you?" I ask, feeling simultaneously guilty for putting her at risk and angry at how cruel these men are.

"No, because *I* will disappoint *them*. This is my home. This is my grandfather's home. We don't want to lose our jobs. I like living here."

"Lose your jobs?" I ask incredulously. "Before you said that they would kill you if they found out you brought me food and water. They don't sound like men anyone should be working for, let alone living under the same roof. Or were you lying?"

"I wasn't lying. They *would* kill us both, and I wouldn't blame them. There are rules and I broke one of them today by helping you. I *won't* do that again." She reaches for the zipper of my hoodie, her fingers shaking as she slides it downwards. "I'm sorry." Tears well in her eyes and I instantly feel guilt, remorse at pushing her. She's just a child after all.

"I can do it," I retort with a sigh, gently pushing her hands away and pulling off my hoodie.

She nods, turning back to the water and dipping her hand beneath the surface. "It's lukewarm. I'll add some more hot water."

"No!" I snap, then blow out a breath when she gives me a startled look. "I mean, it's fine."

"Then let me take your things," she says, holding her hands out to me.

"I'd prefer to bathe alone."

"I *have* to make sure you're clean," she adds, her eyes telling me what her words do not. If she doesn't, she'll be punished.

"Okay," I say, slowly stripping off my clothes until I'm standing before her naked. I've never been naked in front of anyone, and I feel heat rising up my chest and neck as I hand her my clothes. Nala, sensing my embarrassment, averts her eyes, and turns her back on me so that I can climb into the bath and lower myself under the milky water. The scent wraps around me as I disturb the water, and I momentarily breathe in a deep lungful. It smells so *good*.

"I will make sure these are washed—" I hear her gasp, and I know she's looking at my ravaged back and the horrific scars left by the burns I endured as a child. "Your back…"

"I was burnt in a fire when I was eight. I nearly died."

"Did it hurt very badly?" she asks as I lay back. The coolness of the water, a welcome relief despite the situation I'm in.

"It did, yes."

"Was anyone else hurt?"

"My mother. She died."

"I'm sorry..." Her voice trails off as she frowns. "You've suffered before... I wonder if they know."

"If The Masks know? Would it make a difference if they did?"

She doesn't answer, instead she passes me a facecloth. "For your face... I can wash your hair if you'd like. It feels so much better if someone else does it, don't you agree?"

"I wouldn't know, I've always managed to clean myself."

Her cheeks redden. "Of course you have. Sorry. My grandfather has told me that I must be willing to do everything I can to make your stay here comfortable. He's trusting me with your care."

"Comfortable? We both know that isn't how it's going to be for me, despite this moment of reprieve. Can you tell me what's going to happen, Nala? Who are the Numbers? Are they prisoners like me?"

She shakes her head. "It isn't my place to say. I *can't* tell you. But if there's anything else that you need, I'll do my best to ensure you get it, provided it doesn't break any rules, of course."

"How about a helicopter out of here?"

"I meant like your favourite food, or drink, maybe a book? We have a huge library in the eastern wing of the castle..."

"What about a mobile phone, a computer?"

"I'm afraid not."

"If I wrote a letter home promising not to tell where I am, would you send it for me?"

"*This* is your home."

I don't bother to argue. Instead, I dip the washcloth into the milky water. She expects me to wash, and will wait until I've cleaned every inch of skin as she's been ordered to do, which means that I can't avoid cleaning my face. My heart sinks. So much for keeping my mask in place. "There is one thing I need..." I say, taking a chance, and hoping she'll keep to her promise.

"What is it?"

"I need some foundation for my skin."

She frowns. "You wish to cover the scars on your back...?"

"No. There isn't enough foundation in the world to help with those scars. I wish to cover up this," I say, placing the washcloth over my face and scrubbing at the thick makeup before revealing what I've managed to hide so far.

Her eyes widen, and her mouth pops open in shock. "Oh..." Her voice trails off as she struggles to find the right words to say.

"I'm not as perfect as Konrad thinks, and I'm not sure he'd be all that *kind* to me if he saw what I truly looked like. I'm far from beautiful, as you can see. I don't even want to know how the others would react, but I'm guessing it wouldn't be all that positive."

"No, perhaps not," Nala admits. "I just don't know if..."

"What?" I ask, cutting her off. "Would helping me with this go against their rules?"

"Not exactly. It's just..." She sighs, frowning.

"Maybe bombarding them with all my flaws all at once wouldn't be wise. Better to let them become accustomed to me bit by bit?" I suggest, hating every word coming out of my mouth but needing to persuade her to help me. I need to cover up my birthmark if I'm to remain strong. I need to become someone else if I'm to survive this place and these men.

"Okay," she nods. "Six has a similar complexion to you. Give me a couple of minutes. I'll go fetch some foundation from her room. I'll be back."

"Six?"

Nala nods. "Yes. She's nice. You'll like her."

"You mean I'm going to meet her?"

"This is your home now, and the Numbers will be sharing it with you. Of course you'll get to meet them," Nala explains.

"*Them*? How many are there?"

"Twelve."

"Twelve...? So I'm one of them now..."

"No. You're *Zero*. You're here in The Masks' quarters. You're *different*." With that she squeezes my arm and rushes from the room, leaving me pondering why, if I'm so different, have I been named after a number as well.

CHAPTER 7

CHRISTY

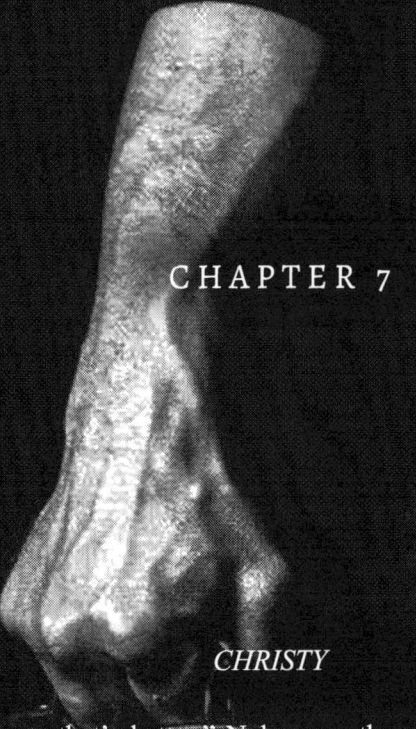

"There, that's better," Nala says, then immediately blushes. "I didn't mean… I just meant…"

I wave away her embarrassment, staring at my reflection in the mirror and my perfect porcelain skin. There's no hint of a birthmark in sight. This foundation has even better coverage than the one I've been using recently. My shoulders relax a little knowing that I have my mask in place.

"It's fine. It *is* better," I say, giving her a small smile as I lock gazes with her in the mirror. She stands behind me, her hands folded in front of her as she waits. For what, I'm not sure.

Dropping my gaze, I rest my fingers on the bottle of foundation. Like the bubble bath in the bathroom, there's no label, and the bottle itself is oddly shaped, like a conch shell you might find on the beach. It has a glass stopper, rather than a screw cap to keep the liquid inside. I don't know of any makeup brand that uses such a design. It seems dated, old-fashioned somehow, even though the contents are definitely twentieth-first century.

"It's pretty, isn't it?" Nala says, taking the bottle from me and holding it in her hands.

"It's unusual. What's the brand?"

"Brand?"

"You know… Maybelline, Rimmel. Perhaps it's Chanel?" I muse.

"Oh no. Thirteen makes it."

"Thirteen? Another Number? But I thought you said there were twelve?"

"Shit," Nala curses, then immediately covers her mouth with her hand.

"Nala?" I question, turning to face her. The soft cotton of my nightgown swishes over my legs as I move. The material is loose and drops to the floor and the sleeves are long, reaching my wrists. It sits high on my neck too, covering up every inch of skin, but the material is thin, hinting at my nakedness beneath. I'm not sure what The Masks are trying to achieve by making me wear this, but if it's to make me feel uncomfortable then it's definitely working. "Nala, please. I didn't tell them about the fact you visited me in the dungeons. I promise, I won't say anything."

She grimaces, then eventually nods. "Thirteen is like you, I guess."

"Like me?"

"Yes. She doesn't perform like the others do."

"Perform?" I ask, so many questions swirling around my head. "Perform for who? What do you mean?"

"She's here because of what she can do as much as the other Numbers are, except her gift is a little different."

"Her gift?"

"She looks after the Numbers in a way. She makes things…" Nala unfurls her fingers around the bottle of foundation. "This for example. All the makeup. The bathing milk you washed in. Perfume. Ointments, lotions and healing balms, that kind of thing. She's never had to entertain the guests like the others. The Masks wouldn't make her, she's too…"

"Too what?"

Nala pulls a face, biting her lip. "Too precious. *Fragile*. She's their family now."

"Family? Yet she's called Thirteen. What's her real name?"

"No one but The Masks knows and they don't call her by her name because she *wants* to be known as Thirteen. When she arrived here a year ago she came of her own accord. This is her home by *choice*."

"So it isn't home by choice for the other Numbers?" I ask, knowing it to be true.

Nala chews on the inside of her cheek. "At least not at first. It's different once they understand…"

"Understand?"

"They want to be here," she continues, ignoring me. "It'll be the same for you, eventually."

"Wow," I say, unable to wrap my head around all the new information or Nala's naivety. She's young, yes, but she must understand what is and isn't right. Then again, if she's lived here all her life, then her impressionable mind can easily be indoctrinated. Perhaps her bringing me food and water was simply a kindness, not an indication that she understood the gravity of my situation and wanted to help me out of it.

"May I brush your hair?" she asks suddenly, clearly wanting to change the subject. She reaches for the antique brush resting on the vanity, hesitating when I stiffen under her touch. "It hurts, doesn't it?"

I nod. "The skin has long since healed on my back, and the doctors tell me I shouldn't feel sensation given the damage to all the nerves, and yet I do."

"I'm sorry," she says, handing me the brush so that I can pull my long hair over my shoulder and brush it myself.

"Why?"

"You've suffered. Just like them…"

"The Numbers?"

She opens her mouth to respond, but the sound of a door opening and closing, and footsteps entering the room beyond the bedroom, stops her. Her eyes widen and she swallows. "They're here."

"You're afraid of them…"

"Nala!' Konrad calls, making us both jump. "Bring Zero out."

Nala bites her lip again, then holds out her hand. "It's time."

I take her hand, having no other choice but to do his bidding and follow Nala into a sitting area that's decorated similarly as the bedroom. I would've been impressed by the high ceilings and all the natural light coming through two huge windows to my right if I hadn't been so utterly terrified by the three men standing before me.

"Leave us," Konrad says, jerking his chin towards the door.

"Yes, Sir," Nala replies, her eyes downcast. With one last squeeze of my hand, she scurries out of the room leaving me alone with my three masked kidnappers.

"Sit," one of the men demands. If memory serves me right it's Leon, though I can't be certain given the mask he's wearing covers every inch of his face. "I said, *sit*," he bites out, immediately getting my back up.

"If you treat me like a dog, then I'll behave like one," I snap back, baring my teeth.

Konrad scoffs, removing his mask. "I told you she was argumentative, Leon."

Leon. So I was correct.

"And if you behave like a dog then we'll treat you like one. Maybe she should be collared and put on a leash?" Leon suggests. He looks over at the third Mask, Jakub, waiting for his command.

Jakub nods, jerking his chin at Konrad. "Do it," he rumbles, his accent thick, dark. It sends shivers down my spine.

"Collar and leash?" I question, my gaze flicking between the three men. "You can't be serious?"

"Deadly serious," Konrad retorts, winking at me before turning on his heel and leaving the room.

"No—"

"The sooner you learn that we always follow through on a threat, the better," Leon warns, cutting me off as he removes his mask, revealing the man hidden beneath.

I inhale deeply, my chest filling with air as he fixes his gaze on me. He's beautiful, *perfect* but like most alluring things, there's a catch. He might have a jaw sharp enough to cut, dark eyebrows that frame stunning green eyes, full lips, a flop of ebony hair that falls perfectly around his handsome face, and a dimple in his chin that most women would want to lick, but that doesn't hide the truth of who he is.

It can't hide the fact that this man is *soulless*.

My skin prickles as he cocks his head to the side and slides his gaze over me in one slow sweeping motion. Straightening my spine, I raise my chin. "I am not someone you could put on a leash. I *will* bite."

"Oh, I'm counting on it," he retorts with a sharp grin as he sits down in the centre of the large roll arm sofa and spreads out his arms along the back. My fingers curl into fists as his gaze focuses on my bare breasts beneath the cotton nightgown I'm wearing. I'm acutely aware that my nipples are hard, not because I'm turned on, but because I'm suddenly cold. It's as though The Masks have sucked all the warmth from the room and shrouded it in darkness.

"What do you think, Brother?" he asks, turning his attention to Jakub. "Will she keep us entertained or will that perfect mouth of hers seal her fate far too early?"

I settle my gaze on Jakub, focusing on the quietly controlled man in the corner of the room. His stature is slimmer than his brothers, more lean athlete but with broad shoulders. He's tall and holds himself with an air of confidence that is neither cocky nor vain, just absolute.

"I think she's trouble," he observes, his accented voice taut with tension. "I think she doesn't understand what we're capable of. I think she believes that she is stronger than we are."

"Yes," Leon agrees. "We'll have to do something about that..." his voice trails off as I meet his frosted gaze. My spine tingles with the threat.

"I won't make this easy for you," I mutter.

"Będziesz posłuszny," Jakub says, drawing my attention back to him. I've no idea what he's just said, and I don't care to know either. I'm more concerned about the fact that he's approaching me. "Będziesz posłuszny," he repeats, removing his mask. He chucks it on the side table beneath the window, then locks me with his steely gaze. "You *will* obey."

Despite having met the masked version of him in my visions over the past two years I'm taken aback by his appearance, by his *youth*. I'm guessing he's in his early twenties like me, as opposed to late twenties like Konrad and Leon appear to be. It surprises me that as the youngest, he's clearly the leader of the trio. Then again, there's something innately commanding about his presence, and it isn't just the way he holds himself, or the barely contained monster lurking beneath his skin. It's much, much more than that. Refusing to kowtow to his demands, I shake my head. "No."

"Wrong answer," he retorts, and before I can even turn and run, he's wrapped his fingers around my throat and has me pushed up against the wall, nose to nose. I feel his steady breath on my skin as he glares at me. "You will obey. You will do what we tell you to do, when we tell you to do it," he continues, his hazel gaze pinning me to the wall as much as his body is. The unusual golden colour of his eyes, flecked with deep browns and dark greens, reminds me of the forest surrounding the castle.

"Every time you refuse our commands, you will be punished. Every time that mouth runs away with itself, you will pay the price. We are not men who you say no to. Understand me?" He releases the pressure on my throat slightly, and I draw in a ragged breath. "Well?"

"I understand," I reply through gritted teeth.

"You may be Zero to Konrad, but you're *Nothing* to me, and you'll be treated like nothing until I decide you're worth something," he says, sliding his hand from around my throat and into my hair. Grabbing a handful, he yanks my head back, pressing his body against the length of mine before dragging the tip of his nose up my exposed neck, breathing in deeply. "Do *not* fuck with me."

I let out a gasp as he bites down on my earlobe, drawing the fleshy part between his lips. "Please," I beg, hating myself for being so weak. Anger burns in my stomach, but this time I clamp my mouth shut knowing that unlike Konrad, Jakub doesn't do well with someone combative. That's abundantly clear.

"My brothers may need someone to toy with, and *that* is why you're still breathing, but know this, *Nothing*, I will have no problem teaching you a lesson if you speak to me with disrespect again," he warns.

Pig.

My hands itch to push against his chest, to shove him off, but his threat and the lazy way he trails his lips across my cheek prevents me. When he reaches my mouth, his lips hovering just over mine, my heart stops beating altogether and for the tiniest moment, no more than a millisecond, my body concedes and I allow myself to accept whatever is about to happen.

Our lips meet.

Time stills.

Breath hitches.

Everything fades away as the scent of fresh pine leaves and damp earth rises up from his pores.

He smells like... *life*. Familiar, yet frightening.

My pulse thumps in my neck as he draws in a deep breath, his eyelids fluttering closed.

"What is that...?" he mumbles, breathing me in.

When his tongue slides across my lower lip, my mouth parts of its own accord. When his fingers loosen in my hair, the tension in my muscles releases. When his hand cups my arse, squeezing me through the thin material of my dress, an ache forms between my legs.

"Here we go... *Brother*—?!"

Time speeds back up, untethering us from the strange attraction that has wound its way around us both like the snake around Eve's heart. My stomach lurches as reality seeps back in. *What the hell was that?*

"Fuck!" Jakub swears, releasing me with a shove as he steps back.

My back slams against the wall behind me, pain shooting down my spine as nausea twists my stomach. Did we just kiss? Did I *want* his kiss? Jakub strides over to Konrad and snatches the leather collar and lead from his hand, chucking it at Leon who catches it.

"That was quite the show, Jakub," Leon remarks, one brow arched as he rises slowly to his feet, and snaps the leather between his tattooed hands. Dark swirly shapes cover the back of both hands, creeping up each finger. They remind me of reeds in a pond, the kind that could drown you if you happened to get tangled up in them.

"I thought we agreed not to indulge until Zero has learnt her place," Konrad remarks, folding his arms across his chest and levelling his gaze at Jakub.

"We *did*. That was... What the *fuck* did Thirteen do?"

Konrad frowns. "Do?"

"I can smell one of her damn lotions on Nothing's skin," Jakub accuses, jabbing a finger in my direction. "She smells like... like. Fuck this!" he rages. "Leash her. I need to speak with Thirteen." With that, he grabs his mask and storms out of the room, slamming the door behind him.

"Well, I'll be fucked," Konrad smirks, darting his gaze from Leon back to me. "Looks like you got under his skin, Zero."

Leon shakes his head, snorting. "Doubtful. He seems more pissed with Thirteen. He doesn't like to be caught off guard. Besides, she's not really his taste."

"He looked pretty caught up to me. You've got to admit, she's quite alluring, isn't she?"

Leon runs his gaze over me as he fingers the leather collar. "Maybe."

"Come on, Brother, you *must* see what I see," Konrad continues. "All that fiery red hair and long limbs. Aren't you just the least bit curious to find out what she looks like beneath that dress?"

"Not really. I am interested in how loud she screams though," he retorts, stalking over to me.

My mouth parts, a cutting retort on the tip of my tongue, then I remember what Nala had said and instead I force myself to be quiet.

"Where do you think you're going...?" Leon asks as I slide along the wall, backing away from him. A wide grin splits his handsome face. It's the kind of smile girls with no sense would fall for, only seeing the beauty and not the beast beneath his skin. There's a reason why some of the deadliest things are so alluring.

"I—"

"Running wouldn't be wise..." He pauses, cocking his head and dropping his smile. "What should I call you?" he muses, thumbing the leather collar in his hand. "Looks like Jakub thinks you're *Nothing*, and Konrad has already named you *Zero*…"

"How about Christy?" I say, instantly regretting my moment of bravery.

His lip curls. "How about *Nought*?"

"Nought?" My throat closes over and tears prick my eyes. I see what this is. Take me away from the people I love. Strip me of my name, my clothes, my identity. Make me a number. No, make me less than a number. To them I'm no better than an animal, a dog they can leash and force to obey.

I'm *Zero*, *Nothing*, *Nought*, to these men.

"Yes, from now on I shall call you Nought. *Heel*, Nought."

My jaw grits, my nostrils flaring. I look from Konrad's amused gaze back to Leon's cruel one. If they think they can treat me like this, they've got another thing coming. I would rather die than allow them to reduce me to that.

"I said, *heel*!" Leon repeats, snapping his wrist so that the end of the leather leash catches my bare feet. The sharp pain registers within my tormented heart, pushing me over the edge just as my fingers reach the handle of the door.

"Fuck you!" I snap, ripping the door open and slamming it closed behind me.

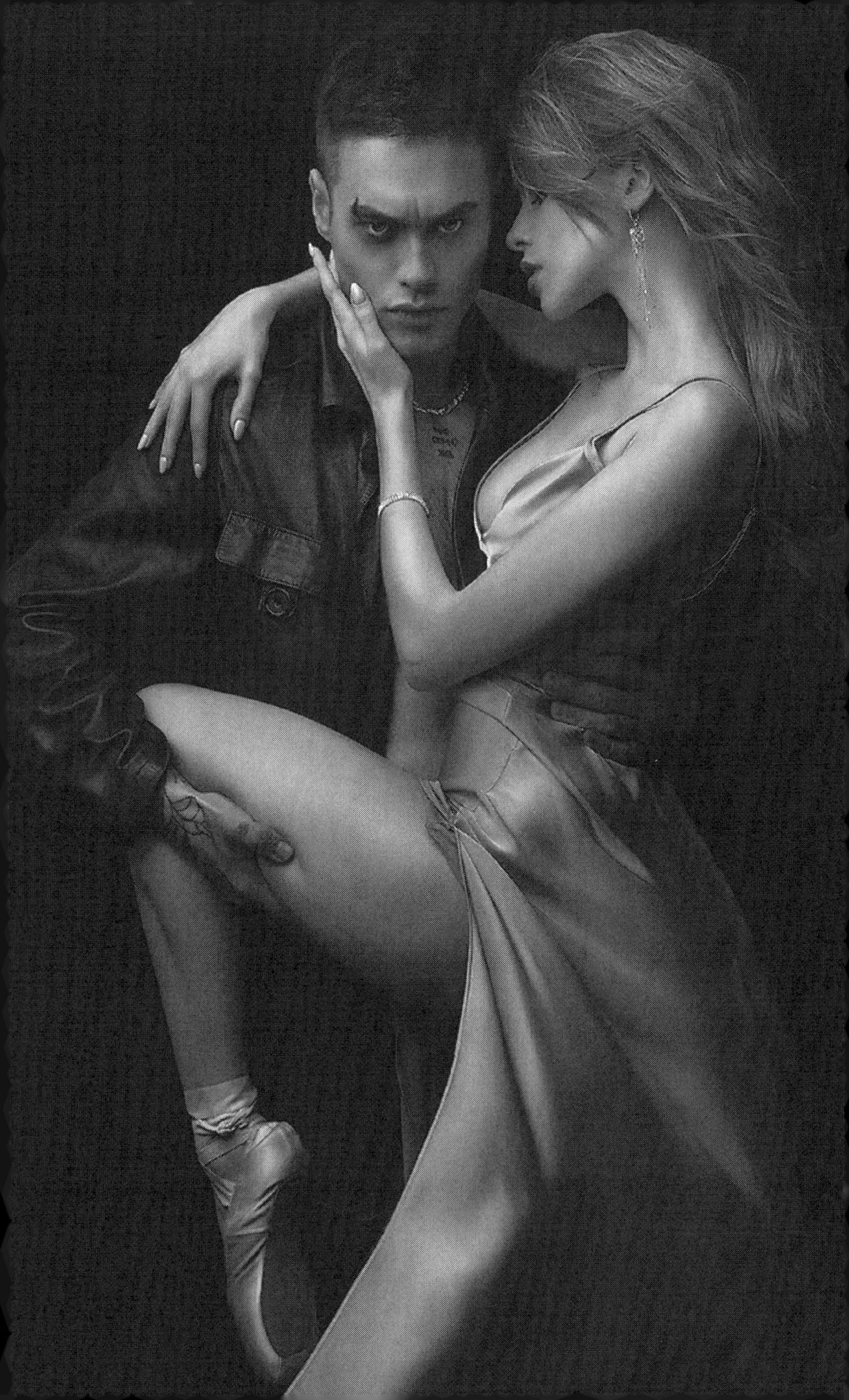

CHAPTER 8

CHRISTY

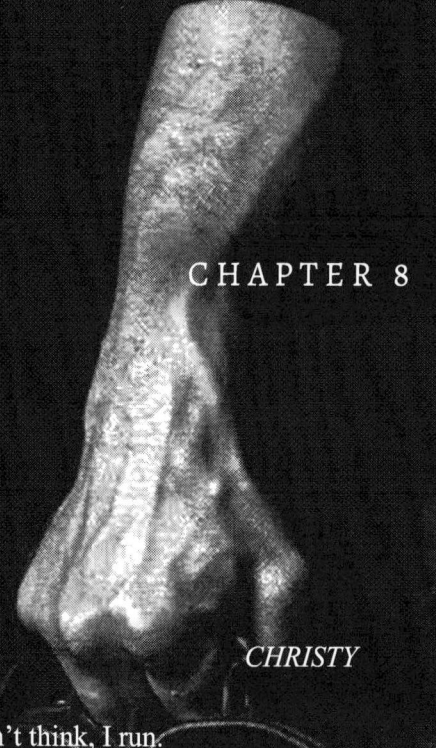

I don't think, I run.
 Hurtling through the bedroom, I push open the bathroom door and within a couple of steps I'm already on the other side of the room and barreling into the corridor beyond. My bare feet slap against the shiny wooden floorboards as I pump my arms as fast as I can, all too aware that I'm being chased.
 Hunted.
A part of me knows that I'm giving them what they want, but I couldn't allow myself to be at their mercy a moment longer. If I'd conceded to their demands, if I'd obeyed and given in, then I would've lost myself forever in that moment.
 I wouldn't have forgiven myself.
 At least this way I go down with a fight. What had Kate always told me?
 "Never let the bastards get you down, Christy, but if they do, you'd better believe you'll get back up and show them what true *strength is."*
 That's how she survived. She fell as Kate and stood up as Grim.

Right now, I don't have any weapons or fists strong enough to fight back with, but I do have courage and the will to survive, probably a whole dose of stupidity too, but my pride won't allow me to abide by their demands. As much as I thought I could, I *can't*.

Fate can go screw her traitorous arse. I don't care what she has planned for me. I don't care that for the longest time I was apathetic, willing to let fate take its course, believing that there was nothing I could do to change it.

I can't be a slave to these men. I won't.

Reaching the end of the long hallway I pray with every single part of me that the door has been left unlocked. My hand shoots out, grabbing the handle whilst my brain registers their footsteps behind me. They're not running, so assured of themselves in their ability to hunt.

My fingers wrap around the metal, my heart pounding in its effort to keep me alive.

"*Please*," I beg.

The handle turns.

A rush of adrenaline fuels me onwards. I race into the outer hallway beyond. The wooden floorboards make way to stone floors, walls and archways. I pay no attention to my surroundings other than the innate instinct to flee from what endangers me the most. If I allow myself even the slightest hesitation, I know they'll be on top of me in an instant.

So I keep going, pounding down stone steps, my feet practically flying across the ground as my hair whips out behind me. When I reach the bottom of the stairwell, I hit a sharp left, following the sudden cold breeze and hoping it means that there's an exit somewhere that leads out of the castle. Right now I'll take my chances in the forest.

I don't look back. I keep running.

I run even though my lungs are screaming and my breath is short.

I run, feeling every inch the prey.

I run, my thoughts sprinting as fast as my legs.

I run through a huge dining hall, with a long wooden table situated along its centre and tapestries hanging on the walls. I run past an empty kitchen, the lingering smell of coffee and vanilla in the air. I run past rooms filled with antique furniture and opulent rugs. I run along corridors with paintings of men and women in various states of undress hanging from the walls. I run until time ceases to exist and I have absolutely no idea where I am.

I run until, eventually, I end up in a large square courtyard, my knees giving out and my lungs busting out of my chest as I fall at the foot of a huge oak tree that rises up out of the stone ground like some prehistoric beast.

Sweat pours from my skin as my hands slam against the ground, the thin cotton material of my dress doing nothing to protect my knees against the gravel. On all fours I hiss and wheeze, my heart and lungs battling to keep me alive. Years of dancing ballet might have made me supple, limber, but it hasn't strengthened my heart enough to give me any real kind of stamina. I sway on my arms and legs, my hair falling forward in a shroud as stars spot my vision and blackness creeps in, threatening to pull me under.

"Get up. Run!" I hiss between every ragged intake of breath.

Pushing upwards, I stumble forward, a sudden lightheadedness making me dizzy. My hands reach out blindly towards the tree, and when my fingers meet rough bark, I press my body against it, welcoming its support. For one precious moment, I close my eyes against my reality and force myself to breathe, to rest.

"I would've at least stopped at the kitchen and armed myself with a knife. That's what I did when I tried to run the first time."

"Huh? Don't you mean the *only* time, Eight?"

My eyes snap open, my anxiety spiking, and with it another bout of vertigo. "Who's that?" I ask, still hanging onto the tree.

"I'm Four, and this is Eight. Nice to meet you..." the woman's tinkling voice trails off as she waits for me to answer.

Shaking more than the leaves clinging to the branches of this great oak tree, I slowly turn around and come face to face with two exceedingly attractive women wearing little more than corsets, stockings and heeled pumps. One is petite, with startling grey eyes and long hay-blonde hair, the other willowy, with ebony skin and a shaved head. Both watch me with interest, not in the least bit bothered by my terror or their state of undress.

"Who are you?" I demand, baring my teeth and scanning the area behind them.

The petite blonde glances at the taller woman and raises a brow before stepping forward. She lowers her voice. Her tone might be gentle, but there's little sincerity in her eyes. "I'm *Four*," she says, pressing the flat of her palm against the dome of her breasts. "And this is my friend, *Eight*."

"You're Numbers."

"Two of them at least," Eight replies, a dazzling white-toothed smile making her even more beautiful, if that's possible. "We live here."

"You mean you're *prisoners* here!" I snap, angry at their apparent calm.

"No," Four shakes her head emphatically. "We live and work here of our own free will. Ardelby Castle is our home, and The Masks are our masters."

"Then if this is your home, and you're here of your own free will, why do you refer to those *men*," I spit, "As your masters? Do they collar and leash you too? Do you heel like dogs like they expected me to do?"

Four flinches at my outrage, but Eight remains stoic. "We've all done many things for The Masks, but they only ever treat you how you want to be treated. Do you want to be treated like a dog?"

"No, of course I don't!" I shout. "Who in their right mind wants to be treated like an animal?"

"You'd be surprised," Eight responds, folding her slim arms across her chest, assessing me with a cool gaze.

"Well, not me. *Never*. I won't wear a goddamn collar or walk on a leash, and I will never, ever heel. They're bastards!"

"Hush now!" Four says, her eyes widening minutely. "Do not disrespect The Masks. It's unseemly."

"Disrespect? Have you lost your mind? Those men, those *monsters* kidnapped me. They've drugged me, chained me up in a cell, threatened my life and my dignity. They've stripped me of my name, *your* names." I pant, my chest rising and falling as my palms press against the trunk and my fingers curl into the bark, little shards of wood sliding beneath my nails.

"We're perfectly sane, thank you very much," Eight retorts, planting a hand on her hip.

"It's hard at first for everyone, but truly, you'll come to love living here," Four adds, her voice sounds so sincere that I want to puke from the lies. "Ardelby Castle is beautiful. We're very lucky."

"They've brainwashed you. Don't you see?"

"No, Zero. We've *enlightened* them," Konrad says, stepping out from behind a column of stone. This time he's wearing a mask that covers the top half of his face. It's white, the bottom curving over the tip of his nose and beneath his cheeks, molding perfectly to his skin. He smiles at the two women and they practically preen in his presence. It makes me sick.

"Master," Eight and Four say simultaneously, dropping their heads and looking up at him from beneath hooded eyes. They both offer him a hand each, and he takes them, his thumb rubbing gently over the backs of their knuckles. It reminds me how someone might stroke a pet. My stomach tightens into knots.

"Thank you for being so welcoming to Zero. She's finding it difficult to... settle in," he explains, glancing over at me, his top lip pulling up in a slow smile. "She'll soon learn that we have her best interests at heart."

"Screw you," I mutter, unable to take my eyes off of him.

Seems like he has the same trouble because he fixes his gaze on me as he lowers his mouth to Four's hand and kisses it, repeating the action with Eight. I watch in sick fascination at the way they tremble under his gentle touch and sensual kiss, and for the briefest of moments I consider striding over to them, ripping their hands from his grasp and shaking some sense into them. The only reason I don't is because Leon steps into the courtyard, collar and leash in hand. He too is wearing the same, snow-white, mask.

"I see you've met Four and Eight, *Nought*. You will be introduced to the others in due course. But first…" he holds up the collar, and steps towards me.

"No!" I snap, edging around the tree, my back scraping against the rough bark. I don't register the pain, only the fear. "No," I repeat.

"You should've kept running," Leon taunts.

"I should've grabbed a knife from the kitchen like Eight did!" I growl back.

Leon laughs. "That was a fun couple of hours. Wasn't it, Eight?"

Eight lifts her head and looks directly at Leon. There's no denying the admiration, awe and lust in her gaze. "Yes, it was. I'd like to do it again some day," she says softly.

Is she flirting with him?

"One day," Leon responds noncommittally, flicking his gaze back to me. My teeth start to chatter, but I grit my jaw tight and edge slowly around the tree, readying myself to bolt. Leon draws his lips back over his teeth, like a shark about to bite. "Right now I have plans."

Out of the corner of my eye I notice Konrad stepping away from Four and Eight, dropping their hands. "Be sure to tell the Numbers that we will be having a *formal banquet* to welcome our new friend."

"Tonight?" Four questions.

"No, Nought has a lesson to learn before we'll introduce her to you all," Leon interrupts.

A look passes between the two men, and Konrad nods. "Indeed."

"A lesson?" I croak, my stomach turning over.

"Off you go," Konrad urges.

"Yes, Master," they agree, before they both give him a seductive smile that leaves no room for misunderstanding. They truly have been brainwashed. Regardless, I don't want them to leave me alone with these men.

"Don't go!" I call, my voice cracking, betraying me.

They leave without a backward glance. My stomach drops, nausea rising.

"Now, where were we?" Leon asks, his eyes narrowing. "Are you going to heel?"

A sudden rush of rage replaces the fear. It obliterates it, sets it alight, burns it to ashes. With my next shaky breath I dig deep, drawing on the courage that I know lives within me. Right here and now, I decide that I will not be a victim. I will not *obey*. I refuse to be theirs. I won't be owned by anyone. "Never!" I snarl, pushing off from the tree with a rush of adrenaline and new found energy.

I bolt, running straight into a hard chest. Strong arms wrap around me, holding me tight, and I'm immediately accosted by the smell of wet pine leaves and freshly turned, damp earth.

Jakub.

"Nie powinieneś biegać, *Nic*," he says, before snapping a pair of handcuffs around my wrist. He walks me backwards, shoves me back against the bark, then yanks my wrist into the air and reaches above my head. "You shouldn't have run, *Nothing*," he repeats in English, clipping the handcuff into a metal loop fixed into the tree trunk, his hazel eyes shadowed beneath his mask.

"No..." I whimper, trying to buck him off me, but he pins his body against mine, attaches another handcuff to my other wrist and yanks my arm upwards, clicking it into place too.

"*Yes*," he counters, wrapping his fingers around my throat, stroking, not squeezing. "Perhaps now you'll understand that we mean what we say. This isn't a game. You belong to *us*."

"Konrad said you like the chase," I say through gritted teeth.

"Maybe that was once true. Now I don't like much of anything," he whispers against my lips, a note of sadness in his voice that's too confusing to analyze at the moment.

"Let me go," I beg, the handcuffs digging painfully into my wrists.

"I can't do that."

"Can't or won't?"

"Won't," he replies, so close that I can feel his heart thumping against my breast and the heat from his skin seeping through the thin cotton of my dress. He breathes in deeply, running the tip of his nose against my skin, then steps back enough to pull out a white mask from the back of his jeans. This one completely covers the face and has two red teardrops falling from the section cut out from the eyes, and two holes for the nose. He holds it out to the side and Leon steps up, taking it from him

"Put it on her," Jakub orders.

Leon nods and Jakub steps out of the way so that he can attach the mask to my face. "There, now isn't that just fucking poetic," Leon says, his fingers running down my neck and between my breasts before falling away, leaving a trail of heat in their wake.

"Are you just going to leave me here?" I ask, my voice muffled beneath the mask.

Konrad nods. "Yes."

My chest heaves as I draw in a breath through the small nose holes and try not to panic at how claustrophobic I feel. Digging my bare feet into the roots of the oak tree protruding out of the stone slabs, I force myself to keep calm knowing that my fear is their sustenance.

"This is The Weeping Tree, Nothing," Jakub explains. "It's over a thousand years old and has borne witness to many atrocities, including the hanging of innocent women charged with devil worship and witchcraft. Many, many years ago a foreign nobleman fell in love with a local healer woman named Marie. They were together for ten years, had several children, and lived a happy life until she was charged with witchcraft for curing a family of influenza. In those days, barely anyone survived, but her ability to use natural remedies saved that family. Instead of being praised for her kindness, the family turned on her, afraid they would be charged with devil worship for surviving the unsurvivable. Marie was hung from this very tree."

"That's horrible," I whisper.

He nods, then continues. "Her *goodness* killed her. It is said that upon her death, this tree wept blood. The whole village witnessed it. It was the first and last time that happened. Legend has it that this tree only ever cries tears of blood when a virtuous soul, pure of heart and mind dies beneath its boughs."

"Yet here you are shackling me to this very tree, and for what?

THE DANCER AND THE MASKS

You're no better than the men who hung those innocent women," I accuse.

"I never said I wasn't."

"Then why tell me such a story?"

"Entertainment. Curiosity, maybe," Jakub replies with a shrug.

"Why are you so cruel?" I ask, my teeth chattering with both fear and the feeling that I'm walking on someone's grave.

"This is your home now, it's only right you are aware of its history," Konrad says, backing his brother.

"And your fate," Leon adds darkly.

I snap my head to look at him. "What do you mean, *my fate?*"

He doesn't answer, Konrad does. "Marie's husband was so heartbroken that he bought this tree and the surrounding land in a fifty mile radius, then built this castle so he could always be close to the soul of his wife. This tree hasn't wept blood since she died, even though the legend has been tested often over the years."

"Other people have died here?" I ask, barely able to get my words out I'm so horrified.

"Yes, and many have come close," Jakub confirms, a muscle feathering in his jaw.

Nausea churns in my stomach with the realisation of where this is going. "You mean for me to die here, is that it? This is your revenge on my sister. *This* is my fate?"

Leon steps closer, cupping my masked face. "Everyone has to die eventually."

I snatch my head away. He laughs, and whilst the sound is cruel it's also hollow, lacking any real kind of malintent. Just a bitterness that I don't understand.

"You're *ours* now, Nothing. That means *we* hold the key to your fate. See this as a warning of sorts. We will release you when we think you've understood the gravity of your situation. Take that time to think about how you wish to behave from this moment onwards."

"Please, don't do this!" I cry, all sense of self-worth flying out of the window just as a thunderclap sounds overhead and rain begins to pour in fat, heavy droplets. I'm saturated in seconds, the dress sticking to my naked body beneath, the material becoming see-through. All three men stand and stare, oblivious to the rain as it saturates the four of us.

"You disobeyed us. This is the consequence," Jakub retorts eventually. With that, he turns on his heel and leaves, Konrad and Leon following close behind him.

CHAPTER 9

CHRISTY

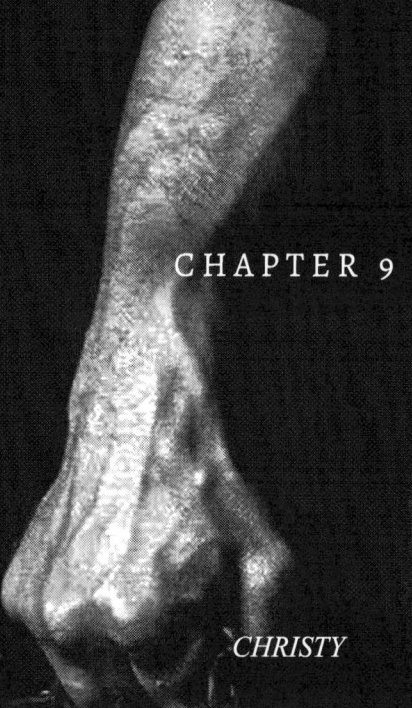

Sunlight streams through the back of my eyelids, waking me from my troubled slumber. I've been in and out of sleep all day, waking up every time my knees gave way and my wrists screamed in pain from having to hold the weight of my body. My arms ache from being held aloft, my wrists are bruised from being shackled so tightly and my fingers are numb. I'm thirsty, hungry, and completely and utterly exhausted beyond anything I've ever experienced before.

The only thing keeping me sane, keeping me alive, is my anger. Even when I withstood the storm that flooded this courtyard with rainwater three inches deep yesterday afternoon, rage and the late afternoon sunshine that broke through the clouds before nightfall had dried me off and warmed my body enough to survive the night. The tree itself acted as a shelter of sorts, the slight curve inwards of the trunk that I'm resting against protecting me from the worst of the elements. Regardless, whilst I'm mentally able to withstand a lot, I know that it will catch up with me eventually. My body always pays the price.

Shifting my feet, I push upwards, my back sliding against the rough bark as I stand on the balls of my feet, trying to ease the pressure off my wrists. A sudden jolt of pain causes me to cry out, but I bite it back, swallow it down and concentrate on seperating my physical self from what hurts. Within a minute or two, I'm detached enough from the pain to not let it bother me. I just need to wait this out. Lifting my head to the sky, I look up at the canopy of branches and leaves and try not to think about which branch those poor women were hung from. Instead, I concentrate on the position of the sun and the shadows in the courtyard. At a guess it's early afternoon. Sighing, I wiggle my fingers and move my body, trying to stretch as much as possible and keep the blood circulating, stopping only when I sense someone else entering the courtyard.

"I'm impressed with your gumption, Nought. Most of the Numbers begged for release within a few hours of being shackled to The Weeping Tree. Yet here you are surviving a whole day and night, not to mention a storm so violent that we lost a few trees in the forest," Leon says as he steps out from behind one of the stone pillars.

"I don't care what you're impressed by," I reply, eyeing him warily. I probably should be more polite, amenable, but I can't bring myself to act that way. I don't have it in me to stop fighting, even if it is only with my words and my attitude.

Leon laughs as he approaches me. He has his hands buried in the pockets of his black slacks and is wearing a white fitted t-shirt that shows off his muscular arms and strange black tattoos that wind up from his fingers, wrap around his biceps, and disappear beneath his top. When I noticed the tattoos on his hands yesterday, they reminded me of reeds in a pond, and that's exactly what they appear to be. Even his mask matches his outfit, with similar imagery painted across its surface.

"By now you should've lost most of the feeling in your arms. It can't be comfortable."

"It isn't."

"And yet there have been no tears. No calls for help. No cries of pain," he muses, stepping closer to me.

"Would that have gotten me set free sooner?" I ask, unwilling to hide the disgust in my voice.

He cocks his head to the side. "I guess that would've depended on which one of us was tasked with watching you. Konrad might've succumbed. Jakub definitely wouldn't have, but me— well, here I am."

"You've been here all this time watching me suffer like some twisted creep?" I interrupt.

"I made my way back here late last night. Though not before taking my time to shower and changing into something less... wet." His gaze tracks over my dress, which has dried off now and is fluttering around my legs in the breeze. "That storm really was very unfortunate, but as much as I'm intrigued to know whether this tree will weep for you, I also *need* you to stay alive. Therefore I stayed with you just in case."

"Are you expecting thanks, is that it?"

"Not in the slightest, though I was getting bored waiting for you to break."

"Then it's just as well you've struck up a conversation because hell will freeze over before that happens."

"Everyone has a breaking point. It's only a matter of time until we find yours, Nought."

"Not me. I won't break. Not now, not tomorrow, not next week or next month. Not in a year's time, not on my goddamn deathbed. I will *never* break," I retort vehemently.

He looks from me, and into the branches above, completely ignoring my outburst. "Yesterday, when my brothers were telling you about the story of this tree, they forgot to mention one very important piece of information."

"And what was that?" I ask, watching him from behind my mask as he steps into a pool of light. The sun catches his hair, the dark strands highlighted with deep brown and mahogany. He has the kind of hair you want to run your fingers through, and the kind of physique that most male models aspire to, but he's no less a predator. He's just wrapped up in pretty packaging.

Dropping his gaze back to me, he continues. "Marie's husband, the rich nobleman, was called Jan *Brov*. This castle, this tree, their love and her death is a part of our history, our legacy. We've *all* suffered because of her kindness."

"You make it sound like she was wrong to help that family?"

"Six months after this castle was completed, and three years after her death. Jan died of a broken heart at the foot of this tree," he says, pointing to my feet. "Right where you're standing, actually. He couldn't live without her, so he slit his own throat and fed The Weeping Tree his heartbreak. In the next five years following his death all but one of their five children perished from disease and illness. The only surviving child, Szymon, grew into a bitter, twisted man who eventually bore three sons of his own. He was cruel and heartless, every last ounce of empathy taken from him because of all he'd endured. One craze-filled night, Szymon beat his wife to death here in this courtyard, and murdered two of his sons, leaving his eldest to carry on the Brov name. Every generation has a similar story, all of them cursed by her kindness and brought up with cruelty and savagery. The Brov's family tree is as twisted as the roots that grow beneath this castle."

"Why are you telling me this?"

"I'm telling you this because kindness, empathy, and *love* doesn't exist inside these walls. It has been eradicated from the bloodline wholly and completely."

"You can't blame Marie's kindness for what happened. She helped those people. She *saved* them."

"And lost herself and her family in the process. For what? All it's achieved is a lifetime of suffering. Generations of it."

"You're using Marie and the tragedy that befell her family as an excuse for your behaviour. Ever heard of the term, breaking the cycle?"

"Don't be naive. You've not lived in our shoes, you've not walked our path or that of the Brov ancestors," he says, stepping closer.

I laugh, I can't help it. "Next you're going to tell me you're not all bad, that you don't kidnap, enslave and coerce. That you don't threaten women with degradation and rape. That you don't enjoy forcing women to submit to your whims, then hire them out to people who pay to fuck them."

"Oh, I wasn't going to say that at all. I'm merely pointing out the truth about us. There's no way out of this. You're no more than entertainment to us. You can fight us all you want. You can cry, and you can scream—God, I *hope* you do—but don't expect anything other than what and who we are, Nought."

"I don't expect anything but cruelty, I don't see anything other than ugliness, and I don't feel anything other than rage."

"You don't seem like the type of person who is strong enough to last the fight," he remarks, almost to himself as he reaches for my tangled and matted hair. "But maybe you'll be the challenge we all need."

"Free my wrists and I'll show you just how strong I am."

Leon tips his head back and laughs, the sound echoing around the courtyard. "I could end this right now with my bare hands around your pretty little throat," he says, his fingers trailing over the column of my neck.

"Then why don't you?"

"Because this is way too much fun." With that he steps back and clicks his fingers, and from the right hand side of the courtyard, Renard and Nala appear. Neither of them acknowledge me other than a cursory glance. He chucks the key to Renard, who catches it. "Get her back to our quarters. Feed her. Make sure she bathes and dresses in the outfit we've left for her. Then take her to our library. Jakub, Konrad and I want to see her dance."

"Yes, Sir. Of course," Renard replies.

"Oh, and Renard," Leon says, addressing his butler but looking at me, "If she escapes in your care there will be consequences. Dire ones."

My heart drops, all thoughts of escape eradicated with his threat. I won't be responsible for their death. Leon knows that.

"Yes, Sir. Understood."

With a terse nod of his head, Leon strides back across the courtyard and disappears into the castle.

"You're shaking," Nala whispers, gently pushing my hands away from the mask, and removing it for me. Her face crumples. "You look terrible."

Over her shoulder I can see my reflection in the bathroom mirror. The foundation I'd so carefully applied has been washed away by the storm, my hair is matted, and dark circles ring my eyes. I've not eaten properly in two days, my shoulders and arms ache, and I'm past the point of exhaustion.

"I've been tied to a tree for the last twenty-four hours, Nala. I'm not sure what you expected," I reply, pushing past her and removing my dress. The bath isn't even halfway filled but I step into it nevertheless, hugging my knees to my chest.

"You didn't do what they asked…" she says, her voice trailing off when she notices the look in my eyes.

"They wanted to put a collar and leash on me. They wanted to treat me no better than a dog. Should I have obeyed? What's next, will I need to lick their hand, shit and piss in front of them?"

Tears spring in her eyes and she looks at her feet, her fingertips clutching the mask tightly. "I'll leave you to bathe. Grandfather has brought you food. It's in the bedroom. The clothes you need to wear are on the bed," she says softly, before turning on her feet and leaving the room, closing the door behind her.

The moment she's gone I allow the tears to fall, sobbing silently into my hands as the water rises up around me. I don't know how to move forward. When I ran, they chased me. When I fought, they punished me. There doesn't seem to be any light at the end of the tunnel, only a long, lonely walk of darkness. I don't know how to fight this. I've only been here a couple of days and already I feel my strength waning, my courage slipping. The only thing I can do is fight one battle at a time. They'll have a weakness, a chink in their armor. When I find it, I'll use it.

With that thought I feel a sense of calm settle over me, allowing me the headspace to wash myself clean. I use the shampoo that Nala placed on a table beside the bath, and rub a healthy amount into my hair. It smells of roses and jasmine, floral and sweet. When I'm thoroughly clean, I climb out of the bath and wrap the towelling robe around myself, then head back out into the bedroom. On the vanity unit is a bowl of pasta with a creamy sauce and a tall glass of water. Despite hating the fact that I'm beholden to these men, I eat every last scrap, cursing every mouthful for tasting so delicious and for providing false comfort, but it gives me much needed sustenance. I can't fight if I'm too weak to stand.

Picking up the bottle of foundation, I spread it across my face, working the liquid into my skin until my complexion has been smoothed out. Once I'm done, I comb through my wet hair and towel dry it as much as possible, then turn my attention to the outfit The Masks have left draped over the end of the bed.

It's not the same dress I've been made to wear up until this moment, but a long sleeved, emerald dress with a sweetheart neckline and floaty skirt that falls just below my knee. It's demure, sophisticated, and not what I was expecting at all. I've been left matching satin ballet slippers, but no underwear. Figures.

Chewing on my lip I mull over my options. I could refuse to do as they ask and be punished once again, try to run and risk the lives of Renard and Nala or do as they want. Whilst I'm grateful they haven't made me dress up in something as revealing as what Four and Eight were wearing yesterday, I'm not foolish enough to think that they won't ever expect me to wear something like that in the future. It's only a matter of time.

Picking up the dress, I finger the material wondering how I'm ever going to escape this terrible place. I can't even bring myself to think about Sandy and Frank, they must be going out of their minds with worry, and Grim… She'll disregard her own safety to bring me home. That frightens me most of all.

Lost in my thoughts, I don't notice Nala enter the room until she clears her throat. "You need to get dressed. The Masks are waiting for you."

I meet her gaze and see the worry in hers. She thinks I'm going to run and whilst I want nothing more than to escape, I can't be responsible for anything happening to her. "It's okay, Nala, I'm coming."

"Thank you," she murmurs, her voice clogged with tears.

Handing her the towelling robe, I put on the dress, wondering how these men seem to know my size given it fits perfectly, then step into the ballet pointes and wind the ribbon around my ankle, securing it with a bow.

Nala's eyes widen. "You look beautiful."

"Shall we go?" I respond tightly.

She chews on her lip, not moving. "They saved me, you know," she whispers.

"Sorry?" I ask, not sure I heard her correctly.

"They saved me from dying."

"I don't understand."

Nala covers her face with her hands and sobs quietly, her thin shoulders shaking as she cries. I sigh, wanting so badly to hate her, to lump her in with The Masks and Renard, but I can't. She's a child. I go to her, placing my arm around her shoulder and guide her to the bed. We sit and I let her cry until her tears dry up.

"You don't have to tell me your story if it's too painful," I say.

"I do. Maybe it'll make you see them differently. They're not all bad. At least they weren't always bad," she adds quietly.

"The Masks?"

"Yes. Renard isn't my blood family, but he took care of me and called me his granddaughter when Jakub, Leon, and Konrad asked him to."

"Why would they do that? How did you come to be here, Nala?"

She turns to face me, grasping my hands in hers. "Jakub found me in the forest as a baby. I was abandoned, left for dead in the roots of one of the trees wearing just a thin babygrow. They can't be certain, but they think I was five or six weeks old. Jakub brought me back to the castle. He was only eight at the time. Konrad and Leon were thirteen, I think."

"Nala, I'm so sorry." I squeeze her hands, urging her to continue.

"For a whole six months they kept me hidden. They looked after me, kept me safe, warm, and fed. They cared for me until one night their father found me in their quarters..." She swallows hard, her eyes brimming with tears. "He wasn't a good man. Not to them, not to anyone."

"What happened?" I ask gently.

"Their father was furious. Renard walked in on him trying to take me from Jakub's arms whilst Leon and Konrad tried to stop him. Renard knew that their father would likely kill me and punish the three of them severely, so he took the blame. He said that I was his granddaughter and that he'd asked the three of them to watch over me. He took the beating from their father, but was allowed to keep me on the proviso that Jakub, Konrad and Leon had nothing more to do with me and I was set to work the moment I could be useful around the castle. I've lived here my whole life. I've seen many things, and very few of them are good," she says, swiping at the tears falling from her eyes. "But I'm telling you, they weren't always this way. They were *good* and kind. Their father beat the kindness from them. Just like his father before him."

"I don't know what to say..."

"I know you hate me for not helping you last night. I know you hate them."

"I don't hate you. You're just a child."

"But you hate them?"

"How can I like men who treat people the way they do? I'm sorry they've had bad upbringings, and whilst that might be the reason why they act the way they do today, it doesn't excuse them for it."

"I understand. It's just..."

"Just what?" I ask.

"They've never let anyone aside from me and Renard into their quarters, and they've never revealed their true faces to *anyone* before. I've even forgotten what they look like."

"That doesn't mean I'm safe around them. It just means that I'll never be able to leave here because I know their true identities. It's another form of control. That's all it is, Nala."

"No. I mean, I guess it could be, but I think it's more than that. You're special, *different,* even if they don't realise that yet. Even if you don't."

My skin covers in goosebumps. She doesn't realise just how different I am. Yet again, I find myself wondering why my path has been crossed with theirs. Why me? Why them?

"What about Thirteen, isn't she special too? You said she was family."

"She's not blood related, at least I don't think so. I don't know her story, but I do know that whilst they care for her in their own way, she has never been invited to their apartment and she has never seen their faces. Only you have. That has to mean something."

"Perhaps," I concede, though what I'm unsure of.

"I know what they've done to you isn't right. I know that keeping you here is wrong. But they care for the Numbers in their own way. They're fiercely protective of them. They'll be like that for you, if you let them."

"They're prisoners, Nala. They're only protective because they're a commodity."

"No. You're wrong. The Numbers are free to leave whenever they want. They *choose* to stay."

"Even if that were true, and the Numbers weren't manipulated into staying here, today Leon threatened both you and Renard. He said that if I escaped in your care there would be consequences. You're just a child. That isn't right."

"They wouldn't hurt me or Renard, not really," she says, but I know she doesn't quite believe it.

"Those boys who took care of you and kept you safe when you were a baby, they're gone. You even said that they'd kill you if they knew you brought me food and water the first night I arrived here. They're not good people, Nala."

"No one can lose goodness. It's still in them. I know it is. They've just forgotten."

"I've seen no evidence to suggest you're right."

Nala opens her mouth to respond, but the door to the bedroom swings open and Renard steps in. He flicks his gaze to our clasped hands then looks up at me. "It's time to go."

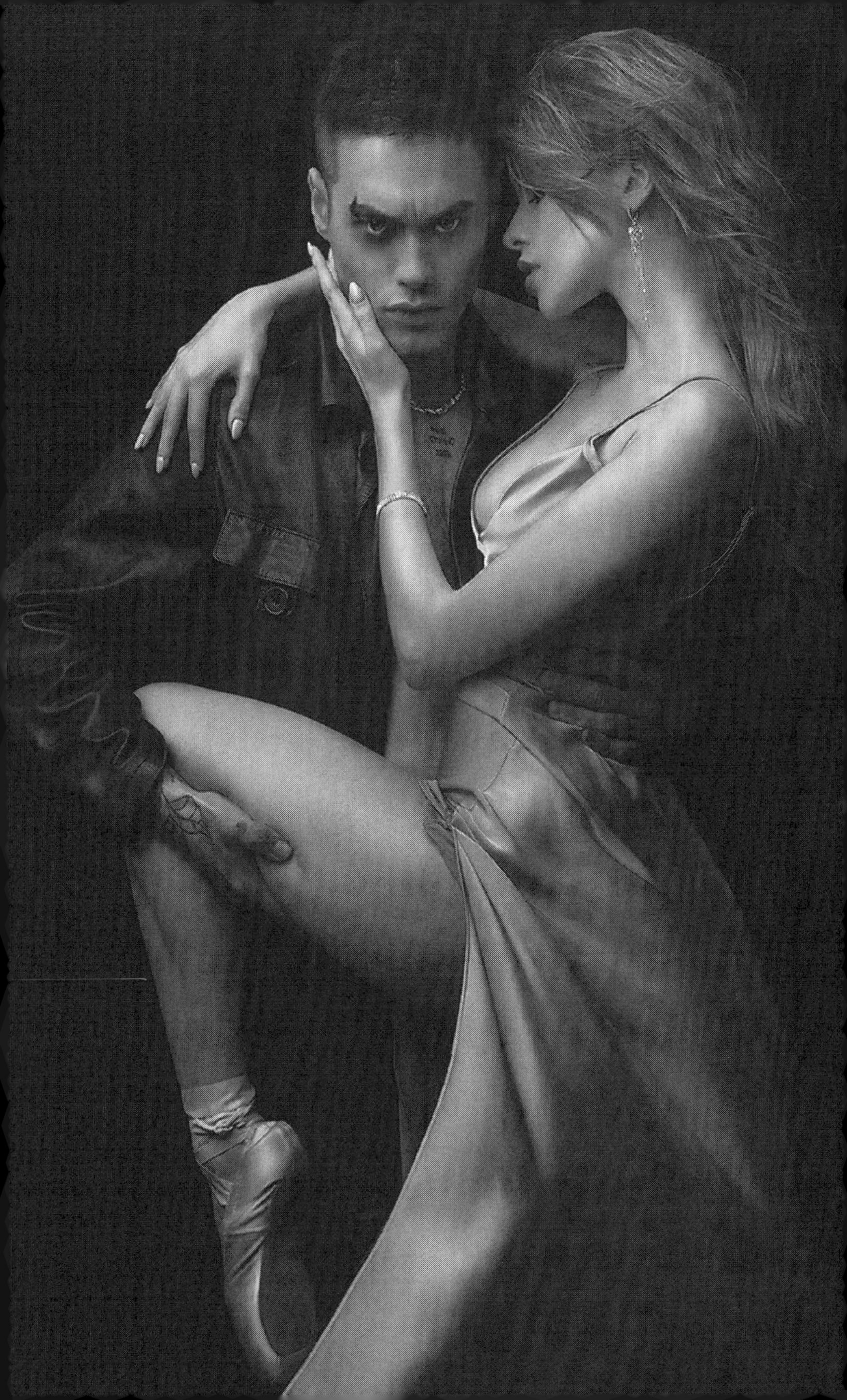

CHAPTER 10

CHRISTY

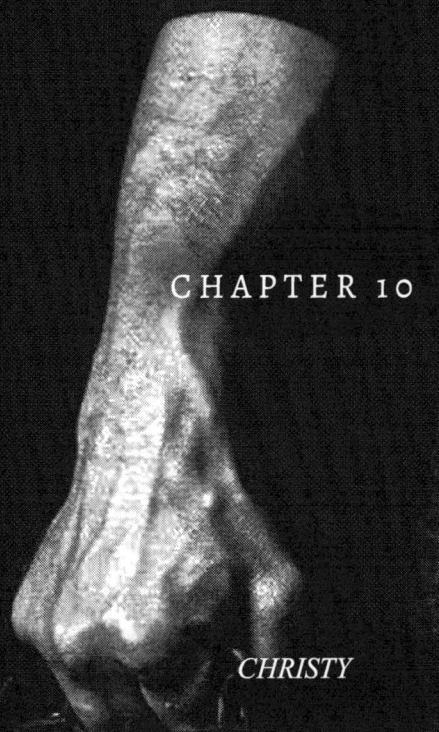

"You're late," Leon snaps as I step into the library situated deeper in their private apartment. Renard is standing directly in front of me, blocking my view of my captor.

"Apologies, Sir. Mistress was fatigued and needed a little longer to rest and recuperate. She is feeling better now," Renard replies, his voice even, neutral. It angers me. I can understand Nala's youthful belief in The Masks' ability to change, but what's Renard's excuse? He's an old man who must understand how the world works.

"Don't apologise on my behalf. I'm not sorry to be late given I don't want to be here at all," I say, stepping out from behind Renard, the heat of the open fire wrapping around my bare legs as I move.

For a moment all Leon does is stare at me from his seat by the crackling flames. In his hand, he holds a crystal decanter and is swirling the amber liquid around and around as he takes his fill of me from behind his mask. Of the three, he scares me the most. He puts me on edge.

"Where are the others?" I ask, trying and failing to hide the tremor in my voice.

"They'll be here shortly." He raises the glass to his mouth and takes a sip, before turning his attention to Renard. Leon jerks his chin. "If you wouldn't mind."

"Yes, Sir." Renard flicks his gaze to me, and I can't help but notice the look of concern in his eyes. Despite it, he leaves me alone with his master, the door closing with a resounding click.

"You look exquisite," Leon remarks. His words might be complimentary, but his tone is not. It's predatory.

"Why am I alone with you?" I ask before I can stop myself.

A slow smile pulls up his lips. "Are you afraid, Nought?"

"I'm *angry*," I say, refusing to look at him or give him the satisfaction of knowing how much he terrifies me. Instead, I allow my gaze to trail over the room. It's a large space, the walls are panelled with dark wood that match the polished floorboards, and three of the four walls are covered in huge floor to ceiling bookshelves filled to the brim with books. The room has one window, but the heavy curtains are drawn, blocking the last of the afternoon's sunlight from the space. Several lamps are dotted about the room giving it a warm, comforting glow. In another world, another life, I would've loved this room. Books are something I treasure, and yet all I want to do is get as far away from this space, and the man who dominates it, as possible.

"You didn't enjoy being shackled to The Weeping Tree?" he asks after a moment, a note of humour in his voice that's as dark as his soul. I snort, not deigning to answer him. "Okay, touchy subject… Let's try again. You seem very interested in these books. We have another library in the East Wing, one that's three times the size of this. If you're good, perhaps Jakub will show it to you. He likes to read as well, you know. At least he did, once upon a time."

"What do you want?"

"You're here to dance for us, of course." He takes another sip of his drink, peering at me over the rim of his glass.

"No. I mean, what do *you* want?"

"Oh," he says, a slow smile spreading across his face. "You think I arranged for this moment alone together, that I'm panting after you like Konrad is?" I raise a brow and fold my arms over my chest, trying not to show my nerves. "It's true, Konrad *is* enamoured. He can't wait to redden that perfect lily white skin of yours."

"I'm not perfect," I mutter under my breath.

If he heard me, he doesn't acknowledge it. Instead, Leon places his glass on the low table in front of him and pushes up out of his chair, striding towards me. Even though every single part of me wants to run, I stay rooted to the spot.

"You think you know me, Nought?"

"I don't presume to know anything other than the fact you're a demented bastard," I hiss.

In a flash, Leon lunges for me, his hand coming up to grasp my throat as he crashes his body against mine, forcing me backwards until my back hits the door. "Fuck, you really do know how to turn me on. Keep going, see how far I like to be pushed."

Our gazes clash and my breath comes out in short, sharp puffs of air as his fingers flex around my throat. "You've got an affliction. You're *ill*."

"You make it sound like there's a cure," he replies, his free hand sliding up my arm and across my shoulder until he cups the back of my head and brushes his lips over my ear. "Are you the cure, Nought? Is that it?"

"No," I reply softly, trapped in his hold. Trickles of fear slide down my spine, but despite that I shift in his hold, turning my head so that my cheek presses against his masked face, and my lips brush against his ear. "I'm your *mirror*."

"What?" he pulls back, his weight lifting off me as he presses the palms of his hand on the door either side of my head. Our gazes clash, but I refuse to look away. I refuse to back down.

"Every wrongdoing, every act of cruelty, debasement and pain that you intend to inflict on me will be reflected back at you. I will never, *ever* succumb to coercion or brainwashing like Four and Eight have so clearly done. I will strive every minute of every day to show you the darkness that swims inside your veins until you see nothing else. Until you *see* who you are. My name isn't Nought. It isn't Zero. It isn't Nothing. It isn't even Christy. I am the magic *mirror* from a fairy tale, I am the one who sees things, who reveals truths, and who never, *ever*, breaks," I reply, pushing off from the door until he's the one who takes a step backwards away from me. "You blame a good woman for your family's pain. But it wasn't Marie. It wasn't even Jan, who died of grief and heartache. It was *Syzmon*. This curse your family has befallen is because one man couldn't see past the pain, and instead of trying to heal, he caused more of it. Just like his children, and their children after that. All the way down to you three. It's been a never-ending cycle of destruction that will continue forevermore unless you face what you are." I breathe deeply, my nostrils flaring as I reach up, my fingers curling around his mask. I push it off his face, chucking it to the floor. His eyes widen with shock, but he makes no move to react, stunned into silence. "So no, Leon. I won't be your victim, your possession or even your cure, but I will be your mirror. I *will* make you see."

His eyes flare with anger, with passion, with hate, but underneath it all there's something else too. *Respect*. It might not be empathy or kindness, but it's a start.

"Konrad was right about you," he eventually says, crouching down to pick up his mask. "You're a worthy foe. I'm going to enjoy breaking you."

"Perhaps," I reply, holding my nerve, aware of how close his face is to my crotch. "Or perhaps it will be me who'll be breaking you."

Looking up at me from his kneeled position, Leon puts his mask back on, securing it behind his head with swift, sure fingers. "You seem very certain of yourself, *Nought*," he says, trailing his fingers over my ankle and up my calf as he peers up at me. His hands are cool, not warm. Smooth, not rough. His touch is gentle, not cruel. There's no ownership in his touch, just exploration. It surprises me, knocks me off-kilter. "But do you know what *I am* certain of?"

"No, what?" I ask.

"That despite your fight, your apparent strength, you're *pliable*. Inside that tough outer casing is someone who's longing to be touched, kissed, *fucked*. You've lived a sheltered life. You've had no lovers, no friends except your dear old aunt and uncle, and *Grim*," he spits out, throwing her name out like a curse. "Admit it, you like the excitement. You crave it."

"Don't flatter yourself. I don't long for anything bar escaping here!"

"Like clay, we can mold you into what we want, what we need," he continues, brushing off my half-truths like confessions in a church. "And you'll love every second of it because deep down, you've always *wanted* to belong to someone. Well, now you belong to *us*. Don't we all just want to belong in one way or another?" he says softly.

Something lurches inside my chest. Something unwelcome. Something I don't want to acknowledge. All those nights I've dreamt of The Masks, seeing them in my visions, all those days these mysterious men have fought their way into my waking thoughts have finally come to fruition. For two years I've lived with these men inside my head, knowing that I couldn't change my path. So why do I persist in trying to do that now? Shouldn't I just accept what's going to happen?

Licking my lips, I flex my fingers uncertain what to do. Fighting someone who is trying to hurt me, who physically restrains me, is easy, but his gentle touch and the truth of his words makes keeping him at arm's length more difficult. I know this man isn't to be trusted. Every cell in my body is telling me as much, yet the way he stares at me, touches me, soothes me with his melodious voice, lulls me into a false sense of security.

His gentleness makes me weak. The irony of that isn't lost on me.

"Get your hands off me," I say, doing the only thing I can in the moment, and whilst my voice is heavy with warning, it's empty of conviction because deep down I know he's right, at least partially. I *have* longed to be touched, kissed, fucked. I'm a virgin in every sense of the word. I haven't lived, not really. I work, *worked* with the dying because I didn't have to share the fact I wasn't living. I've been cared for by my aunt and uncle, by Grim, without even trying to stand on my own two feet. Until The Masks kidnapped me, I hadn't even stepped a foot outside my village, let alone seen any of the world. I've hid, not just because of my physical deformities, but because of who I am and what I can do.

"Am I right?" he asks, refusing to slow the steady creep of his hands towards my virgin pussy.

"You see what you want to see," I lie.

"No. I see the *truth*. I see the tremble of your body as I touch you. The flush of your skin as I edge closer to your pussy. I see the hardness of your nipples despite it being warm in this room. I see your pupils widen with lust. You're *lying* to yourself."

"I tremble because I know I can't win against a man who's physically stronger than me, even though that won't stop me from trying," I counter. "My skin is flushed not because I want your touch but because anxiety is tearing me up inside. My god damn nipples are erect because I'm afraid, not turned on. You're making assumptions based on how my body reacts. Why is that?" I counter. "Does it ease *your* conscience telling yourself that I want this, that I want you?"

He continues to slide his hands up my legs, gently, reverently, and I find my breath catching. I'm caught in his pull, just like I had been in the van with Konrad, and in their sitting room with Jakub. It's no different with Leon, and I hate myself for it.

"You're forgetting one thing, Nought. I have no conscience to ease," he says, his hands stilling.

"You did once," I mutter.

"What did you just say?" His eyes narrow at me and I swallow hard.

"No one is born evil, corrupt, twisted," I reply quickly, not wanting him to suspect that I've found out anything about his past. "What did your father do to you to make you this way?"

"Sold me to The Collector when I was four to pay off his debts," he says casually, as if he hasn't just shocked me to the core.

"Wait. What? But you're *brothers*."

"We are in every single way that matters. But I'm not a Brov, only Jakub holds that title. We are, however, The Masks."

"Konrad too?" I ask, meaning the part about being sold.

Leon meets my gaze and nods. "Yes, Konrad too. Jakub was born the year after I arrived, and Kon was brought here a year after that. He was six when his family sold him to The Collector, the same age as me when he arrived."

"I—"

"Not what you expected?" he asks, his fingers circling over my skin. Soothing, distracting. My traitorous clit throbs.

"No," I admit, trying to figure out if that knowledge changes anything. He may have been stolen too, but he's still the man who kidnapped me, threatened me, chased me and captured me. He's still the man who wants to hurt me despite the gentle way he touches me now.

"You said that you're my mirror, so let me see my reflection in your gaze when I slide my fingers into your wet heat," he says, his voice low, sensual. Full of challenge. "Let me see who's right, me knowing that you want this or you lying about the fact that you don't."

"I don't," I whisper, but even as I say that I can't seem to move, to breathe even. I'm caught in a place of shame, and shocking arousal as his finger traces along the seam of my pussy, and his hot breath flutters against my core.

"You've laid down the gauntlet, Nought. I'm not one to back down from a challenge. The sooner you learn that about me, the better."

With his gaze fixed firmly on mine, his warm finger gently presses against the spot where my pussy lips meet. He rests his fingers there, watching me closely. I fix my face into a blank slate, refusing to let him see how much his touch affects me. He can't know how close to the truth he is. He can't know that I've longed for a man's touch, that a tiny part of me, buried deep in my soul, has wanted to be craved and desired, or that his honesty and insight has touched me more than it should have.

"Stop it," I protest, weaker now.

"I can smell your arousal, Nought," he says, breathing in. My cheeks flush with heat at his proximity. If he were to tip his chin downwards, his lips would be millimeters away from my mound. "You want me to touch you, don't you? You want me to bury my fingers knuckle deep in your ripe pussy and fuck you until your world upends."

"No," I reply through gritted teeth. "I don't." But as I say those words, I don't push Leon's hand away, I don't move as he slides his finger between my folds and finds out just how much I'm lying. Behind his mask, his eyelids drop shut and a low growl rumbles up his throat.

"You're a liar," he whispers, his tongue slipping out from between his plump lips, wetting them. The tip of his tongue runs lightly over the material of my dress, grazing my mound as his fingertip rims my entrance. I have to fight back the moan desperate to release from between my clamped lips, and force myself to hate what he's doing because enjoying this makes me no better than him.

It's *wrong*.

"Stop," I whimper, my hips rocking of their own accord as he presses a damp kiss against my mound, the soft material of my dress adding to the friction.

"Then fight back. *Run*," he says, but it isn't an order. It's a request, almost a plea. Something's shifting. Something fundamental.

"That's what you want," I choke out, barely holding myself together. I feel my seams parting, his words and his honesty, his touch and his attention, snipping at the fraying thread. He gently eases one finger into my core, whilst the pad of his thumb circles my clit with just the right amount of pressure. Two converse emotions war for my attention. Lust and hate.

I hate him. Yet I want to chase the physical feeling, the release he's stoking. I want a man's fingers to make me come. I want the man who's visited me these past two years in my visions to draw out my pleasure. I want *Leon* to make me come. The thought is confusing and gut churning, but undeniable.

Staring down at him, I reach to cup his face, my fingers sliding into his hair. He flinches, but he doesn't stop edging his finger inside of me, he doesn't stop drawing out this potent feeling. It begins to unfurl, the tension in my lower stomach searching for release.

"I can be gentle," he whispers so quietly I almost think I'm mistaken. For the briefest of moments, probably not even long enough to count as one, Leon leans into my hold, his eyelids drooping. He offers me a glimpse of someone I doubt many have seen before, and I know in that moment, I've weakened him. It gives me the strength to do what I must.

"I will *never* give you what you want… You're irredeemable, " I hiss, releasing him from my hold and pushing his hands away, rejecting him, rejecting this.

I *have* to.

His eyes harden. Then, like a switch being turned back on, the bastard returns.

"Then I will *take* it. I will fuck your cunt with my fingers and tongue, and make you scream my name all while hating yourself for liking it so much." His words are crass, harsh, unfeeling, and like a bucket of water over crackling embers, they completely smother any last feelings of desire.

"Fuck you!" I snap.

Bringing my knee up, I slam it as hard as I can into his jaw, hearing the sound of bone meeting bone. His head snaps back, and the force makes him topple backwards just as Jakub and Konrad enter the room.

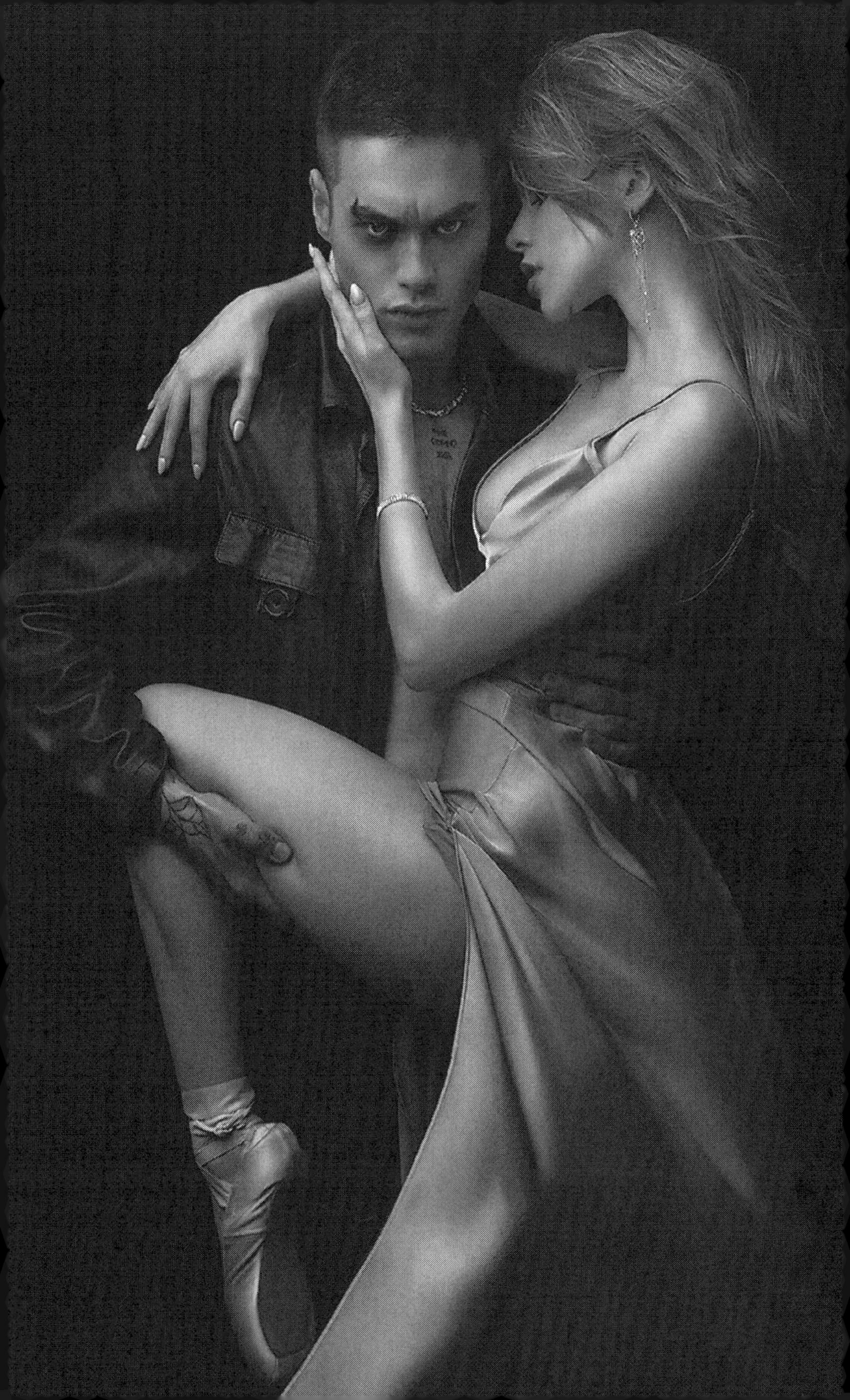

CHAPTER 11

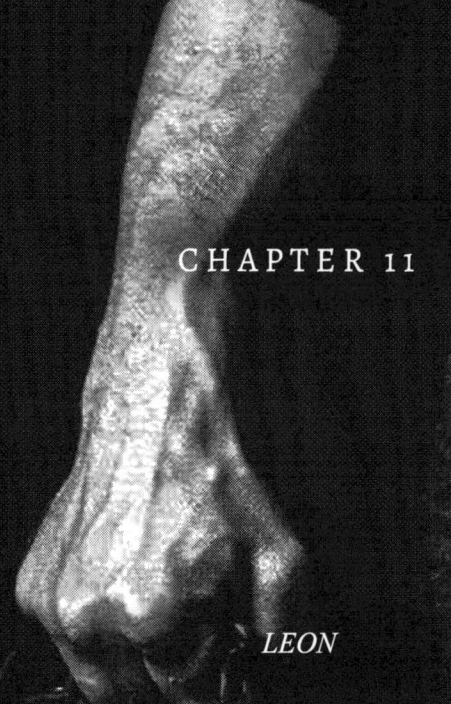

LEON

F*uck.*
Fuck. Fuck. Fuck. Fuck!
Who is this woman and what the hell has she done to my self-control?

She said she'll be my mirror... That she'll make *me* see. What she doesn't understand is, unlike my brothers, I'm not afraid of my reflection. I don't pretend. I know what I am and I happen to fucking like it.

Except for the brief moment when you remembered that kid you were. You didn't like it then.

"Fuck!" I curse under my breath.

This isn't how it was supposed to play out. I was supposed to scare her and instead she has me confessing our history and falling to my knees before her, touching her like she's made of fragile glass, rather than breaking her and cutting myself on the shards.

I don't get on my damn knees for anyone. Ever. Not since...*Fuck, don't think about that. Don't.*

Konrad's deep laughter pulls me up sharp, and I shoot to my feet.

"Looks like someone started the fun without us," he says, eying me as he enters.

"Just making sure she's still got the fight within her. Can't have her *wanting* our touch, now can we? At least not yet, anyway," I reply quickly, sliding my hand in my trouser pocket so they can't see how my fingers glisten with her juices. I grip hold of my cock, telling it to calm the fuck down because getting hard at her soft whimpers and gentle moans is a sign of fucking weakness. Her screams are what I *crave*.

"She just kneed me in the chin for tying up my shoelaces. She *thought* I was going to touch her." My gaze flicks to Nought. She frowns but she doesn't try to out me. Why doesn't she tell them I'm lying? I grit my jaw, the feel of her fingers in my hair and the gentle way she'd held me lingering.

"I'm surprised you're not punishing her for her insolence," Konrad remarks, striding over to the bottle of cognac that I left on the side table and pouring himself a shot. He side-eyes Nought as he passes, but she keeps her gaze fixed on me. Waiting for my next move.

"You walked in before I could. Want to help me, Brother?" I ask, grinning at Konrad. He swallows the shot, the amber liquid matching the colour of his mask.

"Fuck yes."

"Pigs," Nought hisses, her shoulders tensing and her hands curling into fists. She's like a feral cat, her claws unsheathed, ready to protect herself. But feral cats are just domesticated cats in disguise. She'll come to obey sooner or later. I'll have her purring beneath my touch soon enough, and when she trusts me completely, that's when I'll take what I *really* want. There'll be no gentleness then, only need.

"We've been called worse," Konrad says.

"Touch me and I'll rip your goddamn eyes out."

My lip twitches at her fight. I'm beginning to really enjoy that mouth, and I can't wait to find out what she tastes like, but more than that, how fucking loud she screams. "You really are a tease," I say, smirking as I stalk towards her. "But that's okay, they're the most fun."

"Wait," Jakub says, stepping between Nought and me. He lifts her chin with his finger. "Want to tell me what happened, Nothing?" he questions evenly. To anyone who doesn't know him they'd see a controlled man, someone who isn't affected by anyone or anything. Kon and I know differently. Jakub is affected by *everything*. Always has been. He just handles it differently now.

"What he said," she snaps, anger boiling in her eyes. She's trembling with it, and fuck if I don't love the affect I've had on her. She could've dropped me in the shit, but her shame at enjoying what happened keeps her mouth shut. I smile internally. She's not as immune to our attention as she thinks.

"You're certain?"

There's a warning in his voice, despite his even tone. Nought appears to understand its meaning as much as Konrad and I do, despite not knowing him well enough yet. That in and of itself is intriguing. If you lie to Jakub then you have to pay the consequences. I can take the punishment he'd dish out for lying to him. I'd even enjoy it. But Nought? She wouldn't last a minute.

"What can I say, he's an arsehole. I kneed him in the chin."

Konrad roars with laughter, but Jakub just nods his head. I'm not so certain he believes her, but for now he drops the subject. Grasping her elbow, Jakub walks Nought into the centre of the library. It's a large space, the only furniture are the bookcases lining the walls and the four chairs placed by the fireplace, two on either side. Konrad and I sit to the left, Jakub to the right. The empty chair remains out of respect for our father.

"You're here to dance. So dance."

"Just like that?"

"Just like that." Jakub twists on his feet to face me. My little brother, the true Brov heir, meets my gaze with his steely one. "I told you to wait for us to join you before requesting Renard bring Nothing here."

He's angry, he has every right to be. I disobeyed his direct orders. It's punishable, he knows it as well as I do. "You did."

"And yet you decided to do the exact opposite of that?"

"I did." There's no point in denying it. We both know I overstepped.

Jakub nods sharply. "You know what to do."

Without hesitation, I pull off my t-shirt, dropping the material to the floor. Konrad passes Jakub the leash, the very same one Nought was so determined to run from. Out of the corner of my eye I see Nought watching us. Horror rushes across her face as she realises what's about to happen.

"Make sure you really mean it, Brother," I say as I step further into the room and give him my back.

"Don't I always? We learnt from the best, after all," Jakub replies, and I hear the tightness in his voice. Even after all these years he still battles with his love for his father, the man who stripped him back to nothing so that Konrad and I could help rebuild him into the man he is today.

Locking eyes with a trembling Nought, I hear the familiar whoosh as the leash cuts through the air. She flinches, her hand rising to cover her mouth as the first lash stings my skin.

"Ahhh," I moan, the rush like nothing else. I fucking crave it.

"Oh God," Nought cries, unable to comprehend how I could enjoy being whipped. Konrad chuckles, Jakub doesn't make a sound.

Five lashes, that's what I'll receive. Five lashes for disobeying his orders. Jakub doesn't hold back, he never has because he knows as well as I do that I need this. Pain is my medicine. It gives me strength. A focus. It reminds me of who I am.

With every lash a calmness settles over me, the glorious pain ebbing away to reveal that special place I've searched for my whole life. Fucking nirvana. After the fourth lash, Jakub steps out from behind me and walks towards Nothing. He holds out the leash to her. What's he doing? My fucking breath catches in my throat. Even Konrad seems to have trouble breathing.

"Take it," he says.

"W—what?" she stutters, shaking her head and backing away.

"You heard me. Take it."

"N—no. I can't do that. No!"

Within two strides, Jakub grasps the back of Nought's head and marches her over to me. She stumbles from the force, her hands flying out to prevent herself from crashing straight into me. Nought's palms are like fire on my sweat-slicked chest. Her nostrils flare at the touch, her hands lingering a fraction of a second too long before she yanks them away.

"I won't do it!" she says as he grips her wrist and forcefully shoves the leash into her hand.

Jakub leans in and presses his lips against her ear. "You will do it, or you will receive it. Your choice."

"Where?" she asks, surprising us all with her question, her gaze fixed on me.

A muscle feathers in Jakub's jaw, just beneath the curve of his jet-black mask. "Where *what*?"

"Where will I receive it?"

"Your back, same as Leon."

"Then I'll receive it," she says, surprising us all.

"Interesting," Konrad remarks. I can hear the excitement in his voice without needing to look at him. I'm betting he's gagging to be the one to lash her back, then heal her with his false words of affection. Everyone thinks I'm the worst, the most dangerous of the three of us, but at least I don't pretend I'm something I'm not. What you see is what you get. Konrad's still a twisted fuck, he just likes to pretty it up with falsities a little more than I do.

"As much as I appreciate you stepping in, Nought, I can take the pain," I say, smiling like the devil. This is too fucking perfect.

"Don't flatter yourself. I'm not doing this for *you*," she snaps.

"Then who, if not me?" I bite back. This fucking woman.

She swallows hard but she doesn't respond. Instead she shoves the leash back at Jakub, turns on her heel and steps a few paces away from us, giving Jakub her back just like I had a moment before. When she reaches for the hem of her dress, and begins to slide it upwards, Jakub stiffens.

"STOP!" he shouts.

She jumps, her hands falling away and her skirt dropping back down around her knees. When she looks at him over her shoulder, her long flaming hair forming gentle waves down her back, even I have a hard time stopping my cock from twitching. She's fucking growing on me. "What?"

"Czy mówiłem ci, żebyś zdjął sukienkę?" he says, his voice thick with annoyance.

"What? I don't understand?" Nought replies.

"Did I tell you to take your dress off?" he repeats in English.

She shakes her head. "I assumed—"

"Well, you assumed wrong," Jakub grunts. He doesn't want her naked yet, we have a special something planned for that moment. So for now, the dress stays on, though it will do little to protect her from what's about to happen. The material is thin, so she'll still feel the pain, and boy am I ready to hear her fucking scream.

"Oh fuck," Konrad mutters under his breath, handing me my t-shirt as he moves his mouth to my ear. "Ten grand she pukes."

"Twenty she faints before that happens," I retort, pulling on the t-shirt and rolling my shoulders.

"Deal." My brother holds out his hand and I shake it. I don't much care about the money, between us we've got enough to last ten lifetimes. Money doesn't motivate us. It never has.

Jakub doesn't hesitate. He raises the leash then brings it down on her back. The sound of it cracking against her skin makes my blood erupt and my cock stiffen, but the silence afterwards, the absence of sound...

Fuck. I've never been more turned on in my life.

She doesn't make a murmur. Not a whimper.

Instead, she turns around to face us with nothing but hate in her eyes. If she'd softened a little when I'd touched her earlier, testing her boundaries, then she's hardened right back up now. There's no denying that at this moment she is *fierce*. Out of the corner of my eye I see Konrad's jaw drop.

Jakub stares at her for a long moment, waiting for another reaction. I can tell by the tense way he holds himself and the grip on the leash that he's surprised too. That doesn't happen very often. Having lived the life we have, doing what we do, we're all clued up about the intricacies of the human psyche. The Numbers remain here because we've manipulated them into believing what we want them to believe. This prison is successful only because the Numbers no longer see it as one. Take a lion in a zoo for example. It's fed the primest cuts of meat, taken care of and given a certain amount of freedom. The Lion can still be what it is, but has been conditioned to live in a cage. Still beautiful, still full of life, but not free. The same applies to the Numbers. We've given them the illusion of freedom, a life they think they want. We've allowed them to be exactly who they are deep down inside, with their artistry and their sexual proclivities. There are no boundaries with regards to those two things. The only boundary, the one that's most important, is the cage they don't see, the one that keeps them in this castle. So far, only one of them has tested their freedom, or at least the illusion of it, and in the end it wasn't us who caged him but one of the other Numbers.

"Are you done?" she asks, flicking her gaze between us all, before finally resting her eyes on Jakub.

He nods. "Yes."

With a deep intake of breath she shifts her feet, extends her left foot, then rises up onto her pointes and begins to dance, astounding us all once again.

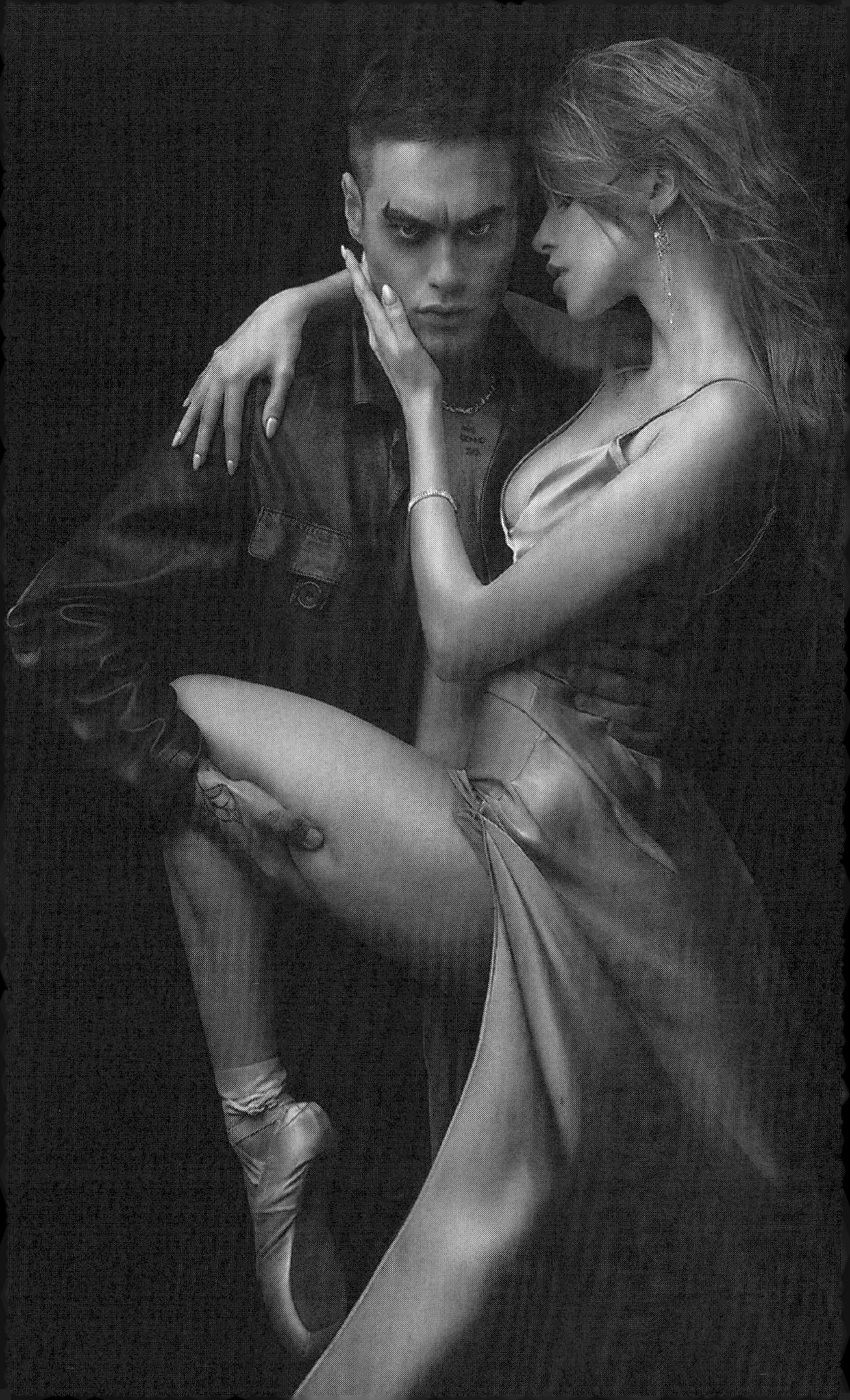

CHAPTER 12

CHRISTY

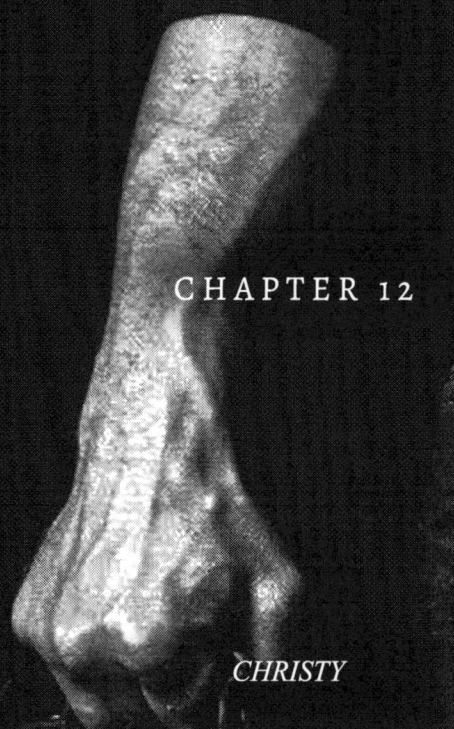

My feet still, the lingering sting of the lash Jakub gave me registering in some distant part of my subconscious. I slam the lid on the pain, forcing it back to where it belongs as I dip low to the ground, my right leg slightly extended, my left knee bent outwards as I take a bow. Not once do I take my eyes off them.

My captors.

The Masks.

Sweat slides down my forehead, a few stray strands of hair sticking to my temple and cheek. I push them off my face as I slowly rise, adjusting my feet into fourth position.

It's been a while since I've danced so freely. More often than not, outside factors prevent me from completely letting go, from breathing *life* into every step rather than simply following them. Believe me, there's a difference. My muscles ache pleasantly, my heart pounds with exertion, but my soul, for the briefest of moments, had flown free.

Dancing has always been a passion of mine. Grim says that I'm good, and yet I've never been able to pursue a career for fear of what doors it will open and the people I might meet, because where people are, so too are more visions. It's why I work with the dying. There aren't any surprises. Death is a finality that even I can't see beyond.

How ironic then that under these circumstances, I'm able to dance with a gravity I haven't experienced before. I'm not certain whether it was the degradation of the stinging lash, being free from the shackles or the way Leon had touched me, but for the first time in my life I didn't hold back. I let everything out, and for the briefest of moments, whilst I danced, I *was* free.

Of course, it was just an illusion.

As The Masks stare at me, I wonder how many more times we'll play this game. I'm not a fool, I understand what's happening here. I'm an expert at keeping myself locked away, imprisoned in a cage of my own making. I've done it my whole life. Leon was right in his assumption that I've lived a sheltered life, but that wasn't forced on me, I *chose* it.

The difference is that it was *my* choice, but being kept prisoner here isn't.

"You're talented," Konrad says, a note of awe and sincerity in his voice. I don't allow myself to bask in it. I know a manipulative prick when I see one. This constant push and pull is part of their mind games, something they no doubt honed on the other Numbers. I've been shackled one minute, freed the next. I've been treated abominably then shown a modicum of decency. This kind of behaviour can wear down the strongest of people until, eventually, they'll believe whatever version of the truth these men tell them. Not me. I'll never lose sight of what this is.

Never.

"How long have you been dancing?" Jakub asks as he rests his elbows on the armrests of his chair, clasping his hands together in front of him. He's looking at me more like a commodity than a possession. I'm not sure that's any better.

"Why don't you tell me? You seem to think you know so much about me already," I counter, refusing to make this easy for him.

Konrad smiles, his uncovered lips pulling back over straight, white teeth. "I don't know about my brothers, but up until this moment, I thought I understood you. Now I'm not so certain. You're quite the mystery, Zero."

"You think?" Leon asks, swirling the amber liquid in his glass. "I'm not sure there's much depth to her. She can dance, but she's nowhere near as talented as the others. She's pretty, but she's not stunning. She's got fight, but I'm willing to bet it won't last. I'm bored already."

I grit my teeth, but don't bite. Leon can go fuck himself.

"Well, *I'm* still interested." Konrad says, trailing his heated gaze over my body. "Anyone who can take a lashing like Zero just did is worth investing more time in. I'd be happy to see how long it would take her to scream, seeing as you've already lost interest in her." Leon stiffens, his shoulders tensing. Konrad chuckles, glancing at his brother. "Yeah, I thought as much."

"She's good enough to be in the show," Jakub says, interrupting them both and leading the conversation down an entirely different tangent. "The Menagerie could do with another dancer. Father must've thought so too, given he died trying to acquire one. Her name is Penelope Scott. I assume you know her, given your sister was so intent on keeping her from us?"

"We haven't met but, yes, I know of her," I say, determined not to give away just how much. She's a close friend of Grim's, as close as anyone has ever gotten apart from Beast. Pen is important to my sister and whilst we've never met, I know a great deal about her and the men she loves through Grim.

"By all accounts she's an exceptional dancer," he continues.

"I wouldn't know. Like I said, we've never met."

Jakub nods, turning his attention to his brothers. "What do you think? Should we put Nothing into the show?"

"No," they both say simultaneously.

"Why?" Jakub asks, the lazy way he twists his head to look at them belies the tension he holds in his jaw. If I'm not mistaken, this seems like some kind of test.

"She's *ours*, remember," Konrad reminds him. There's no denying the possession in *his* voice.

"Yes, and she'll remain ours. I'm merely suggesting that she could perform in the show. That's it."

"And what if *I* don't want to? What then?"

Jakub turns back to face me, steepling his fingers beneath his chin. "Do you honestly think you have a choice?"

I fold my arms across my chest. "I'm not foolish enough to think anything of the sort. I'm simply asking a question. What will happen to me if I refuse? Will you tie me to The Weeping Tree again, maybe you'll lock me up in the dungeons, or wait... Will I be whipped?"

Jakub pushes up out of his seat and strides across the room towards me. "Let me show you," he snarls, grasping my upper arm and yanking me to the other side of the room. Stopping before one of the tall bookcases, he looks over his shoulder at his brothers. "Leon, Konrad, you too."

Leon grins. "Brother, so soon?"

"Why not? She's here now. We may as well show her," Jakub replies, reaching for a red, leather bound book on the shelf level to his shoulder. He pulls it towards him and with a puff of cold air, the door swings inwards revealing a stone staircase that curls upwards and out of sight.

"What's up there?" I ask, knowing that wherever we're going, it can't be good.

"You'll see," he replies, blocking my exit so that I have no choice but to climb the steep, stone steps.

When we get to the top of the circular stairwell, lit periodically by the soft glow of the sunset pouring through slim rectangular windows, a door greets us. It's arched at the top, thick metal hinges are fixed into the dark wood and the surface is gnarly and bumpy just like the bark of The Weeping Tree. I have the sudden urge to touch the wood, and reach out pressing my fingers against the surface.

Behind me Jakub steps close, I can feel the warmth of his breath against my cheek as he slides a large metal key into the lock. "Five years ago a storm brought down several trees in the forest. This door was made from one of the ancient oaks," he explains, turning the key in the lock and pushing open the door. "As was every piece of furniture in this room…"

With his chest against my back, and his hand clasped around my upper arm, he walks me into the room. I draw in a sharp intake of breath at what I'm confronted with.

"No," I whisper, aware of Leon and Konrad entering the space.

"Yes," Jakub replies.

Out of the corner of my eye I see Konrad walk over to the huge four poster bed taking up the centre of the room, big enough to sleep several people. He reaches up and removes his mask, chucking it into a woven basket on the floor beneath the window then sits on the mattress, his hand moving over the bedding leisurely. None of that would've bothered me had I not seen the four rusty chains hanging from the bed frames from metal rings. At the end of each chain is a leather cuff. It doesn't take a genius to work out what they're for.

Konrad catches my eye as he picks up one of the cuffs, fingering the leather almost reverently as Leon approaches the bed. "You are the first woman to enter this space..." Konrad's voice trails off as he licks his lips.

"I don't want—"

"You don't want this?" Leon asks, trailing his hands up the bedpost provocatively. "This is tame in comparison to what's over there." He points to the far left of the room at a huge armoire, also made out of wood. "Jakub, may I?" he asks.

"Do it," Jakub says from behind me.

My throat dries. I don't want to see what's in that wardrobe, and before Leon's even reached it, Jakub leans down, his lips pressing against my ear as his arm wraps around my waist. "You wanted to know what would happen to you if you refused to perform in The Menagerie. Well, *Nothing*," he says, gripping my jaw with his hand and forcing me to look at Leon opening the doors of the armoire, "We'll do *everything*."

Leon stands back to reveal a plethora of instruments. My mouth dries out at what I see before me. There are whips and floggers in various coloured leather. Wooden paddles in an assortment of sizes. Mouth gags, blindfolds, lengths of silk, feathers and nipple clamps. There are several different vibrators in all manner of shapes and sizes. One particularly scary looking one is as long and as wide as my forearm.

"Oh my God," I whisper, all of it shocking, but none more so than the knives fixed to the inside of the doors. I'm vaguely aware of Jakub's fingers circling my hip as he holds me against him. It's a comforting gesture, gentle. I don't trust it for a second.

Leon picks up a knife. His fingers wrap around the leather handle of a particularly sharp-looking blade. It may be only a couple of inches long, but it could do untold damage in the wrong hands.

"We're all partial to a bit of blood play, aren't we, Brothers?" Leon says, reaching up and removing his mask. He places it on the bed and Konrad picks it up, chucking it in the basket alongside his mask. "There's something so erotic about fucking a woman with a knife pressed to the thrumming pulse in her neck. You never really know if you'll finally lose control and let the blade slit her throat."

"Amen to that, Brother," Konrad agrees, getting off the bed and walking over to the armoire. "Though I do love the colour of a woman's skin when it blooms beneath the stinging blow of a paddle."

"You're sick," I say, unable to hide the mounting fear. "How can anyone find pleasure in pain? How can *you*?"

"That's a very one dimensional way to look at the world, Zero. Intense pleasure can be drawn from pain so long as you know what you're doing," Konrad counters. "The three of us are experts in walking that fine line."

"Am I supposed to be impressed?" I counter, swallowing hard as Jakub walks me towards the bed.

"No. Right now you're reacting just the way we'd expected," Leon says, pressing the tip of the blade into his thumb, slicing the pad. Blood oozes out of the cut, trickling down his thumb and hand. He holds the blade out to Konrad, who grins and takes it from him. I watch as he cuts his thumb in exactly the same spot.

"Sit," Jakub demands, twisting my body around and pushing me back onto the bed. I throw my hands out to stop me from falling backwards. Recovering quickly, I move to stand, but Konrad throws Jakub the knife and the blade rushes between us, keeping my arse planted on the bed. Jakub catches it by the handle, a gentle smile pulling up his lips as he removes his mask with his free hand, then turns to face me. It's clear from the look in his eyes that he wants to cut me.

"Don't," I blurt out, holding my hands up defensively and squeezing my eyes shut. My heart pounds in my chest, my throat closes over in fear, but when nothing immediately happens and Leon starts to chuckle, I force myself to look. Jakub holds the blade against his thumb, cutting himself just like Konrad and Leon had. Tipping his head back, there's a look of pure bliss on his face as blood trickles from the wound. I watch it slide down his thumb and drip from his wrist, tiny droplets spilling onto the skirt of my dress. I'm aware of Konrad and Leon climbing onto the bed behind me, and despite the relative warmth of the room I feel nothing but coldness. Goosebumps break out over my skin. I grit my jaw to stop my teeth from chattering. They can't know how afraid I am.

Slowly, Jakub lowers his head, meeting my gaze. He lifts the knife and I swallow hard, waiting for him to do what I know he desires.

He wants to cut me, hurt me. He wants to see me bleed.

I maintain eye contact with him, ignoring the fact that Leon and Konrad have moved to sit either side of me on the bed, and steel myself for what's to come. Only he doesn't cut me like I expected him to do. Instead, he lifts the knife and slams it into the wooden post before grasping a handful of hair and pulling my head back. Pushing between my parted knees, he leans over and presses his lips against my ear.

"If I wanted to cut you, Nothing, there wouldn't be anything you could do or say to stop me," he says, pressing his blooded thumb against the column of my throat and dragging it over the throbbing pulse in my neck. "This room will be our sanctuary. We can be whoever we want to be within the safety of these walls. I hadn't planned on showing you this space so soon, but as you're so determined to disobey every command, now that you're here, you may as well experience a little taste."

"No!" I cry, jerking against his hold, but Leon and Konrad grip my upper arms, keeping me still.

"This time, I'm asking you not to fight," he says, sliding his thumb into my mouth. The metallic taste of blood hits me, and I try not to gag. The urge to bite him is strong, but he shakes his head reaching for the knife once more. "Don't even think about it," he warns, pulling the knife free and resting it against my throat.

Konrad leans in closer, pressing his bloodied thumb against my cheek. "If I were you, I'd keep very still."

"Or you could move, and *bleed* for us," Leon suggests, swiping his blooded thumb across my clavicle.

I choose to keep still.

Jakub watches me, the intensity of his stare cutting deeper than the knife he holds delicately against my throat. "Suck me clean, Nothing," he says darkly, the words filled with sexual connotations. "I want to know what I've got to look forward to."

My mouth pools with saliva as he presses his thumb against my tongue, but given I have a knife held against my throat I really have no other choice but to suck. So that's what I do. I wrap my lips tightly around his thumb, suctioning him into my mouth. More blood weeps from the wound, but I swallow it, never once taking my eyes off him. He tastes like he smells, like a forest after a rainshower, earthy, strangely *warm*.

"Good girl," he whispers, pulling his thumb from my mouth and leaving a trail of blood across my lips. Next to me Konrad groans, shifting position. Before I can even protest, his thick thumb is pushed between my lips.

"Heal me with your tongue, Zero," he says.

It's an odd thing to say, but then again these men are hardly normal. Still, I hesitate, sensing that Jakub must give his permission first. When he nods his head, I delicately lick the pad of Konrad's thumb, tasting him. A mixture of blood and woodsmoke fills my mouth. He groans as

I lick his thumb, the tip of my tongue sliding along the cut before releasing him.

"Fuck," he mutters.

Out of the corner of my eye I see him reach for his crotch, adjusting himself, and despite everything they've threatened, despite the knife pressed against my throat, a tiny part of me feels a sick sense of satisfaction knowing that I'm turning him on. In this moment I don't feel weak, I feel powerful. It's both liberating and unwelcome. Why do these men make me feel this way? I don't feel differently towards them. I still hate them for what they've done, but the woman in me, the one who's only ever known pity or disgust, feels a sense of pride.

"My turn," Leon says, edging closer. He presses his nose into my hair, breathing me in as he pushes his thumb between my lips. "I don't want you to suck, Nought. I want you to *bite*," he growls, the sound rumbling up his throat. Internally I smile, because I'm going to do just that. I press my teeth into the fleshy pad of his thumb and bite as hard as I can. This time blood spurts from the cut, filling my mouth with metallic warmth. The sound he makes is one of intense pleasure. It's *feral*. Shockingly, my toes curl in my ballet pointes.

"That's enough," Jakub snaps and I release Leon's thumb, swallowing his blood like this is something I do every day. My stomach churns, my throat squeezes. God, these men. I hate them, despise them for all they've done, all they intend to do, and yet… There's something primal about this moment that makes me feel more alive than I've ever felt in my life.

What's wrong with me?

"That wasn't so difficult, was it?" Jakub points out, easing back the knife and snapping me out of my thoughts. "You obey and we reward you. How would you like to be rewarded?"

"Sleep. I want to sleep," I reply instantly, heaving out a breath as he stabs the knife back into the bedpost. I need to get away from them. I need to distance myself from these feelings that persist, that I don't understand or even want. I need a moment to catch my breath. I've been running on a few hours of sleep for the past forty-eight hours and I'm exhausted. What little energy I have left is quickly fading, the spike of adrenaline that got me through the past hour or so is leaching from me even as we speak. The lack of sleep and all this stress must be having a psychological effect.

This isn't me.

"Then that is what you shall have… but first," he says, lifting my chin with his hand, "I'm going to claim your first kiss."

Before I'm able to protest, his mouth is pressed against mine in a hard line. He's unforgiving, unyielding as he grips the back of my neck. I whimper against his mouth, my lips parting at the sound, and he takes the opportunity to slide his tongue between them. I open, and he takes.

Then he ravages my mouth. He plunders. He fucks me with his tongue. Konrad and Leon pin my arms, leaving me unable to push him away. I can't even move my head given his hand is clutching me so tightly.

All I can do is let him kiss me. I'm helpless against these men.

His teeth crash against mine, his tongue probes and searches, swooping into my mouth. This is an explorative kiss as much as an angry one, and I wonder if he can taste his blood on my tongue, his brothers' blood.

Does it turn him on?

Do I turn him on?

He bites down on my bottom lip, drawing blood, sucking on it before licking the pain away. His fingers don't soften in my hair with my whimper, they grip tighter.

"Jakub," Konrad warns, but it's as though he's in some far away place, not right next to us.

Jakub's only response is to kiss me *harder*, to plunder my mouth *deeper*. His nose smashes against mine as he bends my head back, shoving his body further between my legs and kisses me until I'm gasping for air. This kiss is invasive, as though he's trespassing on my soul, searching for something.

He obviously doesn't find what he's looking for because he lets me go with a shove, rearing backwards, his eyes blazing. "I have one question that I'm going to ask you, and I want the truth. Lie to me, and

I will allow my brothers to do what they've been wanting to do to you since the moment they laid eyes on you. Believe me, sucking their thumbs will be nothing compared to what they'll make you do. Your throat will be so raw from their cocks you won't be able to swallow without being reminded of them."

Leon chuckles as I drag in a panicked breath. "Fuck yes," he grinds out, lowering his nose to my hair and breathing me in.

"Brother?" Konrad questions, as uncertain of Jakub's motives as I am.

Jakub refuses to look at him. Instead he cups my cheek, rubbing more blood across my skin, marking me with his affliction. "Before Konrad and I arrived this evening, did Leon touch you intimately?" he asks.

"What the fuck?" Leon's grip tightens on my arm as fear wraps around my throat like a snake, constricting my airways. Jakub glances at him, narrowing his eyes.

"Be very, *very* careful how you choose to respond right now," Jakub warns me, fixing me with his stare. I consider lying but what would be the point? Jakub already knows the answer. Bringing me up here, showing me this room, wasn't just a warning of what could happen to me should I disobey them again, it was a ploy to reveal the truth. I can see that now. "Well?"

"Yes," I say.

"Fuck!" Konrad breathes, the tension in the room thickening with every intake of breath. Leon's grip becomes painful, and I don't know whether it's because he's angry at me for telling the truth or is afraid of the repercussions. Either way, I don't care. I don't owe him a thing.

"Take your hands off Nothing," Jakub orders, cutting his gaze to Leon who drops my arm immediately. I automatically reach for the spot, rubbing my fingers over the tender skin. "You don't get to fucking touch her again until I say so. Understand me?"

"I understand you," Leon replies with a terse nod of his head.

"Get out. I'll deal with you later."

"You want me to leave?" The note of incredulity in Leon's voice is hard to miss.

"I want you to get out of my fucking sight!" Jakub roars, all control slipping. I flinch at his wrath, my fingers curling into the bedspread.

Leon doesn't retaliate. He simply nods, climbs off the bed and leaves the room without a backward glance.

"Brother. Be calm," Konrad says, trying to reassure him.

"Be calm? That's twice he's disobeyed me in the past twenty-four hours. Don't tell me to be calm! He's losing control and right now we need to focus. *All* of us. Take him to the lake. He needs to cool off. I will not let a piece of pussy come between us. No matter how fucking tempting."

"Fine, but what are you going to do with Zero?" Konrad asks.

"We're going to have a chat and then I'm taking her to my room."

"Why *your* room?"

"Because I don't trust either of you not to end up in her bed late at night when I'm asleep. My door has a lock and only I have a key. *I* can control myself around her."

"I can too," Konrad counters, his nostrils flaring as he stands.

"Don't bullshit me, Kon. I know you better than you know yourself. You both need to remember what we discussed. She's only *ours* and not just *mine* on the proviso neither of you lose your heads. We have a business to run. That is our priority. Got it?"

"Understood," Konrad responds, and with a brief flick of his gaze to me, marches from the room.

The second the door swings shut behind him, Jakub lets out a long breath then reaches for the knife and strides over to the armoire. Wiping the blade on a cloth he picks up from the shelf, he places it back in its sheath that's tacked to the door.

"If I'm causing so much trouble, why don't you just let me go?" I ask quietly, certain my question will cause me more pain, but asking it regardless.

"Because it's too late. There's no going back now. Since the decision was made to seek our revenge and make you ours, all Konrad and Leon have thought about is what you could give them. They've waited a long time for you. I won't deny them."

"And what, exactly, am I supposed to give them?"

"Their deepest desires…" his voice trails off as he closes the doors to the armoire, then strides back towards me.

"And that's to beat me with those instruments, degrade me, control me, *fuck* me, is that it?"

Jakub laughs, the sound brittle, harsh. "They want far more than that, Nothing. This room is just touching the surface of what they need. This is *tame*."

"Tame?" I shiver at the gravity of his words, at the honesty in his eyes. It's a bitter truth to swallow, and only fuels my need to escape here as soon as the opportunity presents itself. I can't let any of them get into my head anymore than they already have. These men are master manipulators. Who's to say that this conversation right now isn't just another ruse, another way to get me to drop my guard? Right now Jakub and I are having a conversation. It isn't one-sided, it's a sharing of information, and it changes the dynamics, somewhat. But I've learnt many things from being the sister to a powerful criminal, and one of them is to know your enemy. Study them, learn and adapt. They think they know me, but they have no idea. It's only a matter of time before another vision presents itself, and when it does, I'll be ready to use it to my advantage.

"You've lived in a world where vanilla sex is the norm," Jakub continues, oblivious to my internal thoughts. "I'm betting *Netflix and chill* is about as exciting as it gets in your fantasy world." He raises a brow and smirks, but I refuse to acknowledge that he's right. All I've ever wanted was to be with someone who loves the true me, watch movies with them and make love. It sounds so pathetic now that he's called me out. "You care for the dead, so I know that unlike many of the people we come across in our business, you're one of the good ones. Innocent. Kind. *Pure*," he says, looking at me knowingly. "My clients would pay thousands to fuck you just to see your virginal blood on their cocks."

"I'm not a virgin—" I blurt out.

"Yeah, and I'm not a sociopath," he interrupts. "Regardless, you present me with quite a predicament. On the one hand, I want my revenge and thus keeping you here is essential. On the other hand, you're a distraction for my brothers, one I hadn't considered properly. I underestimated how much they needed you, or rather what you represent. They can both become quite obsessive and single-minded in their needs."

"You don't seem too happy about it," I observe.

"Don't misunderstand me, Nothing. I'm in no way saying I care enough about you to ensure your safety. I'm merely telling you the cold, hard truth. My focus is on our business and keeping what we have here alive. Their focus right now is on you, and that's a problem that I need to find a solution to."

"I have one; let me go."

He shakes his head. "I won't do that." Gripping my arm, he pulls me to my feet, then marches me back downstairs, ending the conversation as abruptly as it started. When we reach what I assume to be his room, Jakub pauses. "Did you want Leon to touch you?" he asks, taking me aback.

"No," I reply. "Of course I didn't."

He narrows his eyes at me. "And yet somehow I don't believe you."

"You can believe what you want. I didn't want his touch, like I don't want yours now," I reply through gritted teeth, whilst pointedly staring at his tight grip on my arm.

He frowns, searching my face, not letting me go. "Let me rephrase that. When he touched you, did you *like* it?"

My chest and cheeks flame, a surge of heat rising up my body at his question. Even though my body is giving me away, I'll be damned if I admit that there was a part of me, a twisted, fucked-up part, that did. "No," I say vehemently.

"Another lie," Jakub murmurs before leaning in close and dipping his head. The heat of his breath feathers over my skin, but it's the press of his lips against the pulse point in my neck that has shivers tracing down my spine. He licks me, tasting the blood he'd left there earlier.

"Please," I beg, my fingers curling into the material of my dress as I white-knuckle ride a sudden wave of my emotions that comes out of nowhere. Confusion, despair, hate, rage, *lust*, they all course through my veins as he drags his lips up the column of my neck and across my jaw before hovering over my mouth.

"Don't lie to me again, Nothing," he says softly. "When Leon touched you, you liked it, didn't you?"

With a heavy chest, and bitter tears falling from my eyes, I give up a truth that hurts me deeply. "Yes," I whisper, my voice cracking with pain.

"I know," Jakub replies gently as he rubs the tip of his nose against the bridge of mine. "I *know*." Then he plants a gentle kiss, so unexpected, so incredibly fragile against my lips that I let out a fractured sob that tears my heart in two. Drawing back, Jakub leans around me and twists the handle to his bedroom. "Go to sleep. Rest. You've earned a few days respite at least. We will not disturb you. I'll send Nala."

With that he turns on his heel and leaves me to lick my wounds, the one he and his brothers have so hatefully inflicted on my soul.

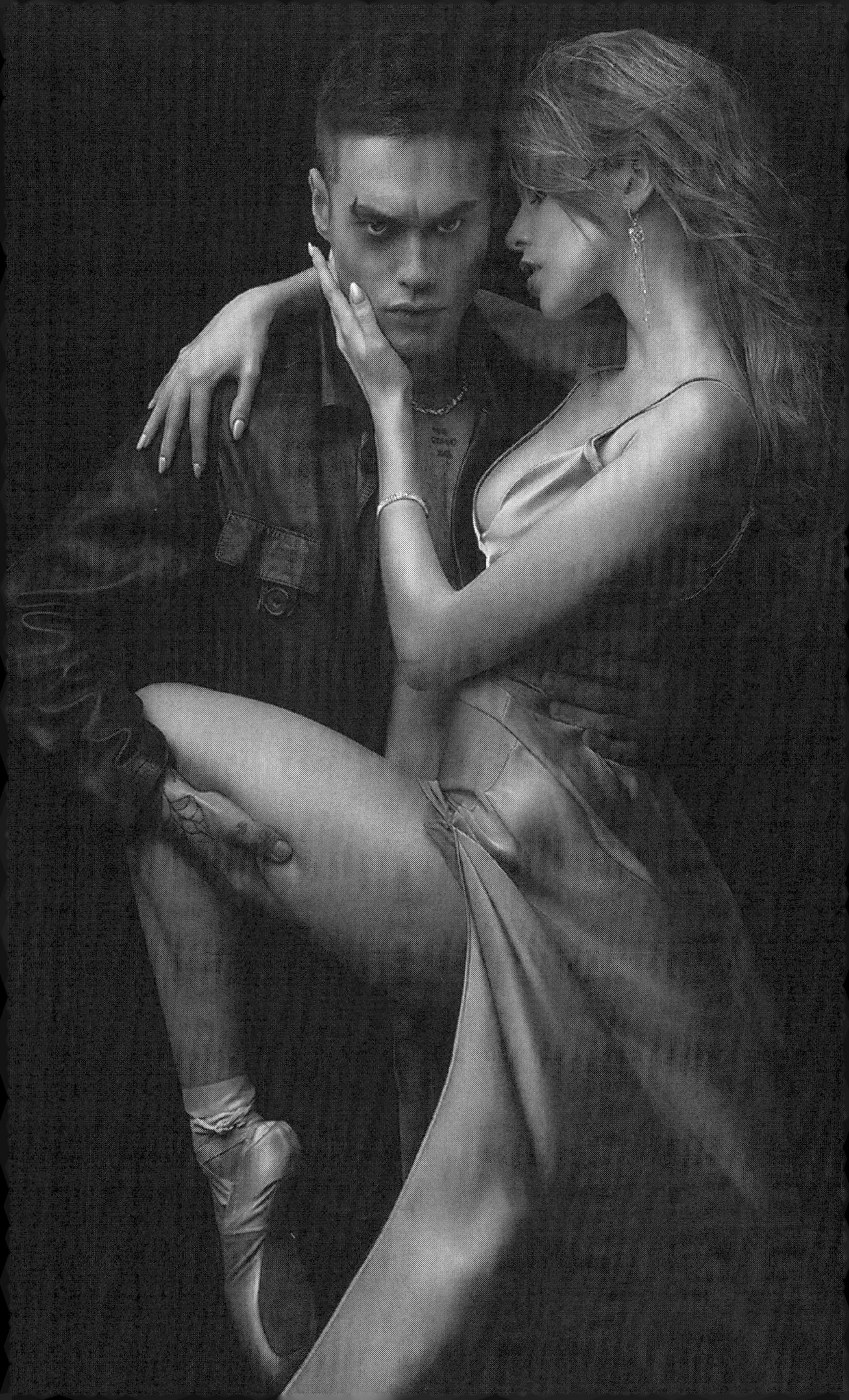

CHAPTER 13

CHRISTY

I float like an apparition, inky darkness making way for muted colours as I watch the scene unfold before me. It doesn't feel like a dream, it feels like a vision and yet this one, this one is different from all the rest. This one is from the past...

"No, Father, please don't. I won't do it again. I promise!" the little boy begs, cowering on the floor. He looks sickly, malnourished. Bruises litter his bare chest and back. Some old, most new.

"What have I taught you, boy?! You don't beg for mercy, and you never, ever, disobey me," the man replies, gripping his son by the hair and yanking him to his feet. "This is your punishment. Take it like a man!"

"I promise to be good."

"Good? I don't want you to be good, Jakub. I want you to be bad. Very, very bad. You cannot be the man I need if your soft heart makes you weak. I will beat the kindness out of you before I ever allow a son of mine to choose kindness over brutality, or weakness over strength. This is for your own good!"

Jakub whimpers, his slim frame shaking. That angers his father. Enrages him.

Pulling back his fist, the boy's father slams his knuckles into Jakub's cheek, sending him flying backwards against the rough ground. He lands awkwardly, his wrist twisting under his weight. The loud snap of a bone breaking pierces the air, and a scream rips out of Jakub's mouth. He throws up, puke spewing out of his mouth and nose in a violent explosion.

"Father!" another boy shouts, stepping forward. He's a little older, taller, more muscular, but still a child. Thirteen, maybe fourteen?

"What, Konrad? What?!"

"Jakub's sorry. He won't do it again," Konrad says, gritting his jaw and lifting his chin. He moves to stand in front of the younger boy.

"Move aside, Son."

Stubbornly Konrad shakes his head. "Don't you think he's had enough?"

"You dare to question me?!" their father responds, raising his fist and slamming it into Konrad's stomach. Konrad doubles over, winded as he sucks in air. Unlike his brother, he doesn't fall. Instead, he stands back upright, fixing his cold gaze on the man before him.

"He's only nine."

"You think I care how old he is? Last year he brought a baby into my home, hid her with your help. It's been a year since that day and still this boy is as weak as he was then. I should've killed her, maybe I still will."

Konrad flinches. "He'll learn. Leon and I will make sure of it. None of us have gone anywhere near Nala. She means nothing to us."

"And what makes you think that you and Leon will do any better, huh? Beating the kindness out of him doesn't appear to be working. He's still a fucking pussy! He couldn't even put that mutt out of its misery. I had to do it!" he spits, a huge glob of phlegm flying out of his mouth and landing on the dead labrador, its brains blown out of the back of its skull.

"We'll deal with him. We'll make him strong," Konrad retorts. His gaze flicks to the animal. There's a hint of sorrow before he covers it up with a firm nod of his head.

"It makes me sick to my stomach that this pathetic excuse of a boy is my own flesh and blood," their father spits, glaring at Jakub who's cowering behind Konrad. "You and Leon aren't even my blood, but you're both more my sons than this gnojek! Get him out of my sight. I don't wish to see him again until he's learnt to do what I ask of him."

"Yes, Sir," Konrad responds.

As soon as their father walks back inside the castle, Konrad drops to the ground beside Jakub's shivering form. "You should have shot her like he asked, Jakub. What were you thinking? He's testing you. He will kill Nala without a second thought if you disobey him again. We have to protect her."

"I know, but I couldn't do it. Star wasn't sick!" he protests, clutching his arm against his chest, tears pouring down his face. "She was pregnant. He wanted me to kill her because she pissed on his rug! I couldn't do it!"

"I know it's hard... But next time he asks you to do something, you have to do it! No matter what." Konrad shakes his head, gently pressing his fingers against Jakub's arm, who winces in pain. More tears fall. "You've broken it."

"It hurts, Kon."

"I know, but I can't take you to Renard to fix it. Not now..." he says, pulling off his shirt and tying it around Jakub's arm in a makeshift sling. "I'll fix you a splint. You'll be okay."

Jakub nods, sniffling. "What should I do? How can I be what he wants? How do you and Leon do it?"

"We do what we have to do to survive. We always have. You must do the same."

"I don't think I can."

"You have to. Turn off everything. Turn off every last emotion apart from the ones that will help you to do what he wants. Become cold, hard, empty. You have to surrender to the darkness, Jakub."

"I'd rather die than become like him!"

"He will kill Nala, and then he'll kill us. Is that what you want?"

"I don't want to be like this..." Jakub cries, more tears falling as a biting wind wraps around his thin frame, making his jaw chatter and his body shake with cold.

"Then become someone else..."

Konrad and Jakub look up at another boy approaching. He's slightly smaller in stature than Konrad, but still big for his age, with the same dark hair, and piercing green eyes. In his hands he's holding a mask. It's black, with two holes for the eyes and two smaller ones for the nose and mouth.

"How long have you been watching?" Konrad asks, helping Jakub to his feet.

"Long enough. It's time. Malik—Father—will kill Nala the next time he refuses to do as he asks."

"I know."

The two older boys look at one another, a silent conversation going on between them before Leon steps towards Jakub and lifts the black mask to his face, securing it behind his head. "When you wear this you become someone else. You're not Jakub anymore. You're not kind or sweet. You're something else. Something dark. Kon and I have one too."

"But I'll still be me underneath... I'll still be me."

"Eventually that will change. You'll wear this until the boy underneath becomes the man he needs to be to survive. Do you understand?"

"I think so... b—but what happens when I take it off? I'll see what I've become."

"Then we don't take the masks off," Konrad adds, swallowing hard as Leon hands him a mask too.

"Never?" Jakub asks.

"Only when we're alone together. The rest of the time we're The Masks," Leon says with a firm nod of his head, securing his own mask in place. "Agreed?"

"Yes," they agree.

"We should go," Konrad urges.

Jakub flicks his gaze to the dead dog, his jaw gritting. Stepping towards her, he lays his hand on her bulging stomach, whispering words that are too private to be heard. Then, agonisingly slowly, he removes her leather collar and leash with one hand, holding it lovingly against his chest. "Goodbye, Star." Climbing to his feet, Jakub faces his brothers and nods.

"Who are we?" Leon asks.

"We're The Masks," all three say in unison, the howling wind dragging the declaration from their lips and throwing it out into the frigid air.

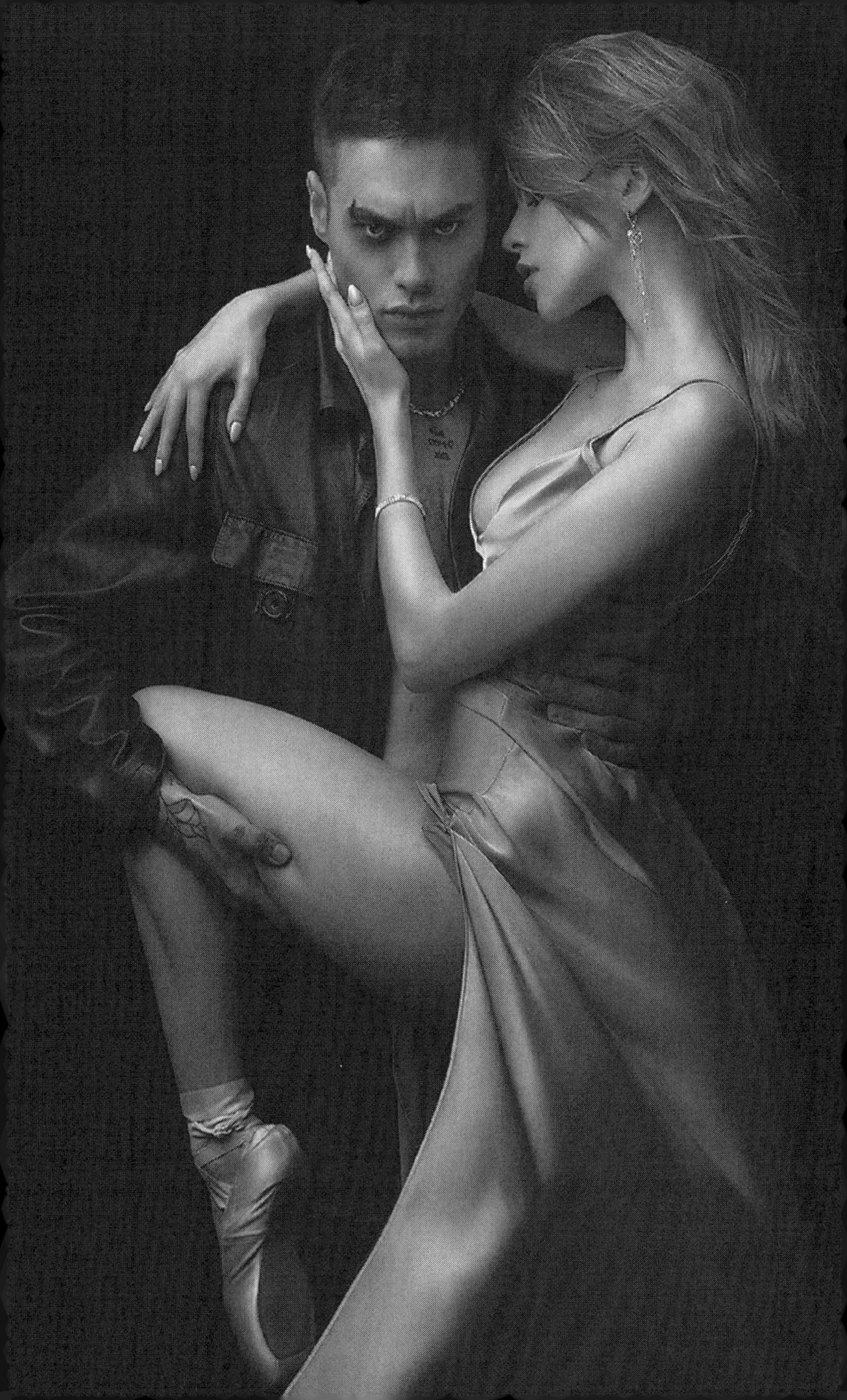

CHAPTER 14

CHRISTY

My eyelids flutter open, the vision lingering like a suffocating blanket. It feels burdensome, heavy. I've never had a vision of something that's happened in the past. Never. Yet, I know that wasn't a dream. I feel the truth of it in my bones. Jakub, Konrad and Leon became The Masks to survive. It's a sobering thought, and I'm not certain how I feel about it.

"Hello," I croak, my throat dry, my body stiff.

"So she awakens…"

I shift uncomfortably, peering into the semi-darkness. "Jakub?" I whisper, confused by the softness in his voice.

"I'm here," he says.

Fear and a lingering sense of sorrow cascades down my spine as he steps out of the shadows and into the muted light. The flickering candles and dying embers of the fire lit in the hearth edging him in the ghosts of the past.

My breath catches in my throat, *this* is how I see him in my visions. Just like this.

"Your mouth is open," he points out.

I slam it shut, drinking him in as he stands before me in a black roll-neck sweater and charcoal trousers, an air of sophistication rolling off of him. There's power too, and a sense of rigid self-control beneath the grey mask he wears. It sits over his nose and cheeks, revealing his mouth and strong jaw.

"What time is it?" I ask, mentally checking myself for any lingering pain. Apart from the usual dull ache from the scars that never quite goes away, and a foggy head from the vision, I feel okay. I'm warm and am lying on the soft mattress of Jakub's bed.

"It's time to meet the Numbers," he replies, stepping towards me.

"Right now?" I push up onto my elbows, shifting backwards on the bed. My head is still groggy, my body feels weak despite resting these past few days and being cared for by Nala. She's been kind, thoughtful, bringing me everything I need to make me comfortable including a change of clothes, even if it is this awful white dress that is apparently my uniform aside from when The Masks dress me up like a doll to appease their whims. She even brought me some books to read and my own foundation so I can keep my mask in place.

"They've been wanting to meet you."

"Dressed like this?" I repeat, groaning as I move, the after effects of the vision lingering. I still feel like a part of me is back there watching those boys take their first step towards the monstrous men they are today. It's a little difficult to digest.

"Exactly like this, but first I want you to lie back down."

"What? Why?" I ask, moving to sit up.

"I didn't get long enough..."

"Long enough?" I whisper, disliking the way his eyes darken as he stares at me.

He cocks his head to the side. "To watch you sleep."

"You've been watching me sleep?" I ask, feeling creeped out. Which seems ridiculous given everything I've been through. It's just that when I'm deep in a vision I'm completely under, oblivious to the waking world around me. *Vulnerable.* My aunt has often said that it's as though I'm in a coma. Nothing and no one can wake me.

"Yes, I wanted to know what you looked like sleeping in my bed. I wanted to know if it would turn me on..." he says without a hint of embarrassment.

"And does it?" I ask, shifting uncomfortably, steadying my voice even though my heart is thumping a million miles a minute. I don't want him to be attracted to me. I don't want to be some kind of experiment, and I definitely don't want him to act on whatever perversion makes him hard, but I ask the question regardless. Better to know what your enemy is thinking so you can prepare yourself for the fight, and I *will* fight.

"No."

There's a bitterness to his response that fills me with both relief and a twisted kind of disappointment. I don't want him to want me, but equally being unattractive when I'm completely bare is hard to swallow, let alone when I've covered up my birthmark to make myself fit the mold of beauty.

"Then what *do* you want from me?"

"*Everything*," he replies.

I try to search for the boy he once was and come up empty. All I see is a man trapped beneath a mask with no wish to get back to the boy who refused to kill his beloved pet. "Everything?"

"I want everything," he repeats cryptically.

"That's an awful lot from someone you refer to as *Nothing*," I say, shuffling sideways away from him. It's only then that I become aware of something tied around my neck. My hands fly upwards, feeling the collar fixed in place. The leather is smooth, supple, worn, and I know without having to see it that it's Star's collar, the very same collar The Masks have been trying to make me wear ever since I arrived here.

"If you remove it, I'll order Konrad to keep you in the dungeons for a week," Jakub says, watching me closely. In his hand is the leather leash, his thumb rubbing up and down the soft leather. It's attached to the collar at my neck.

"I lasted a day. I can last a week," I bite back, my fingers pulling at the collar.

Jakub shakes his head, then yanks the leash, pulling me forward by the throat. I have to follow the movement, or choke. My hands fall away as I crawl across the bed, trying not to stumble as the long nightgown I'm wearing gets caught under my knees. "Not with what he has in mind."

"The other Numbers... they survived, didn't they? What makes you so certain that I won't?"

"Because what he'll do to you will be a thousand times more disturbing than what he did to them. He'll fuck you up in here," Jakub says, tapping his head.

I don't rise to the bait, despite his words making fear pool in my stomach like a rusty nail. I'm no fool, I know I've managed to traverse the worst of their behaviour, that they've barely shown me what they're capable of. It's a strange position to be in, knowing who they are, what they're capable of, but also knowing who they once *were*. I've been given a glimpse of the boys before they became The Masks. That has to mean something, surely? Fate, however cruel, is giving me a lifeline and I intend on grasping it with both hands.

"Why me?" I suddenly ask, shifting my body so that I'm sitting on the edge of the bed, my bare feet pressed against the warm wooden floorboards. My dress lifts, revealing my ankles and shapely calves. I have the urge to pull the dress down. I don't.

"You know why. Your sister ordered the death of my father. This is payback. She took something of ours, we took something of hers."

"No, that isn't what I meant." I almost ask him why he cares about his father's death given he was abused by him, but that would mean me explaining how I know about his father's cruelty and there's no guarantee he'd believe me. Even if he did, it wouldn't make a difference.

"Regardless of what you meant, this is how it is. You are *ours*. That isn't going to change, no matter how much you want it to."

"You keep saying that I'm yours, and aside from the fact that I'm not something that can be owned—" He scoffs at my declaration, but I push on regardless. "Why do you want to own me when you already have the Numbers...?" I haven't even met all of them, but if the rest of them are anything like Four and Eight, then The Masks will have no problems fulfilling their desires, right? Those women wanted Leon and

Konrad. It's not as though The Masks would have to fight for their attention, *steal* it. Then I realise, that's precisely what they want. To hunt, to take something from an unwilling victim. My throat squeezes with anxiety.

"The Numbers aren't ours. They never were. They never will be."

I swallow hard, the tightness of the leather collar reminding me that I'm no more than an animal to them, a creature they can order around and abuse, and yet... This collar, this leash, belonged to a beloved pet, one that Jakub adored. Surely that's significant somehow?

"Who do they belong to, if not you?"

"The Collector..."

"*The Collector?*"

"Our father."

"But he's dead. So that makes them yours now, doesn't it?" I ask, trying to understand his logic, because of course they shouldn't belong to anyone but themselves.

"No. It doesn't. The Numbers belong to *The Menagerie*, to the people who pay big money to come here to watch them, to my father's legacy and what he built here. The Numbers do what they love, they're gifted performers—"

"Performers? Is that why Four and Eight were dressed up like strippers? Is that the kind of performance you mean? They strip and then fuck whoever pays you the most?" I laugh almost hysterically. "They call you their Master but isn't that just a more creative word for *pimp?*"

"You really are small-minded," he remarks, a ghost of a smile playing about his lips. "But yes, they fuck our clients."

Small-minded? This isn't a conversation I'd ever thought I'd have with a man who has me collared and leashed like a dog, but I keep him talking if only to stave off whatever he has planned for me. "So enlighten me."

"Konrad has ordered a formal banquet this evening. You'll be enlightened soon enough."

"You want me to perform in *The Menagerie*? Am I expected to fuck your clients too?" I ask, my voice shaking, my skin growing cold at the thought.

"Like I suggested to my brothers in the library, you won't be for sale like the other Numbers, given you're ours and we don't share unless it's with each other."

"So I'm going to dance then?"

"No. Tonight there will be no guests in Ardelby Castle. Tonight it's just us and the Numbers. Dinner and... well, you'll see. It's your welcome... of sorts."

"Thank God," I mutter, but my relief is short-lived when he lunges forward and wraps the leash around my neck, pulling it tight. My throat constricts as he tightens his grip and forces my chin up. He smiles down at me, his eyes empty.

"Don't relax too much, *Nothing*. Everything you do from now on is for our benefit. If we want to see you dance, you will dance. If we want you collared and leashed, you will gladly follow us wherever we go. If we want you naked and spread open, then you'll oblige. If we want you to scream and cry whilst we fuck you, then you will do exactly that." He releases his grip on the leash allowing it to loosen, and I suck in a pained breath, gasping for air.

"I—"

"Pull up your dress," he commands, cutting me off.

I feel the weight of his stare as he dares me to object. When I don't act immediately, he tightens the noose once again. My throat constricts from the pressure and I know that if I don't do what he says, he'll strangle me here and now without a second thought. The truth of that knowledge is in his eyes as tears form in mine. Yet again, Fate has tricked me. The boy he was is no longer within him. Whatever she had planned, it's too late.

"You need to learn your place," he snarls, twisting the noose ever tighter.

It would be so easy to let him kill me. To end this here and now knowing that my future is going to be filled with more horrors such as this. But I don't want to die. I need to adapt to survive. I need to bide my time so that I can *kill* this motherfucker and his psycho brothers.

That rogue thought settles in my heart like a rock dropping to the bottom of the ocean. It grounds me. Gives me purpose. It makes me strong. I never thought I was a violent person... until now.

"Pull up your dress," he repeats.

I nod, telling him that I will do as he asks. He loosens the noose allowing me to suck in several ragged breaths. Shifting slightly, I curl my fingers into the material of the long white dress and pull it upwards, revealing my bare legs inch by inch. I force myself to do what he wants knowing that I will obey his commands until the opportunity to end him and his brothers presents itself.

When the hem of the dress reaches the apex of my thighs, my hands still. Despite my determination to embrace my newly found courage, I can't quite bring myself to reveal the most private part of me. Leon might have touched it, but no one has seen it.

"Did I tell you to stop?" he snaps, fixing his gaze on my creamy thighs. Tiny freckles are scattered across my skin. Their colour is the shade of my hair. As a child I never paid them any mind until one day a boy at school started making fun of me. He said I had the pox, that I was tainted, that my freckles like my face, were the mark of dark, evil things. From that day onwards, every child at school stayed away from me. Only giving me attention when they were throwing sly kicks and hateful words my way. Now these freckles are just another part of me that marks me as different.

"I want to see your cunt," he demands, snapping his eyes up. "I need to see what has gotten Leon so twisted up. He's seen a lot of pussy over the years, but yours seems to have turned his head more than I expected."

"Leon didn't see my *cunt*," I retort, spitting out that ugly word and forcing anger into my voice. It stops me from being afraid, even though it prompts Jakub to tighten the noose momentarily.

"But he touched it."

"Yes," I whisper.

"What about Konrad?"

"No."

"And there I was thinking he'd broken our agreement too and taken a peek whilst he had you chained up in his dungeon. What did he do with you then?"

"Apart from cutting off a length of my hair... not a lot." My fingers pull at the hem of the dress, yanking it back down.

"Stop!" Jakub suddenly shouts, covering my hand with his. "*I* want to see."

"Don't you have an agreement?" I ask, my pulse thrumming in my neck. When it comes to me, they do things together, apparently. At least they're supposed to.

"Fuck the agreement. Leon's already broken it by touching you," he growls, forcing my hands away whilst still keeping the noose tight around my neck. Gathering up the material in his hand, he lifts the skirt of the dress then stares straight at my pussy. If I'm not mistaken there's a sharp intake of breath, but that could be my mind playing tricks on me given my own ears are filled with the rapid rushing and pulsing of blood from a mixture of embarrassment, shame, and fear. I reach for the hem of the dress, wanting to cover myself.

"Don't you fucking dare!" he snaps. "Now spread your legs."

"No!"

"DO IT!"

Gritting my teeth, I turn my head away and slide my legs open. Heat travels up my chest as fury boils my blood. Today is not the day to fight. I need a plan. I need to be sensible. I only just started to replenish my energy before the vision, now it's depleted once again, but that doesn't make this any easier.

"You're bare," he grinds out, his voice gravelly like stones crunching underfoot.

"What can I say, I prefer to keep my bush under control. Is that a problem?" I retort, my sarcasm helping me to regain a modicum of control and self-respect.

He doesn't respond like I expect him to. Instead he swallows hard, his Adam's apple bobbing up and down as he licks his lips. The energy in the room shifts as he stares at me, his gaze lowering from my pussy to my thighs and legs, then back up again to my face and hair. He reaches for a strand, touching the softness between his thumb and finger before trailing his hot gaze back down to my pussy. His mouth parts, heat creeps up his neck, flushing his skin.

"What?" I bite out, not liking how my stomach tightens and my clit throbs under his perusal.

"You're different…" he remarks, sounding confused.

"I'm sure you've seen a hairless pussy before."

"That's not what I meant."

"Then what did you mean?"

He doesn't answer and there's something about the way he holds himself that tells me he's battling with his attraction. That he's surprised by it, doesn't want it. Well, that makes two of us.

"Lay back," he commands.

"What?"

"Lay. Back!"

The noose tightens, reminding me who's in control. I lay back.

Jakub nudges his way between my parted legs, forcing my thighs further open and my pussy lips to part. I've never felt more exposed, or more vulnerable in my life. This isn't how I envisaged the first time a man would see this part of me.

It twists my guts up.

Churns my insides.

Raises my heartbeat to a thumping so loud I can barely hear anything else.

He stares, and stares and *stares*, feasting on me, *hungry*. I've never been looked at this way before, with interest, with *lust*.

Pity, yes.

Lust, never.

It tips this moment from something disturbing into something shamefully exhilarating.

For the briefest of moments I find myself luxuriating in it.

It's wrong. Twisted. Yet, it's happening.

"You've got a pretty cunt," he says quietly, and there's a hint of something in his voice that I can't quite place. Not admiration, not that, just something. A torrid concoction of embarrassment, fear, and desire licks at my insides as he continues to stare. I force my eyes shut, my fingers curling into the bedspread as I hold on, waging a war with myself and this sudden rush of feelings that have no place here in this room with this man whom I *hate*. "I could take you now. It would be so damn easy."

"I would rather die than let you rape me," I seethe, meaning every last word despite the way my clit throbs and my veins thrum with tumultous heat. Just because my body is betraying me, twisting me up with hormones unleashed in a moment of sheer panic and fear, doesn't mean that I'm willing. I'm not. "So you may as well use that leash to strangle me, because I refuse to let you take the one thing that only I should have the power to give. Believe me when I say, I will fight you until my last breath."

"What makes you think I *want* what you have to offer, Nothing?" he asks, the tone of his voice different, less… cold. I can't help but look at him. When I do, I catch a glimpse of something I don't understand passing over his face. A host of emotions that confuse me, switching our roles, like *I'm* the one holding *him* captive.

The noose around my neck loosens completely as he drops it to the bed and kneels on the floor between my parted legs, still staring at my pussy. It's oddly submissive, but equally he holds all the power. I have none.

"You said you want *everything*…" I choke out, forcing courage into my voice. "You have me lying on a bed with a collar around my neck and the most private part of me on display."

"Your most private part? This is just your body…" he says, frowning.

"It is not *just* my body. This is me. This is *mine*," I reiterate.

"Ours."

"You're looking at me like you don't know whether you want to hurt me or…"

"Or…?"

"Or *pleasure* me," I continue, pushing past the gravel in my throat. "I don't know what to think. What do you want from me?"

If he's affected by my words, he doesn't show it. Instead he rests his hands on my knees, cupping them, firm but gentle. I can feel the calluses on his palms, and I briefly wonder what kind of work he could possibly do to make them so rough. My skin erupts in goosebumps that cascade across my skin like sin in a whore house.

"I'm not like my brothers. What I want from you is far more dangerous than what my brothers need," he grinds out, his fingers tightening over my knees, causing me to whimper and squeeze my eyes shut on him, on this room, on my body and the way it flushes beneath his touch. "Look at me, Nothing!"

My eyes snap open as he presses a kiss against the inside of my knee, his tongue tasting my skin.

My traitorous core squeezes.

"Don't," I beg, my voice cracked and broken, desperate with longing and hating myself for it. Am I really that easy to manipulate? A look of hunger, a gentle but possessive touch, and I roll over just like a dog? This can't be happening. "Don't fucking touch me!"

"You taste just like I imagined," he mumbles against my inner thigh, ignoring my outburst. His mouth moves higher, the soft whisper of his lips doing more damage than any firm grasp or threat to my life.

"And what do I taste like?" I find myself asking, wanting a distraction as he licks and bites, edging his way higher.

"Dangerous."

My pulse runs riot, it gallops and bucks, making me lightheaded as he presses his thumbs against my inner thighs and spreads me wide. My chest, neck and cheeks flame with another surge of heat as he rips off his mask and presses his nose against my mound, breathing me in.

He. Breathes. Me. In.

My heart stutters, and my body shakes with a mixture of self-hatred, lust, and pure physical *desire*.

This is wrong. I should fight...

A moment ago I wanted to kill him, and now...

Now, I want him to taste me.

Taste me.

I lift my head, begging him with my eyes whilst cursing him with my mouth. "I hate you. I will *kill* you for this!"

"Then do it, nothing's stopping you," he taunts.

Fury turns my blood ice cold. He knows he can overpower me. I can't win against him, but I can make him hurt. So I slap him. I push upwards, shove against his shoulders and slap him as hard as I can across his cheek. His head whips to the side, the force of my slap unbalancing him. Surprise lights in his eyes, but he reaches for my hips, holding me down as I try to stand.

"Yes," he hisses, correcting himself as he grabs the leash and tightens it once more. "Fight and die, or keep still and live. Your choice."

"Screw you," I choke out, but I don't fight him when he pushes me back onto the bed.

"Look at me whilst I fuck your cunt with my tongue," he demands, loosening his hold on the leash so I can breathe again.

I meet his gaze as his eyes blacken with need, his pupils blown wide. Then he grins and tastes me, burning me up from the inside out with one firm stroke of his tongue up my tender flesh.

I've never experienced anything like it. My whole body goes rigid at the sudden exquisite sensation. Jakub licks and sucks, plundering my core with his tongue, drinking me up, feasting on my dripping pussy. He kisses and taunts with his lips, teeth and tongue, and it's as though everything that's happened over the past few days incinerates in that moment, swallowed up in fire and smoke, lust and passion. The tip of his tongue rims my entrance and sensation blinds me momentarily as my virginal pussy weeps for him. A hot tear slides down my temple as I try to comprehend what's happening.

No, my mind protests.

Yes, my body retorts.

This is what you've been hungering for, my soul reminds me.

I have the sudden urge to pull him closer, to wrap my legs around his head and grind against his face, taking what he gives, wanting what he offers, hating myself all the while. How can I *do* this? How can I *want* this?

"Hmmm," he hums as he licks me again, a long sweep from anus to clit and back again. If he's the devil then his tongue's an angel and I'm in purgatory caught between heaven and hell.

A heady moan releases from my parted lips. A cry of shame and overwhelming *want*. The noise that rumbles up his throat matches mine, ashamed, shocked, but filled with need.

Unequivocable need.

"Please," I beg, unashamedly rocking my hips whilst tears stream down my face, wetting my hair.

I want to come.

I want to chase the high that Leon started back in the library. No, that Konrad started in the back of the van when he touched me without my permission or consent. I didn't want his touch. I didn't want Leon's. I don't want Jakub's, and yet... I do. I do want it.

I want a moment where I don't feel fear, only pleasure, only acceptance, only *belonging*.

They've already claimed me. I'm theirs, whether I want to be or not. So for one moment in time, I'll concede.

He licks and sucks stoking the flames, making the passion billow and soar higher and higher and higher as his fingers dig into my hips. Jakub holds me steady, forcing me to wait, to succumb to the towering inferno of rage, hate, lust and the heady, desperate need to come.

"Why is this happening?" I moan, feeling my body ripen under his touch.

It evolves, changes. My core tightening then unfurling with sensation. My clit engorges. My pussy weeps. Every curse, every word of hate is obliterated by sensation, by the basic human need to chase pleasure. To feel something exquisite. My legs spread wider, my body concedes, welcoming him, giving him easy access. I open up instead of close down.

I. Let. Him. In.

He rears back, dousing the fire between us with ice. His fingers squeeze the tender flesh of my thighs once, then he lets me go, rocking back on his heels as he drops his head. "Fuck! Fuck!"

"Jakub...?" I question, feeling the shift. Regret, empathy, sadness. It pours from him into me as I push up onto my elbows. My arms shake. My body quivers. My core weeps for his mouth and the orgasm that is just out of reach. "It doesn't have to be this way."

His head snaps up and the look he gives me has me gasping for breath. I scramble backwards on the bed, understanding in that brief locking of eyes that I've stepped over some invisible boundary. I've made a mistake. He means to hurt me.

"Don't!" he roars.

Then he comes for me with steel in his eyes, a burning hatred stuttering across his face.

"Wait! I didn't mean—"

But he doesn't wait. He thrusts his hand out, grabbing my ankle and yanking me back towards him. Then splaying his fingers between my breasts, he shoves me back onto the bed. "Don't!" he snaps. Reaching down he rips up my dress and buries his head back in my pussy and *takes*. He takes my pleasure and twists it up into a dark, devious thing.

The intense white ball that he'd conjured up with his lips and tongue just moments before evolves into a fiery demon, something with the capability of shredding me apart.

His lips scorch. His tongue invades. His mouth burns. His fingers bruise.

And I am putty in his hands.

I don't fight, I gasp.

I don't cry for help, I scream for more.

More. More. More.

Jakub growls, teeth scraping against tender flesh as he eats me out. Wild. Unhinged. Taking and giving, fucking and fighting. My hands fly back to grasp his head, to pull him closer, whilst pushing my hips upwards to meet the frantic way he ruins me with his tongue.

I'm out of my mind with passion, not thinking, just doing.

He doesn't stop me from grabbing at him.

He doesn't stop until I'm jerking in his hold, my back arching, my heels digging into his back as I come.

I come so hard that black spots blur my vision and white noise fills my ears.

A scream rips out of my throat. A wild animal stripped back to her rawest form.

Then he rears upwards and slaps my quivering flesh.

One, twice, three times.

I jerk with every hard slap against my tender, swollen pussy, crying out.

I'm *crying* now. Sobbing.

I've never experienced such wicked pleasure from such a tortured man.

He's ruined me.

Pulling down the hem of my dress so that it covers me back up, he grabs his mask, hiding the fury of his expression. I'm left confused, exhausted from the rush, angry at giving myself over to him so easily. I can't even say he stole my orgasm, because he didn't.

I gave it up.

"Get up. We're late for dinner."

"What's going on?" I ask brokenly, twisted by the lingering sensation of his tongue on me, of the confusing feelings. I still hate him. I still want to kill him. Yet he's just given me the most intense orgasm of my life. I'm dripping for him.

"Do as I say! Get the fuck up!" he snaps, tugging on the leash so that I'm forced to stand and follow him or risk getting my neck snapped. I stumble, my muscles trembling, my heart pounding, my pulse soaring. I swipe at the tears, hoping to God my mask is still in place.

"Jakub...?" Even to my own ears my voice sounds weak.

"Don't call me by my name. I am your Master, not your lover or your friend. From this moment on that is who I am to you. Nothing more, nothing less. You are still *Nothing*."

He's cruel. Cruel for wrapping his dead dog's collar around my neck.

Cruel for refusing to call me by my name.

Cruel for giving me the biggest rush of my life.

Here I am collared and leashed and *panting* like a dog, like a bitch in heat.

My legs suddenly feel heavy, my heart plummets, I can barely put one foot in front of the other as I stumble forward, trying to keep up.

"If you can't walk, *crawl*," he says spitefully, a twisted smile pulling up his lips.

He *planned* this.

This is another trick, another manipulation. I'm a stupid, stupid fool.

I shake off the self-disgust and replace it with hate. It sprouts new shoots, it grows in size, tripling and quadrupling the longer he stares with that cold kind of emptiness instead of the heat he'd lied with before.

Arsehole.

"I will *never* crawl. Never!" I grind out, my spine snapping straight, my jaw gritting with new-found disgust.

"Good, because the moment you stop fighting is the moment this ends. Understand?"

"Completely." This was a test and I failed. I gave in to a lie.

When we reach the bedroom door he hesitates, grabbing something resting on a chest-of-drawers. "Put this on."

"Put what on?" I ask, fighting the sudden desire to claw at him, to *fight* just like he wants me to do. I'm wound up, bound, and raging now that I've blinked back the fog of *his* spell. Beast might refer to me as a witch because of my visions. I might have been chained to The Weeping Tree where witches were hung, but right now, at this moment, *he's* the spellcaster. He's the one who deserves to hang for what he's done.

"This," he says, offering me the item.

I take it from him, confused at first. It looks like a *mawashi* that sumo wrestlers wear, except this is made of soft leather rather than traditional silk or cotton and it has a wider section of leather making up the crotch area. It also has a lock... *Oh, my God.* "This is a—" I begin.

He smirks, eyeing me as I hold onto the offending item. "—chastity belt."

"You bastard..." I hiss, my voice trailing off as I turn it over in my hands, the silver lock that fixes the crotch section to the belt, glints in the candlelight.

"If you want to protect yourself from any more intrusion then I suggest you wear it. My brothers might pretend they're patient men, but I know otherwise."

I scoff, he's no more patient than they are given what he's just done, he's *worse*. "Pot, kettle, comes to mind."

"What, you think because I've tasted you, I can't control myself? Don't flatter yourself, Nothing. I've had better, tasted better, fucked better. I'm doing this for Leon and Konrad. They've waited a long time for you. If they indulge in what they truly want from you too soon then they will lose their focus. We have a big function coming up soon, and I need their heads in the game, not focused on a bit of pussy, however *pretty*," he says, spitting that word out like it offends him. "Put it on!"

Despite his harsh words, the ugliness of the item and what it represents, I can't help but feel a tiny sense of relief. Wearing this will afford me some protection no matter how barbaric the idea of one is. It will buy me some more time. Time to gather myself, make a plan.

"Who has the key?"

"I do, of course," Jakub replies as he pulls out a silver chain wrapped around his neck, a small key hanging from it. "If you want to remain unsullied, then I suggest you obey my every instruction from this moment on or unlocking this belt to piss and shit won't be the only time I'll be freeing your pretty little pussy."

My heart sinks to the bottomless ocean of my soul. It settles next to the promise I made myself earlier. I *will* kill him.

I will kill them all.

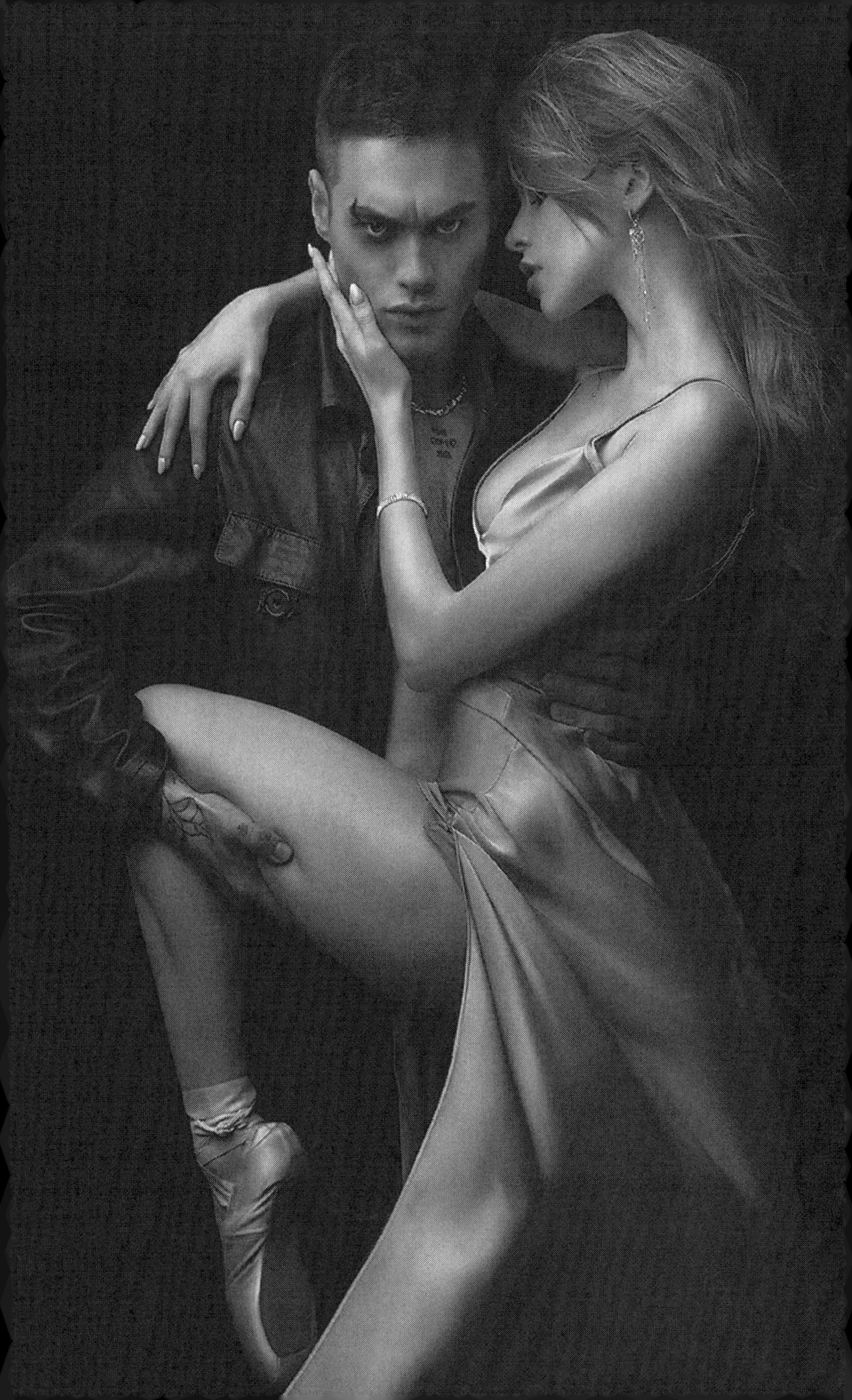

CHAPTER 15

JAKUB

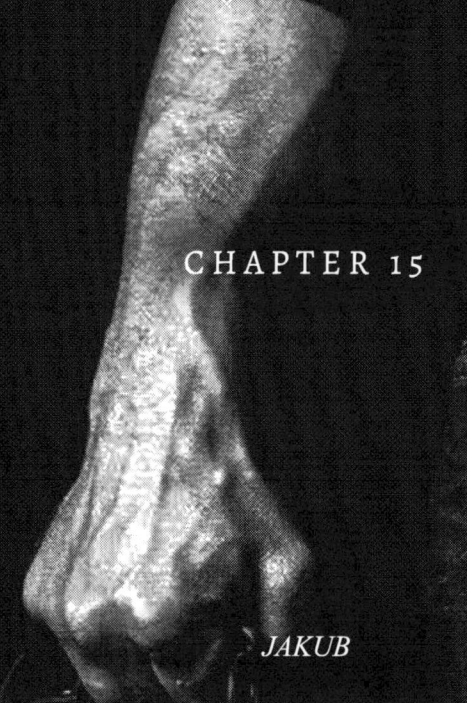

My brothers watch us as we enter the grand hall. Nothing walks to my left and slightly behind me, her movements graceful despite how uncomfortable she must feel wearing the chastity belt. Her footsteps are light, her chin tipped upwards and her spine straight. She is a force to be reckoned with, not just because she's put my brothers under her spell, but because she made *me* feel something other than cold, hard, emptiness.

She's dangerous for us all.

I should've killed her.

I should've put her out of her misery and ended this charade, but something stopped me, something I refuse to look too hard at. She still lives and I have the key to untold pleasures and indescribable pain hanging around my goddamn neck. It weighs me down, a fucking *curse*.

"Nice room, shame about the company," she mutters, her sarcasm fuelling her fire.

She has courage, I'll give her that. It's both irritating and admirable, though it waivers a little when she notices the gilt cage hanging from the ceiling above the large dining table. I hear her gasp when she sees who's inside.

"Nothing, meet Two. She's a trapeze artist and one of the founding members of The Menagerie," I explain, looking upwards, following her surprised gaze.

Two smiles coyly from behind her gilded cage, acting every part the delicate, rare creature she loves to portray. It's part of her act, her charm. Two's slight frame, small breasts and long pale hair piled up on her head in ringlets, appeal to our clients who fantasize about overpowering something fragile. She's just like a pretty bird in its cage, perched on her swing and wearing a canary yellow dress that does nothing to hide her pert breasts and thatch of hair between her legs. She might be in her mid-thirties now, but is still as beautiful as she was when she arrived here eight years ago. Two was my father's second acquisition, but she was Leon's first. He broke her in, and they are still bonded by the experience, though his interest in her has long since waned.

"We were about to send out a search party for you," Leon remarks, sipping a glass of red wine, his cool green eyes watching our every move from beneath the applique mask he's wearing. It covers the top half of his face, the varying shades of gold fabric glued over the top of black molded leather. It's one of his favourites, and the one he tends to wear when we dine with the Numbers. Like me he's dressed smartly, with a fitted black shirt and gold cufflinks that glint in the candlelight. But where he has chosen a mask that is more decadent, my own is a dark grey to match my mood.

"We're here now," I retort, ignoring the challenge in his gaze. It's happening more and more these days, but whilst he and Konrad may be older than me by a few years, I'm the true heir to the Brov dynasty, and long ago I proved myself strong enough to take the seat at the head of this table. I was fourteen when I broke in One, my father's first acquisition, and have sat in this chair ever since. "Shall we begin?" I ask as Nothing stands beside me, her arms folded across her chest. I can feel her anxiety, her anger and fear. It's distracting, but even more so for Konrad who hasn't taken his eyes off her. He's obsessed. I knew it the moment he first laid eyes on her. Leon remains quiet, assessing, but Konrad is barely containing his emotions as he eyes the outline of the chastity belt beneath the material of her dress.

"*What* is she wearing?" Konrad hisses under his breath, knowing full well what it is. Fury paints his face as red as the half-mask he's wearing. Nothing stiffens, feeling the sudden violence of his anger. Despite that, there's a hint of a smile playing around her lips. She's enjoying this tiny victory. I should punish her for it, but I don't.

"It was necessary. Just think how sweet it will be to finally unlock the treasure trove, brother. I can't have any more slip-ups," I say, pointedly looking at Leon who meets my gaze with a hard stare of his own.

Konrad glares at me, but he doesn't retaliate, all too aware of Two hanging above us. Whilst loyal to a fault, she loves gossip. Normally we don't tolerate such talk, but her years of service have afforded her some grace. We're not averse to indulging our Numbers if it's beneficial to us.

"Do you have anything you wish to add?" I ask, turning my attention to Leon, curious to see if he bites. We may have made an agreement as to how we manage Nothing, but ultimately I have the last say, and if I choose to change shit up, then that is my right as heir. Besides, after his bullshit a few days ago he's lucky she still remains ours and not just mine.

Resting his hands on the table, Leon presses his palms against the smooth oak. "Who has the key?" he asks, his voice even.

"I do."

He nods, but doesn't say anything further. Instead, he stares at Nothing, his eyes undressing her. It doesn't go unnoticed that her nipples are peaked beneath her white cotton dress. It's a fear response and not one of lust, but despite that she maintains eye contact with Leon, refusing to submit. It's been a long time since anyone here at Ardelby Castle has had the courage to do the same. Like me, Leon has very few emotions left. Of the three of us, he was the first to discard his humanity like an old coat that no longer fit him.

"Don't think that this will give you any respite, Nought," he says. "There are many things we can do to you despite that contraption."

"Not without my say so," I interject.

"Our agreement still stands." Leon's lip curls up and a sudden flash of anger flares across his face. That in and of itself is surprising, and it takes me aback.

"It does, for now. Ultimately, *I'm in control*, Brother."

Leon taps his finger against the table. "If you say so, Jakub."

Suddenly, the key around my neck feels heavier than it should. I'm aware of the power that holding this key affords, but I'm also aware of the responsibility, not towards Nothing—I care little for her other than what she can provide for myself and my brothers—but to our bond. It is the only thing left that I truly value. Whatever happens, this woman cannot get between us. I won't be drawn in by her reckless courage, freckle-spattered thighs or the way she completely gives herself over to pleasure. I won't.

"Noted," I reply, forcing my fingers to relax from around the leash. I've been holding onto it tightly ever since the moment I clipped it onto the collar around her neck whilst she slept peacefully, as though a monster wasn't hiding in the shadows watching her.

"We should begin," Konrad says, cutting through the tension, eager to start. He may not be able to fully indulge in Nothing like he wants, but he's well aware that there's more to tonight than dinner. It may satiate his appetite a little while longer, or it could do the opposite and fuel it.

We'll soon find out.

Nothing shifts on her feet. A kinder man would remove the collar and leash, and ask her to sit at the table. I'm not that man. Besides, she hasn't earned her place yet. You don't get to dine with The Masks until you've committed to your life here, and I have the feeling that Nothing won't ever dine at this table.

"What should I do?" Nothing asks, her shaking fingers clutching at her dress. She scrunches the material in her hands, her head turned to face me. The length of her hair hides most of her features, but her beauty is the kind that's hard to miss. It's... *disappointing*.

"Stay where you are," I say curtly, before motioning for One—who's been waiting in the shadows all this time—to begin. A beat later, the haunting notes of *The Promise,* a piano piece by Michael Nyman begin to rise up into the air. Despite years of conditioning not to *feel* any kind of emotions other than the ones that have kept me alive, I cannot prevent the hair of my arms from standing on end. Like Leon and Two, One and I have a connection that runs deeper than mere master and slave. Aside from Thirteen, she's the only Number I have any type of relationship with. If you can call it that.

"Oh my God," Nothing whispers, her head turning to seek out the person playing such exquisite music. There's no denying that One is profoundly talented, her music able to capture and entrance. My father knew exactly what he was doing when he collected her. "That's beautiful."

Nothing's shoulders relax, her demeanour altering as the music washes over her. I would bet my collection of curiosities that in this moment, right now, Nothing doesn't feel any fear, lost to the music as she is. Without warning I lean over and grasp her arm, having the sudden urge to see if she reacts physically the same way as I do, and to remind her to never let down her guard. She flinches away from my touch, stiffening when my hand grips her arm tightly.

"What are you—"

"Don't ask questions," I snap.

Pulling up her sleeve, not only is the skin of her arm covered in goosebumps, but more freckles. A pointillistic decoration unique only to her. Earlier she thought I was staring at her perfect, untouched pussy. I wasn't. I was staring at the rash of freckles covering her creamy thighs. They're an abnormality, a random pigmentation of skin. To some they might be beautiful, others unattractive. I'm not sure which side of the line I sit on. Either way, they had me intrigued enough not to want my brothers to completely break her just yet, to *want* to taste her.

Licking my lips, I ignore the fact that her essence is still on my tongue and concentrate on using this moment to play with her head.

"*This* is why One is valuable," I say, running my forefinger over the tiny hairs standing to attention on Nothing's arm. She catches my eye, a note of curiosity on her face. "Men and women have come far and wide to listen to her play," I continue. "They pay a lot of money for the privilege, for this precise reaction. Some even say listening to One play is a better high than an orgasm, and here you are enjoying her talent for free."

Konrad scoffs. "Some of them also pay three times the amount to fuck her whilst she bends over the piano and plays them a tune. All that silky black hair, perfect olive skin and sultry Italian sex appeal means she's one of the favourites." He reaches for Nothing's free hand, flipping it over so her palm faces upwards. She tries to draw her hand away, but he grasps it tightly, then presses the tip of his index finger against the sensitive skin, circling her palm. "Tell me, Zero, does her music turn you on?"

"I don't—" she stumbles, her breath hitching.

"Does my touch make you wet?" Konrad asks. "Imagine me doing this to your clit. Have you ever had a real, earth-shattering, soul-splitting orgasm, Zero? Does One's music make you want to come?"

Nothing's lips part, her eyelids fluttering as she battles against her reaction to Konrad's touch combined with One's music and, no doubt, the lingering effects of my tongue and lips on her sweet, sweet pussy. I don't immediately let her go either, curious to see whether she can handle both of our attention.

"What about this?" Konrad asks, leaning over to press his lips against her open palm, before tenderly kissing the pulse point in her wrist.

She shudders, her body reacting, just like he knew it would. The way her body sways towards him despite her obvious hate confirms my suspicion that until very recently she hasn't experienced being touched by a man before, especially not those who are as skilled in the art of manipulation as we are. We use sex as a weapon, pleasure and pain are the tools in our arsenal. She's no match for us, no matter how strong she appears to be.

"Don't— Don't touch me," she objects, trying once again to withdraw her hand from his hold. This time I can't avoid punishing her. I don't want to. I need to make her pay for her disobedience, for *wanting* what I gave her. How fucking dare she open herself up like that! How fucking dare she give herself up so easily! She was so pure in her lust, so angry in her submission. It was a heady fucking concoction and I hate the fact I succumbed to it.

"I told you, Nothing, you do what we want, when we want it. Put your forearms on the table and bend over," I demand. Konrad lets her hand go and grins. Leon just watches. Silent, emotionless.

"Why?"

"Always with the questions... You really don't get it, do you?" I spit, standing abruptly and grasping the back of her neck. Leaning in close, I rest my lips against her ear. "Put your forearms on the table and bend the fuck over!"

Above us, I hear Two giggling. Nothing stiffens, her gaze lifting upwards briefly, unable to understand how anyone could find this amusing. Then with a heaving chest, she does as I demand and bends over. Her hair fans out across her back, the fiery tresses almost reaching her arse. None of the other Numbers have red hair, so I'm aware of the novelty, one that Konrad's clearly attracted to given the way he's fingering a lock of Nothing's hair reverently. He's always been drawn to fire, to heat and flames. She represents physically everything he wants in a woman.

"Do you want to do it?" I ask him, holding out the leash, giving him the responsibility.

"Fuck, yes," he responds, taking it from me as he moves to stand behind Nothing. She's trembling so much that the globes of her arse wobble beneath the material of her dress.

"Relax, it won't hurt as much if you do," I find myself saying, instantly regretting it when Konrad gives me a sharp look and Leon snorts in derision. Fuck them both, I'm doing this for *them*, not her. "You might want to break Nothing, but you need her to last, at least long enough to get what we all need. Let's not ruin her just yet."

"Right, Brother," Konrad says with a smirk, before crouching down behind her and sliding the dress slowly up her legs and over the mound of her arse. I swallow hard, my cock twitching, not at the sight of the chastity belt resting along her arse crack but at the spattering of freckles over the globes of her cheeks and back of her thighs. I find myself staring at them, at the way they mar her perfect skin. They look like a galaxy of stars… Stars...

Star.

A tremor wracks my body, the violence of it snapping me out of the moment. *What the fuck?* A past memory lingers in the back of my mind, it feels painful. *Why does that word hurt so much?*

"Get on with it!" I snap, not wanting to find out.

"With pleasure," Konrad murmurs, before shifting his position and bringing the leash down against Nothing's rounded arse with a loud thwack. She jerks forward, but she doesn't scream.

Leon sits forward in his seat. Shifting from laid-back to interested.

"Do it again," he demands, his voice low, gruff. I know what he's thinking, that her lack of reaction in the library was a fluke, that she can't be as controlled or detached from the pain as she appeared that day. Konrad flicks his gaze to me, and I nod, giving him permission, wanting to find out just as much as my brothers how much she can take.

Thwack!

Nothing remains silent. Her body isn't tense, it's relaxed. Her eyes stare off into the distance, not hollow, just serene. It's eerie.

Leon's fingers tighten around the stem of his wine glass. "Again!"

I jerk my chin. Konrad brings the leash down onto her arse once more.

Thwack!

Around us One's haunting music rebounds off the high ceiling and walls, the notes building into a crescendo. The combination of Nothing's star-spattered arse—reddened now by the lashes— and One's music is, admittedly, more than a little intoxicating. It's been a long time since I've felt even the slightest attraction to a woman, and it's not a feeling that sits well with me. Attraction is dangerous. It can lead to the kind of emotion that can make a man weak.

I'm not a weak man, and neither are my brothers.

"Again," I say, punishing her for more than her refusal to obey. We're punishing her for being so *strong*.

Konrad whips her twice more until five deep-red slashes mark her arse, obliterating the stars beneath burning comets. Nothing doesn't cry, she doesn't scream, she doesn't even move.

Nothing gives us *nothing*, whilst at the same time telling us everything.

This woman is something else, something *more*.

When the Numbers begin to enter the room, I don't even notice them.

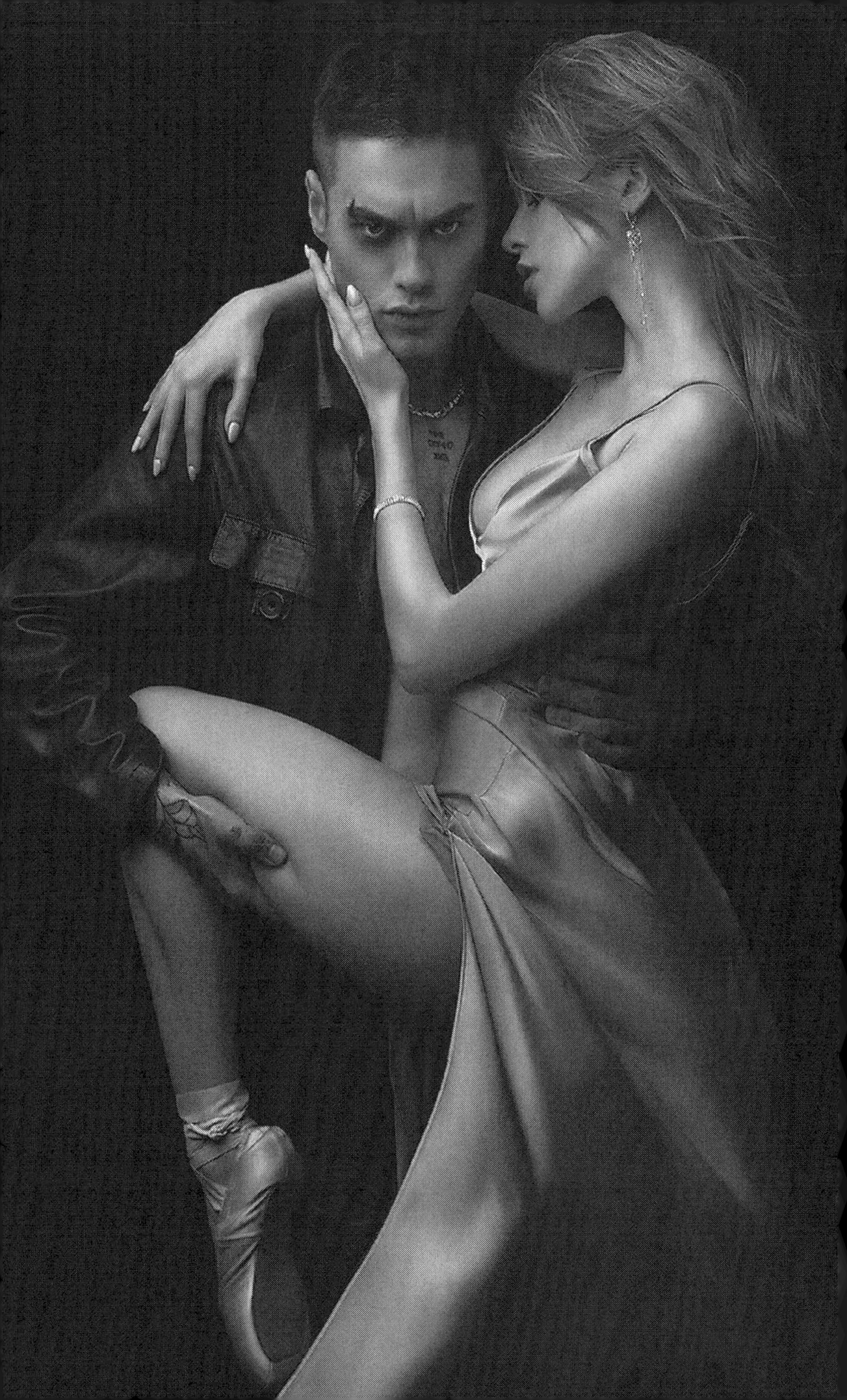

CHAPTER 16

CHRISTY

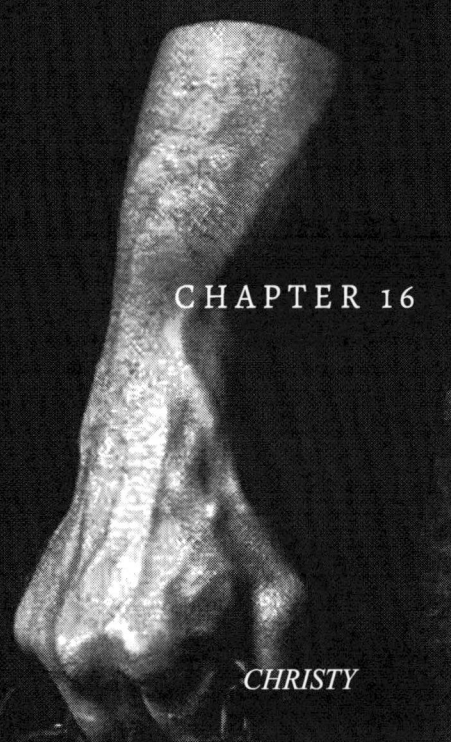

I've often wondered whether pain is relative. Do we all feel it the same way? Or are others just able to endure more? You see, I *feel* the sharp sting as Konrad whips my arse. I *feel* the intense heat that follows. Yet, I'm removed from it. Detached.

It's as though it's happening to someone else.

Thwack!

Thwack!

Thwack! Thwack! Thwack!

My heart thunders, my pulse races, my skin crawls and my legs turn to jelly, but I don't scream or cry or move. I float somewhere away from my body, feeling everything and nothing all at once, a strange kind of euphoria settling over me. The haunting tune might have stopped playing but the rush of listening to such extraordinary music remains. I find myself wanting to meet the pianist, One.

"Climb up onto the table, Nothing," Jakub eventually says, cutting through the tether that held me adrift and yanking me back to reality. His voice is oddly calm, as though he's controlling something inside. I can relate to that feeling. *"Nothing…"* he prompts.

I obey him, not because I've lost the will to fight, because that burns as brightly as I'm sure my arse does now, but because I'm still in that place where peace lives. Where nothing and no one can touch me. Pushing up onto my hands, I climb onto the table, painfully aware that my arse is still on display. The table is so large that I don't disturb the place settings as I crawl across the centre, but it's slow-going. I might not feel the pain, but my body is reacting to it nevertheless.

The Masks watch my every move, and when my dress falls past my arse, covering me up once more, I half expect them to tell me to lift it back up. They don't.

"Stop there," Leon commands, the flickering flames of the candles dotted about the hall are reflected in his eyes as I lock gazes with him.

Twisting my body, I sit with my legs crossed. My arse stings, but I switch off the pain, compartmentalising it until I can deal with it later. "Am I dinner?" I ask, an almost hysterical laugh bursting free from my lips.

Leon tips his head to the side, ignoring my question and asking another. "Didn't that hurt?"

"Yes."

"Then why didn't you scream, cry, make any kind of noise?"

"I don't know," I reply honestly. I really don't know how I do it, much like I don't know why I have visions. It's a mystery.

He nods, seemingly satisfied with my response. Konrad takes a seat next to Leon and I hear the sound of a chair sliding across the stone floor as Jakub sits down at the head of the table, but I don't turn my head to look at him. Instead I concentrate on a flickering candle on the other side of the hall, its light glowing brighter as it floats towards us.

A beautiful, raven-haired woman wearing a black lace dress with no bra or panties glides across the room, appearing out of the shadows like a ghost. Her expression is impassive, neutral, but her dark eyes are sharp and intelligent. She stops behind Jakub, her hand resting on the back of his chair. I have to twist my head to the side to look at them both. They make a beautiful couple.

"This is One," Jakub says, introducing me to the woman who played such beautiful music only moments before. I still feel its effects lingering on my skin like a lover's caress. "She is the matriarch of The Menagerie. She has lived here the longest and has earned her place by my side at this table. One, meet Nothing."

One tilts her head in greeting, acknowledging me. "What can she do?" she asks, her voice heavily accented, sexy, the vowels roll off her tongue in an expressive kiss.

"She's a ballerina. Other than that, not much else."

My nostrils flare at his dismissal, but I bite my tongue.

"A ballerina," she murmurs, eying me. "For the show?"

Jakub nods his head. "I'm considering it."

"Considering it? What is she here for if not for that?" One asks.

"She's here for us. She's *ours*," Jakub retorts pointedly. There's a possessiveness to his tone that doesn't go unnoticed. One's dark eyes narrow, and despite my appreciation for her music, I'm immediately wary of her.

"She is certainly very... *pretty*," she says, her observation not meant as a compliment given the look of disgust on her stunning face. I can only imagine what she'd think if she saw the real me, if my prettiness is as unattractive as her reaction implies. The respect and awe I have for her musical ability is quickly replaced with dislike. Anyone who puts more worth in a person's appearance isn't someone I'll ever get along with.

"Sit, One," Jakub barks impatiently, keeping his gaze fixed on mine. "I'd like to introduce the others and get this evening underway. I'm suddenly *very* hungry."

"Whatever you wish, *Master*," she preens, her fingers sliding along the high back of Jakub's chair and brushing down his arm in a move that is more dominant than obedient. He flinches, his jaw tightening, but he doesn't tell her to stop or punish her for the intimacy. Perhaps he fucks her? The way she looks at him certainly suggests as much.

"Send the rest of the Numbers in," Konrad says, his deep voice echoing around the grand hall, making me jump.

Two arched wooden doors swing open, spilling light into the space from the hallway beyond. A couple wearing barely any clothing walks in. They both appear to be around my age, and both smile warmly, as though me sitting in the centre of this banqueting table is entirely normal.

"I'm Three, and this is Seven," the woman says, tucking a strand of brown hair behind her ear, the ends kissing her chin. Her dress is knee length and a deep scarlet. Like her male counterpart, she is naked beneath it, although he's wearing sheer trousers and nothing else. Heat blooms in my chest and I pray with everything that I am that no one notices.

"Pleased to make your acquaintance," Seven says, dipping his head, a flop of curly blonde hair dropping in his eyes.

"Three is a dancer, like you, though she specialises in Flamenco and latin dances. Seven is a Tenor," Konrad explains. "They often perform together."

"Fuck together too," Leon adds.

I don't respond, I simply watch the beautiful couple take their place at the table, aware of their eyes on me.

"You've already met Four and Eight," Konrad says as the two familiar women step into the hall. Four has her long blonde hair piled up on her head, and her arm looped through Eight's. They're both wearing blue, though the floor length dress Four wears is the shade of the ocean, whilst Eight's is the colour of an inky sky just before night takes hold.

"Hello again," they sing-song, their bare breasts jiggling with every step as they take a seat.

"Four is a violinist and Eight an artist, the kind that uses brushes and paint. Both are exceptionally gifted like all the performers in The Menagerie," One explains.

"How does a portrait artist perform in a show?" I ask, unable to help myself.

"You think that I'm incapable of entertaining people, or keeping their interest?" Eight asks, her voice tight as she helps herself to a glass of wine poured by Renard. I hadn't even noticed that he was in the room.

"I didn't say that."

"Well, the answer to your question is simple. I paint as Four performs. Whatever the client wants, whatever image they require, I paint it."

"She's very good at it," Four adds, smiling at Eight adoringly. "Sometimes she uses the Numbers as a canvas too. It's *thrilling*."

Any further questions I might have are prevented from being asked when two blades thud into the table top either side of my hips. A scream rips out of my mouth and everyone laughs, with the exception of The Masks and the woman who strides into the room wearing absolutely nothing but two leather straps criss-crossing her chest, and heeled biker boots. She's small, lean, muscular, with tiny breasts, a boyish figure, and skin the colour of warm molasses.

Konrad leans across the table and pulls the knives from the wood, grinning widely. "This is Five, our little knife thrower. Don't piss her off." He spins the knives in his hand and offers them to Five over his shoulder. She takes them from him, her strange golden eyes pinned on me, a long black braid hanging over her shoulder. I wonder where she's from. I've never laid on anyone as exotic or beautiful. She's stunning.

"Thank you, Master," she retorts, her voice quiet, respectful, and I can't help but wonder why she doesn't slide that knife across his throat and set us all free. Taking a seat at the table she dips her head reverently at both Leon and Jakub before tucking the knives into her leather belt next to a third that's nestled there. I could look at her forever, fascinated by her exotic beauty, except I'm forced to stop when an equally beautiful woman steps into the room. She's stunning, but the total opposite to Five in every way.

"And this is Six," Leon explains, his gaze lingering on the curvaceous woman who steps into the hall. She has a wild mane of curly dark auburn hair that falls over her voluptuous breasts, accentuating her curves. She's wearing a cream slip and looks like a woman from one of those Botticelli paintings, unapologetically female with rounded hips, stomach and thighs, and more than enough sexiness to send even the most restrained man wild. She's walking sex. She oozes it, and yet she's the first person I've met this evening that doesn't appear wholly comfortable being here.

When she reaches the table, she holds her hand out to me, offering a gentle smile. I take her hand, noticing how our skin is the same pale shade then remember it was her that Nala borrowed the foundation from.

"Pleased to meet you," she says, gently squeezing my hand before letting go. Passing by Leon, she takes a seat to the right of Five. He watches her settle at the table.

"Six is a Contralto. Her voice is pure *sex*," Leon explains. "She fucks like she sings too."

Six remains impassive, her hand reaching for the glass of wine Renard has set before her. She doesn't acknowledge Leon, the other Masks or any of the Numbers, and I immediately feel a kinship with her. I'd bet my life she's not brainwashed like the others.

"And this is Nine, Ten and Eleven," Jakub interjects, a dark scowl forming on his face when One leans over and whispers something in his ear. He grits his jaw, anger burning across his face at whatever she's said to him.

Noticing, Konrad continues with the introduction. "Nine is a contortionist. Ten a mime artist, and Eleven a fire eater. They arrived at the castle at the same time three years ago. Triplets, if you hadn't already guessed."

"You make it sound like they weren't kidnapped like all the rest," I mumble under my breath, my gaze flicking between the three women. They're all tall, willowy, with wavy brown hair and wide green eyes. Their only defining difference is the beauty mark that adorns a different spot on each of their faces. Otherwise, it's almost impossible to tell them apart. All three wear matching gold gowns, their pear-shaped breasts and neatly trimmed pubic hair identical.

"Hello," they giggle, even more saccharin than Four. Despite their apparent lightheartedness, there's an absence in their gaze. It's disconcerting. They take a seat next to each other, still giggling, though their amusement is short-lived when another woman enters the room. She commands the space, her sheer silver dress floating about her legs as she strides across the room in strappy heels, a diamond choker at her throat. She's the only one I've seen wear any jewellery.

"Złodziej," Jakub snaps. "Thief!"

Konrad's gaze flicks to the women entering, his eyes narrowing. Jakub grits his jaw, but when One rests her palm on his arm he bites back whatever he's about to say next. Instead, he stares at One's hand, snarling. One pulls back as though burnt.

"I am Twelve. You must be *Zero*," she asks, cocking a perfectly arched brow, her accent similar to One's, her demeanor much the same. I instantly dislike her.

"No, I'm—" *Christy.*

"Zero," Konrad interjects, preventing me from making a mistake. I'm not sure why he stops me saying my name, given he seemed to thoroughly enjoy punishing me earlier, but he does. Instead he turns his attention to Twelve, his eyes narrowing. "What are you wearing?"

"This old thing," she says, her hands falling to the dress as she lifts it, dropping her gaze coyly. She knows full well he wasn't talking about the dress but the very expensive looking item of jewellery around her neck.

Leon snorts and Jakub scowls, but it's Konrad who takes action. He stands abruptly, grabs her by the hair and forces her face down against the table. I flinch, feeling her warm breath against my hip. I move to shuffle away, but Konrad snarls.

"Stay the fuck where you are," he insists, looking at me but not letting go of Twelve.

She shifts against the table, her hip pressing back against his cock, a smile spreading across her face as she side-eyes me. "*He's mine,*" she bites out.

My mouth falls open in shock at her show of possessiveness over a man who is treating her with such brutality. Why in the world would she think I want this, any of this? I'm a victim, not a threat.

Konrad growls, his fingers yanking at the choker at her neck. He pulls it free, shoving it into Jakub's hand, then presses the length of his body against hers, his mouth against her ear. "How many times do I need to tell you, Twelve, you are no more mine, than I am yours. *You* belong to The Menagerie, to any one of our clients who pays handsomely to fuck that desperate cunt. This is the last time I shall tell you this. Next time you need reminding of your place, it won't be a week in my dungeons that you'll endure," he warns, lifting his gaze to meet Jakub, who nods his head, "But a night in the forest with Jakub."

Twelve sucks in a shocked breath, her passion and fire put out by the threat. Why is a night in the forest with Jakub scarier than a week in the dungeons with Konrad?

"No, I didn't mean it..." Her voice trails off as Konrad's hold tightens. A look passes between him and Jakub.

"You didn't mean to steal what belongs to me?" Jakub asks, taking Konrad's place behind her. His fingers grasp the back of her head, as he pulls her upright against him. The room quietens, the change in atmosphere darkening. Jakub holds his hand out to Konrad, who places his flick knife in his palm before pressing the edge against her throat. She whimpers, her dark eyes somehow fixed on me. For a moment, I watch in sick fascination, unable to move, afraid to gain his attention and feel his wrath.

"Tell our new acquisition what rule you've broken, Twelve?" he asks her, his voice controlled, sinister in a way that makes my skin grow cold.

"I shall not covet what isn't mine and never will be."

"That's right," Jakub says. "What else?"

"To never steal from my Masters."

"Then tell me now why I shouldn't cut your throat and let you bleed out for breaking those rules..." Jakub asks, pressing his lips against her cheek, whilst the tip of the blade nicks the olive skin of her throat.

"One of the staff forgot to close the cabinet after cleaning. I saw it and—"

"Thought you'd take it?" he sneers, pressing the knife in further.

Her eyes widen in fear, her nostrils flaring as she realises her mistake. My wariness of her is replaced with pity. "Don't!" I say, unable to help myself. Out of the corner of my eye I see Six snap her attention to me. She swallows hard.

Jakub narrows his eyes at me, but pulls back the blade at Twelve's throat. "Are you daring to tell me what to do?" he asks, his attention focused on me now.

"She's scared," I say.

"She has every reason to be," Konrad adds, though I refuse to take my eyes off Jakub.

"I just *miss* you—" Twelve mumbles, a silvery tear leaking from her eyes and sliding down her nose. If this isn't Stockholm syndrome, I don't know what is.

"Here's the thing, Twelve, I don't miss you, or want *you* for that matter," Konrad snarls. "Get out of my fucking sight!"

The relief I feel is palpable. If she isn't here, then she's safe. At least for now. Of course it was foolish to believe The Masks would let this go so easily. What happens next makes my stomach fold in on itself.

"No," Jakub snaps, causing Twelve to wobble on her feet and look between the two men. "This is a punishable offence. Renard!" he commands, folding away the knife and handing it back to Konrad.

"Yes, Sir?" Renard responds, appearing out of nowhere like an apparition.

"Wheel in the Stocks and bring me the Cat-o'-nine-tails."

Stocks? Cat-o'-nine-tails? Jesus Christ.

"Surely, you're not going to...?" My question trails off as I see the look of sheer malevolence in Jakub's eyes. Konrad and Leon are no different.

When Renard hesitates and the other Numbers mumble under their breaths, Jakub roars. "NOW!"

Renard nods, rushing off to fetch the items requested as Jakub focuses back on Twelve, whose eyes are wide with a mixture of fear and triumph. "Do not look at me! You *stole* from me, and you're going to pay for it right here and now!"

"Yes, Master," Twelve mumbles, her body trembling.

For a moment I think it's fear, but then I notice the flush of her cheeks, the way she licks her lips and stares at Konrad with undeniable lust in her eyes, and understanding hits me that it's desire causing her to shake. This is exactly what she wants. I swallow hard, not understanding how anyone could *want* pain. I've suffered so much of it in my past, still do. Pain is the last thing I will ever seek out from another person.

"Jakub, you know how much I love dishing out punishment, but I'm not in the business of giving Twelve what she wants."

"I'm well aware what Twelve does and doesn't want, *Brother*," Jakub snaps. "But I see this as an opportunity to demonstrate the rules all the Numbers must live by to our newest acquisition—"

"Acquisition?! I'm not an object, I'm a person!" I snap, unable to control my outburst.

"You *are* an object, and will remain an object until we decide you're worthy of becoming more than that," Leon interjects cruelly.

"Indeed," Jakub agrees. "So far allowances have been made for your minor misdemeanors." He looks pointedly at me as though I should be grateful for being tied up to The Weeping Tree, whipped just now and scared out of my mind from the moment I arrived here. "It's about time Nothing understands her place, and I think this is the perfect opportunity to do that."

"I agree," Leon adds darkly, cutting me a look that has a shiver running down my spine. I don't even want to know what thoughts are going through his head right now.

The sound of metal wheels passing over the wooden floor of the grand hall heralds Renard's return and snatches Leon's attention away, allowing me to let out a shaky breath. I watch in sick fascination as the old butler arranges the stocks which, contrary to my imagination, are not made from wood like I've seen in history books, but from metal.

Without even having to be asked, Twelve removes her dress, then positions herself in the archaic contraption, placing her head and wrists in the corresponding grooves. Renard locks her in place, the iron bar securing her. I swallow hard at the way she widens her stance, displaying her beautiful body for everyone to see. She looks at me with a slow smile, and triumph in her eyes when all I feel is pity and growing horror.

Konrad holds out his hand for the whip, but Jakub shakes his head. "No. Leon will be dishing out the punishment."

I hear Twelve's sharp intake of breath and see how she strains against the stocks holding her in place. "But, I thought—"

"You thought that your beloved Konrad would be the one to whip you raw, huh? Well, Twelve, you stole from me. That means I choose who whips you. Leon…?" Jakub says, turning to his brother who takes the Cat-o'-nine-tails with a smile so sinister that my blood runs cold.

Leon holds the implement reverently, his fingers running through the lengths of leather and the tiny silver balls attached to the end of them. "With fucking pleasure, Brother," he drawls.

"Don't do this," I exclaim. "Don't hurt her!" My mouth is dry, my voice weakened by the unfolding events, but I can't just sit here and say nothing, do nothing.

Leon turns his attention to me. "One more word from you and you'll be next. Understand?"

I nod, blinking back the tears as I look between the three men and Twelve whose whole demeanour has changed. She's afraid now. Very afraid.

Leon stalks towards her, his tall frame lithe, lethal. The whole room has quietened, the atmosphere has shifted into something dark and sinister. I shift on my arse, sucking in a sharp breath from the pain, reminded of it in this moment of sheer terror that Twelve feeds us all.

Konrad snaps his head around to look at me, a question in his eyes. "Are you okay?" he asks gently, and I have to blink back my shock.

Am I okay?

Is he insane? Of course I'm not okay. My arse is red raw and I'm about to witness a woman get flogged by a man who's clearly filled with bloodlust. My mouth opens to respond but slams shut as Twelve screams, the Cat-o'-nine-tails spreading red-hot fire over her skin.

Leon tips his head back and lets out a sigh. "One," he says, eyes burning hot as he focuses not on Twelve, but on me.

"Five lashes. Five lashes to remind you of the rules, Twelve, and to ensure Nothing here is aware of the consequences of breaking them," Jakub says, as Leon fondles the lengths of leather waiting for further instruction. One leans over and whispers in Jakub's ear. He nods, then says, "After every lash, I want you to repeat the rules, Twelve."

"Yes, M—master," she stutters, trying to control the wobble in her voice.

"Given Leon has already started, you should repeat the first rule..." Konrad prompts, folding his arms across his chest, the muscle in his jaw feathering as he grits his teeth.

"The first rule is to *always* obey The Masks," Twelve says, her whole body stiffening as she waits for the next lash. Jakub doesn't warn her to relax like he did me, he simply nods at Leon who whips her again. Another scream releases from her lips. It takes her a moment to catch her breath, but eventually when she finds the strength, she continues.

"The second r—rule is to not covet what isn't mine and never will be."

Leon is even more brutal this time, the third lash cracking against her skin like a thunderbolt. Her scream is loud enough to shatter windows.

"The third rule is..." Twelve sobs, her voice breaking with pain. "...To n—never steal from my Masters—"

She's barely finished her sentence and Leon is bringing down the whip. The bloodcurdling scream that erupts from Twelve's lips has me choking on my own sob and blinking away the tears threatening to fall. I have to remain strong. It seems even more important now than ever before.

"The fourth rule is to respect my fellow Numbers. We're f—family."

Another lash, more tears. She's crying harder now. I feel her pain, *hating* these men on her behalf because she's too brainwashed to do the same.

"And the final rule?" Jakub prompts, his jaw tight, his words tense.

"To n—never break those four rules, but if we do, then to expect s—severe punishment."

My gaze is drawn to the Cat-o'-nine-tails that Leon clutches in his hand, tiny droplets of blood dripping from the leather. Drip. Drip. Drip. I can't take my eyes off it, or how his hand is gripping the handle so tightly the veins in the back of them are protruding against his skin.

"Oh God," I murmur, dragging my gaze to Jakub who shifts in his seat.

He looks at Konrad who's been quiet all this time, to Leon who's breathing heavily, his chest rising and falling, then back to me. "Contrary to what you believe, this punishment isn't the norm but it *is* necessary. Twelve understood the rules, and she *chose* to break them. This is the consequence."

"It's *barbaric*," I hiss, my gaze cutting to Twelve who's barely able to keep her body upright. Blood trickles from the lashes across her back and nausea rises up my throat.

"We provide a home, shelter, food, and warmth. The Numbers are well cared for, they perform in The Menagerie doing what they *love*, and they fuck our clients because they *want* to, not because we force them to," Jakub continues.

I don't buy that for one second, but I don't question it. Too shocked to do anything but sit here and listen to his bullshit lies. Jakub turns to Renard, who has been waiting in the shadows. His expression is tight, but he's not foolish enough to express whatever thoughts are going through his head right now.

"Sir?" Renard asks, waiting for instruction.

"Take Twelve to her quarters. Lock her in."

"Yes, Sir," he nods, flicking his gaze between Jakub and Konrad.

Konrad's nostrils flare, and I'm not sure what's going on, but it's clearly some unspoken conversation that I can't interpret. "After the meal I will send Thirteen to deal with Twelve's wounds."

Twelve sobs, her heartbroken words tumbling from her lips. "No, please, I need you," she cries.

"And that's precisely why I'm sending Thirteen. Do not covet what isn't yours," Konrad grinds out, reiterating rule number two. "What happened here today is on *you*, Twelve."

"Take her to her room," Leon orders, dropping the Cat-o'-nine-tails on the floor and taking his seat back at the table. He leans forward and brushes his fingers over my knee, the darkness in his eyes abating, and for the tiniest moment I see something odd in his piercing green eyes. It's as though he's seeking my reassurance.

"Don't touch me," I sneer, flinching away from his touch. I don't want him to touch me. *Ever*. He snorts, sitting back in his seat, that fleeting look replaced with hardness.

"You heard Leon," Konrad adds.

"Yes, Sir." With a dip of his head, Renard unlocks Twelve and guides her from the room. She cries out with every step, her pain punctuated with sobs.

Silence descends as we all watch them leave, broken only by the light steps of another woman approaching the table. She passes Renard and Twelve, stopping briefly to whisper something into Twelve's ear, a look of practised calm on her face. I watch as she caresses the bare skin of Twelve's arm, my eyes zeroing in on how she appears to be rubbing something into Twelve's skin. No one but me appears to notice the strange exchange, but there's no denying the air of calm settling over Twelve despite her horrific injuries.

As Twelve leaves—the door to the Grand Hall shutting behind her and Renard—the woman approaching smiles gently, her attention fixed on me. She's dressed differently to the others, her clothing hides rather than reveals. She's wearing a cream silk shirt, tucked into a floor length navy skirt. Her light brown hair is hanging in a loose ponytail and her heart-shaped face is pretty but not stunning like the others.

"This is *Thirteen*," Konrad says, getting to his feet.

She gives him a gentle nod of her head, and he welcomes her with a kiss to her cheek. Leon and Jakub follow suit as they all greet her like she is more than just a Number. Then I remember what Nala had said. Thirteen *is* different from the other Numbers. Unlike me, unlike the others, she isn't a possession, she's *family*.

That thought makes my heart squeeze in pain, remembering my own.

CHAPTER 17

CHRISTY

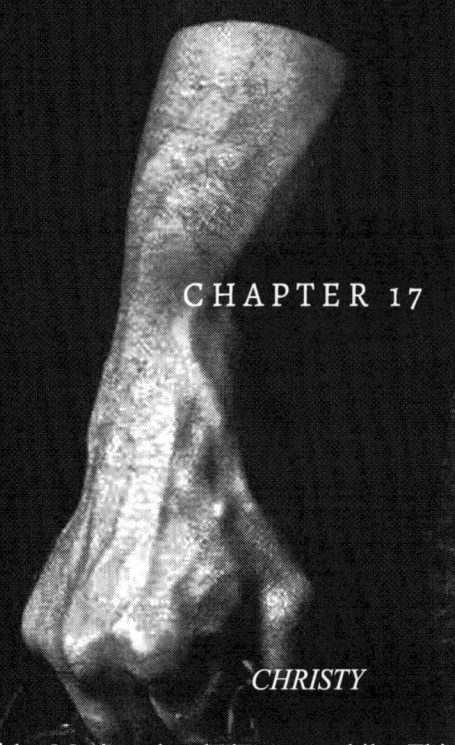

The Masks take their seats whilst Thirteen stands before me, her unusual grey eyes watching me carefully. She reaches for my face, her fingertips sliding over my skin as she cups my cheeks, and presses her mouth against mine, the act taking me off guard. I want to push her off me, then I remember who she is to The Masks and how they whipped me for talking back earlier, how they just flayed the skin on Twelve's back, so I don't.

Her fingertips gently stroke my skin as the tip of her tongue edges its way between my lips. Around us some of the Numbers giggle, and I hear one of The Masks clear their throat, a sound that is more warning than anything else, but she ignores them all. My lips part of their own accord as I accept her kiss even though I'm confused by it. My heart hammers in my chest as her tongue slides over mine and warm liquid rushes into my mouth. I struggle a little, but she holds me firm until I have no choice but to swallow or choke. The sweet taste of watered down honey, and something else I can't place, washes over my tastebuds. When she's certain I've swallowed whatever she's just fed me, she strokes my tongue gently with hers once more then pulls back.

Something shifts in her gaze and without opening her mouth, a thousand words are spoken, some innate understanding passing between us.

Trust me, her expression says.

With an almost imperceptible nod, she draws her hands back and steps away, taking her place at the table. The skin on my back smarts, and my pulse thrums with a truth I'm yet to uncover.

"Now that we're all here, the feast can begin," Leon says, his eyes focusing back on me. Despite the pretty hue, there's a darkness to them that's undeniable. Whatever chivalry and respect he'd shown to Thirteen, it's gone now, completely obliterated by the deviant need he hides within. "Lay down, *Nought.*"

"W—what?" I stutter.

Konrad smirks, picking up the discarded leash. "You heard him. Lay down." I see the threat in his eyes, and the desire to whip me again. It reminds me of my recent debasement and I bite down on the sudden cry of pain as I shift position, obeying their command. I do it not because I can't take another punishment but because I don't want to be humiliated in front of these people. "Five, if you please," Konrad says.

From the corner of my eye, I see Five stand and move around the table, as comfortable in her nakedness as I am wearing clothes. A thread of jealousy assails me. I may have accepted who I am, but I've never been completely comfortable in my own skin. This woman isn't confined by her looks, she commands attention. The jealousy I feel is quickly replaced with trepidation as she reaches for a knife from her leather strap. What do they mean to do to me?

Sensing my urge to bolt, I feel strong hands wrap around my ankles and know without looking that it's Jakub. His callouses scrape against my skin, sending shockwaves of sensation through me. I can't quite figure out if his touch is revolting or, God forbid, pleasurable. Either way, that brief physical reaction is replaced with fear as Leon presses his hands on my shoulders, pinning me to the table.

"You might want to keep still," Leon says, drawing delighted laughs from some of the Numbers, though, tellingly, not all.

"What are you going to do to me?" I whisper, hating how afraid I sound.

Konrad chuckles. "We're here to eat dinner... so that's what we're about to do."

"You mean—" Tears burn my eyes, pooling on my lashes as disbelief washes over me. Surely they aren't going to...? I struggle against their hold, a burning desire to fight is raging beneath my skin. I will *not* die like this.

Konrad pins down my bucking hips, his smile widening as he looms over me, his dark hair flopping forward over his blood-red mask. "We're not cannibals, if that's what you're thinking, Zero."

"Oh God," I exhale, instant relief making my body go lax. For a terrible moment I *had* truly believed that I was their dinner.

"God won't help you, though if you ask for the Devil you might be rewarded," Leon says, his upside-down face smiling down at me as he rests his hands against my shoulders.

"As you know, Zero, we do have a thing for blood," Konrad interjects. "There's something so carnal about making a woman bleed, don't you think?"

"No," I bite out, swallowing hard, my anger only tempered by the feel of a sharp, cold blade at my throat.

Five appears above me, her long braid tickling my cheek as Konrad and Leon lean back, giving her space. "Keep still," she warns, her dark eyes flashing with sympathy. "I won't hurt you."

"Okay," I whisper, something in her gaze telling me that I should trust her. Maybe it's because I know she's a victim like me, or maybe it's because of the warmth in her dark eyes. Either way, I don't move.

Gripping the high collar of my dress, she holds the knife vertically towards my throat then slices through the material. When the tip of the knife kisses my breastbone, she pulls back just enough for me to breathe again. My pulse thrums loudly in my ears, and before I can even take a breath, her deep berry lips are pressed against mine in a kiss so warm and kind that I barely feel the nick of the blade as she makes a tiny cut in my skin, just over my clavicle.

"I'm sorry," she mutters against my mouth before pulling back and resting the knife on the table beside my head.

She just cut me! I want to ask her why, but she steps out of the way, returning to her seat as Konrad removes his hands from my hips, grabs the material at my throat, then yanks hard. The dress splits down my middle, the sound of cotton tearing, reverberating around the hall.

A sudden rush of cold air rolls over my skin, fear and the change in temperature causing my nipples to harden into puckered points. My chest heaves, and I automatically reach up to cover my breasts, but Konrad is back, pinning my arms to my sides. He leans over me, his mouth just a centimetre above mine.

"Jakub may have locked up your cunt, but we all get to feast on your skin whilst we eat tonight, Zero. So be good, accept what's happening, and we'll make sure you're rewarded."

I want to tell him to go fuck himself, but my tongue suddenly feels heavy, my limbs too, as warmth spreads out from the place Five cut me. The need to fight back recedes to some distant place in my mind as a languid sensation washes over me in its place. I feel everyone's eyes on my exposed skin, but I don't try to cover up. Instead, I bask in this feeling as he sits back down, never once taking his gaze off of me. My toes curl, my skin tingling with the strangest sensation. It's as though I'm lying in my garden back home, nothing but the summer sun warming my naked skin. I'm relaxed, content. The heat of his gaze, of *their* gazes, feels good. It feels better than good when it should terrify me.

"Everyone," Jakub says, an instruction to do something, though I've no idea what.

I'm vaguely aware of Jakub and Leon removing their hands, and a frown creases my forehead in the absence of their touch. Why do I want it back? Why do I let out a whimper as though I can't bear to not have them touch me again?

Somewhere deep inside I know I've been drugged, that the knife Five had cut me with was laced with something to relax me, to make me accept the unacceptable, but I can't seem to even summon up the energy to care. So when One stands, her long black hair whispering over my bare breasts as she leans over me, my skin prickles and I remain still, content to just lie here. She pinches my chin between her thumb and forefinger, then lowers her luscious lips to mine. Her kiss is soft, warm, but it lacks the kindness that Five had shown me. Even in this state, I'm aware of that fact.

"Welcome," she murmurs. Her thick accent is molten lava, a warning, as she picks up the knife and nicks my skin just above the curve of my left breast. I don't register the sharp sting. I don't even feel any blood pooling, and that's not because I think I've imagined the cut, but because I'm floating on a cloud of indifference so unexpected that all I can do is lay here. More heat rolls out from her cut, adding to the intensity of the first.

"Pain and pleasure are the foundations of our existence, Zero," Konrad explains, the throaty sound rumbling up his chest.

"It's fundamental to the harmony of this place. Accept their welcome and you'll be rewarded," Jakub adds.

I do as he asks, *unable* at this moment to protest. Somewhere in the back of my head an angry little voice is telling me to fight back, to fight this strange floating kind of sensation, but another part of me, a bigger part, is unwilling to move a muscle. I'm not even sure I could if I tried.

One by one each Number welcomes me, always with a kiss on the lips, a cut to my skin, and a few muttered words. Some are more genuine than others. Six, Three and Seven are kind just like Five. They greet me with gentle kisses, sweet words and the barest of cuts. Four and Eight are indifferent, and Two makes a show at having to climb down from her cage to greet me. She takes a seat at the table with a huff after sliding the knife over the protrusion of my hip bone. I know without looking that it's deeper than the rest.

Nine, Ten and Eleven go through the motions but lack any kind of empathy as they kiss, cut and greet me. I get the impression that this is all just a game to them. Something to laugh at, to giggle about like children beneath their hands. They lack depth, or maybe they're just too scarred by being here under the thumb of these men to behave any other way. Not that it matters, I'm beyond the point of caring about anything or anyone right at this moment.

"These are the Numbers," Jakub says, interrupting my thoughts with his accented words. "You will respect their place here, and their decision to remain. They do not need saving. Understand?"

I nod my head. "I won't save them…" The words fall out of my mouth and yet they don't feel like they belong to me at all.

"You will live alongside the Numbers for as long as *we* decide," Leon adds, the threat in his voice unmistakable, though I'm not clear if it's my life he's threatening or Jakub and the power struggle they appear to have going on.

"The Numbers have earned their place here. They are valued," Konrad continues. "You, however, have yet to earn the right to sit at our table, to eat with us. The first rule is simple. Obey our command."

Obey, there's that word again. It's filled with meaning, strained at the seams. They want me to submit to their authority, accept my place here whether it be as a Number, an object of desire, of lust and hate. I should feel more fear. I should be terrified, in fact, but I'm not. Their words, whilst disgusting, do not disturb me like they have done so before. The edge of my fear has been removed, the heart of my hate quietened, allowing me to dive beneath the surface of my emotions into the core of how I truly feel.

Obeying someone's demands means not thinking about any other option. It means allowing another person to take the lead, to let go of any responsibility to others, to myself. In a weird way it's a freedom of sorts. A freedom to exist without consequence because the responsibility is firmly on someone else's shoulders. My whole life I've been conscious of everyone else, bombarded by visions I don't wish to see, of futures that aren't my own. I've been responsible for people's happiness and it's a burden that has been exhausting to carry. Would it be so wrong to give up that responsibility? Would it be so bad to give over the power to someone else just for a time? Those thoughts surprise me, the clarity of my new understanding a double-edged sword. I'm aware that the drug could be skewing my views but equally, at this moment, I don't care.

"Lay still whilst we eat. Let us fill our stomachs with sustenance, whilst we feast on your body with our eyes," Konrad murmurs.

He reaches for me, his fingertips sliding over my cheek and down my neck until he reaches the first cut made by Five. A trail of heat follows his touch, my body relaxing under his command, my muscles feeling heavy under his scrutiny. I watch as he swipes at my skin and lifts his finger to his mouth sucking on my blood he collected there. I feel his hum of appreciation low in my belly.

"Delicious," he says. "I wonder if your cunt tastes as good."

Without warning, my clit pulses at the memory of Jakub's lips against my delicate flesh. I react instinctively, squeezing my thighs together, the supple leather of the chastity belt tight against my core and providing friction in an already overly sensitive area. The sudden jolt of pleasure batters at the anger I've felt ever since they stole me, carving another notch into the thickened wall encasing my resolve to stay strong, to never accept my place here. Konrad has barely touched me and my body is reacting without my consent. I *hate* that. At least, I think I do.

Enough. That little voice inside my head grows louder, refusing to sink beneath this new sensation, this fakery. *Fight*, it says. *Don't let them control your pleasure too.*

It's enough of a jolt to make me ignore my pulsing clit and focus on the injustice of the situation, the reality. This isn't about my pleasure. This is about their control.

"Dinner is served," Renard says somewhere from the other side of the hall as it fills with men and women carrying trays brimming with delicious smelling food. I turn my head, watching them spill into the room. They're dressed just like Nala had been. The women are wearing black knee length dresses and white pinafores, and the men, black suits with a white shirt and tie. A golden crest of three masks is embroidered on the breast pocket of the mens' jackets and the lapel of the womens' dresses. Steam rises up into the air around me as they place plates piled high with sliced meat and vegetables onto the table. I'm vaguely aware of my stomach rumbling, and realise that despite Nala bringing me food earlier today, I didn't eat any of it. Not a crumb.

I watch with my head tipped to the side as Leon and Konrad are served lamb chops covered in gravy and steaming vegetables dripping in butter and herbs. My stomach contracts with hunger as I watch them eat, and I have the sudden urge to reach out and snatch a potato dripping in gravy from Leon's plate. He catches my eye, spearing the potato and takes a bite, chewing slowly. My lips part as saliva pools in my mouth.

"Are you hungry, Nought?" he asks me.

"Yes," I admit, my tongue peeking out from between my parted lips.

Leaning forward, he rests the gravy-soaked potato against my mouth but when I go to take a bite removes it quickly. My tongue darts out, lapping at the gravy left behind on my lip. The meaty taste explodes on my tongue and I almost weep at the loss of something that's far more meaningful to my sense of survival than hunger. By allowing him to see my weakness, to tease me with something I want, I've let him control me. I should've grabbed the fork from him and slammed it into the back of his bastard hand.

"Be a good girl then, and you'll be rewarded." He smiles, then eats the remainder of the potato, reminding me who has the ultimate control.

Turning my gaze away, I blink up at the gold cage hanging above the table and try to focus on anything but the way I feel and the hunger in my belly. Around me the Numbers and The Masks feast on their dinner, their enjoyment interrupted only by the seemingly pleasant conversation. I don't pay attention to what they're saying, unable to grasp hold of anything more than a few words here and there. Right now, my body feels even less of my own than it does when I'm recovering from a vision. It's both as heavy as the manacles that were wrapped around my wrists and ankles in the dungeons, and as light as one of the dust motes falling from the ceiling above me now.

Time passes, plates are cleared and I find myself drifting in and out of consciousness, bound only to the present moment by a casual touch here and there by the hands of my tormentors. Every now and then, Jakub's calloused fingers reach for my foot or ankle, the rough skin of his palm passing over mine and sending bolts of unwanted electricity up and down my spine. His touch is certain, meaningful, but controlled, as though he's going through the motions but refusing to reveal his true intentions. He lies with his touch. Hiding his wants and desires, suppressing them in the moment. The fighter in me wants to kick out, to shove my foot in his food and ruin it, to make him reveal what he's hiding, but the heavy fog of this drug has reduced me to someone compliant, pliable. Again, it should scare me. I should be frightened, but I don't even feel that.

Konrad is less restrained than Jakub. He touches me regularly and often. A hand pressing against my stomach, a finger trailing over my hip bone, another sliding under the leather belt at my waist. There's a sensuality to his touch, but I'm not so under the influence of this drug that I'm fooled into thinking it's affection. Ultimately, this man wants to inflict pain. That's where his predilections lie.

Leon, however, his touch is more like a lightning bolt, certain in its intent, ruinous in its motives. There are no lies with his touch, only truth. I feel his thick fingers in my hair, twisting tightly as he leans over me to grasp another slice of meat rather than wait for a servant to dish it up for him. At one point, he grasps my chin and slides his gravy-soaked finger into my mouth, the taste bursting on my tongue, reminding me that I'm only fed because they allow it.

"Are you ready for dessert?" Renard asks after a while.

Everyone at the table stops talking, tension winding tightly in the air. My eyes flicker open. I hadn't even realised I'd closed them.

"We are," Jakub responds, an edge to his voice that makes my skin prickle with foreboding. "Leave us!"

One by one the Numbers bid their farewell to The Masks, a solemnness following them out. The staff clear the table around me until all signs of dinner have been removed. They retreat back into the shadowed corners of the hall, departing through doors I can't see, into corridors that I've never walked down, until it's just me alone once again with The Masks, naked, vulnerable and entirely at their mercy.

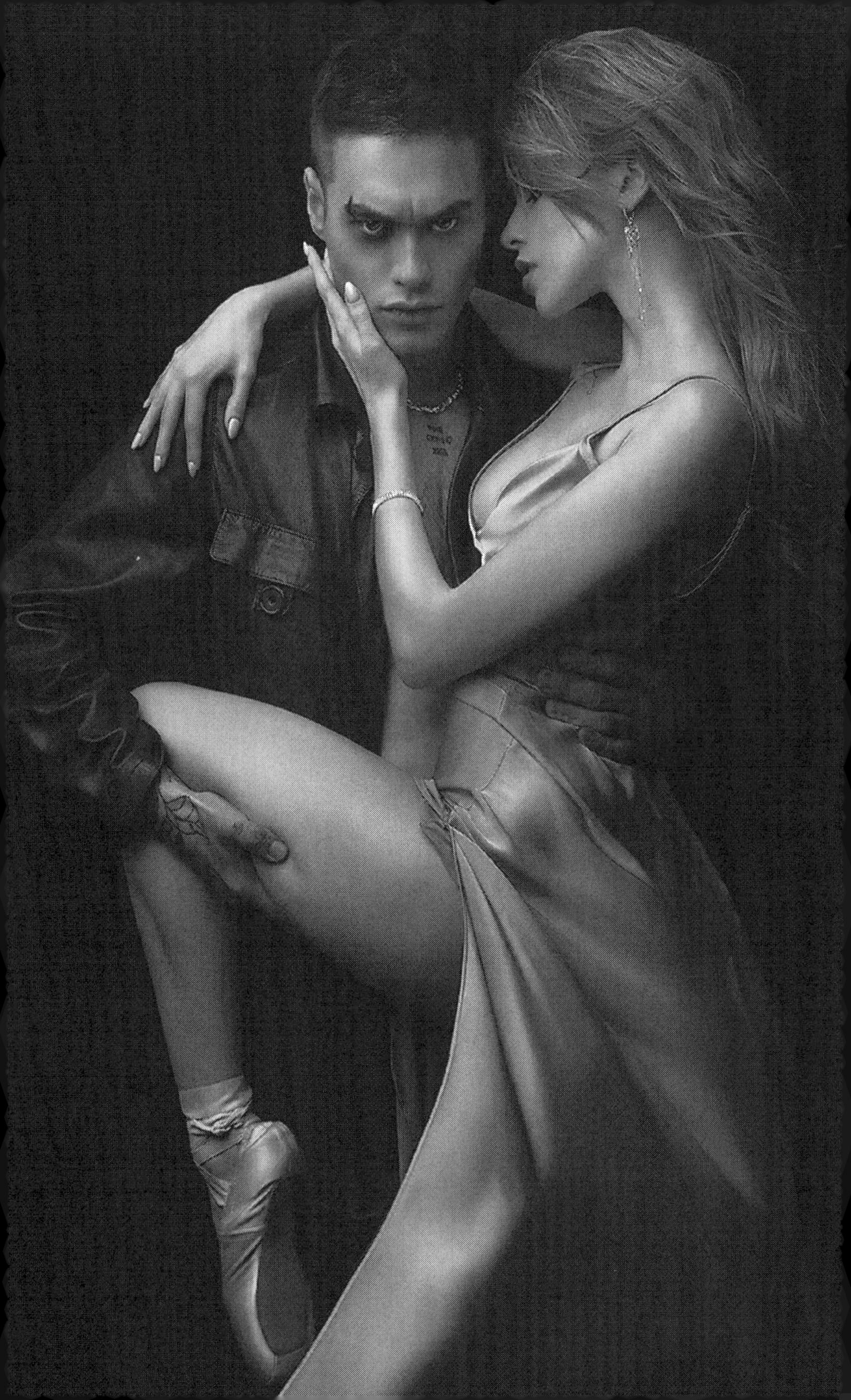

CHAPTER 18

CHRISTY

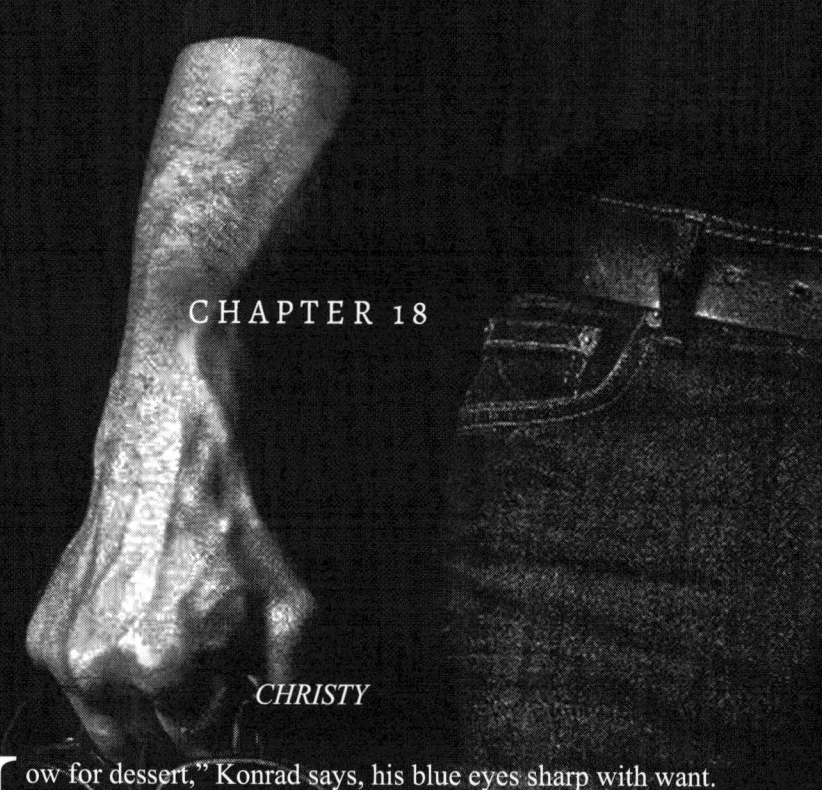

"Now for dessert," Konrad says, his blue eyes sharp with want. The effects of the drug continue to incapacitate me. My limbs feel heavy and my head groggy. Getting away from these men is no longer an option. I simply can't move.

"Please," my voice is slurred, my tongue heavy. That inner voice battling with my body's need to obey. Begging these motherfuckers isn't something I want to do, but it happens regardless. My physical strength has been overpowered by this drug that I've been poisoned with. "W—what have you d—done to me?"

"Thirteen is truly gifted. She has the ability to make any manner of drugs, and all of it using natural ingredients. If you haven't already guessed, Five's blade was steeped in something to relax you. There's no running now, Nothing," Jakub says, wickedness lacing his voice with poison just like the drug is lacing my veins in the same way.

"How could she?" I mutter, heartbroken by her betrayal. Why had she looked at me the way she did? Like she understood my predicament and wanted to help me, and yet it was her drug that made me feel this way, that's put me into this vulnerable position. I can't even try to fight back.

"If she'd been born in the wrong century, there is no doubt that she would've been accused of being a witch and hanged from The Weeping Tree for her skill," he continues, oblivious to my disappointment.

"She's a witch?" I mumble, spots of light dancing in front of my eyes as I try to make sense of what's happening.

Konrad stands, looming over me. "Not like the ones you might find in fairy tales, Zero. She's a healer for want of a better word."

"A healer?" I laugh, and the sound is bitter. This isn't healing, this is aiding and abetting monsters who imprison and control, who manipulate and coerce, who *hurt* people. She's no better than they are.

"She calls this particular elixir *The Quickening*," Leon explains, his thick fingers sliding through my hair, pulling the strands so that my scalp tingles. I feel the weight of his hands, the intention in his movements, and it sends a wave of warmth cascading over my body. It's not a reaction I want or understand, but it happens regardless. "You may feel heavy, sleepy, relaxed right now," he continues. "But soon the drug's true purpose will reveal itself. Be ready, Nought. This is the one and only time we can guarantee that you'll enjoy what's about to happen. This is our welcome."

I almost say that Jakub has already given me that back in his bedroom, but then that would be admitting out loud that I enjoyed it, that a tiny part of me craves that feeling again.

"No! Don't!" I protest weakly. Forcing my lips to move, I glare at Jakub standing before me. "This isn't what I want."

Jakub's eyes flash with anger. "Even under the influence you are still so argumentative. We are giving you a *gift*, Nothing. Accept it."

"Rape isn't a gift. Touching me without my permission isn't a damn g—gift!" I stutter, stumbling over my words, trying desperately to force my arm to move so that I can knock away Konrad's fingers as they trace my rib cage. Instead, a languid feeling rolls over me at his touch, sparking sensations of pleasure that floods my sex. A rush of anger fires up inside my chest. Is this what they mean by the drug's true purpose? The Quickening makes your body relax until you're unable to control it anymore, then it makes you feel pleasure when you otherwise wouldn't?

Don't lie to yourself, you've already proven how much you enjoy their touch.

I close that thought down, refusing to acknowledge it. "H—how could she?!" I bite out, forcing the words through heavy lips and a slack jaw, trying in vain to ignore my pulsing clit.

"Thirteen?" Jakub asks, taking my hands in his and pulling me upright. Even that simple touch is like a beacon to my pussy. Heat rushes to my core at the simple contact. I want to snatch my hands away, but can't even do that.

"Yes," I spit. It takes immense effort to lift my head and look at him. My torn dress hangs open, and my breasts feel heavy, swollen, as I sit with my legs stretched out on the table in front of me. Jakub glances at my chest, at my peaked nipples before lifting his gaze back to mine. My body feels like a ripe fruit, ready to be plucked, tasted, but inside I feel rotten to the core. None of this is right. None of it is real in the true sense of the word. It's a lie. If I had all my faculties then there's no way I'd be reacting this way to their touch. I'd be disgusted. I *would*. "How could she?"

"Because we asked her to, because she's our friend."

"*Friend?*" The laughter that leaves my mouth sounds light, carefree, but it wasn't meant to. The drug turns my hate into smiles and laughter, just like it turns my physical disgust into acceptance and pleasure. Internally, I'm cursing that bitch, Thirteen. Goddamn her. She's a traitor to the sisterhood, to humanity. How can she willingly be friends with these *monsters*?

"She understands what we are," Leon adds, a reverence to his voice that surprises me. I manage to twist my head to look at him, and he meets my gaze with a hard look, making me wonder if I imagined it.

"What, perverted psychos?" I spit out.

Konrad laughs, not in the least bit bothered by my insult. He shucks off his dinner jacket and hangs it over the back of the chair, then rolls up his shirt sleeves, revealing thick forearms, dark hair and protruding veins. My core tightens. "Thirteen knew us before—"

"Before?" I ask, my single-word question a fumble of vowels and consonants. I sound drunk.

"Yes, before we—"

"Kon. Enough!" Jakub warns, his eyes flaring with anger.

His fingers tighten around mine, his thumbs pressing painfully into the back of my hands as he tries to control his outburst and steady me at the same time. Why he even bothers is beyond me. I'd thought I'd seen the tiniest shred of humanity in him before, when we'd been alone together in his room, but I realise now that was just me projecting. I'd held onto the kindness of the boy in my vision, and for a moment allowed that to blur the reality of the man he's become.

"What? She won't remember any of this in the morning. What difference does it make?" Konrad counters, sliding off his loafers and climbing up onto the table behind me, placing his legs either side of mine. The width of Konrad's chest and shoulders make me feel tiny even though I'm not, and when his arms wrap around my stomach, holding me firmly all I can do is let him. I don't fight it. Even my internal voice quietens, subdued by this drug, his gentle touch, and the lack of pain I usually feel when something is pressed against my ravaged back.

"Regardless, Thirteen's past is her own. She wouldn't share our story any more than we would share hers," Jakub reminds him, removing his mask and laying it on the table. His cheeks are flushed, and little rivets mark his face beneath his cheek bones where the mask has been too tight. I have the sudden, insane urge to touch it. To run my fingers over his skin, to see whether he is in fact human and not a monster disguised as one. Then again, aren't humans and monsters one and the same? Everyone is capable of monstrous things, there are just some who're better at hiding their demons than others.

"Your mask," Leon remarks tightly, jerking his head towards the discarded mask.

Jakub rolls his shoulders, then his head. "Don't worry, Brother. I've given strict instructions that no one is to enter this room on punishment of death."

Punishment of death?

Fear trickles down my spine, making my body quake. Konrad notices, and his large hand presses against the centre of my chest, warmth seeping into my skin. I wonder if he feels how my heart thunders, how it fights for me, reminding me what this truly is when every other part of my body has been hoodwinked by this drug.

"Your fear is warranted, Zero. Your instincts are entirely correct," Konrad mutters into my ear knowingly, his warm breath tickling my neck, making goosebumps chase across my skin. "But as much as we are bad men, as much as we want to take from you, use you up for our own gain, that day isn't today. Soon, but not today."

"I don't believe you," I whisper, swallowing the lump in my throat as his fingers spread out across the centre of my chest, almost touching my nipples but not quite. My body hums with feeling, the heaviness that had hindered my every move, now making way for rolls of pleasure that lap at my senses, confusing me. My internal voice gets quieter and quieter as the wash of feeling and sensation gains strength. "You mean to rape me."

"Maybe I'm lying. Maybe I'm not. I guess there's only one way to find out," Konrad says, his voice sensual, sexy. Despite everything, despite all that they've done, all that they plan to do, his voice calls to something deep inside of me, to a part of me I hadn't known existed until now.

"No!" I whisper. "No." This is the drug. This isn't me. *It isn't.*

"We like to play with our toys," Leon continues, reaching up to remove his mask. He shakes his head from side to side, his black hair whipping around his head with the movement. "If you haven't already guessed, we're not just about the physical, but the mental too. Fucking your cunt isn't the only goal we have in mind. Fucking with your emotions, your mental state, your *soul*, it's all fair game now that you're *ours*."

"I *hate* you. I will always hate you, and one day… when you least expect it. It won't be Grim who takes your life—because believe me, she's coming—it'll be me!"

Leon throws his head back and laughs. The sound buries itself deep inside of me and settles in my core, the drug twisting my reaction to his cruelty and making my pussy weep for him. "You don't have it in you, Nought," he goads, getting in my face, his beautiful features twisting into something so ugly that he needn't wear a mask to disguise it. He's already a monster. There's nothing human left within him.

"Trust me. I do!" I counter, scraping every last ounce of fight in me and hurling it back at him. "I will *kill* you!"

Leon's green eyes ripple with excitement and before I know what's happening, he reaches out and grasps my chin roughly, slamming his mouth against mine. The force of his kiss is so violent that even Konrad sitting behind me is knocked backwards. I'm vaguely aware of the growl ripping out of Konrad's chest, reverberating into my back, but it's soon overshadowed by Leon's tongue forcing its way between my lips as he tastes me. A groan rumbles up his throat as he kisses me like he wants to crawl inside my body and tear me open from the inside out.

It's all teeth and tongue. Violence and hatred. His fingers bite my skin, the sharpness of his stubble rubbing me raw as he devours my mouth.

Heat floods my chest, burning my insides as my body reacts to his passion. It might be born on the back of violence and hate, but it doesn't matter to my traitorous pussy because she's flooding and pulsing. I've never been kissed like this before. I've never been kissed in a way that rips open my chest, yanks out my heart and pulverises it into a bloody mess. If I could reach for him, and claw at his face to pull him closer, tighter against me, I would. All rational thought, all need to fight him off, to kill him, incinerates in this moment. Something else takes over.

Something dark, devious, twisted and corrupt. With just one kiss this bastard makes a mockery of me. He couldn't have hurt me any more if he tried. When he pulls back, his plump lips curl up in a sneer.

"Now tell me again how much you want to kill me."

I'm panting just as much as he is as we stare at one another. I have no words. I have nothing I wish to say to the man who has just kissed me like I'm both his sworn enemy and heavenly match. I hate myself. Him.

With a snort of derision, Leon turns to Jakub. "We always said we'd strip her bare, *together*. Are you truly going to take that from us after everything we've endured?"

For a moment, Jakub's jaw tightens and I swear I can hear the grinding of his teeth as he considers his brother's request, remembering what he's already done. He looks at Konrad behind me then. Finally, he flicks his gaze to me and nods.

"Any actions I take are with you two in mind. Tonight we will strip her completely bare, like we discussed, but neither of you will fuck her until *I* say so," Jakub says, ripping his gaze away from me and back to his brothers. It's a minor reprieve, one I didn't expect, but I'm not foolish enough to think I'm safe, given the look on Leon's face.

He grins. "No *fucking*. Got it."

"Otherwise we can indulge?" Konrad asks, his fingers swirling over the bare skin of my chest, heating me up. My body shudders under his touch. Fucking me with their dicks isn't the only way they can hurt me. I don't even want to know what they have in mind, given their armoire filled with implements that terrify me.

"Within reason," Jakub agrees, before undoing the necklace and fisting the key in his hand. He walks around the table, sliding his gaze up my bare legs before focusing on the lock. "She's still intact. I want her kept that way."

"You mean she's a virgin?" Konrad asks, surprised.

"Come on, Brother, you must've guessed," Leon says, and I can feel him smiling even though I can't see his face.

"Yes, she's a virgin," Jakub confirms, locking eyes with me.

Konrad buries his face in my hair and breathes in deeply. "She's made for us."

"I hate you," I grind out, despite my toes curling with pleasure as Konrad slides his hand lower, his lips grazing the sensitive skin on my neck. My body rolls with his touch, undulating beneath his palm. I cry out, every nerve ending coming to life, tiny sparks of electricity firing beneath my skin at the barest touch. Even the cool air that circulates around such a large room makes me shudder with intense need. This fucking drug, it's twisted me up inside.

"And so it begins…" Leon smiles lazily, his palm smoothing up my leg, his fingers gripping and releasing the flesh of my inner thigh as he stakes his claim on me too.

"You're all bastards!" I feel as though I'm shouting but it comes out as a whimper, there's no force behind it, only *need*.

"It's true, we are," Konrad agrees, pressing featherlight kisses against my bare neck. "Keep hating us if it makes you feel better. In fact, if you want to survive here I suggest you never stop."

"She isn't strong enough. She'll cave. She'll lose this spark, this fire. She'll come to heel just like all the rest," Jakub remarks coldly, reaching for the lock on my chastity belt and pulling on it so the leather between my legs tightens against my pussy. My core spasms, my clit thrums with the pressure, but I bite down on the cry of pleasure. I swallow it down, bottle it up.

He tugs several times, sending sparks of fury and lust right to my core.

I will not let them take another orgasm from me.

I refuse to give them that.

I won't let them fool me into thinking this is anything but assault.

Right now my body isn't my own. This is a synthetic reaction, a chemical misfiring.

My muscles begin to tremble with the effort to hold back, to ignore the growing inferno between my legs. Jakub places the key in the lock, turning. A small click sounds and he pulls at the leather revealing my glistening pussy to them all.

"Fuck," Konrad groans, his hand sliding towards my wet heat. "Look at her pretty, pink lips. She's already aroused."

I close my eyes as he parts my outer lips and gently presses the pad of his finger against my swollen nub. The sensation blinds me for a moment as I jerk against his hand. My body loves the feeling, craves more pressure, but my heart, my soul, they're like tiny birds frantically flying against the walls of my rib cage, dying to burst free, to escape, to rip at their faces with claws and beaks.

"Look at her. So fucking wet," Leon growls, his hand squeezing my breast now as he watches his brother finger me, the deftness of Konrad's touch stoking the beginnings of another orgasm just like that, like it's as easy as whipping me. Perhaps it is. Perhaps I really was made for them after all.

No! That tiny voice inside my head shouts.

"You're n—nothing more than thieves. You're s—stealing something I should only have the right to g—give!" I say out loud, stumbling over the words.

"And it feels so fucking good," Leon says bending over me, his green eyes cutting a path to my soul as he lowers his lips to my breast and sucks my erect nipple into his mouth. He licks and nibbles, all the while pinning me with his gaze, daring me to object. I let out a whimper as he tugs my nipple between his teeth and smiles up at me, edging this moment in pain.

Delicious pain.

I shudder. My body's reaction to their touch taking over the dying embers of my will to fight.

"Did you know that Leon can make a woman come just by playing with her tits? He's really fucking good at it," Konrad taunts as Leon proves his brother's point and moves his hot mouth to my other nipple, capturing the one he's just taunted with his teeth between his finger and thumb, sending shockwaves of pleasure to my core. When his tongue slides across the mound of my breast and licks at the drying blood from the cut One inflicted, I'm fighting the urge to concede. To just let this happen.

To let them steal an orgasm just like they stole me.

"She's already succumbing. It's so fucking *easy*," Jakub remarks whilst Konrad continues to finger fuck me, burying his thick finger into my pussy, but stopping just before he breaks through the delicate wall of my virginity. I feel a slight pressure inside of me where he pushes gently against the boundary, testing the thin barrier.

"The Quickening will do that, Brother," Konrad says, his voice taut with restraint, his body trembling beneath me as he holds back from taking my virginity with his hands.

"I'm not so sure the drug can be blamed for it all," Jakub responds, cutting a look my way. I know he isn't talking about right now, he's talking about earlier. I hadn't been drugged then. He sounds disappointed, angry even, but it doesn't stop him from lowering his mouth to my ankle and trailing hot kisses over my skin. His mouth is both ecstasy and anguish. It's heaven and hell.

"I'll never succumb," I bite out, detaching myself from my body's pleasure the same way I can detach myself from the pain.

"You already are," Leon laughs, sucking my nipple and the flesh of my breast back into his mouth.

"I don't mean physically," I bite out, writhing beneath their talented hands and mouth.

"You might steal my pleasure, but that's it. That's all. I will fight, every step of the way. *Always*. Until my last goddamn breath!" My clit pulses but I refuse to pay it attention. Every stroke of Konrad's finger, every firm grasp and lick from Leon and every kiss Jakub presses against my thighs, assails my senses. I burn for them, because of them. I'm wet even though I should be as dry as sandpaper.

It angers me.

I'm livid.

I'm past the point of fury. Beyond the point of self-preservation.

This is it. Right here and now, I need to take my power back.

But right when I think I might be able to do that, an orgasm rips out of me, taking a scream with it that shatters the air and splinters me into a thousand sharpened pieces. I imagine them raining down over us, cutting these men, slicing them up and shredding them just like they've shredded me.

This isn't pleasure that's come from a place of care and attention. My orgasm has been coerced, fooled, dragged out of me by men who don't deserve to bask in it. My body trembles, shaking, utterly at their mercy as I ride the wave, floating on the ebbing tide of my orgasm as it ripples over every inch of skin.

"That wasn't so bad, was it?" Konrad whispers, still stroking my dripping core, dragging out the orgasm as much as possible.

I don't answer, I can't. A heavy fatigue settles over me and any moment now I'm expecting it to pull me under, to make me forget, to leave me vulnerable and at their mercy. God knows what they'll do to me now that I'm like this. I hear their voices as though far away, capturing words here and there. They're discussing what to do next. Leon and Konrad argue that I'm ripe for the taking, Jakub protests. Like cowards they want to steal my virginity whilst I'm not awake enough to protect it, and there's me thinking they want the fight.

Well, fuck them. Fuck that.

"NO!" I roar.

Something inside me shifts, clicking into place. My mouth fills with the sudden, sweet taste of honey, reminding me of Thirteen's kiss. Her eyes had told me a truth I didn't understand at the time, but as I lay here weakened by their touch, a sudden, potent, oxygen-stealing inferno rages inside my chest, eviscerating The Quickening's power over me.

I realise then, with utter clarity of mind, body and soul, that Thirteen had given me something to counter the effects of the drug. The sweet liquid she'd trickled into my mouth with her kiss has finally freed my muscles, my lips and mouth. I can now move without the heavy weight keeping me pinned to the table.

I *can* fight back.

Courage flares. "Get your motherfucking hands off me, you sick, fucked-up excuse for men!" I scream with every last ounce of disgust and rage I feel, kicking out and landing the heel of my foot on Jakub's chin. His head snaps back and I see the surprise in his eyes before he stumbles backwards from the force of my rage. I don't think, I act, and crash my head back against Konrad. He cries out, probably in shock more than pain, but it's enough for him to release his arms. Without thinking I raise my fist and aim it square at Leon's cheek, pain radiates from my knuckles all the way up my arm, but I ignore it.

Then I leap off the table and run.

My feet slap against the cold stone as I run blindly towards a shadowed corner of the hall. Behind me The Masks get to their feet and I hear the shock in Leon's voice. "How the *fuck* is she awake? The Quickening is supposed to knock her the fuck out after she comes."

I don't bother to listen to the response. I need to get out of here.

The first door I come across is locked, but I refuse to give up. I move to the next door, my torn dress flapping out behind me like a boat sail in the wind, but that's locked too.

Still I run, this room becoming another cage I can't escape from. I'm aware of The Masks watching me, their greedy eyes devouring my fear. I know this is exciting for them, that I'm feeding into their desires, but that innate need to escape, to get as far away from them as possible won't allow me to sit back and wait for them to hurt me further, not now that I'm thinking clearly. I need to give myself a fighting chance. I can't allow myself to give in like I had in Jakub's bedroom.

Running, I keep trying every door until I've made a full circle of the hall. Panting and angry and scared, I press my fists against the first set of doors I came across and start pounding against the wood until my fists are bruised and my voice is hoarse. Tears stream down my face, and I swipe at them not caring that I'm rubbing away the makeup I'd so carefully applied earlier today. Not caring that they'll be able to see my true face.

Drawing in a deep breath, I realise that's the only thing I have left. The true me. The ugly scarred back, the port wine birthmark. The strange eyes and fiery red hair and freckles that mark me as different.

I thought that by hiding, I would regain control, power, but that was before I understood what motivated them. If I disgust them, then I may save myself from the worst kind of torture. Sure they could kill me, but at least they won't steal my virginity. At least I'd be spared the pain and degradation of that. The Masks thrive on beauty. Feed off of it, capture it, contain it. They sell beauty to the highest bidder. It's what they *want*. Well, my beauty is fake. It's a lie.

Ripping off what's left of my dress, I spit onto the material and use my tears and spit to wipe away as much of the foundation as I can, then discard it before stepping out of the shadows, completely naked.

My head is tipped down slightly as I pad across the floor to where the three of them stand, my hair covering my face in a shroud. I'm shaking so hard with anger that my teeth chatter, adding to the lie. My stance is one of defeat, but that too is a fabrication. Let them think I've given up. I want to see the shock on their faces when they finally see who I really am in all my naked glory. They wanted to strip me bare? Well, they're going to get more than they'd bargained for.

"Have you given up so soon, Nought?" Leon goads, buying into the lie.

"I must say, it was fun whilst it lasted," Konrad adds, his thick voice as cruel and as sharp as the snap of the leash as he slashes against my bare leg. I barely register the pain.

Jakub steps forward. I know it's him because I recognise the shoes he wears: expensive leather loafers that kiss the floor lightly as he moves.

"For a moment there, I thought we'd finally met a worthy foe. Alas, jesteś po prostu rozczarowanie, Nic." He reaches for my hair, fisting it. "You're just a disappointment, Nothing."

"Oh, I hope so," I reply, stoic, strong, unflinching in my determination to reveal my true self as I lift my head and meet his gaze.

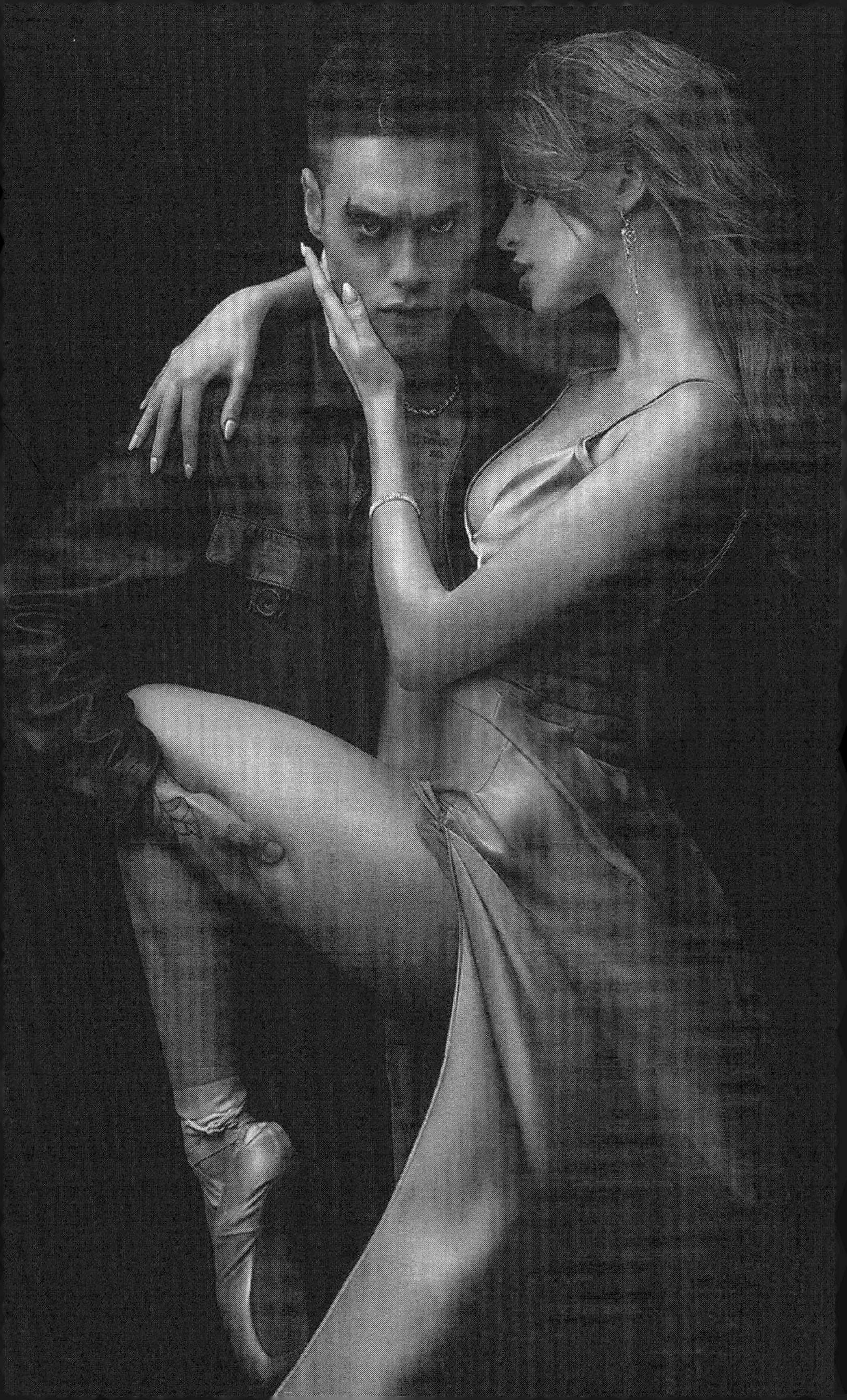

CHAPTER 19

JAKUB

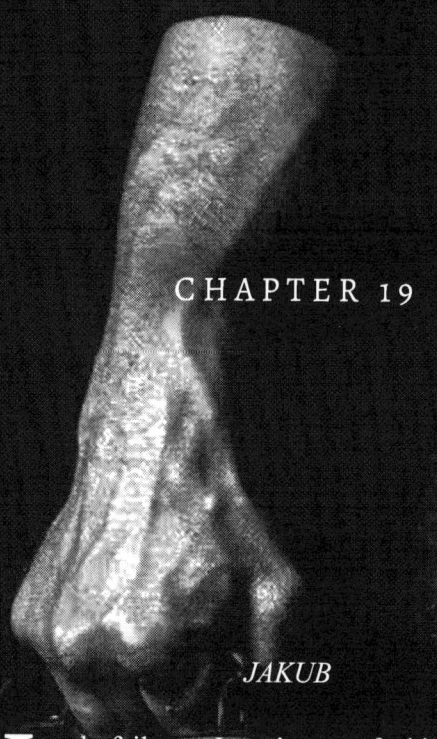

Words fail me. I can't even fucking breathe. Who is this creature standing before me? What the fuck am I looking at?

Nothing's eyes glower with fury. The intensity of her hate is powerful enough to make me pause. But nothing prepares me for the sheer fucking *beauty* of her birthmark. One she's been hiding from us. I swallow hard, time standing still as I drink in the deformity. I'm greedy, feasting on her appearance, seeing her in a new light. I have to blink several times to make sure I'm not imagining it, but every time I open my eyes she's still marked, still flawed, still my kind of beautiful. The redness of her birthmark is almost purple in places. I'm sure many people would find her uncomfortable to look at.

I don't. *I don't.*

I want to touch it. I want to touch her. This is nature messing with genetics, meddling with society's ideal of perfection, and fuck if it doesn't turn me on. My father spent years searching for the most beautiful men and women. He brought them back to the castle, used and abused them. Then, when he'd finally beat the beauty from their skin and discarded them—because in the end their beauty wasn't enough—he took his wrath out on me. His obsession with perfection was a disease, one he fed regularly. I grew up hating beauty because all it brought me was *pain*.

"Jakub, what is it?" Leon asks, approaching us, drawing me away from my thoughts momentarily. I hear the caution in his voice, the concern. I've no idea what he'll think, whether he'll be disgusted or intrigued, either way I'm not ready to share her with them just yet. I force her backwards into the shadows of the hall, until she's seeped in darkness just like me.

"What are you doing?" she asks, trembling under my touch. I hadn't even noticed I'd put my hands on her. My fingertips tingle. My cock fills with blood, punching against my trousers in an effort to get to her.

I *want* her.

Earlier I'd fucked her cunt with my tongue. I'd wanted to take her first orgasm as my own. It'd pissed me off that Leon had touched her before me and I wanted to take something for myself, but now? Now this new yearning to claim her as *mine* overwhelms me.

"What the fuck, Jakub?" Konrad says, his footsteps coming closer too.

"Czekać! Wait!" I say, needing a moment.

I need to fucking think. I need to decide how to play this. I may be the youngest, but I'm the true heir and as such I have to maintain what we've built here. We stole this woman with nothing more than the need to exact revenge and yet, she's only been here a matter of days and she's already fucking with our heads.

Konrad has fallen for her beauty, or at least the accepted side of her. He gets his kicks out of uglying up beauty temporarily with bruises and slashes from his whips and his paddles. It's why my father loved him so much. Konrad will use pain to punish, just as Leon does. Their only difference is where they draw the line.

Konrad might be obsessed with marking something pretty, but he's also turned on by the healing process. He thinks I don't know about his cravings, but I've seen the way his gaze lingers on the Numbers after he's made them come with both pain and pleasure down in the dungeon. I know how he loves to watch Thirteen tend to their wounds whilst pretending he's making sure they're still able to perform in The Menagerie, to fuck our clients. Before Thirteen arrived and became the Numbers' unofficial healer, Konrad would insist on being in the room with the Numbers whilst a maid applied arnica to their bruises and washed their welts and cuts. He would pace up and down like a caged animal, chomping at the bit, wanting to be the one to soothe and pacify but always holding back.

Konrad is a man of two halves, but has only ever revealed the darkest side to the Numbers.

He'll chase and capture, whip and torture, but he also wants to *heal* and *venerate*. He finds peace in the process and, I suspect, the tiniest shred of humanity. It's why Twelve stole from me to get his attention, why she accepted the punishment because she wanted *his* attention specifically. She wanted to push him into revealing his other side. Of all the Numbers, she's been the closest to seeing the gentler side of his nature, but now that his attention is fully on Nothing she's had to take drastic action. Of course her plan backfired. Twelve's in love with a monster who's equally brutal as he is gentle, and who has no interest in her.

Leon, however, is just a monster. Just pain and darkness. He wants the fight. He wants the screams and the tears. He wants his victims to beg for mercy and never give it. He likes the power that he wields. Two, Six and Eight only survived him because he was more afraid of our father's wrath than he was concerned for their lives. He never overstepped the line. Father understood that whilst Leon did not share his blood, he shared his darkest desires. So after Eight, Leon's skills have been put to better use elsewhere. If a client disobeys our rules, he's the one who deals with them.

Ends them.

The Masks have become feared and respected because of his thirst for violence. Now my father's dead, there's no telling what he'll do. Beautiful or ugly, deformed or perfect. Neither version of this woman that stands before me now makes a difference to him. Nothing won't be safe with him. Not ever.

"Brother, what is it?" Konrad insists, impatient now.

I swallow hard, trying to figure out what the fuck I'm going to do. "She's..." I can't even bring myself to speak. Instead, I press my fingers against her birthmark, unable to control the tremor in my voice.

"I repulse you..." she murmurs.

I nod my head, even though that's a lie. "She's marked. *Deformed.*"

The words come out as a snub. They're hurtful like I intended, because I cannot let *her* know that she is anything more than a toy to play with. Too much hangs in the balance. We can't afford to be distracted past the point of exacting revenge. Besides, my brothers and I made a promise to each other a long time ago that no one would come between us and I'm going to stick to it, regardless of how my cock twitches and my fucking dead heart stutters back to life. We will stick to the plan, we will *use* her, then we will *discard* her.

That's it.

"You're an arsehole," Nothing says, her jaw gritting as angry tears form in her eyes. This time she lets them fall, and I feel the jewelled drops warm my hand. I want to lick them from her skin. I want to know what sin tastes like.

Resisting the urge, I drop my hand and step back. "No, I'm your worst nightmare."

"What do you mean, deformed?" Konrad snaps, stepping up beside me at the same time as Leon does. "Let me see!" he reaches for her, pulling her out of the shadows and back into the light.

"Get your hands off me!" she growls, her temper flaring once more, and I can't help but notice how her birthmark darkens with the emotion. I swallow hard, and bite down on the inside of my cheek until it bleeds.

"What the fuck?" Konrad reaches for her, his hands gripping her shoulders as he turns her to face him. "Who are you?" he asks, anger rolling off him.

She laughs, more tears welling. "*Yours*? Or am I no longer

desirable? Am I too disgusting, *deformed,* for men like you to fuck now that you've seen my true face?"

Konrad's jaw grits, then he pinches her chin between his finger and thumb and twists her head from side to side. "You hid."

"I'm not hiding now," she replies, jerking her chin from his hold, but he lunges for her, his hand curling into her hair as he yanks her close.

"You shouldn't have hid," he grinds out, then smashes his lips against hers in a kiss that is as punishing as Leon's was, just in a different way.

I've watched my brothers kiss women—fuck them—before, but I've never seen them act like this. Leon kissed her like he wanted to ruin her, end her life. Konrad kisses her like she's an anchor and he's a boat cast adrift, like she keeps him afloat, alive somehow. Two polar opposites but both of them are punishing. Nothing fists his shirt, her knuckles white, her body stiff until it isn't, until she's melting in his hold. Then he lets her go with a grunt and she wavers on her feet, hands still raised, eyes blinking, face flushed, nipples erect.

"Screw you," she hisses, wiping her hand over the back of her mouth, fury painting her features—her skin—with a pink blush. She looks from Konrad to me, finally resting her gaze on Leon. "Don't you have anything you wish to say?"

Leon's quiet for a time, assessing her. Then he rolls his shoulders and bares his teeth in a way that is more animal than human. "Looks like we're not the only ones wearing masks."

She snorts, her gaze trailing up and down his body. I've never seen anyone as brave as her when it comes to Leon. Though I suppose there's nothing more dangerous than someone who believes they've got nothing left to lose. "Fuck you."

"No, you're the one who's well and truly fucked now," he replies, a dark laugh bursting from his lips.

"Is that so? Well, *Leon,* this is me. Every last deformed and scarred part," Nothing taunts, throwing her arms out to the side. She lifts up onto the ball of her left foot, and turns gracefully until she has her back to us. I watch as her long red hair sways over her arse, revealing the red stripes of Konrad's lashes and the shapely curve of her long legs. Next to me Konrad groans, and I know he wants to run his tongue over the welts marking her skin. I'm about to ask what she's doing when she reaches for her hair and pulls it over her shoulder revealing a back so ravaged by scars that I have to force myself to keep rigid and not fall to my knees in reverence.

"Still want to fuck me now?" she asks.

Yes, I think. *Yes I want to fuck you. I want more than that.* But I'm stunned into silence.

We all are.

I take a step forward, but Leon's hand flies to my shoulder, squeezing tightly. He holds me firm, understanding me at this moment, understanding the danger this woman brings to our status quo, to our life we've made here. She's suddenly turned from a plaything to tease, torment and cast aside, to something infinitely *more* dangerous.

We stare at her, unable or perhaps unwilling to break the spell she's put us under. I don't know for certain how my brothers feel, but I can guess their thoughts are as tumultuous as my own.

This woman. She's not what any of us expected.

Beside me Leon twitches, the muscles in his body taut with tension. He's barely holding on and I know he's close to exacting his revenge on Nothing for the death of our father in the only way he knows how. Violently. Right now he's her biggest threat.

Konrad, however, is perfectly still. He's assessing what he sees before him, trying to figure out how she'll fit into the way he sees the world, and me? I both want to throttle her to death for causing this friction and fuck her until I can't see straight. Of the three of us, it's Konrad who eventually breaks the silence, who acts.

"I didn't know you were burnt in the fire too," he comments, stepping up behind her, his voice soft, sympathetic. *Jesus, fuck.* She's his wet dream come true.

Nothing looks over her shoulder at him accusingly. "How did you know about the fire?"

"We do our research. How do you think we found you, Zero?" His fingertips feather over her damaged skin in a way a man might touch his lover: gently, and with affection.

"Well, your research wasn't very extensive given you didn't know about this. Perhaps you should've dug deeper," she retorts, jerking away from him.

"Don't," he warns, gripping her upper arm and holding her firm with one hand as he traces over every bump and swirl of skin with the other. Her chest heaves, her breathing becomes more ragged. His touch is no longer pleasurable, that's for sure. However she managed it, The Quickening has left her system completely. Right now she wants to fight him off, she may still do that. A large part of me wants her to because I know if she did, Leon would end this here and now and we could forget about all the ways she's fucking with our heads.

"Grim was good at hiding your past, just not good enough at keeping you hidden," I say, my eyes drinking in every inch of her scarred skin. I can't seem to look away. From just beneath her shoulder blades to a few inches above her hips, her back is completely covered in scars reminding me of the whorles and grooves that form the thick bark of the trees in the forest surrounding the castle. They're almost too painful to look at. There's no doubt that she would've suffered immensely. My black soul finds a sick kind of peace in that, and my cock. Fuck, I'm harder than I've ever been in my life.

Konrad releases her from his hold and she turns around to face us, backing away. None of us move to go after her, stuck in place with shock, and dealing with our own perverse reactions to her disfigurement. Leon clears his throat, tension rolling off him. I glance at him, and for the first time in my life, I can't fully read his intentions. I'm not sure if he wants to fuck her or kill her. Probably both. Either way, he's resting on a knife's edge. So you can imagine my surprise when Leon doesn't lunge for her like I expected him to, and instead asks her a question.

"How old were you when it happened?"

"Aren't you supposed to know that already?" she retorts, folding her arms across her chest in an attempt to comfort herself.

"I wasn't interested in your history before."

"And I'm not interested in telling you either—"

"But I *am* now," he says, cutting her off. "Tell. Me!"

She flinches at his anger. "I was eight. The fire took my mother's life and gave me third degree burns, some sections of my back were classified as fourth degree."

"Where did it happen?"

"What difference does that make?" she counters.

"Answer the damn question!"

"My childhood home in Ilfracombe, Devon."

Leon's fingers momentarily grip me tighter. I glance at him. "Brother?"

Ignoring me, he keeps his gaze fixed on Nothing. "How come you didn't die?"

"What kind of question is that?" she asks.

"Your mother died. Why didn't you?"

She swallows hard, her eyes filling with tears. "I don't know. I don't remember getting out of the house. When the fire brigade found me I was passed out, lying on the wet grass at the bottom of my garden by our pond. They thought I'd run there to soothe my burns. My nightie had melted into the skin of my back from the heat of the fire."

Leon's jaw grits so hard I can hear his teeth grinding.

"Your scars are some of the worst I've seen," I say, drawing Nothing's attention away from Leon. She may not know it, but he's acting stranger than usual. I don't understand why he's so interested in her story. He couldn't give a fuck before.

"Over the years I've had extensive skin grafts from donors to aid healing. But this is as good as it gets."

"Is that why your pain tolerance is so high?" Leon cuts in, "Because of what you've endured?" He keeps his fingers wrapped firmly around my shoulders, holding on tight, but this time I'm not sure if it's for my benefit or his.

"I don't know."

"But you *can* tolerate high levels of pain, yes?"

She swallows hard, taking another step back, sensing that the monster prowling beneath his skin is close to revealing itself. Now I understand his sudden interest. Earlier, Nothing hadn't reacted to the lashes Konrad gave her. She somehow managed to detach herself from the pain. That intrigues him.

"Why do you want to know?" she asks.

He smirks, letting go of my shoulder and stepping towards her. "Because, Nought, you haven't deterred me or my brothers. If anything, revealing your true self makes us want you *more*, not less."

"No," she shakes her head, tears cascading down her cheeks as she stumbles backwards, her knees giving way. "All the Numbers are beautiful…"

"I don't give a fuck about the Numbers. You, Nought, have suddenly become a very, *very* fucking interesting toy indeed."

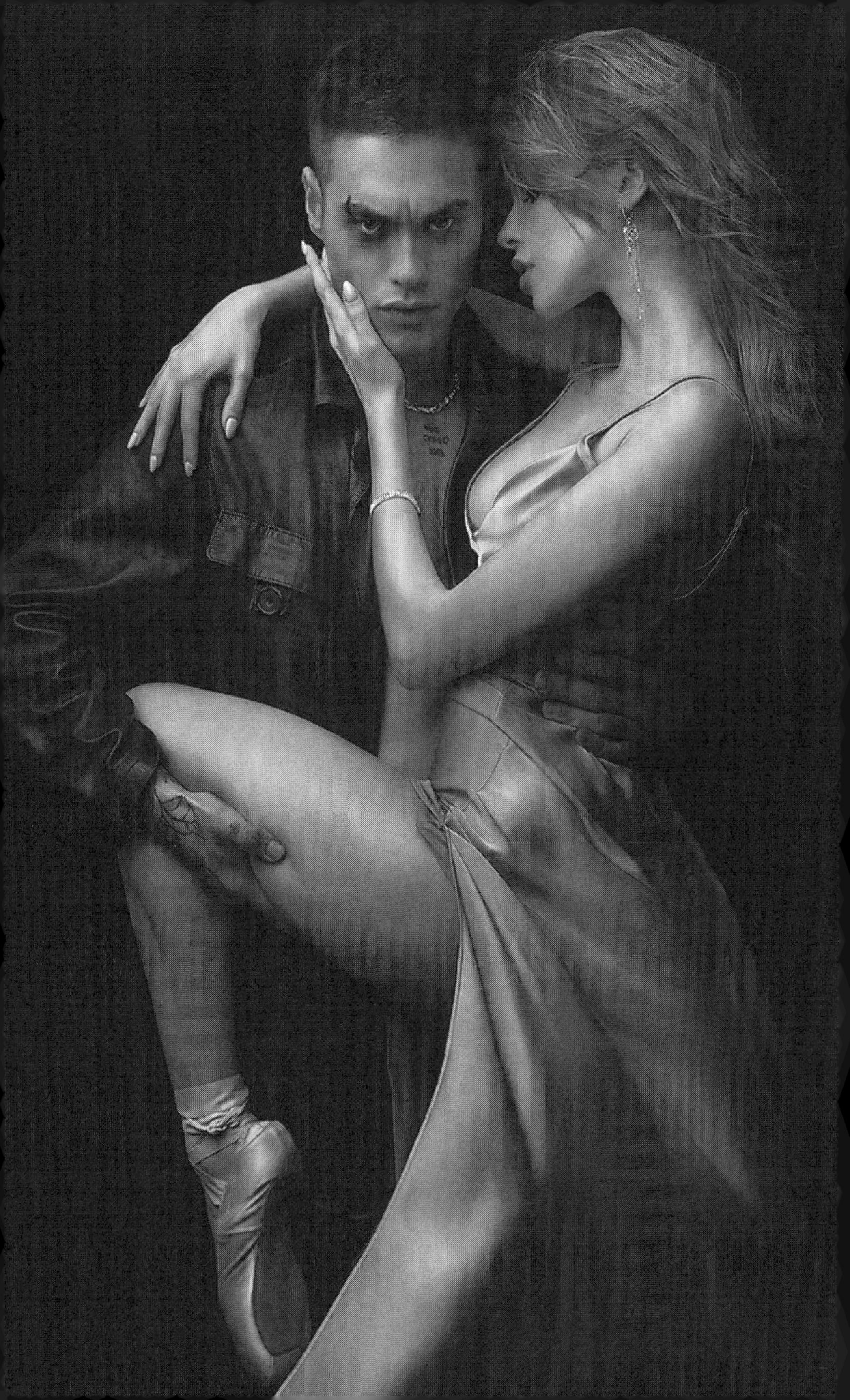

CHAPTER 20

CHRISTY

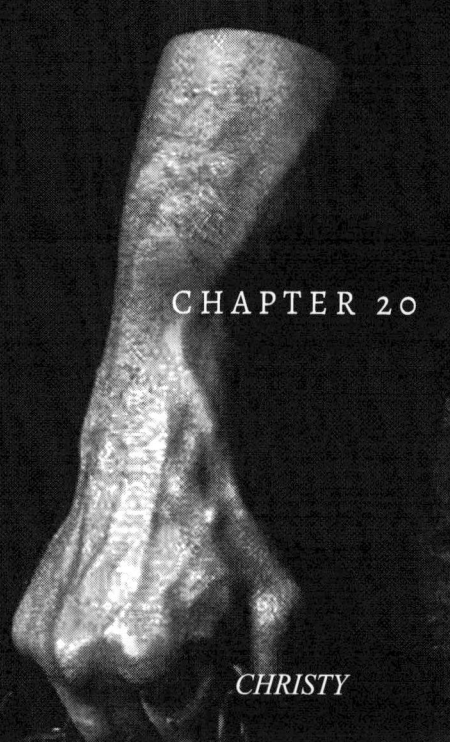

"No," I breathe out. This can't be happening. They were supposed to be revolted by me. I would never have revealed my true self if I'd known. What have I done?

"How many times do we have to tell you, Nought? *No* isn't a word we understand," Leon says, and with every step forward, I take another step back. "I want to fucking touch you again. I want to plunder your mouth and drink from your soul. Fuck, I want to do very, *very* bad things to you."

His eyes flick from my lips to my pussy and a concoction of heat and shame fires inside my belly. I don't want his attention, but my body remembers how it felt to be kissed by him, touched by him. It was like swimming in the ocean with a shark, you know it has the power to bite you, kill you, but despite that the rush is *thrilling*, addictive. That kind of fear, it can make you feel alive when the possibility of death is so near.

"No!" I repeat, louder this time, more for my own benefit than anyone else.

"Leon," Jakub warns, stepping forward. "We have an agreement."

Jakub flicks his gaze to me, the muscle in his jaw leaping. For the briefest of moments, indecision crosses his face. I don't know quite what to make of him. One minute he's handing me a chastity belt to prevent his brothers from raping me, and the next he's removing it so they can all get their kicks. A moment ago, he'd said I was marked, *deformed,* and yet he looks at me like he *wants* me. Now here he is trying to prevent Leon from acting on his perversions. Of the three, Jakub's mind games are the worst. At least with Konrad and Leon I know what their true intentions are.

"You said no fucking," he replies, a wicked smile pulling up his lips.

"You will have your time with her. That time isn't right now."

Leon's fingers curl into his palms, but he halts his path towards me when Jakub steps in front of him. "Are you stopping me from what is rightfully mine?" he challenges.

"The question isn't whether I'm stopping you, Brother, but whether *you* can stop?" Jakub counters, pressing the flat of his hand against Leon's chest. "Because I'm getting the distinct impression that now you've had a taste of Nothing, you won't be able to. Need I remind you that she's *ours*, not yours? We all know what would happen if you truly let go."

"Then why dangle the carrot if we can't take a damn bite?" he retorts, angry now that his toy has been taken away from him. "What the fuck was the purpose of today, huh?"

"He's got a point," Konrad interjects as he approaches us with the leash. He has it wrapped around both hands, the leather taut between his fists. "Don't tell me that you'll be able to stay away from her now, not after this."

Jakub squeezes the bridge of his nose, sucks in a deep breath then holds his hand out to Konrad.

"Give me the leash," he demands.

"What do you intend to do?" Konrad questions him.

"Give. Me. The. Damn. Leash!"

Konrad slams the leash into Jakub's palm, and for a moment I think they're going to fight. Instead, Jakub ignores Konrad's aggression and grabs the back of my head. His fingers squeeze my scalp, his scent cloaking me in rich earthy tones as he invades my space with the length of his body. "My gut is telling me that I should take this leash, wrap it around your throat and end this now for all the trouble you're causing."

"So end it," I whisper, meeting his gaze. "Because I'd rather die than suffer your vile fantasies."

"And yet..." he continues, lowering his mouth to my cheek. "Like my brother, I'm not in the business of giving people what they want. Especially when we still need our revenge."

"W—what?" I stutter, my breath hitching in my chest as his erection presses into my stomach and his lips slide over my birthmark, trailing heat across my skin and causing shivers to cascade down my spine. He's turned on by this, by my *fear*.

"Killing you would be a kindness. I'm *not* a kind man," he says, his mouth hovering over mine as his fingers begin to massage my scalp. It's a gentle touch, soothing and completely contradictory to his words and his threat. "Not anymore." He whispers the last part so quietly that I almost think I've misheard, but when he pulls back I see a glimmer of the boy he once was. He's buried deep, but faintly present.

"Give me your shirt," he says to Konrad, jerking his chin.

"My shirt?"

"Yes, give me your damn shirt. Right the fuck now."

Konrad scowls but obeys Jakub, pulling his shirt free from his trousers and unbuttoning it before handing it to him. He's bare chested, a smattering of dark hair covering his well-defined pecs and abs. Curling my hands into fists, I look away, focusing on Jakub.

"Put this on."

"Fine!" I snatch the shirt from Jakub, sliding my arms in place and buttoning it up, trying not to breathe in Konrad's spicy scent. The shirt swamps me, hitting mid-thigh. He steps close, his eyes locking with mine.

"You missed one," he says, buttoning up the top button, making sure I'm covered up. Luckily for me Konrad is a big guy, and despite the shirt being fully buttoned it's not tight around my throat like the collar is.

"What the fuck is this? What are you doing? We're not done here," Leon says, grinding his teeth in agitation. Clearly he enjoyed seeing me naked. I should hate that fact. I *do* hate that fact. Yet, in a small twisted way I also like it. I like the fact he wants to see me naked, that he's so pissed off that Jakub's covered me back up. God, what is wrong with me?

"We *are* done here, and we have a new plan," Jakub announces, clipping the leash back on my collar and dragging me towards the table.

"What fucking plan?" Leon questions as I try not to trip over my feet in my haste to keep up with Jakub. I'm not sure whether it's the after effects of The Quickening, the antidote that Thirteen had fed me, the stress, or a combination of all three, but my muscles feel weak once more. Regardless, I'm still here. I'm still breathing. I'm still intact, mostly.

"Our father often tested us," Jakub says, "He pushed our limits, taught us how to be the men we needed to be in order to survive in a dog-eat-dog world. Recently we've lost our focus. This will give it back to us. We'll all be stronger for it afterwards."

"Or dead," I murmur under my breath.

If Jakub hears me, he doesn't acknowledge it, instead he shoves the chastity belt into my hands. "Put this back on."

I take it from him, stepping back into the disgusting contraption even as relief floods my veins. He clicks the lock in place, then picks up his discarded mask and puts it back on before twisting on his feet and walking back across the hall with me in tow.

"What are you going to do, Jakub, take her back to your bedroom? She won't last the night."

Jakub stills, turning to face his brothers. "Which is precisely why I'm giving her to Thirteen. *She'll* hold the key."

"For how long?" Konrad questions, a muscle in his jaw flexing.

"Until the night of the Ball."

"Fuck," Leon mutters as Jakub yanks on the leash, walking me from the room just like a dog commanded to heel.

∽

WITH MY JAW gritted tightly and fighting the urge to cry, I walk beside Jakub through another section of the castle I haven't seen before. There's more life here, and every now and then I see a glimpse of a member of staff going about their business. Which means, if I can see them, they can see me. Heat blooms across my neck and chest at the thought of more people seeing me collared and leashed like a dog. The only saving grace is that Konrad's shirt is long enough to hide the archaic device that simultaneously takes away my freedom to make my own choices and protects me, at least temporarily, from The Masks' thievery.

"Everyone will see," I hiss, dipping my head and folding in on myself.

"And...?" Jakub retorts tightly, pulling on the leash so that I keep up with him.

"Why do you insist on humiliating me? Isn't it enough that you've stolen my dignity and self-respect? Now you're parading me around like this, like some trussed up animal. How dare you!" I hiss, ducking my head as a middle-aged man steps out of a door further along the corridor. A servant, given his attire. Before I drop my gaze I see the unmistakable look of horror, pity and *disgust* on his face. Jakub sees it too.

"What the FUCK are you staring at?" he roars.

"Nothing, Sir. *Nothing*," the man says, dropping his gaze.

It was the worst possible thing he could've said, using Jakub's name for me like that. Coming from this servant it wasn't meant as an address, but that doesn't matter to him. Dropping the leash, he strides over to the man, grips him by the throat and shoves him up against the wall with a thud.

"Don't fucking look at her, don't speak her name. Do *not* fucking think about her, understand me?!" he roars, the man's face turning red under Jakub's tightening grip. For a horrifying moment I think he's going to kill him. Instead, he releases his grip and steps back, chest heaving and body taught. "Get the fuck out of my sight!"

The man doesn't need to be told twice. He scrambles to his feet and retreats into the room he stepped out of, disappearing from view.

"You didn't have to do—"

"How dare he fucking look at you like that!" he roars back, cutting off my sentence and grabbing the leash, pulling me alongside him. He storms down the corridor taking a hard right, then entering a large room that allows me a view of a patio terrace and the gardens to the east of the castle through a set of french doors. I barely get a chance to absorb the rows of low, neatly trimmed hedges and rose bushes before Jakub is shoving open another door and pushing me into a dimly lit hallway beyond. Stumbling forward, I reach out to steady my fall but Jakub wraps an arm around my back causing me to jolt in his hold. He shudders with the contact, whipping his arm back as much as I leap away from him.

He can't even bear to touch me.

"Last door on the left," he bites out.

It's an order for me to keep moving, so that's what I do. At least I'll be in relative safety when I get there. Thirteen had shown me compassion, kindness, and God only knows I'm desperate to feel safe right now. Well, as safe as I can be in a castle run by three sadistic men.

I lift my fist to knock on her door, but Jakub makes a tutting sound and shoves it open. I guess she isn't afforded any privacy either despite her being *family*.

"What the hell…?" I say, my voice trailing off as I step into the room, quickly realising this isn't Thirteen's room at all but something altogether different.

The door slams shut behind me and I'm aware of Jakub twisting a key in the lock, but for the life of me I can't even begin to worry about his intentions as I'm too caught up in what I'm seeing.

The room is filled with glass cabinets containing all kinds of strange objects and curiosities. In the cabinet closest to me there are human and animal skulls of varying shapes and sizes, displayed with jewellery and trinkets that hang from the skeleton teeth and drip out of hollowed eyes. I notice a pair of earrings that look eerily familiar to the necklace Twelve was wearing and see a spot next to it that's suspiciously empty. This is where she must've stolen it from.

"Twelve's actions go against everything we've built here. She's lucky she isn't dead for stealing this," Jakub says, pulling the necklace from his pocket. I watch as he unlocks the cabinet and rests the necklace next to the matching earrings, before locking it again, pocketing the key.

"What you did—"

"Was necessary. These jewels belonged to my mother. Twelve knew that. They're *sacred*," Jakub insists, trying to justify what happened.

"It isn't right. What you do here, it isn't right," I whisper, refusing to hear the emotion in his voice. I don't care about his reasoning. Twelve's back is ripped and raw, bloody and split. Nothing justifies that. Nothing.

"You don't understand," he says, his frustration clear. I catch myself wondering why he even cares about what I think. I'm no more than an object, after all.

Refusing to engage further, I stare at the pretty jewels sparkling under the soft lighting, so starkly beautiful against the whitewashed bones of the dead. I'm no expert, but I'm guessing they're the real deal.

On the shelf below there's an ornate clock, its hands made of tiny bones, thin and delicate but strong enough to carry the weight of time. Next to it is a dagger with a strange-looking leather handle. I peer closer, the incident in the corridor forgotten momentarily as I press my fingers against the cool glass.

"Oh my God," I mutter, my stomach churning at the fine hair I see covering the handle and a portion of what looks like a butterfly tattoo still visible in the darkening skin. "Is that *human* skin?"

"Yes," Jakub answers from somewhere behind me.

Swallowing hard, I snatch my gaze away from the disgusting item, turning my head, only for my eyes to fall upon another cabinet containing a gorilla's foot, the grey-black skin aged and worn. Next to it lies an elephant tusk, ingrained on its surface are crude images of men and women fucking. A stuffed cat with a huge body and tiny head sits next to a dog with two tails and six legs. There's a whole shelf filled with ivory carvings, the figurines might be fucking but they don't appear to be enjoying it, every expression is one of torture and pain.

Tripping over my feet, and painfully aware of Jakub watching me, I move towards a third cabinet stacked full of glass containers filled with dead insects and reptiles. There are beetles and butterflies, snakes and lizards but like everything else in this room, they too are distorted in some way. They're deformed, *twisted*.

I spin on my feet, feeling Jakub's eyes on me as I try to absorb everything I'm seeing. I can't seem to process it all quickly enough as my gaze flits from one item to the next. In the corner of the room there's a whole cabinet filled to the brim with China dolls. Every single one of them is decapitated, their heads resting by their side, their eyes watching me as I step closer to look, then back away, my pulse jumping as their black, beady eyes follow my every step.

"Jesus," I mutter, walking deeper into the room.

Another cabinet displays a large glass orb with a real, human eyeball floating inside of it, all of the optic nerves and sinewy tissue still attached. Next to that are several jars containing fetuses in different stages of development, preserved forevermore in formaldehyde. I don't know a great deal about the natural development of the human fetus but I do know that they shouldn't have five limbs, three arms or two mouths, like those I'm seeing before me.

I swallow hard, my gaze flitting from one strange object to the next, finally landing on a tiny human head. It's shrivelled, the skin puckered, the eyes non-existent, dark hair drawn up into a tight bun. My hands fly up to cover my mouth as I try not to throw up.

"What is this place?" I whisper, jerking backwards into a hard chest. I hold in a screech, spinning around to face Jakub.

"These are my things. They're *mine*," he answers, stepping closer, crowding me, pushing me back against the cabinet. I suck in a shocked breath from the cool glass touching my skin and the sudden rash of phantom pain that forces its way into my consciousness.

"Why am I here? I thought you were taking me to Thirteen?" I ask, pushing the pain away, locking it up and refusing to acknowledge it. My senses are overloaded, I can't deal with the pain on top of that right now.

"I was."

"And you're not now?" I question, my voice trembling.

"I wanted to show you these."

"To frighten me?"

"No, to explain. To see if you understand."

"I don't. I *don't* understand. Why do you keep dead fetuses, a human head, a knife that's handle is made of *human* skin?"

"Because I appreciate the unusual. Covet it."

"It's *perverse*."

"Why? I thought you, of all people, would understand."

"*Understand?*" I draw in a shaky breath, anger flooding my bloodstream. "What, because I'm deformed too? Is that what you mean?" He cocks his head, looking at me curiously. He doesn't have to speak for me to know the answer. "Is *this* what my future holds? Do you mean to use and abuse me then stuff me like that dead cat and put me in a cabinet, or pickle me in formaldehyde like those fetuses? Is that your plan of revenge? Maybe you'll use my skin to make a handle for a knife."

He makes a humming noise in the back of his throat, one that should terrify me but only seems to fuel my anger. The sick, twisted, bastard. "Now that you mention it..." He grins, making sure I see that stark cruelty in his eyes, the edge of mania.

Refusing to let him see my fear, I continue on with my tirade. "You put the Numbers in a show to perform for perverted men and women, because they're *beautiful*, talented. But me...? I'm only good enough to be sneered at, *stared* at, like some curiosity, is that it?" I accuse, all the years of hurt that I'd thought I'd dealt with bubbling up to the surface. It doesn't matter that my life is in mortal danger from Jakub, from these men. Right here and now, that's what fuels my sudden rush of anger.

"I already said that you'll be performing in the show."

"So your patrons can see the twisted and ugly in order to appreciate the flawless and beautiful? Will it make the Numbers more valuable when they're compared to me, huh?" Jakub's nostrils flare, his mouth snapping open, but I cut him off. "You call me *Nothing* because to you I'm worthless, and the irony is you didn't even realise just how much until I revealed my true face and showed you my skin. Even your servant understood that when he called me by the name *you* gave me."

"No. I'm not putting you in the show to show off your flaws…"

"Then *why*?!"

Jakub's jaw grits, his eyes flashing beneath his mask. I'm right. I know it. He means to humiliate me even more. I guess revenge is fucking sweet.

"Get on your knees, *Nothing*," he grinds out, his fingers flexing then curling into fists.

"Why?" I duck away from him, sliding out from between him and the cabinet, putting a few paces between us.

"*O Kurwa*! Get on your damn knees!" he roars, reaching for my shoulders and forcing me to the floor. My knees crack painfully against the wooden floorboards, my tits bouncing from the force. "No one gets to call you *Nothing* but me. No one."

"I don't understand."

Grabbing my jaw, he tips my head back. "He *eye-fucked* you! I should've fucking killed him!"

"Eye-fucked me? Are you insane?" I counter, pissed off at his anger, at his twisted up view of what just happened. "That man looked at me just like every other person in my entire goddamn life has. Like. I. Am. Nothing!"

Jakub's fingers dig into my skin as he searches my face. "You don't get it, do you?"

"Get what?" My lips begin to tremble, but I press them into a harsh line and blink back the years of rejection and loathing trembling on my lashes.

"Your *allure*, Nothing."

"Allure?" I laugh and it's bitter and caustic. "I'm marked, *deformed*."

"Yes!" he agrees, pissing me off even more.

"I'm trussed up like an animal. You have me on a fucking leash, for crying out loud! There's no allure, just disgust, *pity* if I'm lucky. What the hell did you expect?"

"I expect my staff to look the fuck away! No one can look—can *lust* after you unless I say so!" His fingers grip me tighter, his teeth grinding as he tries to get a hold of himself.

"Yet, you parade me around like a dog," I continue, shaking my head. "You want to put me in The Menagerie like some freak, but now you're pissed off that someone *actually* looked at me? You're unbelievable!"

"And you're a fucking cock-tease!" he bites back, pushing his thumb between my lips and pressing my tongue down so I can't respond. My teeth clamp down as I glare up at him, meeting fire with fire. Spite with spite. He's fucking insane. I might be the one with a back covered in twisted, scarred skin but he's the one who's fucked up on the inside. I've done nothing to warrant such an accusation. I'm just trying to survive.

Fuck you.

"It's my turn," he suddenly snaps.

Turn?

My internal question is met with the sound of his belt unbuckling. I try to release his thumb, but he hooks it over my lower teeth, keeping my jaw in place, pinching my chin.

"I gave you something and now I want something in return," he says, removing his thumb and unzipping his trousers, pushing them and his boxers down so he can release his cock.

"You stole that orgasm from me. You drugged me!" I hiss, glaring at him and not his cock that's inches from my face.

"I'm not talking about that. I'm talking about the one you gave up in my bedroom!" he counters angrily.

"Gave up?!" My stomach rolls over, sickness rising up my chest.

He's right. I did give it up. There was no drug to soften my body, heighten my senses, make me pliable. I gave him my orgasm willingly.

"Yes. Let's level the playing field, shall we? I'm taking what's owed to me."

I suck in a breath, trying to back away on my knees, away from the angry, violent-looking dick he wields like a weapon. It's long, hard and girthy; the bulbous pink head leaking pre-cum. Being in this position—on my knees with his cock in my face—is both terrifying and intensely intimate all at the same time.

This is the first time I've seen a cock in real life. Sure, I've watched a few pornos, more out of a sense of curiosity than anything else, but that's nothing compared to what I'm seeing now.

I have the sudden, ridiculous need to touch it. *Him*.

"Suck it," he grinds out.

"No!" I shake my head, but he grips my jaw once more, tipping my head back.

"Take my cock and suck me off. Right the fuck now."

"You said you wouldn't!" I hiss through gritted teeth.

"I said I wouldn't allow any of us to *fuck* you. I didn't say anything about getting my dick sucked."

"You're a sadist."

"I'm far worse than that, Nothing. So much worse," he warns me, passing the smooth head of his cock over my lips. I try to turn away but he releases my jaw and grasps the back of my head instead, keeping me in place. My scalp tingles as he tightens his fingers around the strands of my hair. I can taste the saltiness of him, the masculinity and power as he spreads his pre-cum like gloss across my lips. He shudders, his dick jerking upwards, hitting the tip of my nose as he glares at me with glittering, ravenous eyes.

"*Ssij mnie!* Suck. Me. Off!" he translates, a desperate almost pleading look in his eyes that belies his harsh order.

He wants me.

His cock is hard.

He's *desperate* for me.

Deep down inside, right in the very dark recesses of my soul, a tiny flame alights. I've often wondered what it would feel like to have a man's dick between my lips. How it would feel to have their cock heavy and erect on my tongue knowing I'd made them feel that way. Would I choke? Would I drool with saliva? Would I be turned on knowing the man I was sucking off was delirious with desire?

All those thoughts twist inside my mind as I shake my head, making it difficult for him to defile me further. I can't ever let him know what I'm truly thinking, how fucked up I really am. "You put that in my mouth and I will bite it the fuck off!" My temper flares as I bare my teeth at him, showing him that I mean every word. At least part of me does.

"You bite me, and I'll make you suffer."

"You won't be able to when your dick is bitten in half, you fucking perverted psychopath!"

"Grim will pay for it. Konrad will ruin her in his dungeons whilst her *Beast* watches, and then Leon will unleash his demons on them both whilst *you* watch. Are you willing to let that happen over a blowjob?"

"Don't count on it," I snarl, feeling the heat of my anger rushing up my neck and cheeks as I press my hands against his thighs trying to stave him off. "My sister isn't to be fucked with, and neither am I, you demented piece of shit!"

Jakub's eyes flash with hunger, his gaze locking on my birthmark as his chest heaves. I match the ragged, heavy rise and fall of his chest as we face-off. For long moments he just stares at me with his dick clutched in his hand and his gaze pinned on my birthmark. If I didn't know any better I'd say he was entranced, staring at me just like I was staring at all the horrible objects he keeps locked up in this room.

"Stop it," I find myself saying, hating the way he's looking at me. I feel degraded, stripped bare, less than human somehow.

"Do you know that when you're angry it gets darker?" he comments eventually, releasing my head and running his fingers over my skin. He's gentle, almost reverent, and I tremble under his touch, transfixed, horrified, *confused* by the look in his eyes, the change in them.

"What?" I mumble, taken aback by the sudden one hundred and eighty degree turn. The anger and desperation he'd worn so well is now replaced with awe and appreciation.

"Your birthmark, the colour deepens the angrier you get. Does it do that when you display other emotions? What about happiness, fear, *pleasure*?" he muses, his thumb pressing against my cheek, right across the bone, fascinated by something that has only ever caused me heartbreak. "The colour here is just like the centre of your cunt when you come, ripe like a fucking plum."

"And...?" I snap back, not sure how to take him but unable to avoid the way he leisurely strokes his cock. My knees are still planted on the floor, my arse resting on my heels, the sting from the whipping I had earlier still smarting my skin, but I'm unable to move.

I *should* fight back. I *should* run.

In the end, I do neither of those things because what he says next freezes me to the spot.

"...And it's fucking *beautiful*," he mutters, shaking his head as though trying to fathom how that can be. How he could even voice such a thing to the woman he despises as much as I despise him?

"Beautiful?" My voice is incredulous.

"*Yes*, beautiful." Shifting slightly, he takes his cock and gently runs it over my birthmark, his eyes heavy-lidded. He's turned on by my birthmark. But that can't be right. This is another manipulation, another lie. Isn't it?

"You're cruel," I counter, hating the way my eyes prick with tears at the falsity of his words and the degradation of his touch.

"You think I'm lying? You think I'd be this hard if I wasn't telling the truth?" he asks me, reading my thoughts as he rests the tip of his cock against my lips once more.

I don't respond, not trusting that he won't invade my mouth the second I open it. Instead, my fingers curl into his thighs, bunching the material of his trousers that rest there. I ignore the sudden pain in my hand from punching Leon so hard and hold on for dear life.

"Look at this room, these things. I'm not like everyone else, *Nothing*, and neither are you," he whispers, gentler now. There's a subtle change in him, one that softens the harsh cut of his jaw, and the tight press of his lips. Even his fingers soothe, stroking my head, no longer yanking at my hair. "Open up for me. Let me know what it feels like to bury my dick in your mouth and come all over your tongue like you came over mine, and I swear to you on my brothers' lives I will not touch you again until the night of the Ball."

My breath stutters, my traitorous core throbs, remembering their touch despite not wanting it. I remember the way they'd made me feel not minutes ago when I'd been under the influence of drugs. They'd taken a piece of me with their thieving lips and hands, and I despise them for it. Yet, here I am on my knees with Jakub's cock pushing gently against my lips, considering his request. I'm not an idiot, I know that he could take what he wants regardless. Maybe that's the key. Fighting him is only fueling the need he has within him. I can take control back by allowing this to happen. It can be on *my* terms.

"What about Konrad and Leon?" I ask, my lips grazing the tip of his cock as I speak.

He shudders, pressing his eyes shut briefly. "They won't touch you."

"And you really believe that?"

"Yes," he grits out, but there's no denying the uncertainty in his eyes. He doesn't believe they'll be able to stay away any more than he has been able to do the same. I'm in this room on my knees, after all.

He licks his lips, waiting. He doesn't force his cock into my mouth like I expect him to, he just stares at my birthmark, my lips, my eyes, like he's not sure whether what he's seeing is real or a fabrication of his twisted imagination. We're at an impasse, one I don't understand given his tendency to take. Then he curls his fist and gently, ever so gently, runs his knuckles over my birthmark and says; "That collar you're wearing, it belonged to my dog, Star. I loved her. She was the only beautiful thing I owned. It's an honor to wear her collar."

My mouth drops open in shock, hanging slack, wide. I should've known better, because he takes that as an opportunity to slide his dick between my parted lips, sighing as he slips inside my mouth. The salty, warm taste of him assails my senses as I draw in a sharp breath, shocked by both the invasion and the confession. Jakub rests his velvety dick on my tongue, a vulnerability shadowing his features beneath the mask he wears. He hadn't meant to say that, but now he's filled the silence between us with a secret so thick I'm almost expecting him to use Star's leash to kill me.

He doesn't.

And I don't bite.

Call it instinct, call it obedience, call it survival, maybe even strength, *power*. Either way, I don't do what I threatened. Instead, I curl my tongue around his thick, veiny dick and suck.

He groans.

I lick.

He moans.

I scrape my teeth lightly over his sensitive skin.

He tucks his jaw into his chest and shudders.

I peer up at him from beneath hooded eyelids, through lashes still wet from the tears I've shed, and boldly take his cock in my hand. I grip the base and he jerks from my touch, letting out a sigh that cuts through my anger and seeps into my chest, burrowing there, uninvited, unwelcome but there.

With a new sense of purpose, I concentrate on giving him the best blowjob of his life. I've never done this before, but I'm a fast learner, listening to the sounds he makes, studying how he reacts to every lick and suck. It's such an intimate act and there's a level of trust involved.

I could bite him.

He could choke me.

But the fight has gone, the distrust between us has been pushed aside.

Right here and now, I'm just a woman giving a man a blowjob.

Giving him pleasure, not pain.

And just like I did, *he* concedes.

Shoulders dropping, mouth going slack, Jakub drops the veil a little, imparting me with the gift of his pleasure.

There's a power in that. A shift in the dynamics. He might not think so, but it's true nevertheless.

Suddenly I'm no longer a victim. His dick, the most delicate, private part of him, slowly, gently invades my mouth, sliding deeper. I should be disgusted, saddened. I'm not. I feel powerful because this time he yields and *I* take. I draw out his orgasm with a tongue tasting his cock, a mouth filled with saliva making it slippery and hot for him. He doesn't seem to care about my inexperience, not going by the way he moans and gently cups my head. Jakub keeps his gaze fixed on me, never once breaking the connection.

I lick and suck, feeling infinitely more powerful than I had in the dining room not minutes ago.

His dick grows, hardening, filling with blood as I hollow out my cheeks.

"That's it, Nothing. Just like that," he croons, a tentative longing in his voice as his hips rock and the tip of his cock edges down my throat. I gag as he hits the back of my throat, so he stills then pulls back giving me the chance to breathe as I lick his rigid heat, sucking more cum leaking from his slit. "O, kurwa! *Fuck!*"

As his fingers curl tighter into my hair and he pushes his cock deeper into my throat, I understand what he needs and we somehow find a rhythm that becomes more and more frantic the nearer he reaches his peak.

He isn't the only one turned on either.

My already swollen, puffy clit is twitching, needing friction as my hips rock in time with his. With my free hand, I grasp the chastity belt and pull it up revelling in the feel of the leather tight against my pussy, the welcome pressure.

"You want this...?" he questions, through a lust-filled haze. There's surprise in his gaze, confusion, maybe even a little bit of anger. My eyes shutter closed, not wanting him to see how much this turns me on. I don't want to be reminded of my position here, or of the truth of this fucked-up moment. I want to take what I can from it. I don't want to be a victim. I need to feel in control.

Reacting to the reality of the moment, I suck harder, wanting him back where he was, trussed up with desire and lust, bound by sensation and hunger.

Helpless to it like I had been.

I don't want the truth. I don't want to be reminded of what this really is.

My fisted hand slides over his slick cock as my head bobs up and down, up and down, in my frantic need to get back into the headspace where this is okay and I'm not being abused. Releasing the chastity belt, I grab his balls and gently massage them, remembering how I'd watched a porn star do the same to her partner. It has the desired effect.

"O, kurwa!" he cries, his dick bobbing in my mouth as cum shoots out in a stringy wave, hitting the back of my throat. The new sensation makes me gag, but he holds me in place so I'm forced to swallow every last drop of his salty, musky cum. His whole body trembles, and a sense of ownership rushes up my spine, surprising me with its intensity.

My gaze locks with his and a flare of understanding flashes between us before it is gone.

"No, teraz ty też masz część mnie," he says on a shaky exhale of breath, sliding his wet dick out of my mouth. I frown, reaching up to wipe the saliva and residue from my lips. "There, now you have part of me too."

CHAPTER 21

CHRISTY

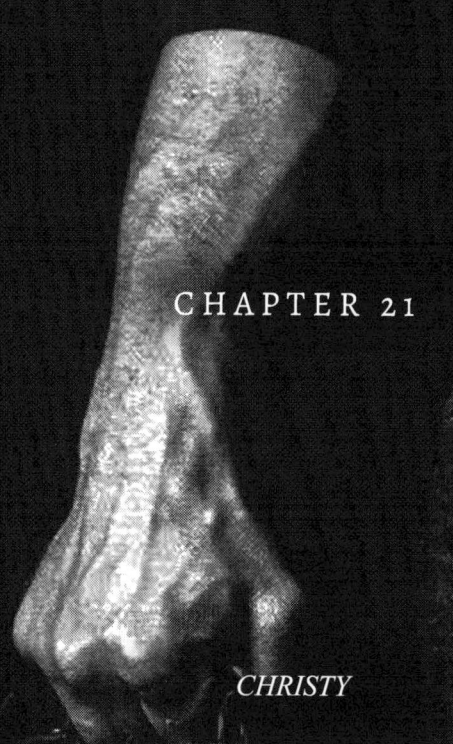

Jakub's knuckles rap against the thick wooden door before us, the sound cutting through the silence that we've been cloaked in ever since he led me from his room of curiosities. We wait, me still on a leash, and Jakub refusing to look anywhere but ahead of him. "Thirteen, hurry up!" he demands when she doesn't open the door right away.

The faint sound of footsteps approaching moments later seem to appease him as he side-eyes me, his anger evident in the tightness of his jaw and pursed lips. I keep a straight face even though I'm smiling internally, knowing that I've won at least some of my self-respect back. He'd meant to debase me, humiliate me, fuck my mouth and make me choke and gag, but instead, I'd made him confess something personal. Unbeknownst to him, it was something that I already knew. I'd stolen a part of him, just like he'd stolen from me.

"You're still Nothing," he says cruelly, reading my expression, sensing my triumph.

"And you might hide behind your mask, but you're more transparent than any man I've ever met," I blurt out, unable to help myself. I'm not sure why I insist on poking the bear, but it feels good. No, it feels better than good. It feels great.

This time he turns to face me completely, smirking whilst Thirteen, apparently, takes her damn time to open the door. "What men? Beast? Your uncle, Frank? Because we both know they're the only men you've got to compare me with. *Pathetic*," he goads.

I scowl, pressing my lips together at his scathing look. "They're both more of a man than you'll ever be!"

"Don't presume to know me, let alone lump me in with them. Just because you've sucked my dick doesn't suddenly make you an expert on who I am. Both your uncle and Beast are under the thumb of their women. That will *never* happen with me," he retorts. "I will never be controlled by a woman who so easily falls to her feet at a compliment filled with *lies*. You think I'm actually attracted to you? You stupid, naive little girl."

"Oh, yeah? Didn't seem that way a few minutes ago!" I retort, anger rolling off me to hide the hurt that insists on settling in my stomach, as if I actually care what he thinks of me.

He tips his head back and laughs, reminding me of so many people who've done the same over the years. I raise my hand, ready to strike him but the door swings open precisely at that moment, preventing me from acting on impulse.

Thirteen coughs, dragging our angry gazes to her. She stands before us hazed in white light from a huge window streaming sunlight into the room behind her. She looks almost ethereal, giving off a sense of serene calm, like an ocean breeze gently cooling heated skin. Instantly I relax, relieved to have another person capable of stepping in and stopping The Masks, or at least respected enough to be listened to. She's dressed in a simple pair of brown slacks with a white t-shirt that dips between her breasts in a low V, her feet bare. In her hands she holds a sprig of rosemary. Its distinct smell rises up to greet my nose.

"Thirteen," Jakub says in greeting, his voice as tight as his body. You wouldn't think he'd just come down my throat.

She smiles warmly, her kind eyes flicking between us both, before resting on my face. There isn't any disgust or pity as she absorbs my birthmark. I'm grateful for that at least. Jakub yanks on the leash, pulling me forward. She doesn't say a word and betrayal seeps beneath my skin at that.

"Nothing will be staying with you until the Ball," he says, filling the silence. "I'm going to speak with One in a moment. I've decided she *will* perform in The Menagerie. She needs to be put to good use."

Thirteen raises her brows in surprise but remains quiet whilst her eyes doing all the talking. They're very expressive. If I didn't know any better, she's questioning his decision.

"She won't be available to our guests. She's *ours*." Jakub explains, not bothering to hide the possessiveness of his tone. I snort, unable to help myself. He couldn't even cope with a member of staff looking at me, how the fuck is he going to deal with his *clients* doing the same?

Jakub's jaw jumps, but he doesn't respond, clearly trying to save face.

Thirteen nods, the slight tightness around her eyes relaxing, but still she doesn't say a word. She simply takes the leash from Jakub so he can unclip the necklace holding the key to my chastity belt.

"Take this. Look after it. Do not, under any circumstances, give it to Leon, Konrad or myself. I will take it back the night of the Ball."

Clasping it in her hands, she fastens it around her neck, the key nestling between her breasts. Jakub locks his gaze on it and for a moment we all just stand, waiting for something to happen. I half expect him to snatch it back from her, given he seems so controlling, but he doesn't. He simply nods, glares at me one last time, then stalks off down the corridor grunting at Seven who appears out of a door further along the hallway. He baulks, stepping out of Jakub's way before casting a surprised look at me.

Once he's turned the corner at the end of the hallway, Thirteen removes the collar from around my neck and slides her cool hand into mine. Relief washes over me as I rub at my skin. Thank God I don't have to wear it any longer. Squeezing my fingers gently, she guides me into her bedroom, shutting the door behind us.

"Who are you to these men?" I ask, not bothering with niceties. I need to know if she's a friend or a foe. I'm confused by her relationship with them. They trust her, that much is obvious, and yet they probably shouldn't have, given what she did to help me.

Shaking her head, she lifts a finger to her lips and guides me further into her room. It's well kept, large and as beautifully decorated as The Masks' apartment, but way more feminine. Her room has a soul, *purpose*. Plants of all different species hang from hooks fixed to one of the walls, some are completely dried, others are in the process, their scent filling the air and reminding me of the meadows filled with wildflowers back home. Below the drying flowers is a huge worktop that stretches from one wall to the other. On its worn surface are all manner of glass containers filled with herbs and vegetation. Seeds and husks. There's a pestle and mortar situated in the centre of the table, mixing bowls, spoons and knives, and jars filled with strange coloured liquids of varying consistency. At the far end, by the open window, is a tabletop gas burner. Its flame is lit and a medium sized copper pot sits on top of it, steam rising up from the liquid.

"What is this place? Who are you?" I ask again.

She drops my hand, turning to face me, shaking her head and tapping her lips with her forefinger. I frown, not understanding. "Is this place bugged or something?"

Smiling, she shakes her head, her pretty grey eyes lighting up from within. Clearly I amuse her. I'm not sure I'm in the mood to be the brunt of such hilarity.

"Then why aren't you answering me...?" I ask, frustration and anger leaching into my voice. She taps her lips again, urging me to understand, and then it dawns on me, she can't speak. "You can't speak?" I repeat out loud.

She sighs, shaking her head. *No.*

"You *can* speak?"

She nods, biting on her lip.

"Then why don't you?" She shakes her head harder, tapping her lips, pleading with her eyes. "Ah, I see. You don't *want* to..."

She nods, squeezing my arm gently before turning on her heel and walking over to the opposite side of the room where her bed and wardrobe is situated. She grabs a pale pink kaftan from the wardrobe, bringing it to me. I take off Konrad's shirt and put it on immediately. The material is made of silk, its scent heady and perfumed like this room. I instantly relax, my shoulders dropping in relief.

"Thank you," I mutter.

Taking my hands, she urges me to sit on the bed, I wince in pain, suddenly reminded of the tender skin from the lashes to my arse and the fact I punched Leon. Funny how the pain returns now even though it was absent the whole time I was with Jakub. She frowns, pointing. *Where?* Her expression seems to say, *Where is your pain?*

"I punched Leon," I say, pointing to my right hand. Her eyes widen in surprise, then she blinks a little before gently pressing her fingers over my knuckles. It's a little sore, but nothing too painful. She frowns then holds up her hand, wiggling her fingers, indicating for me to do the same. I copy her, and wiggle them well enough. Holding her thumb up, she gives me a small smile and nods. She doesn't think anything's broken.

Bringing her hands together, her palms facing upwards, she gestures again. The action reminds me of Oliver Twist asking for more, and I realise that's exactly what she means. Do I have any more pain?

Nodding, I stand, lifting up the hem of the kaftan and turn my back to her, showing her the lashes to my arse. Thirteen huffs out a breath and when I look at her, her expression changes from serene to troubled. With a shake of her head, she strides over to her worktop and reaches for a blue bottle, its contents hidden by the dappled glass. Snatching it up, she returns, then reaches for the hem of the kaftan.

"Wait, I can do it," I say, understanding that whatever's in the bottle it's something she thinks will soothe my skin. "I don't want you to touch me!" She stiffens, apologising with her eyes and hands me the bottle, pointing to a door in the corner of the room. I'm guessing it's a bathroom. "Bathroom?" I ask.

She nods. *Yes.*

"I need to pee," I say, quietly blinking back the sudden tears at the look of empathy on her face.

She nods her head, grasping at the key around her neck and

unfastening it. She hands it to me, jerking her chin as she wraps her fingers around mine and pushes my closed fist towards my chest.

Here.

"Thank you," I mutter.

Entering the bathroom, I push the door shut behind me as more tears pool in my eyes, blurring my vision and preventing me from seeing my reflection in the mirror hanging above the sink. I let the tears fall, allowing myself a moment of sheer misery, letting the emotions so bound up inside of me, out. Anger, pain, anguish, shame, *hate*, it all falls from my eyes, giving me desperate release. It's cathartic.

A couple of minutes pass and I feel immeasurably better for it. Crying is cathartic so long as it doesn't feed someone else's twisted fantasies.

Placing the bottle on the counter, I pull up the kaftan and unlock the chastity belt. It falls to the floor with a thunk and I step out of it, kicking it aside. After relieving myself I strip off the kaftan and wash using the soap left beside the sink, needing to scrub The Masks from my skin even if I can't scrub them from my memories. I don't bother asking permission from Thirteen, I just do it. I get the feeling she wouldn't mind anyway. She seems kind, sympathetic to my situation, and I resolve to find out as much about her and The Masks as I can, despite her refusal to speak.

I've heard of selective mutism. I know that it often occurs on the back of something traumatic, but I've never met anyone with the condition before. Of course, she could be being deceptive, but somehow I don't think that's the case. I might have little reason to trust her, but my gut instinct is telling me she's trustworthy. Right now, that's all I've got.

Drying myself off on a hand towel hanging from the back of the door, I reach for the blue bottle and twist off the stopper, pouring the unknown liquid into my hand. Its consistency is thick, opaque, but it smells like the sea, salty and fishy. Wrinkling my nose, I smooth the liquid onto my arse, wincing at the initial sting that quickly fades to a cooling sensation. The pain instantly eases, the recent events dampened by the soothing concoction. Once I've covered all of the sore skin on my arse, I pull the kaftan on, pick up the chastity belt, wipe it clean and step into it, clicking the lock in place. I might hate this contraption, but if it keeps those monsters from taking what isn't theirs then I will gladly wear it.

By the time I'm finished, Thirteen is sitting on a stool in front of her worktop stirring two cups of what looks and smells like peppermint tea. As I approach she hands me one. I take it from her, breathing in the fresh scent. My eyes flutter shut as the smell conjures up memories of my aunt and uncle who loved to suck on mint sweets. My throat tightens and a sob escapes my lips. I swallow it down and blink back the tears.

Thirteen smiles kindly, pressing her fingers against my hand, jerking her chin. *Drink*, she urges.

"Thank you," I mutter, taking a sip and humming my appreciation as the sweetened peppermint tea permeates my taste buds. The consistency reminds me of the liquid she'd poured into my mouth with her kiss and I find myself asking her about it. "You gave me something to counteract The Quickening, didn't you?"

Her hand stills, her cup of tea midway to her mouth. She sighs, placing it on the worktop. She nods, *Yes*.

"Why?" I ask.

She frowns, chewing on her lip. I'm not sure if her hesitation is because she doesn't want to tell me why or if she doesn't know how to explain without words to make communicating easier. After a beat she reaches for a pencil and pad that appears to be filled with recipes, then flicks to a clean page.

No one should have the right to choose taken away from them, she writes.

"Yet you make a drug that does exactly that."

She shakes her head, furiously writing. *The Quickening isn't meant to be used to trap and ensnare. It's supposed to be used to enlighten, to heighten sensation to a willing participant. It's for pleasure.*

"I see," I reply, cutting her a look. "Surely you understand, given who The Masks are, that they would abuse such a drug?"

I wait for her to respond, to scribble her reply. Instead she sighs heavily, and places the pencil on top of the paper, apparently not willing to answer. Part of me wants to persist, to make her reply, but another huge part is tired. I'm tired of being held prisoner in this castle, exhausted from the constant emotional and physical battle with The Masks, and fatigued with trying and failing to understand why the Numbers stay when they appear to have every opportunity to escape.

She reaches for me, her fingers gently squeezing my arm. Her grey eyes tell me to trust her, that she knows what she's doing, that she has my best interest at heart, but trust has to be earned, and whilst she's helped me this one time, it doesn't mean she won't turn her back on me the next. I step back, putting some distance between us.

Reaching for the pencil once again, she writes: *Trust me. Please.*

The Masks trust her, which counts for a lot given the type of men they are. Yet, they're my captors, my *enemy*. Why on earth should I trust her when her loyalty lies with those wankers?

"I don't trust anyone here," I say. It's a lie, however, because my gut is telling me to trust her and my gut has never, not once, been wrong.

Then trust your instincts, she writes before gently tapping her finger over my heart then my temple as though reading my mind. We lock gazes, and after a beat she holds out her hand, her palm facing upwards. I understand what she wants, and despite not really wanting to give her the key, I do, my gut telling me that it's far safer in her hands than it is in mine.

CHAPTER 22

JAKUB

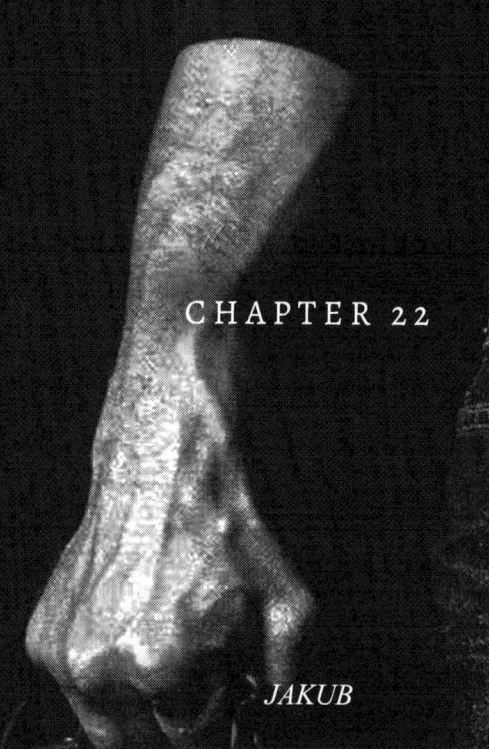

"You wanted to speak with me?" One asks, stepping into the library.

She's changed from her outfit earlier and is now wearing a white, knee length gown with red flowers embroidered across the hem. It's far more demure than anything I've ever seen her wear before and I can't help but wonder if this is her way of trying to attract my attention. I can't remember the last time she wore white. It's been years. I guess Nothing's arrival has stirred up more than just Twelve's jealousy.

"Sit. I have things I wish to discuss," I say curtly, giving her a cursory glance as I take a sip of the third glass of brandy I've drunk since my interaction with Nothing. Despite the heat of the brandy burning my throat and the pleasant warmth it's spreading through my limbs, it's done nothing to ward off the hunger I feel for her. For *Nothing*.

My cock is *still* hard.

"Of course," she replies, walking towards me gracefully, her long limbs shapely. Everything about her is perfect, from her long black hair to her pert breasts, neat pussy and flawless skin. Age has done nothing to take that beauty away from her. If anything, she's grown more beautiful. It helps that she's had access to every possible potion and lotion from Thirteen who, in another life, would be a millionaire by now. Fortunately for us, Thirteen has never wanted more than what she has. Content to be here in this castle with us and not *them*. My brothers and I are well aware of how valuable she is and we treat her accordingly.

Taking a seat opposite me in a high winged-back chair, One crosses her legs at the ankle, and places her long piano-playing fingers over the end of each armrest. I notice that her nails are painted a bright red, reminding me of the times when they had dug into the flesh of my arse, puncturing my skin as I rutted into her. I was a boy then, a fucking child who'd been conditioned into seeking her out whenever unwelcome emotions had begun to creep back in.

From the ages of thirteen to eighteen, whenever I felt myself weakening I'd beat, then fuck One like a wild animal. In return she'd marked me with her talons, staking her claim on me. For five years I used her but that stopped when I realised fucking her wasn't working anymore.

That fucking her made me feel worse. Not better.

With age came realisation. She used me, like I used her. She abused me, like I abused her.

The thought of touching her now turns my stomach.

"Jakub?" she asks tenderly.

It's rare when she calls me Jakub and not Master, but I'm beginning to understand that this is her attempt at reminding me of our bond. Neither Konrad nor Leon were permitted to fuck the Numbers after their initial breaking-in. Only me. I'm the true heir to the Brov legacy and that gave me some allowances. I took advantage of that fact today so I could fuck Nothing's mouth without feeling guilty about it.

Except I *do* feel guilty.

Not because of what I took from her, but because I went behind my brothers' backs. Because I broke *our* rules. The ones we agreed upon together before we brought her here.

Fuck.

"Jakub?" One repeats, cocking her head to the side, her berry-red lips parting on a breath as she watches me. She's fully aware of her sexual prowess, and is an expert at using it to her advantage. Of all the Numbers she's coveted the most, followed by Six as a close second. Both are innately sexual. One overtly so, Six without even realising it.

And Nothing... She has no idea just how fucking tempting she is. How much power she could wield if we don't watch our step. Right now she's oblivious to it, but I'm acutely aware of her ability to completely ruin everything we've established here.

I need to keep my head.

I need to stay the fuck away from her.

And most of all, I need to make sure my brothers don't lose sight of what's important: our business, what we've built here, and our bond.

Putting Nothing in The Menagerie will mean she's not readily available if one of us were to slip up. I know very well that if we'd kept her in our apartment she would've already been shackled to that bed and fucked to within an inch of her life.

It's better this way. For all of us.

Even her.

"Jakub, you seem... out of sorts. Can I help with anything?" One asks me, her sexy accent rolling off her tongue, dripping with sexual innuendo.

It may work on the clients we invite to the castle but it won't work on me, not anymore. I'm not that teenager who revelled in beating then fucking a sexy Italian woman almost twice his age. Those days are long gone.

I don't need her that way. Not anymore. But I should indulge her efforts, if only to keep her on my side. She is, after all, the mastermind behind The Menagerie. With as much effort as I can muster, which is pretty fucking small, I plaster a rare smile on my face and say, "You look beautiful, One. Is that a new dress?"

She smiles, though it doesn't meet her eyes as she shifts in her seat, uncrossing and crossing her legs, all the while flashing me the dark slash of her pussy. "It is, thank you..." Her voice trails off as she stares at me.

"What is it, One?" I ask, giving her a moment of my interest, even if it is fake.

"I don't have to be beautiful for you. You understand that, don't you? Whatever you need I can give you." She looks up from under her lashes, her tongue running over her bottom lip as her fingers tighten on the handrests.

She's overstepped, just like she did in the Grand Hall when she touched me when she shouldn't have. She knows it. I know it. At some point I need to address that, but now isn't the time. Instead, I allow myself to look at One, to really look. She's still as stunning as she was when she first arrived here.

The first time I was forced to fuck her, I threw up. I threw up not because I beat her, marked her skin, bruised her and made her bleed. I threw up because I had to put my flaccid dick in her pussy and make myself come whilst my father fucking watched.

It was the single worst experience of my life.

But each time it got easier. With her help, I was able to switch off my thoughts, my churned-up feelings, all the *weakness*, and just fuck her. I owe her at least a little grace for that.

"I'm well aware of what you're able to provide," I reply, with a dip of my head. "But what I need from you remains the same as it has been these past five years. I will not cross that line with you. We will never be intimate again. *Never*. The Menagerie is your priority. Do you understand me?"

One fixes a smile on her face, but I see the darkness in her soul beneath the pretty facade. My father saw it too and that's why she survived unlike all the others before her.

"I understand. So what can I do for you then?" she asks after a long stretch of silence when I try not to think about the fact I had Nothing on her knees sucking my cock in the room of curiosities only a few hours ago. It was supposed to be a form of punishment. It was supposed to scare Nothing into submission, remind her of her place. Somehow, it managed to have the opposite effect. She might've been on her knees, but at that moment, when she coaxed an orgasm out of me after years of abstinence, she had all the power.

"Nothing will be taking part in The Menagerie. I want her to dance." *I need her out of the way.*

"And when the show is over...?"

I meet One's gaze, lifting my brows at her audacity. She already knows that Nothing won't be available to our clients. I made that perfectly clear in the Grand Hall. Bringing up the subject again rankles me. "No. As I already said, she is *ours*. She will perform on stage and that is it. Do I make myself clear?"

"As you wish." She dips her head in acquiescence, but despite her carefully relaxed demeanor, she can't hide her jealousy. It's plain as day.

"Thirteen is responsible for Nothing whilst Leon, Konrad and I concentrate on the Ball and all the arrangements needed to make sure it runs smoothly. There is a lot of work to be done. Thirteen will remain in charge of her at all times apart from rehearsals where you will ensure she's kept under control. If she goes missing under your watch, there will be consequences. Dire ones."

"I'm willing to help with *whatever* you need," she replies, keeping her expression neutral despite the insinuation.

"Offering yourself up again, I see," Leon says, stepping into the room and interrupting our conversation. He smirks, looking between us both. I can feel the tension he brings with him from the other side of the room. This is worse than I thought.

Downing the rest of my drink, I jerk my head at One. "We were just discussing Nothing's role in The Menagerie. She will rehearse with the Numbers and spend the rest of her time with Thirteen until we're ready for her."

"Of course you were," he responds dryly as Konrad steps into the room behind him. He looks as haggard as I feel. We need to get our shit together, and fast.

"I could use a fucking drink," Konrad says, clamping a hand on Leon's shoulder and forcing him further inside the room. Leon bares his teeth at Konrad, that familiar gesture telling us all where his head's at.

He's in a mood. A dangerous one.

"I want Nothing in rehearsals tomorrow morning," I say to One in a clipped tone. She knows me well enough to know that this is her cue to leave. My brothers and I need to talk. Alone.

One dips her head and rises to her feet. "Goodnight," she says before strutting past Leon and Konrad, her long dark hair swaying across her back as she walks.

I wait for her to leave, and for Konrad to lock the door behind her, before pulling off my mask.

"So what the fuck now?" Konrad asks, swiping a hand through his thick dark hair as he slumps in the chair One had just vacated. "I've had a fucking hard on since she came all over my fingers."

"Nothing's changed—"

"You can say that again!" Leon practically roars, cutting me off. "That woman who stood before us in the Grand Hall was not the same fucking girl we kidnapped." He grabs the bottle of brandy from the side table and takes a deep pull from the bottle, not even bothering to pour himself a glass. He's in shock. Well, that makes three of us.

"She's still Grim's sister. She's still our revenge," I remind him. "Focus, Leon."

"Did you not see her face, her back?" Konrad asks, knowing full well that I did.

"You know I did, but this changes *nothing*," I repeat, all the while knowing it could change everything.

Leon passes Konrad the bottle of brandy then starts pacing up and down the room. "Don't fucking kid yourself, Jakub. I saw your reaction."

"It was a surprise. Granted. But it means nothing. She's here for one reason and one reason only. *Revenge*," I repeat.

"You said she was *ours*," Leon reminds me, his tone mocking, as though he already knows what I did in my room of curiosities. "You said we could have her the way we wanted. We fucking agreed, Jakub, and now you've moved the damn goalposts to suit you."

"No," I retort, shaking my head. "I'm doing this for *us*. We must concentrate on the Ball. When it's over you'll get what you need. Both of you."

Leon snorts, shaking his head. He doesn't trust me to keep myself in check. He's right not to.

I've already broken our agreement. I fucked up.

I let her wrap her lips around my cock. I relaxed enough around her, trusted her enough not to fucking bite me, and she made me come.

She made *me* come.

A man who's been celibate for the last five years. A man who's had zero interest in fucking until her. Until she came into our lives with her fiery hair, her witchy eyes, and mesmerising flaws.

Truth be known, tasting Nothing's pussy had been fucking heaven, and that was before I'd even seen her true face.

I wanted her to disgust me, but she didn't.

She fucking didn't.

It had taken everything in me not to fuck her on my bed. Instead I'd feasted on her, and fuck if I don't want to do that again, and again, and again.

Then to make matters worse, I worshipped her mouth and her lips and her tongue with my dick behind my brothers' backs. I stroked her goddamn tonsils with it, and she took me, opened up to me and all the while her birthmark deepened in colour.

Fuck, I'd come so hard I nearly lost my goddamn footing.

I hadn't lied when I said I'd given a piece of myself to her. It wasn't meant to be a crude remark. I was being fucking honest because at that moment, when I'd relaxed enough to come, to pour my seed down her throat, Nothing had become *everything* I've been searching for my whole damn life.

"You're making a mistake," Konrad grunts, taking a long pull from the bottle. "Grim is looking for her. We're running out of time."

"By the time Grim finds out where she is, it'll be over. You'll have got what you wanted," I say with a confidence I don't truly feel.

"That's it, then? You've made your decision?" Leon asks, gritting his jaw so hard I can hear his teeth grinding.

"Nothing performs in The Menagerie this weekend as discussed. She stays with Thirteen. Then we'll all get what we need on the night of the Ball," I confirm, standing.

"And Grim?" Konrad asks.

"Will die the moment she sets foot in this castle," I reply, refusing to acknowledge the fact that not only have I hidden my encounter with Nothing from my brothers, but that I've broken our agreement to experience her together.

Konrad blows out a breath. "Fine. As you wish."

"Leon?" I question, meeting his angry gaze.

"Understood," he bites out.

"Good," I say with a terse nod of my head. "I suggest you find something to occupy yourself in the interim. No slip ups."

"No slip ups," they repeat as I stride from the room and head straight for the forest.

CHAPTER 23

CHRISTY

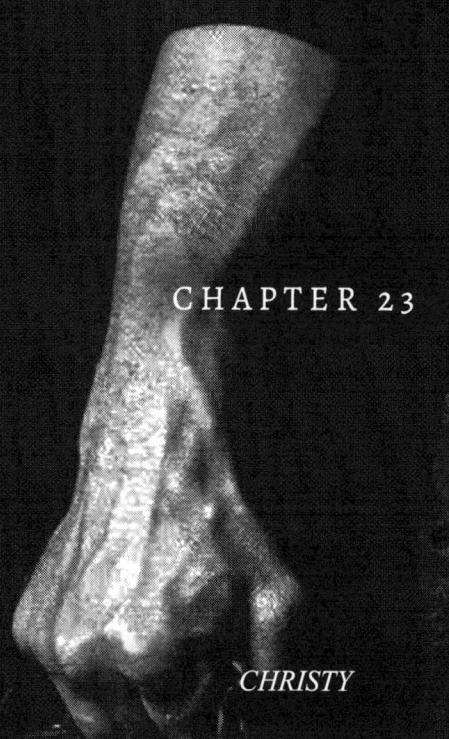

"Rise and shine!" a familiar voice says the next morning. Far too chirpy given the circumstances.

"Go away, *Nala*," I groan, trying to wrestle back the covers from her as she sits down on the edge of the bed and grins at me. "What are you smiling about?"

"You, performing in The Menagerie, of course!"

"Leave me alone."

"Nope. No can do. One has sent for you."

"I don't care. Tell her I'm not doing it."

Nala tuts. "She'd *love* that. You really don't understand how things work here, do you? I thought you were smart."

"What's that supposed to mean?" I ask, sitting up. Next to me the bed is empty. Sunshine pours through the gap in the curtain telling me it's way past dawn. "Where's Thirteen? What time is it anyway?"

"Which question would you like me to answer first?" Nala sasses with a grin as she pulls back the duvet. Her happiness should be infectious, but a heavy weight sits inside my chest this morning that cannot be shifted, *won't* be shifted until I'm safely home and The Masks are dead.

"Where's Thirteen?"

"In her allotment collecting some more herbs."

"Allotment?"

"Of course. She's got an acre of land dedicated to growing her herbs and flowers. I'm surprised she hasn't mentioned it."

"I'm not. I'm still a prisoner here, Nala. Besides, Thirteen doesn't really say all that much," I point out.

In fact, after our brief, stilted conversation yesterday, Thirteen hasn't made any effort to communicate further, choosing to leave me with my thoughts and immerse herself in her alchemy. I spent the whole of yesterday afternoon and most of last night thinking about how I can escape this place, or at least get word to Grim, and coming up empty. When I did finally manage to fall asleep my dreams were filled with The Masks.

Not visions, thank God, but dreams.

Dreams of me shackled to the bed in their room of sin. Dreams of their mouths pressing against my tender flesh, licking and sucking, fucking and searching. Dreams where I'm crying out for more, not cursing their names. Dreams that confused me, that have twisted me up inside. I feel exhausted by them.

"I'm tired. I just want to sleep," I say, feeling the weight of my situation sit heavily on my shoulders.

"Sleep is for the dead. Get up. Get dressed. It doesn't have to be all doom and gloom, you know," she says with a youthful exuberance that pisses me off.

"You're infuriating, do you know that?" I grumble, forcing the memory of those dreams aside whilst trying to pry the duvet back out of her hands and failing to even grasp it as she yanks it to the floor.

"Renard has mentioned it once or twice." She grasps my hand, pulling me upright.

"Nala!" I wince, reminded of my humiliation as I swing my legs over the side of the bed at her insistence. Thirteen's tonic has been incredibly soothing and I'm more than certain without it I'd be in a much worse position, but despite how gifted she is, there isn't anything that can completely heal a bruise or in my case, a whipped arse, in just a few hours. I'm not going to be able to sit comfortably for a while yet. Then again, this is nothing to what Twelve endured. I wonder how she's fairing this morning. The poor woman must be in agony.

"Penny for your thoughts?" Nala says, opening the curtains fully and allowing the autumn sunshine to pour into the room.

"How's Twelve?" I ask.

Nala chews on her lip. "She's been better, but she has Thirteen tending to her wounds so I know that she'll be fine."

"What they did was horrific." I swallow hard, reminded of the blood dripping from the Cat-o'-nine-tails. Leon might've wielded it, but all three of The Masks were responsible.

"It was," she agrees, wincing at her memories of that night.

"And you still think they're redeemable?"

"One wants you dressed and downstairs in the studio in an hour," Nala says, ending the conversation abruptly. "I've brought you breakfast and Thirteen has left you some clothes to wear." She points to a loose, knee length, navy skirt, white t-shirt and ballet slippers draped over the armchair that's situated by the window.

"I asked you a question, Nala—"

"Thirteen also gave me the key so you could, you know…" Nala replies, refusing to engage in a conversation that will make her uncomfortable. She's still holding onto the hope that The Masks will change, *can* change. For now, I let it go.

"Is that allowed?"

Nala pulls a face, understanding what I mean instantly. "The Masks gave you to Thirteen, didn't they?" I nod in agreement. "Then I guess she's allowed to do what she sees fit, right?"

"I guess," I respond, not entirely convinced, but going with the flow regardless. I'm grateful for the clothing and the ability to use the bathroom and freshen up. Two basic human comforts I'd taken for granted before arriving here. Funny how a thin piece of material can help protect you against the world, but as I use the bathroom and then pull on the clothing left out for me, that's exactly what it feels like: armour.

"Now you eat up. One is renowned for her punishing rehearsals. You'll need your strength."

"But the Ball isn't for a while yet," I say, dropping the key to the chastity belt into the pocket of my skirt. The sooner I can give it back to Thirteen the better. As random as this sounds, I don't feel safe keeping hold of it, not when The Masks could take it from me, then take what they want.

"Oh no, you misunderstand. They're not rehearsing for the Ball. The Menagerie will be performing this weekend. We have a small number of guests arriving Saturday."

"Saturday?! But that's in just a few days time."

"Yup. Ardelby Castle is going to be a hive of action as we all prepare for the occasion," she says breezily as if this weekend's spectacle isn't about the Numbers performing for dirty men and women who want to use them up and fuck them.

"Just perfect," I mumble, pulling at the hem of my skirt.

Nala, sensing my discord, sets about tidying up the room whilst I sit and eat the scrambled eggs and bacon she'd brought me. Even though I've only been here for a little while, it feels so much longer than that, despite only seeing a fraction of the castle and none of the grounds surrounding it. If I weren't a prisoner held captive in these walls then I might've appreciated my surroundings. Loved them, even. As it is, every room I enter, every corridor I walk down, every view I look out upon is just an illusion of freedom. I wish the Numbers understood that. Maybe then we could work together to escape.

"So, Grandfather told me you're a ballerina," Nala says as she escorts me to the studio half an hour later.

"I've never danced professionally. It's a passion of mine, not a career."

"Apparently Jakub was impressed."

"He was?" I find myself asking as we descend two flights of stone stairs that lead towards another courtyard, smaller than the one The Weeping Tree grows out of. Sun streams from above, the warm air lifting strands of my hair and making the silk skirt I'm wearing flutter around my knees.

"*Of course* he was! Why on earth would he put you in The Menagerie if he didn't think so?"

"Because I'm a spectacle, a *curiosity*," I say, pointing to my birthmark.

I'm not seeking her approval, anyone's for the matter. I accepted my appearance a long time ago. I don't despise it, I really don't. It's just these men are fucking with my head, bringing out long since buried insecurities. I'm pissed off at myself for letting them get to me.

"You're *not*, she protests."

"Listen, I'm well aware of how people view me," I say.

Yesterday Jakub had called me naive, *stupid* for believing his words of appreciation. He was right. I might have gained some control sucking him off and taking his pleasure, but he'd snatched that back the second he'd opened his mouth. I was so fucking foolish allowing myself to believe his lies, because for a brief moment I *had* believed them.

"The Masks are all kind of messed up over you. They've never behaved like this before."

"Like what?"

"Like their heads are elsewhere. Leon spent all his spare time yesterday in his gym working out until he could barely stand upright. Konrad disappeared into the dungeon for hours on end, which ordinarily wouldn't be unusual except for the fact he was *alone* down there, and Jakub…"

"And Jakub?" I prompt.

"Well, he spent all of last night in the forest. Actually, he's still there. The last time he disappeared for days in the forest he came back even more surly than when he left."

"What does he do there?"

Nala shrugs. "I've no idea, but everyone keeps out of his way when he returns."

"I see," I reply, not really seeing at all.

"Like I said, you've totally messed with their heads, not to mention the fact that you're *dancing* in the show and *not* doing the other... *stuff*. I overheard Jakub speaking with One yesterday. He was adamant that you perform but aren't available for anything else," she explains brightly. "See, he *likes* you. They all do."

I raise a brow at her. "I couldn't care less if they like me or not, Nala. I'm still getting out of here."

"But..."

"But what? Do you think because I'm not actively trying to escape every second of every day, that I'm okay with being here, that I don't want to go home? They've *hurt* me, Nala."

I don't say that they've also brought me pleasure, both stolen and given. She doesn't need to know any of that, and I certainly don't want to pay it any more attention than necessary.

"Hurt people, *hurt* people," she says softly.

I snort. "I won't feel sorry for them, so don't even try to change my mind." Despite my determination to remain unforgiving in that respect, I'm briefly reminded of the boy Jakub was in my vision: bruised, undernourished, and afraid. My heart pangs in sympathy for that boy and what he must've suffered. But I quickly shove it aside. *No.*

"Okay," she mumbles, clearly hurt by my refusal to accept my life here.

Stopping in front of a door to our left, I can hear the haunting notes of a piano being played and just like the other day, chills run down my spine at One's incredible talent.

"She's a gifted musician," Nala says, smiling gently, affected by the music just as much as I am. There really is something uniquely beautiful about the way the notes lift into the air and caress the senses. My skin tingles with the emotion her music invokes, the hair on my arms lifting just like they had in the Grand Hall.

"Yes, she is..." I agree, my voice trailing off at the look on Nala's face. "But?"

"Just watch your back with her. She's used to being number one, and now you're here. Well..."

I shake my head. "I'm Nothing, Zero, Nought," I remind her. "Or have you forgotten that?"

Nala reaches for my hand and squeezes it gently. "You're far more than that and you know it."

With that she twists on her feet and walks off down the corridor, leaving me wondering how a sixteen year old child could be more insightful than many adults twice her age.

∽

THE MOMENT I step into the studio, the music stops and every single Number turns to face me. They're all present, each of them in varying stages of undress, presumably a dress rehearsal given their choice of outfits or rather, lack of them. Even Thirteen stands to the side of the room, dabbing ointment onto Twelve's raw back. I swallow hard at the deep welts and the lashes that criss-cross her olive skin, wanting to reach out the hand of friendship but knowing it wouldn't be well received.

"Welcome, Zero. We're pleased to have you join The Menagerie," One says, drawing my attention back to her. She has a smile fixed on her beautiful face but it doesn't cover the fact she's shocked by my appearance. There's a manic, almost unhinged part of me that wants to shout *surprise* and wave my hands in the air just to see their reaction. Of course, I don't.

"Yes, we're happy to have you," Three adds, her welcome sincere, unlike One's.

"I'm not," I reply tightly, gritting my jaw and willing myself to keep my head held high. They can all look at me with pity in their eyes, and some with barely veiled hatred. I don't care. I'll never be one of them. I will never be a part of this willingly. "I had no choice but to take part in the show, and I'm not going to pretend that this is something I'm happy about because I'm not."

"Don't you dare fuck this up for us," Eight interjects coldly, her bare tits wobbling as she slides into a cupless bra, supported by nothing more than leather straps. "You might turn your nose up at us, thinking you're better because you don't agree with what happens here, but this show is our life and there isn't one person in this room who won't kill you if you cause us issues."

"Don't speak for me," Six snaps, glaring at Eight.

"Or us," Seven and Three add.

Eight snorts, rolling her eyes. "Why am I not surprised? You three just love a lost cause. Well, if Zero fucks up, you can be the one who deals with the aftermath of that because I sure as fuck won't be volunteering for a whipping when our Masters lose their shit again."

"That's enough, Eight," One says, rising gracefully to her feet and ending the argument with a sharp stare. "We're a *family*, remember?"

Eight huffs, busying herself getting dressed whilst One wanders over to a rail of clothing on the far side of the studio and starts flicking through the rack. She pulls out a rose-pink, floor length dress made of silk. It has thin spaghetti straps, a low back, and a slit from thigh to ankle. It's pretty and something I would never dream of wearing. Folding it over her arm she walks towards me, a smile fixed on her face.

"Due to her injuries Twelve is unable to partake in the show this weekend. So you're a welcome addition," she says, handing me the dress.

"What's this?" I ask, taking it from her. It looks expensive, and far too revealing.

"What you'll be wearing to perform in."

I shake my head. "No. I can't wear this."

One raises her brow, her long dark hair falling over her shoulder as she cocks her head and narrows her eyes at me. "You will wear what I tell you to wear."

"You don't understand. I *can't* wear that," I insist. It's bad enough that I have to be in the show, let alone wearing a dress that will do little to cover up the scars on my back.

One steps closer, dropping her lips to my ears and lowering her voice to no more than a whisper. "You will do as I say, Zero, or I shall make your life here very, very difficult. I am the matriarch, the founder of this show. Jakub and I have a special bond. If you refuse my *request*," she says, punctuating the word with sarcasm, "Then I will make sure that you suffer injuries far worse than those inflicted on Twelve."

Spinning on her feet, One sashays towards Five who has been quietly watching our exchange the whole time. She gives me a terse nod of her head, her dark eyes not giving anything away. Yesterday she had treated me kindly, or as kindly as she could given the circumstances. Today, she's closed off.

No matter.

Forcing steel into my spine, I take the dress and stride over to Thirteen who's still religiously applying ointment to Twelve's ravaged back. "Here," I say, holding my hand out so Thirteen can take the key. She smiles at me, screwing the lid back onto the ointment and handing it to Twelve before securing the necklace safely around her neck. I can't help but glance at Twelve's injuries, my stomach roiling. Some slashes are deeper than others. In the worst parts, the skin is split, scabs forming. Those will scar.

"Don't look at me like that," she hisses, glaring at me over her shoulder as she pulls on her shirt, wincing as the material slides over her skin.

"I apologise," I mumble, understanding what it feels like to be gawked at.

"Why? I *earned* these stripes. Can you say the same?"

"What's that supposed to mean?" I say, aware that Six is approaching me.

Pressing her cool hands on my arm, she draws me away from Twelve, towards a non-hostile corner of the room where Three and Seven are standing. Her eyes are kind, concerned, as she lowers her voice and says, "Don't engage. Twelve is hurting right now. When she gets like this she's spiteful. She doesn't like to play second fiddle to The Masks' attention."

"But I don't *want* their attention," I reply tightly. "I was kidnapped, for crying out loud!"

"Regardless, they've claimed you in a way they've never claimed any of us. Twelve doesn't like it," Seven says, his arm wrapping around Three as he hugs her into his side.

"What do you mean?"

Six pushes her auburn hair behind her ear and folds her arms across her chest, pushing up her already ample cleavage barely covered by the blue corset she's wearing. "I can tell by the look in your eyes that you think The Masks indulge their... *needs* with us." Her voice trails off as she waits for my reaction.

"Well, don't they?"

"No. They don't seek sexual pleasures from any of us outside of the first time," Three explains.

"First time? So you *have* been used by them?" I ask, confused now.

"When a Number first arrives here one of The Masks is tasked to—"

"Let me guess, torture then fuck you?" I interrupt.

"It isn't like that," Six insists. "After the initial welcome, they don't indulge again."

"Twelve was the last Number to have any sexual contact with one of The Masks, and that was two years ago when she first arrived here," Seven says, his gaze flicking over to Twelve who's watching us all with narrowed eyes. "She was assigned to Konrad, and grew attached to him. Up until a few months ago he was taking her into his dungeons regularly."

"To *fuck*," I point out.

"No, for *punishment*. She's been trying to get him to fuck her ever since her first time with him. But he won't indulge her. Then when she realised he wasn't going to give in, she's been doing everything in her power to piss him off so he'll keep punishing her. That's kind of her thing. Only he stopped doing that too a few months ago."

"*A few months ago?*"

"Yes," Six says with a heavy sigh. "You don't know this, but you've been a thorn in Twelve's side since before you even got here. Six months ago when The Masks finally found you, Konrad cut all ties with Twelve. It broke her. She's in love with him."

"Do you... *Love* him, any of them?" I ask, dumbfounded.

"I thought I loved Leon once," she says with a soft smile and wistful look on her face.

"*Leon?*"

"Yes, Leon. Why is that such a shock to you?"

"Are you kidding me? Did you not see what he did to Twelve yesterday?"

"She broke the rules..." Six's voice trails off as she chews on her lip. "Twelve knew what she was doing. Like I said, she's been trying to get Konrad's attention, and it worked, just not quite in the way she wanted it to."

"That's messed up," I mumble, unable to fathom how she can be okay with this, how any of them can.

"When you accept your place here, you accept the rules. In return we get the freedom to express ourselves the way we choose with no judgement or limitations. It's a good life," Seven insists.

"Why Leon?" I ask Six. "Of the three, why was it him you thought you loved?"

"He broke me in," she replies instantly.

"Broke you in? You make it sound like you were a horse and he's a trainer." Six chews on her lips, her cheeks flushing as she glances at Three and Seven. "Tell me I'm wrong."

"It isn't quite like that," Three says.

"Not *quite* like that? What did Leon do to you, Six?" I ask, my throat tightening at the look in her eyes. It's as though she's battling with herself, with the truth that hurts and the lies she's told herself so she can accept what he did to her, and her life here.

"He broke me down, and then he built me back up into who I am today. I'm *stronger* for it. Each of the Numbers have had a similar experience, though not with the same master."

"Were you not strong before?"

"No. I wasn't."

"Don't you want to go home?" I whisper, looking between them all, wanting to shake some sense into them.

Seven grinds his teeth, squeezing Three tighter to his side. "No. This is our home, and the Numbers are our family, just like One said. It may not seem like it, but it's true."

"But The Masks are your masters, right? So does that make you their slaves?"

"I suppose you could see it like that," Three says gently.

"I'm not certain how else I'm supposed to see it. As far as I can tell, this place works because they hold power over you. They've *broken* you, forced you into submission, and you've just accepted it."

"You make it sound ugly, like we've given up part of ourselves," Six says, a look of confusion on her face.

"But you have. You've given up your *freedom*. More than that," I continue, gripping her arm and urging her to hear me, to understand.

"You're wrong. I wasn't free before I came here. I was trapped in a relationship with a man who owned me in the worst possible way. I was *dead* inside. The Collector took me from a loveless marriage and gave me a gift by bringing me here. I didn't know it at the time, but I do now. I see," Six protests.

"Do you hear yourself? The Collector took you which is just another word for *stole*. You said you were trapped in a marriage with a man who *owned* you. What's the difference? You are no less owned now."

"The difference is, I'm *happy* here, Zero. You will be too, if you just let yourself," she says, frustration clear on her face.

"No, I won't," I retort, shaking my head and glancing over at One who's currently talking with Four, Eight and the triplets, Nine, Ten and Eleven. "And One, how does *she* feel about it all, about me?" I find myself asking, her warning still ringing in my ears.

Three chews on her lip. "One has lived here the longest. This is her home, and The Menagerie is her life. She will do whatever Jakub asks. She always has. People come from all over the world to see us perform in The Menagerie. That's down to her. She's not only a gifted pianist but incredibly creative. It's a spectacular show."

"You respect *her*?" I ask, in astonishment.

"We all do," Six agrees, not quite able to meet my gaze. "One's priority has always been The Menagerie, *us*. We're a family whether you choose to believe that or not. If you're not a Number then you're an outsider, and she doesn't do well with outsiders, unless of course it's a client and then she does whatever the hell they want. Even if you never like her, you'll come to respect her like the rest of us, eventually."

I shake my head. "I won't, not ever. I'd sooner go home! All these problems I'm causing with The Masks, with the other Numbers, would be resolved so easily if they just let me go."

"It doesn't matter what you want," Seven says, cutting straight to the point. "The Masks have already claimed you as *theirs*."

"I don't want to be theirs. I don't want any of this!"

Six heaves out a sigh, squeezing my arm gently. "Do you honestly think that matters to them?"

"No, I don't, but that doesn't change the fact that it matters to *me*. I am not theirs. I never will be."

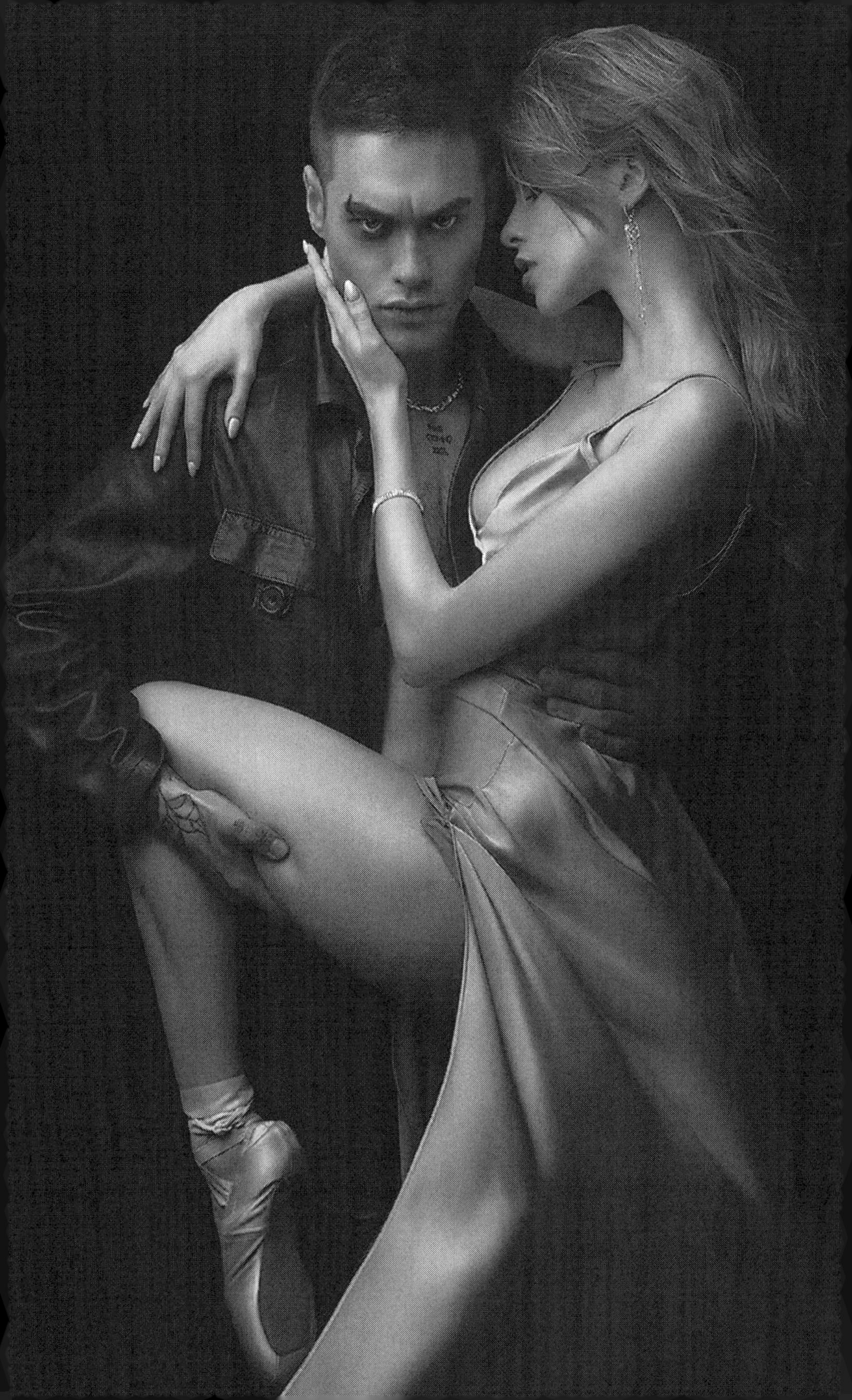

CHAPTER 24

JAKUB

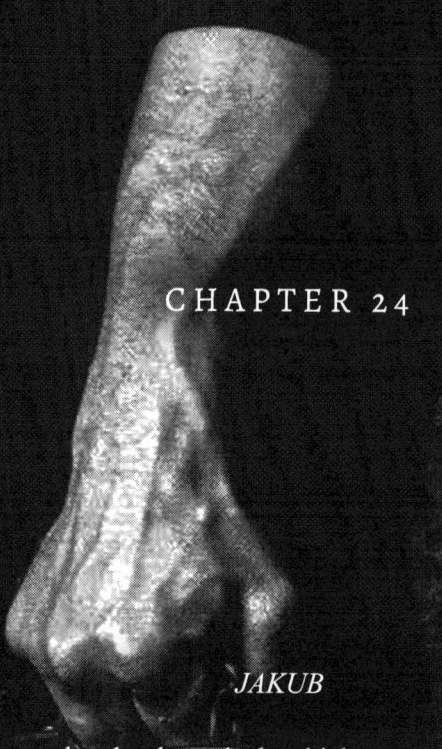

Dawn breaks through the thick canopy above my head, rays of sunlight heating up the mossy, damp earth I'm lying on as insects and wildlife come to life around me. A mosquito lands on my forearm, puncturing a slither of skin that isn't covered in a thick layer of mud. I don't flick it away, content to watch it feed from me as I slowly wake up, revelling in the aches and pains that I feel from hours spent roaming the forest.

Once the mosquito has drunk its fill and flies away, leaving a tiny droplet of blood on my skin, I push up onto my hands and knees. My fingers curl into the dirt as I lift my head and breathe in deeply, marvelling at the way this place, of all places, is where I go to exorcise my demons.

Once upon a time, I hated this forest.

I hated the tiny cabin situated right in the heart of it. The one that still stands. The one that has my blood encrusted in its walls.

I hated the smell of earth and mud.

I hated the river that runs through it, and the twisted trees that loom overhead.

Now I *want* to be here.

It's no longer the place my father had to drag me kicking and screaming as a boy so he could teach me how to be a man.

Now it's my sanctuary.

After cutting off One five years ago I needed an outlet. I needed somewhere to shed my emotions and rid myself of weakness. My father was right to be persistent with his lessons. He understood that what I needed was to be reminded of my base needs, my animal instinct, my need to fight.

Fuck emotion.

Fuck feelings that mess with your head.

Fuck love.

Fuck that most of all.

I came here to deal with my unwanted emotions, to purge them from my system because even now, even after everything my father taught me, they still fucking haunt me. It's been a fight I've had to battle every fucking day of my life.

And now *she's* here, it's only gotten worse…

Fuck that. Screw her.

I won't allow her in my head a second longer.

Gritting my teeth, I stand, the muscles in my legs trembling from the exertion. I'm naked, covered head to toe in mud, my skin cut up from the countless times I've caught myself on low-hanging branches and prickly shrubs as I've run through the forest trying to free myself of this excess energy, these unwanted feelings.

The only thing I'm wearing is my smartwatch and that's telling me I need to get back to the castle because later today I have a business meeting to attend to in the city. Which is just as well, because, despite feeling more myself, I *still* need the distraction.

Guilt, anger, motherfucking lust, it all battles for my attention and whilst I might've rid myself of the tiny scrap of empathy I was beginning to feel because of her, those other feelings stubbornly remain.

"FUCKKKKKKKKK!" I tip my head back and roar into the forest, sending ravens up into the air, squawking and cawing over my sudden outburst.

She came all over my face and I liked it. I took her to my room of curiosities then fucked her mouth with my dick.

Then I hid what I did from my brothers.

I LIED to them.

And you lied to her too, a tiny voice inside my head says.

"Shut the fuck up!" I shout, slapping myself so hard that I stumble sideways. That little voice inside my head, the one that's been taunting me ever since we took her is determined to make me crack.

"Leave me the fuck alone!"

I can't. Look at yourself. Look at what you've become.

I'm a Mask. I'm Jakub-fucking-Brov.

You're your father's son, but you don't have to be.

"I want to be."

You don't.

Fisting my hands I head towards the nearest tree, yank at a low-hanging branch and rip it away from the trunk, then I hit myself across the thigh as hard as I can with it.

The pain registers, but it's not enough.

You remembered Star. You told her about Star. That means something.

"Zamknij się! SHUT UP!" I shout, hitting myself again and again, not caring that I'm running low on reserves, that I'm a step away from passing the fuck out. I don't care so long as it sets me free from this voice, from these feelings I don't want or need.

He killed Star and he beat you.

My throat tightens at the memory of that day when my father shot Star in front of me. Tears burn the back of my eyes but I refuse to feel the pain.

She was just a dog. She was *nothing*.

She was everything.

"Nie! No!"

I hit myself again.

He hurt you, but you don't want to hurt her, do you?

I hit myself harder, dropping to my knees from the force, panting. My chest heaves, my face is wet with tears as I let go of the branch. "I don't give a fuck about her!" I shout, bashing my fist against the tree trunk over and over again, not caring that my fists become torn and bloody.

You're lying. You want her.

I push the top of my head against the rough bark of the trunk and press my eyes shut, drawing in deep breaths, trying to temper the raging emotions within me. It's been almost two whole days since I came into the forest and it's never taken me this long to get my feelings under control.

Never.

I need to figure out how to stop this. I haven't become the man I am today so that a woman like her can bring me to my goddamn knees. My watch vibrates again, reminding me that my time is up. I have business to attend to. I have to go.

But first…

Opening my eyes, I stare at my cock. It's thick and hard, and like the rest of me covered in mud.

I've been hard since I fucking left her with Thirteen.

Hard. Engorged. In fucking pain.

I've leaked pre-cum every time I've imagined the taste of her pussy. My cock jerks, and my balls tingle as I remember how her birthmark darkened in shame when she had sucked me off.

You want her, my inner voice reminds me.

"Yes, I want her," I hiss, fisting my cock roughly. "Of course I want her! She's a piece of ass. Nothing more."

A piece of ass you actually want to fuck.

"Shut the fuck up!"

You feel things… You don't want to, but you do.

I yank at my cock, ignoring the voice and instead wank myself off imaging her tied to our bed, spread open and covered in our cum. I imagine Konrad using a paddle on her bare arse and Leon taking a blade to her scarred skin. I imagine my teeth making little indents in her rounded tits and her pussy weeping for us. I imagine her screaming in pain, in ecstasy. I imagine her tears, her sobs, her cries for us to stop, to keep going. I imagine cutting my initials into her skin with the knife I keep in the room of curiosities, eternally marking her.

You won't hurt her. You won't do it.

Gripping my dick tighter I push that voice away and imagine fisting her hair as I fuck her from behind. I imagine my brothers watching me take her virginity with jealousy in their eyes, because it is mine. *Mój.*

Her virginity is fucking mine.

See, she's already getting between you.

"No!" I grind out, battling with my conscience.

You gave her the chastity belt to save her from Leon and Konrad. You gave Thirteen the key to save her from yourself. You didn't tell your brothers about what you did because you knew they'd want the same, except they'd be rougher with her. You know that.

YOU CARE.

"I don't fucking care!" I shout, quickening my pace, tightening my grip as I grab my balls with my free hand and grit my teeth. I force the voice out of my head and try to recapture the fantasy I'd conjured, because it does turn me on. I do want to fuck her until she screams, I do want to share her with my brothers. I want to mark her. I want to see her marked by them. I want her whimpers. I want her kisses and her delicate flesh fluttering around my cock. I want to press my hand against her birthmark. I want to kiss her flaws and rub my cock over her scarred skin.

I. Want. It. All.

"Fucckkkkkk!" I grind out, my eyes rolling, my head falling back as the tendons in my neck flex with my orgasm. I come thinking about how much I want it all. How much I want *her* and how fucking wrong that is.

Drawing myself up on unsteady legs, my nostrils flare as I draw in a deep breath, coming to the only conclusion I can in the moment. I need to tell my brothers what I did. I need to tell them the truth.

No! My inner voice argues. *They'll hurt her.*

"Yes," I reply, feeling stronger for it. "I'm going to even the score. Konrad and Leon can have her too. I won't stop them."

Twisting on my feet, I stride back towards the castle, that voice in my head getting quieter and quieter the nearer I get to my home. By the time I reach our quarters I'm back to my old self, my dark heart safely tucked inside the thick bars of its cage.

CHAPTER 25

CHRISTY

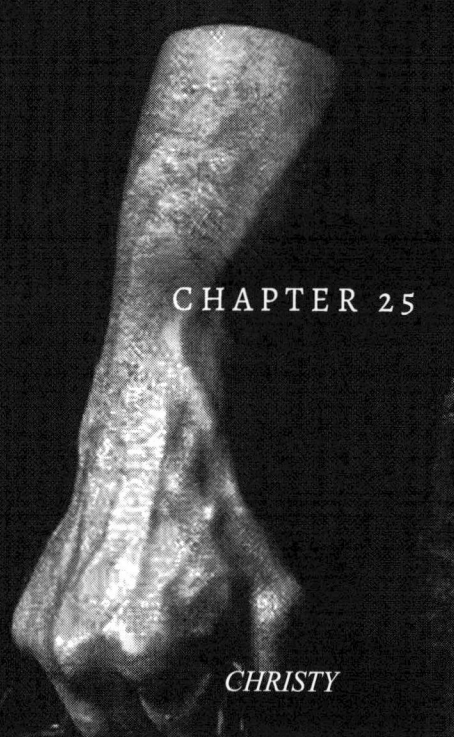

For two days I have lived side by side with the Numbers, rehearsing with them in the studio only returning to Thirteen's room to sleep and eat.

I don't see The Masks and the Numbers don't speak of them either.

Begrudgingly, I have to admit that the show One has put together *is* spectacular. It isn't just a series of routines, but an intricate marriage of gifted performances from each of the Numbers.

Aside from a few short appearances throughout the show, I have a solo dance routine right in the middle of the set to break up the acts performed on either side. One gave me carte blanche to choreograph my own routine, and a large part of me has found a huge sense of achievement in that, a *freedom* I've not felt before.

It's a dangerous feeling, one I refuse to get used to.

I won't lie, however. Over the past couple of days I've caught myself looking forward to performing in the show, then hating myself for it.

It feels like I'm giving up, that I'm giving in by taking part, by doing what The Masks have demanded. The only thing I'm holding on to is the fact that, unlike the other Numbers, I realise that's part of the manipulation. I'm not a fool. The Masks, with the help of One, have coerced the Numbers into obedience by giving them what they desire most: freedom to express themselves doing what they love. It seems unutterably cruel, an illusion made up of smoke and mirrors. Though, I guess that's the whole point.

Despite that knowledge, I've trained alongside the rest of the Numbers without complaint, playing my own game of obedience whilst I bide my time until the night of the show. *This* will be my chance to escape. The Numbers and The Masks will be too busy entertaining their clients to keep their eye on me. Thirteen is planning on keeping Twelve company for the evening, and the staff will be making sure everything is as it should be for the arrival of the guests.

It's the perfect opportunity to run.

It might be my *only* opportunity, and I'll be damned if I pass it up because I'm afraid I might fail. This brief moment of obedience, of achievement—however warped it may seem—won't stop me, because unlike the rest of the Numbers, I have a family outside of these castle walls that love me, miss me, and I *need* to get back to them.

"Good work, Zero. I'm impressed," One says as I finish up my routine, my thoughts whirring with plans of escape.

"Thank you," I mutter, crouching down to untie the ribbon from around my ankles as sweat trickles down my spine and sticks my hair to my forehead. Her words are kind, but her tone isn't. She's as masked as Jakub, Leon and Konrad are. But I see through her to the woman underneath. It seems unfathomable somehow, that something so pure can come from a woman who trades in dreams and illusions just like The Masks. The bottom line is I don't trust or respect One, even if the rest of the Numbers do.

"Are we done for today?" Ten asks, breaking the awkward silence between One and me as she stretches her arms above her head, her small tits bouncing as she moves from side-to-side. Her sisters are bare chested too as they change from one outfit to another. Of all the Numbers they're the oddest. Talking in tandem, finishing off each other's sentences. They're like one person cloned, without any defining personality traits to separate one from the other. It's bizarre.

But no more bizarre than the fact I've seen all of the Numbers in various stages of undress over the past couple of days, to the point where I no longer feel embarrassed looking at them naked. They're comfortable in their skin in a way I wish I could be.

"Yes. We're done. You're free to leave. *All* of you," she adds, when Three, Seven and Six linger, waiting for me. "I wish to speak with Zero alone."

"Zero?" Six asks, tentatively, a question in her gaze.

"She's fine!" One snaps, brooking no arguments. "Get changed, go to your rooms, eat, and get a good night's sleep. We have one last rehearsal tomorrow in the theatre before Saturday's performance."

"Theatre?" I ask.

"You didn't think we performed for our guests here, did you?"

"I suppose not," I agree, wondering where the theatre is located in the castle and marvelling at the fact they even have one.

It takes a few minutes for all the Numbers to change and leave. Once they're gone, One turns her attention back to me as I slide out of my pointes and stand, revelling in the feeling of wiggling my toes, easing the throb in my feet. I've not danced this much in years and the rigorous training and rehearsals over the past couple of days have taken their toll on my body, specifically my feet which are bruised from constantly dancing in pointes. My toenails are cracked and bleeding, and I have blisters covering my heels and almost every toe knuckle. But it's a good kind of pain. The kind that comes from a sense of achievement, much like a carpenter might feel from the calluses on his hands when building a piece of furniture from scratch.

"It's such a shame. You really could have fit in so well with us," One says, her fingertips grazing against the strap of the satin pink dress she gave me to wear two days ago. This is the first time I've worn it and she didn't bother to hide her surprise or her disgust when she saw my scars.

"You think I'm ugly," I say, knowing it to be true.

One flicks a strand of long dark hair over her shoulder, her almond eyes assessing me. "What I think doesn't matter. If Jakub wants you to perform in the show, then you'll perform in the show."

"Do you always do what he says?"

"Yes."

I shake my head, turning my back to her as I pull up my dress and hang it up on the rail with the other costumes the Numbers will be wearing, quickly covering back up with a long, navy-blue, knee length dress Thirteen gave me to wear. I've not seen her all day. She's been tending to Twelve's wounds that have become a little infected according to Five, who alerted Thirteen to the fact this morning.

"Will there be anything else?" I ask.

One narrows her eyes at me, considering her answer. "I think, perhaps, we should find you something else to wear for the show," she says, her dark eyes filled with a malevolence that has me taking a step away from her. "No one needs to see your scars. You understand that we have a certain standard to uphold."

"Whatever you want," I reply tightly, refusing to bite. "I didn't want to wear this dress in the first place."

"Agreed. She's to put on something else," a deep, familiar voice says. "Make sure she's covered neck to toe. We don't need the clients seeing her flaws."

I stiffen at the roughness of Konrad's voice and the guarded look on his face as he stares at me.

Fuck him. Maybe I should wear the dress after all, if only to piss him and his arsehole brothers off.

One's eyes widen with shock before she schools her features and turns to face Konrad as he strides towards us both. He's wearing a plain blue half-mask that both matches my dress *and* his sweater. Not that I give a damn. I couldn't care less about what he chooses to wear or how handsome he looks with his hair slicked back off his face and his short scruff neatly trimmed. His good looks are just another disguise used to lull everyone into a false sense of security.

"Good afternoon, Konrad. Is there something you need?" she asks him, her accented voice dropping an octave or two. For all her sophistication, she's not particularly subtle with her eagerness to seduce him. Looks like Twelve isn't the only one who wants to be fucked by him.

"Other than you leaving... *No.*" He lets that hang in the air, unperturbed by how her cheeks flame red at his rebuff.

"You want *me* to leave?" she questions, caught between embarrassment and shock. Seems to me that she's not used to being dismissed in such a manner.

"I have something I wish to discuss with Zero that doesn't concern you," he explains.

Her brows raise. "And what about Jakub? Does it concern him too?"

"One, you may be the matriarch of the Numbers, but you are not and never will be more than what we *allow* you to be. Don't forget your place, and never question my intentions again. Understood?"

"Understood. I shall leave," she replies with a tight smile, cutting her gaze to me momentarily.

Despite her clear dislike for me, I don't want to be left alone with Konrad. "I'd rather you stay," I say quickly.

Ignoring my plea, she folds her arms across her chest and says, "Zero is due a toilet break soon. It's been a while since she last relieved herself." And just like that she makes me a lesser human, reminding me that I'm no more than a pet.

"You have the key?" Konrad asks sharply, his eagerness to get hold of it obvious.

"No. Thirteen does."

"Then I will ensure Zero is back in Thirteen's care in good time to piss and shit," he replies, my cheeks flaming with embarrassment as he jerks his chin towards the door. "Out."

"Yes, of course," she says tightly, throwing one last look my way before exiting the studio.

Konrad waits for the door to slam shut before he returns his attention back to me. His slow perusal has me stiffening with fear, my mouth drying. Swallowing hard, I straighten my spine and fix him with a heavy stare.

"What do you want?" I ask, stepping out of the corner of the room, instinct telling me that I shouldn't allow him to trap me there. I can't help but wince at the pain in my sore feet. I really need to soak and wrap them. Hopefully Thirteen will have some kind of ointment to help heal the blisters and cuts, or at least dull the pain. In fact, I'm counting on it.

"How are rehearsals going?" he asks, throwing me off balance with his question as he takes in my appearance. His nostrils flare when he sees the state of my feet. "One has certainly been working you hard."

"She has," I reply tightly. I'm not sure what I expected, but a polite conversation wasn't it.

"Is that all you have to say?"

"I'm not sure what you want me to say."

"Aren't you enjoying being able to dance, being a part of something? It must be better than spending your time with the dying. What kind of job is that anyway?" he asks, tucking his hands in the pocket of his jeans.

The act is as casual as the clothes he's wearing, but for some reason it makes me more nervous around him, not less. "A job I no longer have, thanks to you!" I snap. "And I would enjoy being able to dance more if I were back home with the family I love."

"Hmm, back to that again."

His tone of voice irks me. "*Back to that again?*" I repeat, shaking my head with incredulity. "You think that by giving me a few days of peace and the ability to dance that I would just roll over and do what you want. Unbelievable."

He shrugs. "Well, you haven't tried to run these past couple of days. Seems to me you're settling in rather well, Zero."

"Screw you," I mutter, stepping around him and immediately gritting my jaw on the sudden feeling that I'm walking on broken glass. "This conversation is over."

Until it isn't.

I feel the rush of warm air moments before Konrad sweeps me off my feet and clutches me against his chest, his musky scent filling my nose. "I'm going to fix up your feet," he says gruffly, his deep voice rumbling through his chest and into my body.

"I'm perfectly capable of doing it myself," I snarl, trying to twist out of his hold, but he just grips me tighter, his fingers digging painfully into my flesh.

"Keep doing that, Zero, and see where it gets you," he warns, lowering his mouth and brushing his lips gently against my forehead. There's a sweetness to his kiss, despite the way he bruises my flesh. The two sensations fight for dominance, my body reeling from both the abuse and the affection. Neither are welcome.

"Put me down."

"Believe it or not, I'm not in the mood for a fight."

"I won't fight you," I insist, lying through my teeth. Jakub had promised he'd keep them away. He lied. Instinct tells me that if I don't get away from Konrad then something bad is going to happen, something I might not recover from. He's on edge, despite the smiles and the fakery.

"Why don't I believe you, Zero?" he murmurs just as Leon enters the hall.

My heart stills in my chest as I take in his appearance.

It's not his clothing, which is as casual as Konrad's, but his mask that makes my breath hitch. It's jet black, shaped into a demon's face with teeth that drop over his top lip and silver-tipped horns that are pointy and sharp as a knife. His mask is terrifying, reflecting the monster that resides within him.

"NO!" I shout, bucking in Konrad's arms as my heart drops the beat fear holds captive, rattling my ribcage with dread.

"You really don't get it, do you?" Konrad grinds out, keeping me gripped in his arms despite me thrashing around like a fish out of water. "You're *ours*."

"Help!" I scream, calling for someone, *anyone* to intervene as Leon strides towards us both. "Please, help me!"

"Nobody's coming, Nought. Thirteen is looking after Twelve, and Jakub is attending to business in town. For a couple of hours you're ours to play with," Leon says, grasping my jaw roughly and pressing his body against my side, so that I'm sandwiched between the two powerful men.

My hands fly up as I push against both their chests, trying to shove them away, feeling claustrophobic, unable to breathe, frantic with fear. "You had an agreement," I say, grasping for something, *anything*, to stop them from acting on their base needs.

"Which Jakub broke the second he put his cock into your willing mouth," Leon sneers. "I heard that for a virgin you're quite the whore."

I drag in a breath and stop fighting, too surprised to do anything else but question him. "How did you know about that?" I whisper.

Konrad lowers his head, his gaze sharp, unyielding. "Jakub just told us about your little indiscretion. He gave us permission to even the score. He *left* you with us, Zero."

"No!" I whisper.

"Yes! Now you're ours for the taking." Leon grins and places a rag over my mouth, a poisonous, caustic smell assailing my nostrils before darkness claims me.

CHAPTER 26

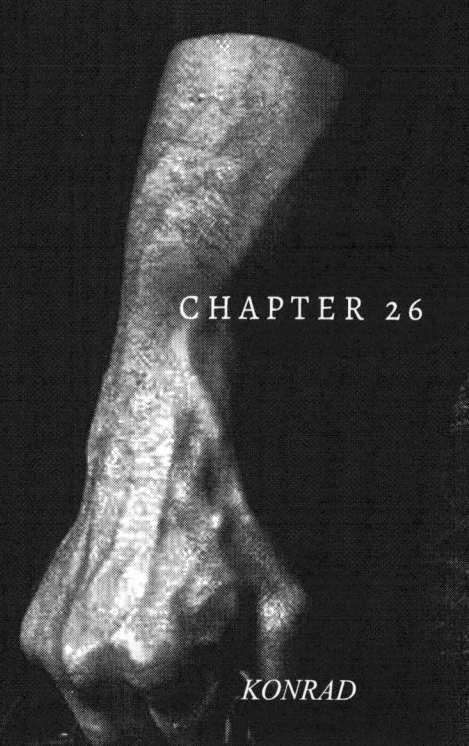

KONRAD

Naked and strapped to the St Andrew's Cross I keep for special occasions such as this, Zero's eyes flutter open. She's only been out twenty minutes, but long enough for Leon and I to undress her and fix her in place, spread-eagled, vulnerable and locked in this cell with us. Down here in the dungeons no one will hear her scream, and fuck if that doesn't make me hard.

She moans, her head swaying between her shoulders as she fights her way back to consciousness. Her back is bare, her scars a tapestry of healed trauma against her otherwise perfectly smooth skin.

When she'd turned her back on us in the Grand Hall, baring her secret, there wasn't a dry cock in the room. She'd thought we would be disgusted, but fuck, her scars had the opposite affect.

Leon saw pain endured and overcome.

Jakub saw beauty within the ugliness.

And me? I'd seen something that still needed healing.

Inflicting pain might harden my dick, but healing the wounds I make gets me off.

"Please…" Zero moans, her long, fiery hair tickling her bare breasts as she lifts her head and fights to stay awake.

"Shh, take it easy," I whisper, pressing my lips against the pebbled flesh of her arm. Tasting her sweetness. My tongue licks over her skin, loving the way she trembles beneath my touch.

"D—don't."

The sound of her voice is both ecstasy and agony. I've thought about nothing else since the evening in the Grand Hall when she came so beautifully beneath our touch then fought so valiantly to regain control of the situation. She will never know, but in that moment, when she bared her true self to us, she'd owned us. All three of us, *including* Leon. And no one has ever owned him.

Keeping away from Zero hasn't been easy. Never before has a woman got beneath our skin quite like she has. Jakub was right, she *is* a distraction. A dangerous one.

Saturday night we've got clients arriving to watch the Numbers perform in The Menagerie, and to indulge in pleasures afterwards. We need our heads in the game, but keeping away from Zero has had the opposite effect.

For the last few days we've been a trio of fucked-up-ness.

In one last ditch attempt to get control of the situation, Jakub confessed to what happened between them in his room of curiosities. Short of fucking her or killing her, Jakub gave us carte blanche to take what we need in order for us to get over these sudden debilitating feelings.

Feelings that The Masks are *not* supposed to have.

It's a solid plan, but it's fucking flawed.

Jakub's a damn fool if he doesn't see that.

Zero is damaged by her past. She's deformed by her birthmark and scars, but still undeniably beautiful, and different enough to be classed as unusual with her red hair, strange eyes and body covered in freckles.

She's Jakub's perfect woman.

She's *our* perfect woman.

And fuck if my cock doesn't weep for her.

I've been hard, *manic,* since that night she bared herself, crazed and out of my damn mind. Countless times I've headed towards Thirteen's room only to return to my own so I could wank myself off with violent tugs, and curb my need for her.

Right now I want to thrash her raw for making me feel this way. I want to redden the skin on her arse and thighs, then I want to soothe and heal the parts I break, stitch her up, and piece her back together only to do it all over again.

It's a sickness. A *need* that I must fulfil.

If I'm feeling that way, then fuck knows how Leon is faring. By the look on his face, not well.

He's been like a bear with a sore head, working out in his gym until he passes out, all so he can keep away from Zero and not let loose. Admittedly, him being here is a risk, but at least I'll be able to stop him should he go too far. The fact of the matter is, we both tried to stay away, but the second Jakub admitted what he'd done, it was game over.

He took from her. Now it's our turn.

"It's time," Leon remarks, pushing off from the wall and testing the lock on the door.

"It's secure. No one can enter," I reassure him.

Down here, in my domain, our masks have been removed. We won't be interrupted.

Stepping in front of Zero, Leon lifts her chin, studying her face, then says, "Hello, Nought. Konrad and I are so looking forward to playing with you."

"No!" she shouts, jerking in his hold. Her skin flushes from her feet upwards, tingeing her in a shade of pink as pretty as the dress One picked out for her performance this weekend.

"*Yes*," he croons, stroking his fingers down her ribcage and skirting across the side of her gently rounded stomach.

"Don't fucking touch me!" The chains rattle in her attempt to free herself, and her head snaps upwards as she realises that she's once again held captive. "You *arsehole*!"

"*Arseholes*," Leon corrects, casting a look at me. "You've got two for the price of one. Think you can handle us?"

"Not able to manage me on your *own*, is that it?" she taunts, fighting with her words.

Leon laughs, his fingers digging into her chin as he plants a hard kiss against her mouth, forcing his tongue between her teeth and fucking her lips like a demon possesed. She stiffens, her muscles straining beneath her skin as she tries to rip her face away from his. Leon, however, doesn't let up. Grasping her roughly, he kisses her like he fucks. Brutally.

I can't say that my cock isn't hard, because it is.

She screams into his mouth, and he jerks away."Fuck, *yes*! Do that again," he hisses, his lip bloody from where she's bitten him. "Your fight is one of the things I fucking love about you."

"Love? You wouldn't know the meaning of the word, you sick prick!" Zero spits venomously.

Leon grins, his teeth stained red. "You're right, I don't know anything about love, but I know a great deal about *pain*. You've no idea how much I crave yours."

"Leave me the hell alone!" she shouts, trying in vain to release her wrists and ankles.

The sound of the chains rattling makes my cock leap with anticipation. Today Leon and I will inflict pain and draw out her pleasure. Then I'll heal her wounds, soothe her, care for her, fucking *dote* on her.

"We don't want to," I say, pushing off from the wall. I move around her, my fingers trailing over the bare skin of her arse, then up across her ravaged back. Her teeth chatter from the contact and the fear. "You can fight this, but it will only hurt more. Just let this happen, Zero, it doesn't have to be all bad. We can make this good for you."

"It will never be good for me. *Never*," she seethes, her lips tainted with Leon's blood.

She looks wild. Fucking beautiful despite the birthmark marring her skin. I've no doubt if she wasn't chained up she'd fight us until her last breath.

"Then we will take your pain, and gorge on it, if that's what you want," Leon says, reaching out and twisting her nipple hard.

She cries out, her spine arching. "I don't want to feel pain, you arsehole! I've lived through enough of it!"

Leon flinches as though slapped. Then he schools his features. "Too bad."

"Let me counter it with pleasure," I jump in, wanting to soothe, to ease the growing tension. I replace Leon's fingers with my mouth, sucking her puckered nipple between my lips and gently easing the throb with my tongue. She bucks against the cross, but I reach around her back, pinning her in place so I can suck and tease. Taste and lick.

"*Please*," she whimpers, her teeth grinding together when Leon twists her other nipple.

"Please what, Zero?" I press, trailing my finger around her areola, spreading my saliva into her pink-tinged skin.

"Don't hurt me." Her voice cracks on a sob, and Leon tips his head back revelling in the sound.

"That's like asking me not to breathe. I *will* hurt you, Nought, but Konrad will counter that with pleasure. That's all we can offer," Leon says, stripping off his t-shirt and baring his chest to her.

Taking that as my cue, I begin to undress as well.

"What are you doing?" she asks, her eyes frantically flicking from me to Leon and back again as we both strip naked. It's a shame she's still trussed up in that chastity belt, but Jakub was right to do what he did. Fucking her will only release the beasts within us, so for now this will have to be enough.

"This is how it's going to go," Leon says, lazily stroking his cock as he addresses her, the muscles of his chest and thighs rippling beneath his black tattoos. Of the three of us, his skin is covered the most. Black reed-like tattoos wind up from his feet, legs and torso. He's never told me the significance of them, and I've never asked though I suspect it's to do with the underground lake he loves to swim in. "For every cut—"

"*Cut?*" she screeches, her voice pitching higher as she cuts him off.

"For every cut I give you," he continues, rubbing his thumb over the thick head of his dick, smearing pre-cum, "Konrad will pleasure you."

"No, *please*," she whispers, tears pooling in her eyes and tipping over her lashes.

Unable to help myself, I lick them from her skin, my tongue trailing across her cheek towards her plump lips. Capturing her mouth with mine, I kiss her, pushing my tongue past her lips as she sobs.

"Concentrate on me, on the pleasure I will give you," I say, pulling back slightly so that I can cup her face. "Trust me to take care of you, Zero. I *will* take care of you."

I'm asking a lot. There's no reason why she would trust me, but right here and now, I'm the lesser of two evils. I think she knows that.

Out of the corner of my eye, I see Leon reach for his knife that's resting on the chair behind him. Its blade is no bigger than a few inches, but it's sharp and entirely deadly. In the wrong hands it could do untold damage. In his hands, it *has* done untold damage, but I know my brother, he won't kill her... Not yet, anyway.

The thought of him unleashing himself completely on her quickens my pulse, stirring up unwelcome feelings. Feelings I haven't experienced in a very, very long time.

I push them away forcefully.

"Oh, God," she whimpers.

"Look at me. Concentrate on me, okay?"

"Okay," she nods, her gaze flicking back to mine. Her strange eyes cut me deeper than a knife ever could, slicing right into the black tar of my soul, slashing through the viscous darkness, twisting, churning me up.

Fuck, her eyes are so expressive. *Haunting,* actually.

Ever since we stole her she's haunted my dreams. I've dreamt about her eyes welling with tears, her lips wrapped around my cock, her hair fisted in my hand. I've lain awake at night fantasising about fucking her pretty pink pussy. Taking and giving. Fucking and fighting. I've orgasmed into my fist like a fucking teenage boy remembering the lashes I'd given her and imagining how it would feel to do it all over again. I've practically lost my mind thinking about healing the wounds I inflict.

Inflict pain, then heal. Whip, then soothe. Fuck roughly, then carress gently. I'm a man of two halves. Black and white. Yin and Yang. I can separate both sides of me. Be one or the other at any given moment. Leon, however, is Yin. All darkness. Jakub is the grey in between, a mixture of both. He doesn't belong with light or with dark, only the shadows.

Truth be known, Zero's sunk so deep into my head that most days I feel like I'm fucking drowning. I need to anchor myself, and she's going to help me to do that. Right the fuck now.

With her face clasped gently in my hands, we breathe in tandem, a steady rhythm linking us in the moment. She searches my face, frowning. Her hot breath tickles my face, sending goosebumps scattering over every inch of my skin. Fuck, this woman makes me insane with want.

Blinking back her shock at Leon caressing the skin of her back, Zero clears her throat, struggling to comprehend what's about to happen. "Who hurt you?" she asks, her voice soft, gentle, kinder than I deserve as she stares at my scar. She's trying to take her mind off what's about to happen, knowing that soon Leon will hurt her. I understand that. I indulge her.

"A client got out of control. He broke our rules and almost killed Eleven. I fought him, he cut me."

"What happened to him?"

"Leon killed him," I say, pressing my lips against hers.

"He deserved it," Leon mutters. Her body quakes beneath his touch as his fingers trail over her scarred skin, searching for the perfect spot to cut. "The fucker wouldn't take no for an answer. He hurt Eleven..."

"And yet, you're hurting *me*," Zero whispers.

"Yes," he admits. "But it's not the same."

"It isn't? How so?"

"Because Eleven wasn't his. You, however, are *ours*."

"Even when I don't want to be?" she asks, her voice quivering as he traces her ruined skin with his fingertip.

"Especially then."

"Then nothing I say will stop you. Just do what you need to do. I want it over with," she says, steeling herself, blinking back the tears, toughening up. The transformation is exquisite.

She might've shown her fear, but now she shows her courage.

Taking that as his cue, Leon raises the knife, and locks eyes with me. "Take a deep breath, Zero. I'm going to cut you now," he whispers, before sliding the knife across her skin a few inches beneath the base of her neck where the burns start. It's a small cut, no bigger than half an inch, but it bleeds beautifully.

Leon's gaze is transfixed on the spot as he watches her blood rise to the surface then spill in tiny droplets down her back. Zero gasps, her eyes widening, her muscles flexing, skin flushing. Her mouth pops open and I kiss her, swallowing her pain, consuming it. My tongue soothes her whimpers as my hands gently cup her breasts.

"That's it. Easy now," I say against her blush lips.

We all take a breath, centering ourselves back in the moment, then with a wicked grin, Leon bends over and licks the cut he made, sliding his tongue along the slit, tasting her essence. He's fucked up like that.

He wasn't always that way.

Leon used to be the kind of person who protected the people he loved from pain. The amount of times he shielded Jakub and me, accepting our punishment from The Collector as his own. He did it out of love, knowing that of the three of us he was the strongest. That he could take it.

But it fundamentally changed him.

The lessons we endured. The teachings our father bestowed upon us.

It changed us all.

A switch was flipped in our minds. Turning off compassion and empathy and replacing it with a craving for twisted, dark things. The men we are today are so far removed from the boys we once were, it's as though they never existed. Our father wiped them off the face of the Earth and the three of us grew up in their place.

Stronger. Tougher. Fucked up. Less... *human*.

Knowing that, understanding who we are, I kiss Zero deeper, getting off on her whimpers that she's so desperately trying to hold in, revelling in the growing heat from our combined bodies locked in this cell together. My cock fills with blood, my erection punching the air, weeping for her.

I fucking weep for her.

Pre-cum dribbles from my slit as blood dribbles from her cut. It feels right somehow, Leon cutting her, marking her, whilst she conjures up our pleasure with her pain.

Everything needs balance. Of the three of us, I'm usually the best equipped to provide that.

Tonight, however, we work together. Leon punishes, whilst I pleasure.

Kneeling on the cold stone floor, I fist my cock, covering her nipple with my mouth, swirling her rosy tip with my tongue, sucking and coaxing. I'd told Zero that Leon can make a woman come just by playing with her tits, and he can, but so too can Jakub and I. We were taught from a very young age how to fuck a woman right. Our father knew the power inflicting pain could wield just as much as he understood that pleasure can be used to manipulate and coerce. He made sure we experienced both from the women he brought home for us to practice on. By the time One arrived, we'd all fucked dozens of women, our adolescent bodies experiencing the kind of pleasure only men should.

What can I say? We had a fucked-up childhood like that.

As I cup the globes of Zero's breasts, squeezing gently, Leon makes another small cut. She shudders against the cross, her tits wobbling, thighs trembling, a soft whimper escaping her lips.

Lowering my hands over her rib cage towards the waistband of her chastity belt, I give it a gentle tug. The leather is soft, pliable, but too tight for me to access her pussy and pleasure her with my fingers. That doesn't mean I can't rub her over the leather though, or use the chastity belt as friction against her cunt.

Licking and sucking on her tits, I rub my fingers between her parted legs, making sure to pay attention to her clit with my thumb. Even with the leather separating us, I feel the heat, smell the heady scent of her arousal. She moans softly, her head resting against her arm. Lips parted, eyes unfocused.

Leon licks at her blood, his tongue smeared claret as he fists his cock. Then he makes another, deeper cut and I watch as he covers his palm in her blood and grasps his cock, using it to slicken himself up.

Twisted motherfucker.

He wants her virginity, and this is his way of staking a claim. Well, he can enjoy fisting his dick covered in her blood from the cut he made, because I'll be fucked if he takes her virginity.

That's all *mine*.

"Fuck, yes," he groans, locking eyes with me.

There's a challenge in his gaze. I know what he's thinking: can I override the pain he's dishing out? It's a tough ask, given I don't have every inch of her at my disposal, but I've never shied away from a challenge.

Lifting upwards, I kiss her again, tugging on her breasts, her nipples, pulling on the chastity belt and capturing her whimpers. Her body is lax, loose, not strained as I'd expected.

She's responsive, but not pliable.

She's taking as much as she's giving.

When I kiss her, she kisses me back, her tongue searching, her moans sending red-hot lust straight to my cock. My balls tingle and without thinking about what I'm doing, I break the kiss and slide my fingers into her mouth.

"Suck," I demand.

She sucks, wetting them up good.

Fisting myself, I kiss her.

She groans, I moan.

I drop to my knees again then slide my tongue up the inside of her leg, her scent like raspberries and sunwarmed skin. When I reach the apex of her thighs, I run my tongue over the tendons stretched taut from her position, showing me a sliver of her outer pussy lips. I lick her there as Leon cuts her back again. She lets out a cry of pain, and I drop my dick, wanting her pleasure more than my own. Adjusting my position, I press the pads of my thumbs against her pussy and find her clit pressing against the leather, rubbing in small, circular motions with just the right amount of pressure.

"Please," she murmurs, but she's not pleading for us to stop this time, she's pleading to come.

Sweat beads across her forehead. Her eyes are heated, angry, but lust-filled.

This is turning her on.

"You like this?" I ask, but it's more of an observation really. "You like the pain and the pleasure?"

"No!"

"You're lying," Leon says, bringing the blade up to his palm and cutting into the flesh. With blood dripping from the cut, he reaches around and slides it up her neck, marking her with his blood. "You like being touched like this, *cut* like this. There's a need in you, Nought. We can sense it. *I* can sense it. You're not as pure and innocent as you'd like us to think. You're different too."

"No. You sick fuck. No!" But even as she's cursing him, she's opening her mouth and wrapping her tongue around his finger, sucking his blood like she's been into blood play her whole damn life.

"Do you want us to stop?" I ask her, grasping her breast and drawing her nipple into my mouth.

"Yes..." she hisses.

"Liar!" Leon insists, withdrawing his finger and pinching her other nipple whilst he whispers in her ear. "You want to feel alive. Nothing does that quite like being strapped to this cross with one man desperate to fuck you raw and the other wanting to bleed the life from your veins. We both want you but for very different reasons."

"You want to kill me?" she asks, tears seeping from her eyes.

"I want to do so many fucking things to you, Nought. So many fucking things... I want to put my dick in your mouth and watch you choke on my cock. I want to take your virginity and smear myself in your blood. I want your tears and your cries of pain. I want your silence. I want you to scream my name with fire in your blood and violence in your soul. I. Want. It. All."

"*No*," she whimpers, tears streaming from her eyes.

"But I can't have any of that right now because you don't just belong to me, you belong to Konrad and Jakub, and they need you too."

Leon reaches up and grabs her hair, fisting it. Pulling her head back he bites her neck, sucking and licking and running his lips all over the tender flesh. He tugs her earlobe between his teeth, before scraping his stubble over her birthmarked cheek. Despite her fear, she moans at his attention, at mine. She's so fucking twisted up by the fear, pain and pleasure, that she can't unravel herself enough to fight back with words.

She's lost herself in the moment.

And if that isn't freeing, I don't know what the fuck is.

Right now she's more free than she's ever been in her closeted little life.

"Fuck!" Leon grinds out, fisting his bloody dick violently as he lets her hair go and loses himself to the moment too.

He jacks off whilst I coax out her pleasure, his free hand sliding over her back, smearing blood over every inch. As far as I can tell, he's only made two shallow cuts and one deeper one, but her groans of pain would indicate that it isn't just the sting from cuts that hurt her, but him simply *touching* her back. But how is that possible? She said that she was eight when she was burned in the fire, that was years ago. How can her scarred back still cause pain?

Then it dawns on me. It's *psychological.*

Her pain is in her head.

And fuck if my dick doesn't grow in size at the thought. "Jesus, *fuck*," I mutter.

When I look up at her bowed head, her hair hanging around her face in a curtain, I see how her gaze goes in and out of focus. It's as though she's trying and failing to switch off the pain. We'd all witnessed how she'd done exactly that when I'd whipped her in the Grand Hall a few days ago, but she's finding it difficult to do so now. The pleasure she's feeling is keeping her in the moment, anchoring her in her body. She's riding the knife edge, literally, and there's something so fucking hedonistic about that.

"Leon. She's trying to escape. Cut her again," I demand.

He's already pressing the tip of the blade into her skin before I've even finished the sentence. "There, that's it. Bleed for me, Christy," Leon says, too in the moment to realise what he's just said.

Christy.

Fuck!

Her spine bows, her tits pressing into my face as her head tips back. Dropping the knife to the floor with a clatter, Leon presses up against her back, and wraps his hand around her throat. I meet his gaze, recognising the hunger in his eyes, the need to own and destroy, for violence, but there's a shadow of something else too. He wants to keep her. He wants to keep the girl, Christy, not the Number.

"You're ours. For as long as we live and breathe!" he says possessively, and with that promise he bucks against her ravaged and bloody back squeezing her throat, strings of cum spurting all over her as he orgasms.

Moments later he steps beside me—his cock covered in their blood, his release—and does something that surprises me. Leon cups Zero's face and kisses her with utmost care. He isn't rough, he doesn't take, he *gives*. He gives her a sweet, loving kiss as his thumbs stroke her cheekbones gently, reverently.

For the first time since we became The Masks, I see Leon the boy and not the man and in that defining moment, I know one thing; we're all fucking screwed.

"Make her come," he demands.

I don't hesitate, I make her come.

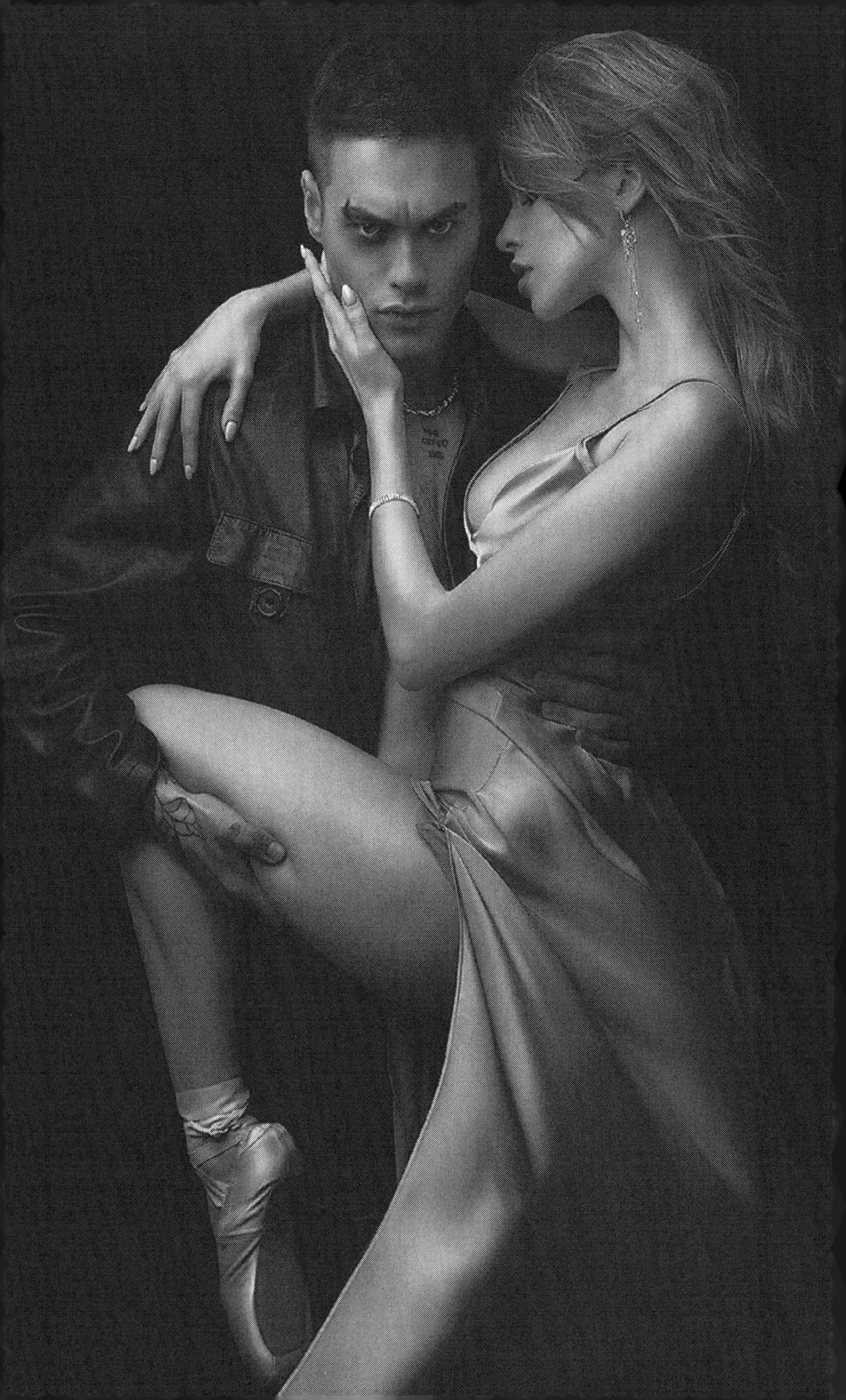

CHAPTER 27

CHRISTY

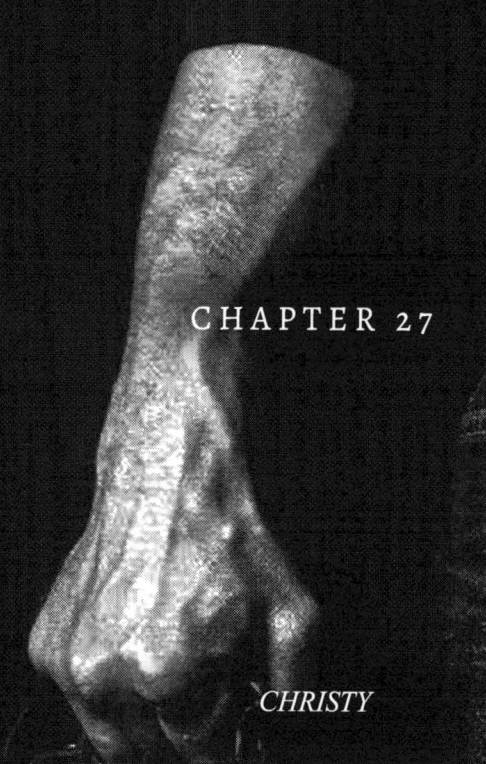

Lying face down on Thirteen's bed naked bar the chastity belt, I stare off into the distance, listening to the rain as it lashes against the window. Fat droplets roll down the windowpane and somewhere in the distance thunder rumbles as Konrad inspects the cuts on my back now that I'm clean from the shower.

"I need to stitch up this cut Leon made," Konrad says, brushing my damp hair off my face. "It's deeper than the others. Those will heal up on their own."

Thirteen slams something down on the worktop behind us. Since finding out what happened she's made it perfectly clear with her actions that she's unhappy with the events of this evening. It surprises me, given she did nothing to prevent Leon from whipping Twelve's back bloody and raw. So why are a few cuts on my back any different? The truth is, they're not.

"Leon held back, Thirteen…" Konrad says, his voice trailing off when she snorts with contempt. Leaning over me, he brushes his knuckles across my bare arm. "It could've been a lot worse."

I'm not sure what he wants me to say. Thank you? Not going to happen.

"Just sew me up, please."

From the moment he unlocked my wrists and ankles, Konrad has been nothing but attentive, affectionate, *caring*. He carried me up to Thirteen's room and stayed by my side, giving me sips of water, feeding me small bites of the ham sandwich Nala brought up half an hour ago. He's shown me nothing but care, a stark contrast to what I've experienced since arriving here.

But it's all a lie.

It isn't a selfless act. He doesn't truly care about me, about what they've all put me through. This is about him *getting off*. I'm as certain of that as I am of Leon's need to inflict pain through violence. The pair are twisted bastards and Jakub is no better, seeing as he gave me over to them. He broke his promise.

Behind us Thirteen brews a concoction to soothe my cuts and encourage healing. She's furious with him, with Leon, that much is obvious, but she's also angry at herself.

She feels responsible for what's happened to me.

She isn't.

The Masks are.

I am.

The need to survive is a funny thing. Since I've been here I've gone through a gamut of emotions. I've oscillated between fear, anger, *and lust* until I've felt sick with it. But one thing has remained constant: my need to go home.

Just because they've made me come, have given me pleasure in situations I'd never dreamed would be pleasurable, doesn't mean I want to stay. Just because they've all kissed me like I really am theirs, that I belong to them, doesn't mean I do. Just because my visions have been telling me for years that The Masks are my future, doesn't mean I want them to be.

I might be *theirs* but I'm aware that there is a time limit on that ownership.

That at some point in the near future, they're going to kill me.

I've seen it in their eyes. It's an inevitability.

Maybe that's why I haven't had any more visions. I can't see into the future if I don't have one.

"Thank you, Thirteen," Konrad says after dropping the wet cloth back in the bowl sitting on the side table and taking the tray from her which holds a needle and surgical thread.

She breathes out a huff of air and sits on the bed beside me, holding my hand. Her gaze is filled with apology, regret. I don't bother to try and reassure her that I'm okay because I'm not. Nothing about what happened today was okay. Nothing.

Konrad and Leon think that because I came, because I *chose* to take some pleasure from the situation, that I'm beginning to accept my place here. They couldn't be more wrong.

I'm going to destroy them.

Not Grim, not Beast, but me.

Me.

Because something else happened in that cell today that made me realise the power *I* hold.

Leon might've cut me, he might've made me bleed, but he didn't come out of the experience unscathed. He called me *Christy.*

I got to him.

And if I can get to him, then I can get to Jakub and Konrad too.

"I'm going to sew you up now," Konrad says, echoing Leon's words when he was about to cut me. I nod my head, keeping my gaze fixed on the rainclouds, grey and stormy, just like my heart. "Thirteen, you can leave us."

She looks at me with concern lingering in her eyes. If I asked her to stay, she would stay and I have a feeling not even Konrad could make her leave.

"It's okay, go."

"I won't hurt her," Konrad says, sounding sincere. She must believe him, because she nods, squeezes my hand then leaves me alone with a monster.

"She cares about you," Konrad remarks the moment the door clicks shut. "You seem to have an uncanny ability to make people do that. What is it about you, Zero?"

"Thirteen cares about all the Numbers," I say, forcing myself not to register the pain as his fingers rest against my back.

"She does. She's a good person. Fuck knows why she came back here..."

Konrad's voice trails off, distracted by the task at hand. I feel the sharp sting of the needle passing through my skin, but I allow my eyes to drift shut, and do what I couldn't do in the dungeon, and compartmentalise the pain.

"Came back here?" I ask softly.

"Our families have history, let's just leave it at that."

"They're okay with her being here?"

Konrad laughs. "I doubt they even know where she is."

I don't press for further information, sensing Konrad clamming up. Instead, I lay still as he sews me up. With each stitch his breathing seems to get heavier and the tension in the air thickens. I'm facing the opposite way from him but there's no doubt that he's getting turned on.

It's bizarre. Twisted.

"There, all fixed," he says eventually, his voice tight with lust.

When I hear the sound of his zipper undoing, I can't help but shift position and turn my head to face him. He locks eyes with me as he pulls his dick free from his trousers, fisting it at the base.

He doesn't say another word, and I can barely even gather my own thoughts as his gaze flicks to my back and he starts to slowly move his fist up and down his cock. Konrad's mouth parts as he licks his lips and reaches with his free hand to run his fingers over my scarred back, circling the cut he's just stitched up. It's all I can do not to bolt off the bed.

"Fuck, Zero. I've never wanted anyone more in my life," he admits, rubbing his thumb over the slit of his dick. "I want to fix you so bad. I want to hurt you and fix you, then hurt you and fix you all over again."

I watch him as he jerks off. He's big, just like Leon and Jakub, but where they have been circumcised, he still has foreskin. For a moment

I allow my gaze to linger on his dick, fascinated by the way his foreskin stretches and gathers as he moves his hand.

It's sexy, there's no denying that. A man who looks like him, is as virile and as masculine as he is, fisting his cock and getting off because of me, is a turn on. It's another new experience, but I'm well aware that it's just one more mindfuck. It's one thing to let these men take my pleasure when I have no other choice, but another thing altogether if I allow myself to give it up without force. I can't allow myself to cross that boundary again if I'm to remain strong enough to fight them.

"Why do you want to hurt me, then fix me?" I ask, gritting my teeth as I push up onto my elbows.

"I don't know. I just do," he replies, his hand pumping faster. "I want to spank you raw, I want to whip you until red welts rise across your creamy skin. I want to cut you like Leon did. I want to take my cock and rip through your virginity. I want to bury myself balls deep in your virgin cunt and dirty up my cock with your blood," he says, panting now as his breaths become more uneven and his eyelids droop. "Then I want to soothe you, lick your pussy better, treat your wounds, and take care of you. I want to *heal* you."

His free hand rests on my lower back as his fist pumps up and down, drawing out his pleasure. I can't comprehend why hurting me then healing me turns him on so much, but it does. Watching him become unhinged, with his cock in his hand and his eyes hooded makes me feel a little more in control.

He's vulnerable right now.

He's giving up his desires, his secrets, and is jacking off without even trying to take anything further from me. It's not what I expected. Not at all.

Testing the boundaries of his restraint, of my hold over him, I push up onto my knees and turn my back to Konrad, pulling my hair over my shoulder. Looking back at him, I lick my lips and smile softly, playing him at his own game. "I want you to come," I whisper.

"Fuck! Fuck!" Konrad grinds out through clenched teeth as his hips jerk. "Turn around, Zero. Turn the fuck around. I don't want to come over your wounds."

Shifting on the bed, and ignoring the way my pulse rises and my heart pounds, I turn to face him just as he tips his head back and orgasms, covering my chest with his thready, white cum. I watch him as his cock jerks with the aftermath and his chest heaves, feeling a knot in my chest unravel a little, feeling as though I've clawed back some control.

Leon and Konrad might've strapped me to that cross, cut me, debased me, forced me to come, but here in this room I've claimed a little self-respect back. It doesn't matter that I'm covered in his cum. What matters is the information he's given up, the insight into his psyche.

Tucking his cock back into his trousers, Konrad turns on his heel and heads into the bathroom, coming back out a few moments later with a damp cloth. Avoiding my gaze he silently cleans me up. He's gentle, solemn, and thoughtful.

It's strange.

"I need to put some ointment on your wounds and the blisters on your feet," he says, evenly. His mask firmly back in place.

"Okay," I murmur, lying back down whilst internally smiling at this small victory.

Konrad takes his time applying the ointment Thirteen prepared, talking to me in a soothing voice that does little to calm my determination to ruin him.

All three of them.

Those are my last thoughts as I fall into a deep, restless sleep.

∽

GRIM PACES UP AND DOWN, *her hand waving in the air as she shouts into the phone. "I don't give a FUCK, Arden Dálaigh! We're going with you. She's my sister."*

Beast steps in front of her, shaking his head. "Let them do this. Think of Iris, Grim. She needs you here."

"Give me a moment, will you? I'll call you back," Grim says, punching the end-call button. She glares at Beast. Her eyes are

bloodshot, ringed with dark circles. "This is non-negotiable. We're going with them. No one fucking kidnaps my sister and gets away with it. I'm going to put a motherfucking bullet in each of them. I need to make sure they're dead."

"And Iris?"

"Pen and the Breakers have already agreed to look after her. I refuse to leave my sister another day longer with those men. Not one more day. You hear me? It's been a month, Beast. A month! I've let her down."

"You don't even know if what Arden has found out is true. She could already be dead," *Beast says gently, reaching for her. Kate whacks his hand away.*

"That girl is a survivor. She's not dead."

"They will ask for another debt. You already owe them one. Let me handle this. I'll take a team. I'll go get her back."

"You don't know the exact location of The Masks' castle. We've looked everywhere. This is the only lead we have, and I refuse to let it go. Besides, Arden won't give up the location just like that, not when they can extract another debt from me. We have no choice."

"There's *always* a choice," *Beast says, gripping her shoulders.* "We can get Christy back. Us, not them."

Grim locks eyes with Beast, and for a fraction of a second, hesitates. "No! We need the Deana-Dhe. You know it, and I know it. This may be our only opportunity to get into the castle unnoticed."

"Grim, you're not thinking straight. This is an 'invite only' Ball. They'll see us coming a mile away," *he adds gently, tipping her chin up so he can look into her eyes.*

"This is a masquerade ball. We can hide in plain sight."

"Think about this carefully," *Beast insists.* "Think about Iris. If anything goes wrong, she'll be an orphan. Is that what you want?"

"Christy needs me. I won't leave her to rot in there. I won't. If anything bad happens, our baby girl has a ready-made family to take care of her. I don't leave anyone behind, especially not family. So you're either with me or not. No matter what, I'm *doing this.*"

Beast grits his jaw, swiping a hand over his face. "You're right.

Fuck, I'm sorry. Goddamn those fucking pricks. I'll take their masks and shove them so far up their arses they'll be choking on them!"

"That's the spirit!" Grim replies, a little laughter breaking through the anger.

"Well, if we're doing this, we could use some back-up. It's about time you told Ford about his sister, don't you think? If Pen and the Breakers are looking after our princess, then perhaps Asia will be willing to loan us her delinquents? Those fuckers know how to fight."

Grim nods her head. "I'll call him later today, but first Arden..."

Locking eyes with Beast, Grim presses redial on her phone, only she doesn't get a chance to speak because Beast snatches it from her and says, "Arden, we're coming with you to the Ball. Oh, and you make this my debt, not Grim's, got it?"

"Beast? What the fuck?!" Kate shouts the moment he's clicked off from the call.

"There was no way in hell I'd let you owe those twisted fucks another debt. This one's mine. We'll get Christy back together. Got it?"

"Got it," Kate nods, then accepting Beast's hug murmurs, "Hold on Christy, we're coming."

∞

"KATE!" I shout, sitting bolt upright in bed. My skin is covered in sweat, my heart pounding loudly in my chest as I blink back the vision and try to reorient myself in the room. It's dark outside. A full moon sits like a pendant in the night sky flooding our room with silvery moonlight. Konrad is long gone and Thirteen stirs, reaching for me, her cool fingers wrapping around my arm.

Nightmare? her expression seems to say.

"A bad dream," I lie, getting out of bed and padding over to the window. "Just a bad dream."

Pressing my forehead against the cool glass I blink back the tears, remembering how Kate had looked, going over in my mind what the vision had shown me.

"It's been a month," she'd said, which means this vision takes

place almost two weeks in the future. Two weeks where anything could happen... *"She could already be dead."*

"Oh God," I mutter, closing my eyes against the tears, and trying not to focus on the fact that Beast could be right and I might only have days left to live, hours even.

Behind me I hear Thirteen moving about. She clicks on the gas burner, striking a match. The familiar sounds of her brewing some tea does nothing to help soothe my racing thoughts.

"It's about time you told Ford about his sister, don't you think?"

Ford? I have a *brother*? Kate has kept him from me... Why?

Pressing my palm against the windowpane, I swallow hard. What other secrets has she been keeping from me? "Damn it, Kate!" I whisper.

Thirteen presses her fingers against my shoulder, making me jump, the after effects of my vision making me feel even more on edge than I already am. She hands me a mug of chamomile tea and I take it from her automatically. I feel like a robot. My body is moving as it should be but everything else feels disconnected.

Drink, she urges, pressing her fingertips against my hand holding the mug.

I take a sip, drinking but not tasting.

Tipping her head to the side, Thirteen's eyes scan my face. She's worried about me, I can see that plain as day, but I don't feel like having a conversation with her. Not right now. Not whilst I have all these thoughts in my head and pain in my heart.

Turning my attention back to the view before me, I allow my thoughts to roam. Who is Arden Dálaigh, and the *Deana-Dhe*? Why is Beast so worried about them helping Kate to find me? And what debt are they talking about?

"Arden, we're coming with you to the Ball."

The Ball. *Fuck!*

Kate and Beast are coming to the Ball. That's their way in, but I know The Masks, this is their domain, they'll kill them both the second they step foot in the castle.

"I need to get out of here!" I say, frustrated tears prickling my eyes, but even as I say the words I know it's useless to try and run without a plan.

I need a way out. I need help.

I could wait for my sister and Beast to turn up and hope we'd all survive, or I could take matters into my own hands. I saw the fear on Beast's face, he's not a man who scares easily, so whatever is going on with these mysterious Deana-Dhe, it can't be good. Beast said that he didn't want Kate to owe them another debt, so he's taken it on himself. He doesn't have to do that, but he's going to, for Kate, for me. They're putting themselves in danger and I can't let either of them owe anyone a debt. Kate can't leave Iris. I *have* to get out of here.

I have to.

But the vision was in the future which means I haven't managed to escape... or I'm dead... or I'm on my way back to her and she doesn't know it yet. I'm hoping for the latter, because the other two options are inconceivable to me.

"You know I won't stay here, don't you?" I say, my breath fogging up the windowpane.

Thirteen sighs, and even though I don't turn to face her, I know she's nodding her head.

"My sister is looking for me. Her name is Grim and she's a very dangerous woman. She won't rest until she finds me, and when she does, Thirteen, she'll kill The Masks, maybe even die trying. I *have* to leave before that happens. She's a mother. I have a niece. I can't be responsible for making her an orphan. I won't."

Thirteen grips my arm, forcing me to face her. *No*, she protests, shaking her head.

"She *will* kill them," I insist. "You care about The Masks. I don't know why, but you do, and if you care about them, then you'll help me to escape. It's the only way, Thirteen. Will you help me?" I ask, trying to make her see reason. God only knows that The Masks deserve Kate's wrath, *mine*, but I have to try and stop Kate and Beast from coming here. I have to. It's too dangerous.

For a long time Thirteen just stares at me, her grey eyes silver in the moonlight as she tries to decide what to do. Eventually, after what feels like forever, she picks up her pencil and pad and writes; *I'm so sorry. I can't help you. Not with this.*

"Then The Masks will die, and you'll be lost."

Thirteen presses her lips into a hard line, scribbling frantically. *I won't be the one lost without them.*

"The Numbers will learn to live in the real world again. They'll have normal, *healthy* relationships where they're not hired out like prostitutes and reduced to no more than a number," I say through angry, gritted teeth.

Thirteen huffs out a breath, then writes something else, showing it to me. *I'm not talking about the Numbers. I'm talking about you.* She stabs the pencil against the word 'you', emphasising her point.

"Me?" I laugh, I can't help myself. I laugh until tears cascade from my eyes and drip from my jaw bitterly.

Yes, you! She nods, pressing her finger into my chest. Fury in her gaze, but also heartache, *heartbreak.*

"You're wrong. I'll be *free*," I snap, swiping at my eyes, but even as I say those words, *mean them*, somewhere deep down inside, my gut is telling me that she's right.

And that, that's the most fucked-up thing of all.

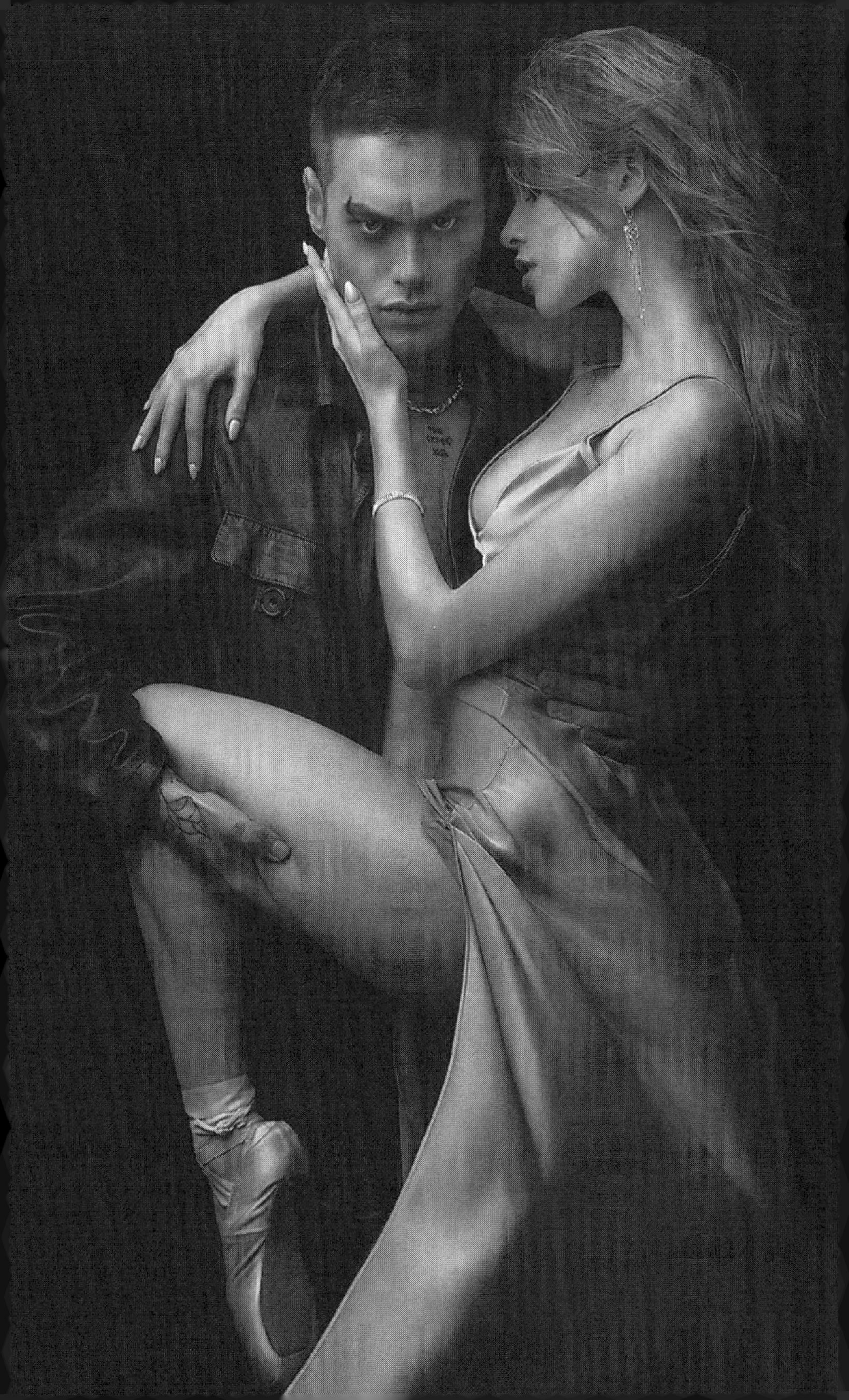

CHAPTER 28

CHRISTY

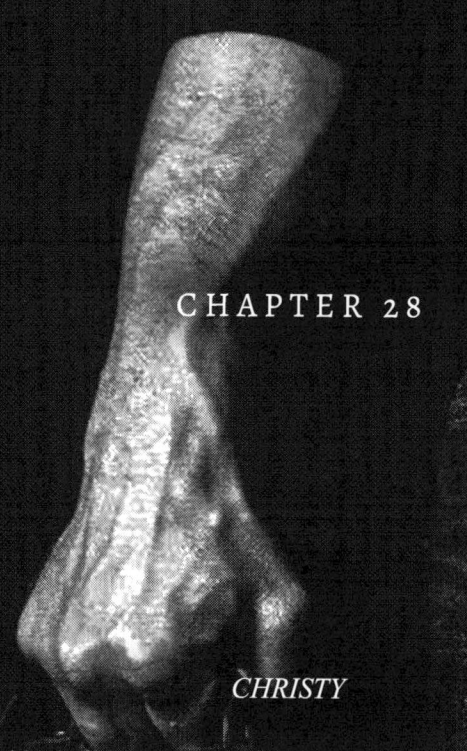

Thirteen taps my arm, drawing my attention back to her. She's mixing up a new solution, another ointment to combat the infection Twelve has picked up from her wounds. I see the worry in her eyes as she points to a vial of clear liquid sitting on the workbench in front of me.

"You want this?" I ask, picking it up.

She nods. *Yes.*

Passing it to her I sit in silence content to watch her working and find myself wondering how she ever came to be here. Is it because she's a healer, using natural herbs, plants and flowers to mix up lotions and potions to cure and soothe all manner of ailments? She has value in that respect, one I suspect is priceless, given the nature of what happens here. Imagine explaining Twelve's injuries to a doctor. Not likely.

Thirteen is essential to the inner workings of this place.

I have to admit, she's extraordinarily talented at what she does. Add in perfumes, body lotions, shampoo and conditioners, and makeup to the list of things she can produce, and she's more of an alchemist.

Thirteen's knowledgeable at what she does, has been willing to let me watch her all morning, but avoids all explanations of how she'd learnt her gift.

"It's kind of magical, what you do," I say as she sprinkles ground-up basil, rosemary and sage into her pot of bubbling liquid.

She shakes her head, picking up her pen and scribbling on the pad next to her. *I'm only using what Mother Nature gifted us all. If that's magic, then I guess I'm a magician.*

"Or a witch?" I say, catching her eye.

That too, she writes on her pad.

Even the most talented cosmetic scientist wouldn't be able to do half of what she does with more advanced equipment in a laboratory. Her kind of gift is beyond anything explainable by human laws, much like my visions are. In that we are kindred spirits.

"Leon was right when he said you would've been hung from The Weeping Tree."

She nods, scribbling on her pad. *Yes, there's no doubt. Most witches were simply healers, early scientists. They wanted to help, to cure people.*

"So you're here to cure people? Or is it because you have history with The Masks?" I ask, remembering what Konrad had said about knowing her when they were younger. This is the first time that I've had the opportunity to bring it up, and instantly regret it when Thirteen lays her pen down and picks up the wooden spoon, stirring the concoction and ending the conversation there. I let out a frustrated sigh, knowing that no matter how much I ask she'll refuse to answer questions she's uncomfortable with.

I just don't get it.

She's kind, thoughtful and empathetic, offering me a tonic for the phantom pain from my burns, making sure I'm as comfortable as I can be given the situation. But at the same time she's secretive and mysterious, refusing to give me the answers to questions that would help me deal with my situation and escape The Masks. I get the distinct impression from the constant interruptions from the Numbers over the past couple of days that she's well liked, *loved* even, and I can understand why that is. What I don't understand is why she's here. Why she protects the privacy of The Masks by refusing to tell me their story and why, above all else, she seems okay with what happens in this castle I call a prison yet she calls home. Thirteen knows The Masks aren't good men. I saw it in her eyes when we first met, so why does she protect them?

It doesn't make any sense.

"How old are you, Thirteen?" I ask, trying a different tactic.

Twenty-four in December, she writes, then points to my chest. *You?*

"I'll be Twenty-four next June..."

My voice trails off as my thoughts return to my family, to Grim. Ever since she found out about me she's made sure that we're always together on my birthday. It doesn't matter what's going on in her life, she's there for me with a chocolate cake, presents and stories. She's a good sister. The best.

Thirteen taps my arm to get my attention, then taps my temple. *What are you thinking about?* she seems to ask.

"My family. My sister, Kate. Most people know her as Grim. The Masks do." Thirteen nods, then averts her gaze. "I wasn't lying to you. She *will* kill them, you know. Grim will kill The Masks for taking me."

Flicking her gaze back to me, Thirteen swallows, her grey eyes flashing with worry. She presses her lips into a hard line and frowns, then shakes her head. *No.*

"She will. She'll be looking for me right now, probably gathering an army so she can come here and save me. The Masks are fools if they think she won't come."

Thirteen shakes her head again, more forcefully this time. *No.*

"Why do you insist on protecting them? Do you care about them that much?" I say.

Thirteen takes my hands, squeezing gently. She tips her head to the side, her grey eyes wary, vulnerable for the first time since we've met, as though she's concerned I'm going to somehow turn my back on her for her honesty.

She nods. *Yes, I do.*

"I don't understand why. They've hurt people, hurt me. They've imprisoned me. I'm *Nothing* to them," I say, emphasising the word. "I'm less than nothing. How can you be okay with that? With what happens here."

Thirteen shakes her head, then picks up the pencil and pad, finding a free page to write on. *You don't understand. It's not that simple.*

I scoff, shaking my head. "It seems simple to me. They're *monsters*. Unbearably cruel."

Thirteen's fingers wrap around the pencil tightly, her scribbled words dark against the page in her need to get her point across quickly. *No! You don't see what you've been shown.*

She underlines the last word over and over again and my skin prickles. What does she know? Her eyes meet mine and my stomach lurches. "What are you saying?" I ask.

You have a gift, like me, she writes.

"No," I reply, shaking my head, refusing to acknowledge what she appears to understand. She couldn't possibly know about that.

Yes, she insists, scribbling furiously. *You are different from the other Numbers, to me, even. You're important, but you're fighting your true purpose. Don't. When we fight what we are, who we belong to, there is only pain and anguish. I should know.*

"Is *that* why you're here?" I ask, taking the opening she's given me and diving right in. I avoid everything else. How could she possibly know about me and what I'm capable of? The truth is she couldn't and that makes me distrust this conversation. If she can be evasive, then so can I.

I'm here because I want to be here. Because I had a purpose. I'm staying because I can't go back to where I was.

"How could you want to be here? How can you sit back and watch the Numbers live a life of enslavement, entrapment? How can you allow any of this to happen? You could stop this. You could help us escape."

Thirteen presses her eyes shut and pinches her nose. She's pissed off, exasperated. Well, that makes two of us.

The Numbers want to be here.

"No!" I shout.

Yes! She scrawls furiously.

"They've been brainwashed!"

Thirteen shakes her head. *Every single one of the Numbers wants to be here. You don't understand everything. You don't know everything.*

"I understand that The Masks are sick, perverted bastards! I understand they inflict pain, manipulate, and imprison. Look at Twelve, for crying out loud. Look at what they've done to me since I've been here. They've tortured and debased. They've shackled me to The Weeping Tree, whipped me for speaking my mind, they've cut me open and jacked off covered in my blood. They've stolen my orgasms. They've punished Twelve because she broke one of their rules just to get their attention because she's in love with the bastards. Don't tell me that I don't understand!"

Curling her fist, she bashes the worktop. It's the first time I've seen her lose her temper, and the flash of anger in her eyes reminds me of my own tempered rage. She's not as serene as she presents herself to be.

Did you know that all of the Numbers were sold by their family? Their own flesh and blood didn't want them, she scribbles furiously, her hand flying over the paper.

"And clearly The Collector took advantage of that fact. Rather than setting them free, he passed them off to his sons to degrade and coerce, training their bodies and minds to accept their life here. To become *sex* slaves. Don't try to tell me that what they have here is any better than a family who doesn't care for them, because it's not! They could have been given freedom as the alternative to a shitty home life, not more enslavement!"

Every number wishes to stay. You can ask them and they will all tell you the same thing. Not everything is as straightforward as you believe it to be. Within these walls the Numbers are safe. The Masks protect them. They give them freedom to be who they truly are. Not everyone gets that. There are more walls and chains and prisons where you come from than there are in this castle.

"Bullshit," I grind out. "My family is beyond the boundaries of this estate. They're *good* people. They love and care for me."

Thirteen's nostrils flare. *If that were true, where are they now?*

"Trying to get to me!" I shout, tears pricking my eyes as I grit my teeth and turn my back on Thirteen, striding across the room towards the window. I stare out at the vast expanse of land that stretches on for miles and miles, making me feel even more trapped, not less.

A moment or so later, I sense Thirteen behind me, but I don't turn around to face her. I'm angry, disappointed. I thought I'd found a friend, maybe even an ally, but despite her kindness and empathy she's on The Masks' side. She's bound to them in ways I don't understand and it stops her from seeing the truth of this place and the darkness of their souls.

"I don't want to talk to you. Leave me alone," I say heavily. "You're no better than they are."

She reaches for me, urging me to face her. I refuse, and so, with a gentle sigh, she places an envelope in my hand then leaves the room. I wait until I hear the door click shut behind her before opening it up.

CHAPTER 29

CHRISTY

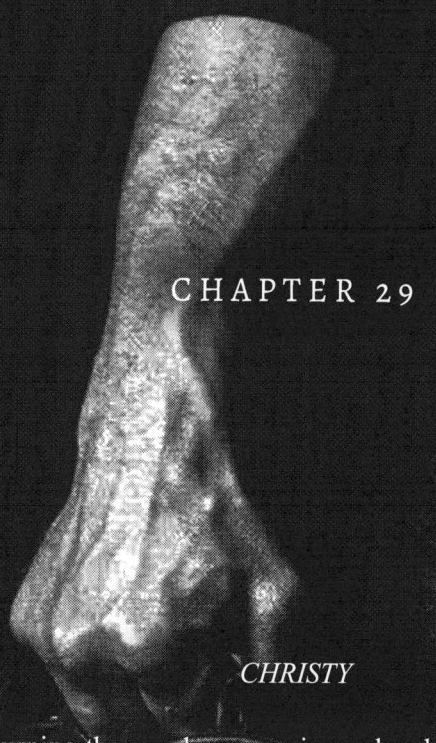

Turning the envelope over in my hand, I notice that it's sealed shut. There's no name on the front, but I open it regardless. The paper is thick, smooth to the touch. Curiosity combined with a growing sense of unease makes me unfold it, my eyes sliding over the neat cursive. There's something familiar about the handwriting and as my eyes focus on the opening line, I begin to read.

To my darling girl,

It's hard to write this letter knowing that the contents of it will break your heart as surely as mine is breaking now. I cannot impress on you enough how much I love you and wish that things could be different, but life doesn't always work out the way we want it to. It's a lesson I'd hope you wouldn't have to learn, but alas, you're my daughter and you're cursed with this gift, just like I am.

My heart skips a beat, my eyebrows pulling into a frown as a memory lurks at the edge of my consciousness. I pause for a moment, trying to remember.

Then it comes back to me in a rush.

I was five, standing in the doorway of my mother's bedroom door as she sat at her desk and cried over a letter she held in her hand. I remember asking what was wrong and she'd smiled, folded up the letter and placed it in an envelope just like the one I'm holding now. Could this be that letter...? With a tremulous intake of breath I continue reading, needing to find out.

> *I've made many mistakes in my life, but the worst one was turning my back on Fate. I thought I knew better. I thought I understood what love was, that it was enough to conquer anything, including her whims, but that's only ever a possibility if the person you love loves you back.*
>
> *You see, Fate didn't want me to fall in love with your father. She had other plans for me. Plans I chose to ignore all because I thought I knew the kind of man your father was.*
>
> *I didn't.*
>
> *To him I was nothing more than a passing fling, a distraction during a time in his life when he needed a warm body to hold onto. But even though he didn't love me, he cares about you enough to keep you sheltered, clothed and taken care of from afar. You might think that's not how a father should behave, and you'd be right, but in his line of work family can be used against you. He stayed away to keep you safe, so I know he loved you in his own way, even though it might not seem like that.*

I take a deep breath, blinking back the tears and pushing down the sudden onslaught of emotion. Kate has only ever mentioned our dad in passing, and never kindly. He hurt her badly. He broke her heart. He wasn't a good man.

> *By the time you read this, you will have already met your sister, Kate. She is your family now. She will look after you and care for you in my*

absence. That girl has the weight of the world on her shoulders, but she is strong enough to endure it. Just like you are strong enough to live a life that will take you on a journey of self-discovery.

Though, I have to warn you. Your path is filled with far more mountains than valleys. You will struggle to overcome many things, my darling girl. It's going to be hard. There will be people who will hurt and betray you, and others who will heal and love you.

My darling, I can't protect you from the pain. I can't stop what's happening, and if you're reading this now, then Fate has already begun to weave her magic, setting you on a new path that will test you beyond anything you've endured before.

Sickness rolls in my stomach at my mother's words, a sense of dread filling me. I swallow it back down, ignoring the crashing beat of my heart and continue to read.

It won't be easy, this new path, but you have to trust me when I say that you cannot stray from it. You must, above all else, follow it to wherever it leads. If I have learnt one thing being a seer, it's this: you cannot run from your future. You cannot hide and you cannot take another path. You may want to fight against it, but it will only cause you more pain in the long run. I know that because I've lived it.

Christy, I've seen parts of your future.

I've seen the castle and The Masks.

I've seen some of the decisions played out by the people around you, and it's costing me greatly not to share them with you, to forewarn you. But I know that if I do, Fate will have her revenge and I cannot risk that again. I won't.

What I can tell you is this: the Masks are bad men. They have been moulded into their father's image. They are cruel and wicked. I've seen just how much.

But that isn't all they are.

There are depths to these men. Crevices that run deep. Cracks line their souls. They are not infallible.

You've been put in their path for a reason, my darling girl, and when the time is right you will understand what that is and what you need to do.

I draw in a shaky breath, my eyes filling with tears at my mother's words because they confirm what I've known all along, no matter how much I wish it wasn't true. The Masks and I were meant to find each other. It doesn't hurt any less knowing that's true. In fact it's worse, because I understand that I never really had a choice.

There's something else too. This letter is in your hands because I made certain that you'd receive it just at the right moment. If everything has gone according to plan, Cyn is the one who gave it to you, or Cynthia O'Farrell as she was named at birth. You might know her as Thirteen. (Yes, I saw her in my visions too).

She is the daughter of Niall O'Farrell and Aoife O'Brien. Aoife was my best friend. She was murdered in a family war between the O'Farrells and the O'Briens when Cyn was just a child. Your fate and hers are intertwined, just like her mother's and mine were. She's here for her own reasons, as much as ensuring this letter gets to you safely.

If you do anything, trust her until you can trust yourself.

Like me, she too has run from her fate, but it will catch up with her. Be a friend to her when that happens. She'll need you.

I frown at that. At my shared history with a woman I barely know. I wonder how she even received this letter and knew what to do with it given she would've been the same age as me when my mother died. There are so many questions I need answers to, but for now I read on.

Lastly, I want to say sorry. I want to say sorry that I'll ignore you when you tell me about the fire. For making you feel like it's nothing but a bad dream. I have to do it. I can't change the course of fate. I can't prevent it from happening. This fire will be the start of your journey and the end of mine.

It has to happen the way it's meant to.

I'm so sorry.

"Me too, Mama, me too," I whisper.

My heart aches at the pain you will endure, and the loneliness you will feel after I've gone.

Right now, I'm writing this letter with you standing in the doorway of my bedroom knowing I cannot tell you what's to come, no matter how much I want to. Your life won't be easy. It will be filled with pain and anguish, but I'm hopeful that it won't last forever. Don't turn your back on your fate like I did. No matter how much it scares you, take the path you've been shown. You have to trust that it will work out in the end.

Right now, you're just a child, a beautiful, funny, kind little girl. I'm so very sad that I only have three years left with you, but at least I have this. At least I have three years to love you and cherish you as much as I can.

I'm so sorry I couldn't stay longer.

Have courage, my darling girl.

Find the truth in your heart. It will never steer you wrong.

But above all else, follow your path, and remember who saved you.

All my love, Mama.

Tears spring from my eyes and fall down my face, dropping to the floor in fat droplets as my legs give way beneath me. My mother knew what was to come. She saw it. She's telling me to stay, to see this through, whatever this is.

But how can I do that? I don't want my future intertwined with these brutal, sadistic men.

Her letter is warning me not to turn my back on my fate like she did, but if she hadn't, she wouldn't have fallen in love with my father, had me. How can that be wrong?

None of this makes any sense.

My thoughts spiral off into a dark place as I capture my reflection in the window before me. Lifting my fingers to my face, I press them against my birthmark. Is this what she was talking about? Did Fate punish her, by punishing me? Or maybe it was the fire that took her life and scarred me. Perhaps I should've died in that fire just like she had.

No, she said that was the start of my journey…

Wait.

I read through the last paragraph again, my heart pounding in my chest and my back prickling with sensation, indicating that something important is just out of reach.

But above all else, follow your path, and remember who saved you.

Remember who saved you.

I read that line over and over again. I thought that she'd meant my aunt and uncle, Kate, but as I re-read the last paragraph again, I know that isn't true. She's talking about the night of the fire.

I was saved.

I was saved by a boy with dark hair and an angry scowl.

Like a wrecking ball crashing through the thick wall of my subconscious, the memory of that night comes flooding back. The pain of it makes me pass out.

∽

"GET UP!" a voice shouts. It belongs to a boy, a boy who's yanking me upwards. His face is completely covered in ash and soot like mine, his hair dark. I don't know who he is or where he's come from, just that he's here in my home as a fire rages around us devouring everything in its path.

"Stop it!" I cry, excruciating pain enveloping me. I stumble, my head falling forward, my hair matted and coloured black from the soot and smoke.

"Come with me. You'll die if you don't!" he demands, his fingers a vice around my arm.

"Get off me!" I pant, trying to run into the flames, but his fingers skirt over my back as he wraps an arm around my waist and hauls me off my feet. I cry out in pain.

So.

Much.

Pain.

"*Mama!*" *I scream as fire licks up the walls and over our heads, its heat overwhelming. I draw in a breath through my mouth only to choke on the fumes, on the heat that burns my throat and lungs.* "*Mama!*"

"*She's gone. You can't save her. Let me help you!*" *the boy shouts.*

"*I won't leave her! I won't!*" *My voice is hoarse, raw from screaming and shouting, from breathing in toxic fumes as my home burns down around us, as pain tries to take me under. My back feels like it's been stripped raw, as though there's no flesh or muscle, only bone. It hurts so bad I black out, then come to almost immediately. Adrenaline and the need to reach my mother overriding everything else.*

"*She's already dead,*" *he cries.*

"*Lies!*" *I kick at the boy, furious at him.*

"*I could let you die! I should let you die!*" *he shouts, but despite his threat, he refuses to let me go. Instead, he lifts me off my feet, sweeps me up into his arms, and jumps through flames, running from the house.*

Outside, cool air hits us both like a soothing mist. Fine droplets of rain from the storm that's been brewing all day drizzles over us. But it isn't enough.

I'm on fire, just like my home. Like my Mama.

I want to die.

Pain. So much pain.

My back is burning.

My lungs are burning.

Everything hurts.

Everything.

Hurts.

The boy runs with me in his arms across the grass and to the large pond that's situated at the bottom of our garden. He strides into the water, dunking my body under the surface.

I scream, my skin sizzling like a piece of bacon in a frying pan.

"*I'm sorry,*" *he mumbles, adjusting me in his arms, but the movement just hurts me more.*

"It hurts."

"I know. I know. Just keep still. I'll help you float."

Black spots blur my vision and I blink them back, trying to stay awake as he cups the back of my head and holds me beneath my knees, careful not to touch my back this time. I don't know how long he holds me like this because time slows to an agonising pace.

"Mama," I whimper, my eyes dropping shut.

I'm dying.

I'm gonna be with my Mama.

I don't fight it. I don't fight as death's fingers slide over my skin and I'm lifted out of the water and placed onto my stomach, the soft grass cushioning me.

"Your back is burnt pretty badly," he mumbles, leaning over me.

I groan with the pain. I don't answer. I can't. I'm dying.

My body surrenders to the darkness, my soul unravelling stitch by stitch. I'm barely hanging onto life when another voice enters the peacefulness. It's foreign, sharp, cruel. Much older than the boy.

"Leave her. We need to go. Now!"

The disgust in his voice jars me, and despite the comforting coolness of death, my eyes flutter open. I see shiny black shoes beneath smart grey trousers walk away across the grass, the man's body outlined in flames as though he's the very devil himself returning to Hell. Then I realise it isn't Hell that's burning but my home, my Mama.

"Mama," I croak.

"Fuck! Fuck!" the boy says. He's still with me, he hasn't left. He drops down beside me, swiping away a wet tendril of hair that clings to my cheek. "I thought you were dead."

"I'm not?"

"No, you're not," he replies, a smile on his lips. "You're stubborn."

"Who are you?" I croak, as he caresses my cheek gently. Nothing seems to hurt anymore. I feel only bliss. Like I'm floating. Is it his touch making me feel this way? Maybe I'm already dead and he's a figment of my imagination. My eyelids feel heavy, darkness is just out *of reach, but I refuse to succumb this time. I want to know who he is. It seems important somehow.* "Who are you?"

"I'm nobody. I wasn't here. You won't remember me when you wake up."

"Because I'm dying?"

"Maybe." *He pauses, cupping my cheek, then he leans over and presses his lips against my ear.* "If you survive, don't *remember me.*"

Sirens ring in the distance, help is coming. "That's impossible," *I reply, blinking at him as he pulls back.* "How can I forget the boy who has eyes so green they're like the fields of Heaven themselves? You're beautiful."

And he is, he's the most beautiful boy I've ever seen.

"I'm not beautiful. I'm far from beautiful. Inside I'm rotten to the core."

"Are you wearing a mask then?" *I ask, my words tumbling out. I don't know why I say that, I just do.*

"Perhaps I should..." *he responds solemnly.*

"No, you're an angel..." *I say, my voice weak. He is an angel. He must be. He saved me.*

The boy shakes his head, sadness creeping into his eyes as a single, solitary tear slides down his cheek. "No, I'm not an angel. My name is Leon. I'm the boy who killed your Mama."

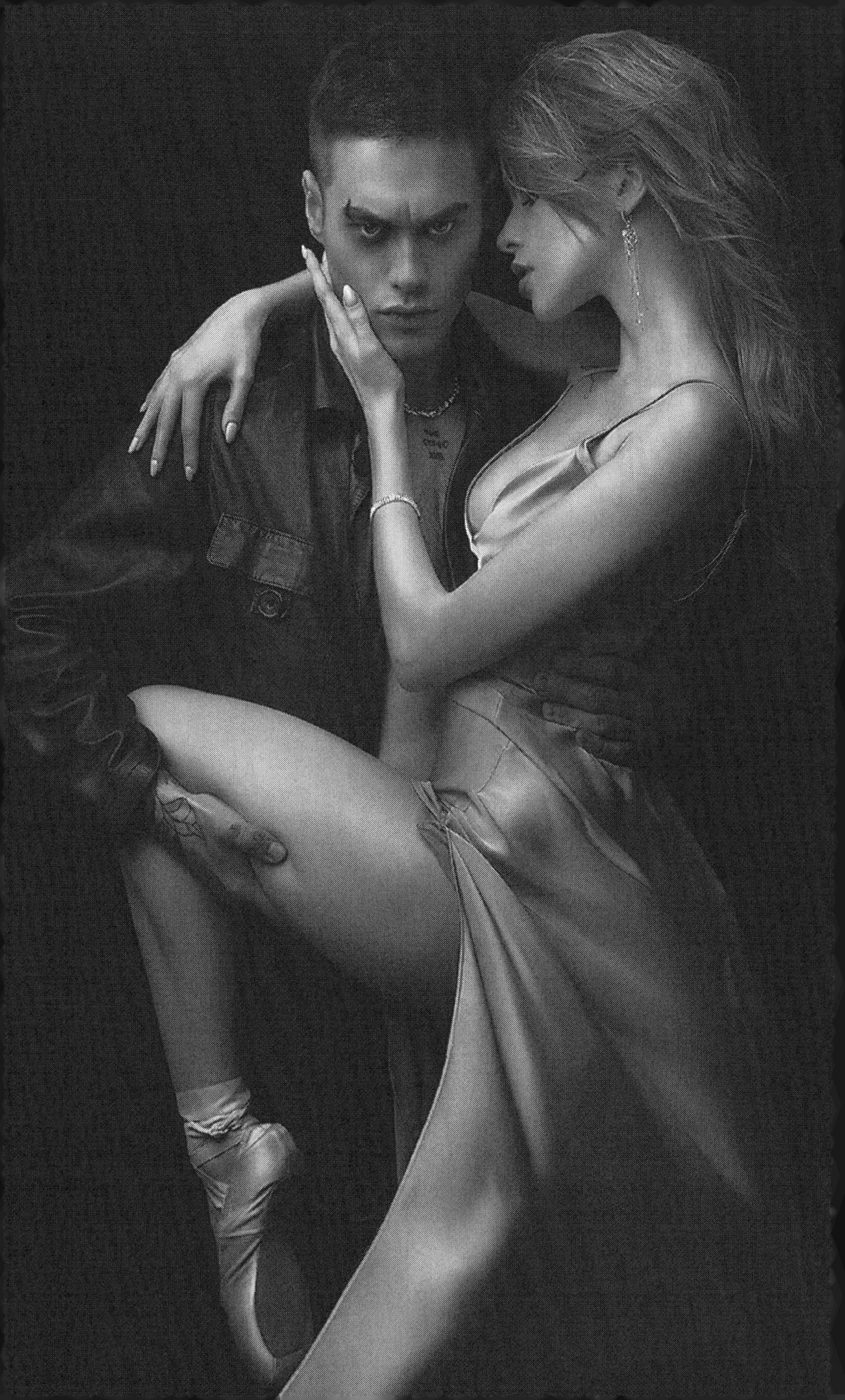

CHAPTER 30

CHRISTY

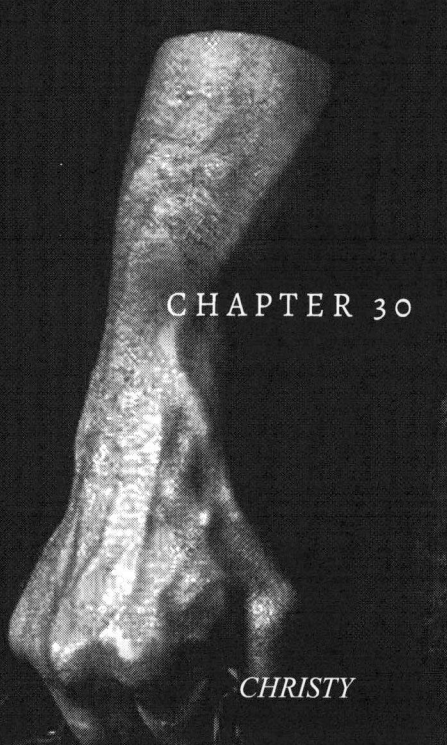

I awaken with a start. Anger blazes, rushing through my veins as fast and as furiously as the fire that had killed my mum and burnt my home to the ground.

I'm raging. I'm a fucking inferno of hate. It billows like smoke in my lungs and boils like lava in my veins. Even the residual pain from the memory smarting my skin isn't enough to stop me jumping to my feet and rushing from the bedroom.

Leon killed my mum.

I'm going to make him pay!

I don't think about anything other than ripping off his mask and looking into the eyes of the angel who saved me and the monster who killed my mother.

My bare feet slap against the stone tiles as I race along the hallway, fury giving me energy. I don't stop when Thirteen steps out of Twelve's room three doors down, her eyes wide with shock. I don't stop when Seven calls after me, or when Six grips my arm as I pass her by.

"Don't!" she says, knowing instantly that I'm on a path of

destruction. She sees the hate in my eyes, understands it and what I mean to do. Either he dies or I do.

"Get off me!" I shout, yanking my arm out of her hold.

When I reach the end of the long corridor and turn left, I run directly into One and Two. Their hands come up automatically, more to protect themselves than me, but when One sees the look on my face, she presses her hands against my chest, holding me back.

"Stop!" she demands.

"Fuck you!" I scream, pushing against her hold. She backs me up against the stone wall, Two helping to hold me in place. They're far stronger than they look.

"Where are you going?" One asks, her cool expression and calm voice like ice over my heated skin.

"To *kill* Leon," I spit, knocking their hands away, aware that the rest of the Numbers have gathered in the hallway. I can feel them staring, and it pisses me off even more. "I'm doing what you're all too chicken-shit to do!"

Two laughs. No, she cackles. "Good luck with that."

One, however, keeps me pinned in place with her penetrating stare. "Do you want to die?" she asks. "I'm genuinely interested, because surely you understand that this will only end in your death. Not his."

"I *want* revenge."

"You will die. He *will* kill you." One persists, her dark eyes lacking any real depth or emotion. She's stating it as a matter of fact, not as a warning coming from a place of kindness.

"I want to see him suffer like I've suffered. I *hate* him!"

"Oh my dear. We've all hated him at one time or the other. The feeling will pass. Now be a good girl and run along back to Thirteen's room. You're a... *mess*." Her gaze roves over my dishevelled hair then focuses on my birthmark. She baulks and it sends even more fury rushing through my blood.

"Don't speak to me like that," I seethe. "Don't dismiss me just because I'm not beautiful like the rest of you. I'm capable of more than you know!"

"Go with Thirteen," she says dismissively, flicking her gaze over her shoulder and nodding.

Thirteen appears by my side, her arm sliding behind my back as One steps backwards. I shove her off me, not caring that she stumbles back into Three, not caring what my mother had written in her letter. I'm too far gone to see anything other than blind rage.

"Don't you touch me! Don't you dare touch me, *Cyn*!" I shout. She flinches, her face paling. I've let her name out, her secret.

I don't care. I don't care.

"Zero—" Three begins, trying to soothe me with her soft voice and concerned gaze.

"My name is CHRISTY!" I shout, panting, wild now. *Rabid*.

"I say let her go." Four shrugs. "At least with her gone, everything can get back to normal. Our Masters have been on edge ever since she arrived. She doesn't fit in here."

Bitch.

"I agree, let her go up against Leon. She won't last five minutes," Eight says, rolling her eyes and hooking her arm through Four's. They turn on their feet, apparently no longer interested.

Good. They can fuck off.

Six steps forward. I feel her empathy, her kindness, and on any other day I might've appreciated it. She opens her mouth to speak but I shake my head. "No!"

"Don't be rash," she says, ignoring me. "Whatever you're feeling, it will pass. We can talk this through. Come with us. *Please*, Christy."

A few of the numbers draw in a surprised breath because of her use of my real name, and it only seems to rile me up further. "That's my name. You all have names. Don't let them take your identity!"

"You know that for us it isn't like that," Six replies gently, holding out her hand. For the briefest of moments I consider taking it, then I push the thought aside. *No*.

"Where will I find him?"

Thirteen shakes her head, warning Six and the rest of the Numbers not to answer me.

"I'll find him with or without your help," I say.

"Truly, you don't want to do this," Three insists, her sweet voice sincere. "Seven tried once too. It didn't go well."

Seven wraps his arm around Three and pulls her into his side. "She's right, it didn't. Luckily for me Three persuaded The Masks to give me one more chance. I'm glad of it. This is my home now. The Numbers are my family. The Masks... my Masters."

I shake my head, my hair whipping around as I look between them all. "This is wrong! Why don't you fight back?!"

"Because we don't want to," one of the triplets says. I don't know which one, but it doesn't really matter, given her sisters are agreeing with her. "This is our home and you're ruining it!"

"I—"

"You'll find him in the West Wing, beyond the library," One says quickly, cutting my rant off and drawing my attention back to her. "There's a door in the back of the library that leads to a gym where he trains—"

"One, what are you doing?" Five snaps, her concerned gaze falling on me. "He *will* kill her." I notice how she reaches for one of her knives strapped to her chest. I'm not sure if she's threatening One, or it's a nervous reaction. I'm assuming the latter when One raises a brow at Five, then turns back to face me.

"Take the stairs at the end of this hall and follow the corridor on the ground floor until you reach the courtyard with The Weeping Tree. The entrance to the West Wing is beyond the red door. You'll find the library soon enough," One continues, stepping aside.

I run, ignoring the calls for me to come back.

By the time I reach the library, I'm covered in a sheen of sweat. The kaftan that Thirteen—or should I say, Cyn—loaned me is sticking to my back. My chest is heaving from the exertion but violence floods my system, giving me the fuel to go on, to see this through. Pushing open the door, I step into a narrow, dimly lit hallway and follow the sound of trap music, it's angry beat the perfect accompaniment to my rage. When I enter the gym, Leon is in the far corner with his back to me, beating the shit out of a boxing dummy. As far as I can tell he isn't wearing a mask which seems out of character, given what I know. Then again, I'm certain none of the other Numbers would be brave enough to enter here without his permission.

Just as well I'm not like them then.

He's bare except for a pair of shorts, his corded muscles glistening with sweat as he moves, showing off his tattoos of black reeds that cover his entire body. They reach up from his ankles, climbing his calves and thighs before disappearing beneath the hem of his shorts only to reappear again at his waist, climbing his back and shoulders.

As I stand here watching him work out, the significance of his tattoos suddenly hits me.

The fire.

The pond.

He saved me.

He killed my mother.

Glancing around the room, I look for something I can use to hit him with and see a broom leaning against the wall to my right. Grabbing it, I stride over to him, my footsteps and angry breaths are drowned out by the music and the grunts he makes whilst working out.

Lifting the handle of the broom, I imagine my mother's agony, and with a roar, I bring it down as hard as I can on the back of his knees.

The way he falls to the floor, grunting in surprise and pain, fuels me on. I don't hesitate. I hit him again, as hard as I can. The wood crashes against his back and he lets out a loud cry, falling forward onto his hands. The smack of the wood against his bare skin is satisfying in a way I shouldn't enjoy, but do.

They say in times of great stress or blind rage people are capable of things they wouldn't ordinarily be able to do. A man could lift a car off his trapped child. A lover could murder the person they love through jealousy.

A woman could beat a man to death with a wooden broom.

Leon collapses onto his chest as I whack his shoulders, his arse and his thighs. A red mist descends and with every punishing blow I scream out words of hate and disgust. They pour from me like blood from an open wound.

"Killer."

Whack.
"Monster."
Whack.
"Pain."
Whack.
"Bastard."
Whack.
"Fire."
Whack.
"Devil."
Whack.
"You. Killed. My. Mama."
Whack. Whack. Whack. Whack.
I know I'm not making any sense, but I don't care. I don't care.

I hit him again, and again, and again. Fury has no boundaries. Rage no ceiling. Violence no walls. I'm lost to it. Completely and utterly lost.

The harder I hit him, the less he responds. His cries of pain turn to grunts, then whimpers, then nothing. Just silence. I expected him to fight back. Wanted it, almost. Yet he doesn't.

He takes every punishing blow that I rain down over him. He just fucking lies there.

"Fight back, you bastard!" I scream, wanting a reaction. Wanting to fight.

But he remains still.

He doesn't try to kill me like the Numbers warned. He takes this punishment because deep down he must know he fucking deserves it.

He. Deserves. It.

I keep going until my arms begin to tremble with exertion, until deep red marks appear across his back and thighs, until his skin splits in places, and starts oozing blood.

Blood.
Fuck!
FUCK!

As quickly as my rage appeared it drains away, taking every last ounce of energy with it. My arms drop as my knees buckle and the broom clatters to the ground.

"Oh my God. Oh my God. Oh my God," I cry, heaving and retching at what I've done.

Tears stream down my face as I swallow down the sickness burning my throat, and crawl towards the man who killed my mother. Overwhelming guilt lacerates my heart as much as I've lacerated his skin. "What have I done?" I pant, my chest tightening. I can barely breathe.

He doesn't move when I lean over him. He doesn't flinch when my fingers reach for his back, tentatively pressing against his bruised and split skin. He remains still as I brush the hair off his forehead.

"I wanted you dead, and now…" I choke on my tears.

His eyes are unblinking, vacant, as I lay on the cold floor, stretching out beside him. I rest my head as close to his as I can, instantly remembering how he'd done the same when we were children.

"You killed my mother," I sob, my heart breaking, my vision blurred from all the tears. "You killed my mother and left me to die. How could you?" I reach for his face, pushing back the hair that's fallen over his forehead, my fingers lingering against his temple. "Look what you made me do. I'm no better than you are."

He blinks and my heart jumps as I pull my hand back. "I told you not to remember me," he replies quietly, his voice broken, cracked, *raw*.

I swipe at my tears, potent relief flooding my veins. "You're not dead," I whisper. I shouldn't feel relieved, but I do. God help me, I do.

"You're wrong, I've been dead inside for a very long time," he croaks, groaning as he tries to lift his head, a flash of vulnerability streaking across his face.

"Why?" I ask. I want answers. I need to understand. "Why would you kill my mother?"

He groans, wincing as he adjusts his position. "You weren't supposed to be there. When I heard the screaming…" his voice trails off as he swallows hard.

"You didn't know?" I whisper, more tears pricking my eyes.

The muscle in Leon's jaw flexes as his eyes flash with guilt. It's brief, but undeniable. "My father told me the house was empty. He lied."

"That was him?"

He nods. "It was a test... I failed."

"Because I lived?"

"Because I *saved* you."

A tiny voice in my head tries to tell me that he's the one lying now, that this is another trick, another manipulation, but somehow I know it isn't. This may be the only truth he tells me, but it *is* the truth.

"Fuck," he groans, blood seeping from the tears in his skin.

"What have I done?" I whisper, the adrenaline that had kept me single-mindedly focused on killing him leaves my body. My teeth chatter and my hands begin to shake as nausea rolls in my stomach once again.

"You took your revenge," he mutters. "I deserved that much at least."

"I should get Thirteen..." I mumble, trying to unravel my feelings. It had felt good to hurt him, to punish him for what he did to my mother, to me. But now that I know it wasn't intentional, that he was a child manipulated by an evil man, it feels different. Wrong on so many levels. "I'm sorry I hurt you."

He frowns. "You are?"

"Yes," I say, meaning it.

"You shouldn't be."

Reaching for him, I run my shaking fingers over his cheek. He flinches under my touch, as though kindness, remorse, *empathy* hurts him. Perhaps it does.

"Why did you save me? Why didn't you let me die?" I whisper, locking gazes with him.

He's quiet for a long time, then finally he says, "I don't know... *Instinct?*"

"Your instinct was to save me?"

"Yes. I heard you screaming and I couldn't..."

"Couldn't?"

"I couldn't walk away, no matter the consequences."

"And what does your instinct tell you to do now?" I ask, swallowing hard at the look in his eyes.

"It tells me to do things that would make you wish you hadn't stopped," he replies, his pupils widening, darkening the green irises, stripping them of colour.

Something shifts in the air, the almost peaceful calm after such a violent act charging with awareness. My skin rises in goosebumps, fear pooling low in my belly. He means to hurt me, and yet he's holding back. The Numbers said he would kill me. This is the perfect opportunity to do that. Right now, he could overpower me and take my life, but he doesn't.

"Why are you holding back?" I whisper, watching him carefully. My body is as taut as a wire, waiting for the moment that he'll attack. Part of me wants him to, wants this over and done with. The other part is preparing to run.

"You want the honest truth?"

"Yes, I want the truth."

He presses his eyes shut, considering his answer. When he opens them again, I don't see a man who wants to kill me, but the boy who saved me and set us both on this path. "Because you've become my mirror, just like you said you would."

I draw in a surprised breath at his confession, at the *humanity* in his gaze, but the longer he stares the quicker it fades and I feel the urgent need to stop that from happening, to keep him in the moment. "Don't leave," I say, touching the man whilst trying to reach the boy. He stiffens again, but he doesn't push me away. Sliding closer, I tentatively press my lips against his and kiss him tenderly.

Maybe it's guilt for hurting him so badly.

Maybe it's madness.

Maybe it's the glimpse of that boy I just saw in his eyes.

Perhaps it's fate.

All I know is that I have the sudden urge to heal what I've broken, to be a better person than the man he's become, so I slide my tongue between his parted lips and kiss him as though I don't hate him, as though my kiss is enough to heal all the wounds I've inflicted on his body.

His mouth parts on a groan as he relinquishes himself to my kiss and adjusts his body so that I'm beneath him. The heat of his chest sinks into mine and something about that seems right even when everything about this should be wrong.

Refusing to unravel my fucked-up emotions, I allow myself this kiss, this moment of healing. I'm no fool, this could all still lead to destruction but I give into the moment, the simplicity of two people offering comfort in the purest way possible. Leon adjusts himself between my legs, pressing me into the cool floor. He kisses me back, and this time our kiss isn't violent, it isn't filled with hate or ownership.

It's not gentle either, it's *searching*.

He kisses me like he's trying to understand something within me, within him.

My body relaxes, my fingers press against his chest, sliding up over his shoulders until I clutch the back of his neck, tugging him closer. I find myself wanting to dive into his depths, so I can soothe away the agony of my scars and the memory of that night. My legs wrap around his waist as I draw him closer to me, the chastity belt digging into my crotch adding more friction. He groans, grinding against me as his tongue searches and soothes, probes and penetrates.

This kiss is electric. Potent. Far more dangerous to my self-preservation than anything I've experienced so far. Ten minutes ago I wanted to kill him. Part of me still does.

But more of me is pulling him closer instead of pushing him away.

The kiss evolves again, shifting gears, and I find myself whimpering beneath him, wanting far more than I have any right to crave.

"Fuck, enough!" Leon says, ripping his mouth away from mine and jumping upwards. He looks down at me with a pained expression. "Get out of here."

"Wh—what?"

"I said, get the fuck out!" He yells, backing away from me.

"Leon," I start, pushing up to my feet. "Let's talk about this—"

"There's nothing to talk about. I killed your mum. You got your revenge."

"If I had my revenge, you'd be dead," I point out, still feeling raw, sick to my stomach knowing what I know, knowing what I almost did, what we've just shared. "But two wrongs don't make a right."

"So fucking pious!"

"I don't believe in God," I reply, taking two steps towards him. "This isn't about a higher fucking power. This is about what happened between us and *why*. I need answers, Leon!"

"You should've fucking killed me, Nought, because I won't ever tell you a thing, and I sure as fuck won't be that boy again," he says, shoving me away. I stumble backwards, my arms cartwheeling as I try to regain my balance.

"Don't do this. Don't be this man! Talk to me."

"If you don't fucking leave right now I will put my hands around your throat and do what I should've done all those years ago."

"Maybe I should let you. At least this will all be over!"

"No!" he shouts, gripping my arms and pushing me backwards. "You aren't just mine."

My toes kiss the floor as I try to keep up with him. When we reach the door he shoves me through it, slamming it in my face. A second later I hear the sound of a key turning in the lock and the screams of a man on the verge of losing his mind.

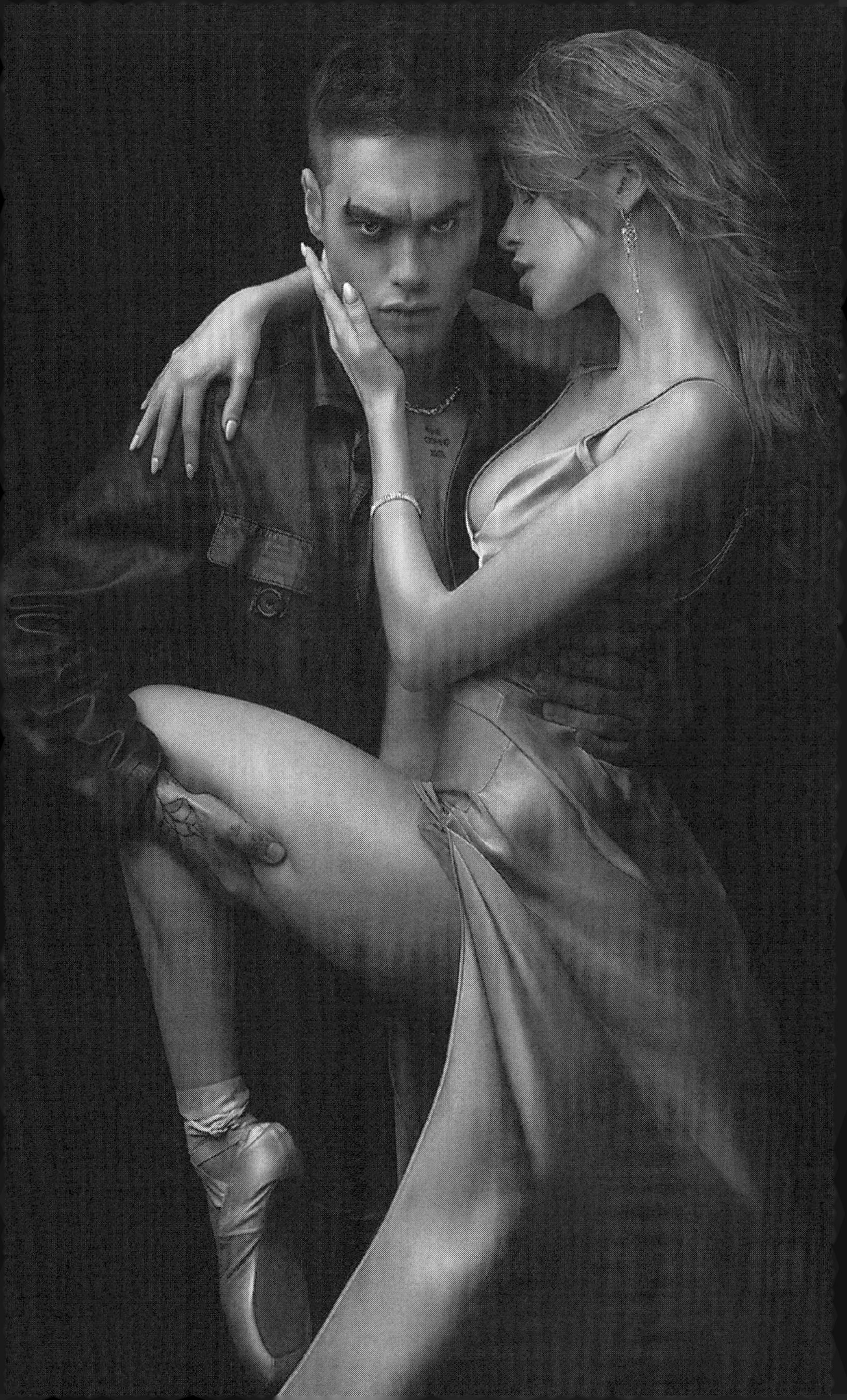

CHAPTER 31

CHRISTY

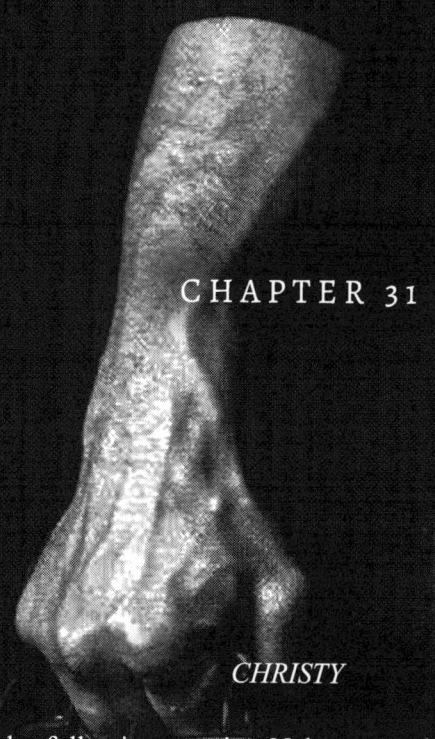

The following evening Nala enters the room with a message from Jakub. "You're to dine with The Masks," she says, holding out a large box for me to take. I'm feeling emotionally exhausted, but that's nothing in comparison to this intense need I have to escape. I have to at least *try* to get away. Time is running out.

"Is that so?" I say evenly, taking the box from her. I glance at Thirteen who's brewing something for Five. She's been quiet all afternoon. Barely talking to me.

"Yes. Cook has been fixing you all a feast. The kitchen smells delicious."

"That's good, I'm starving," I say, trying to temper the sarcasm in my voice.

After my argument with Thirteen last night, the revelations in my mother's letter, and my interaction with Leon, I've had to keep a lid on my thoughts and feelings no matter how difficult that's been. An hour ago, Thirteen applied more of her healing ointment to my back after sewing me back up last night. She didn't ask me then what happened between me and Leon and she hasn't even tried to communicate. Despite her kindness, I can't get over her betrayal. She has the power to help me and she won't.

I don't even know if she read my mother's letter and frankly, I don't care. In fact, I'm hoping that by reading it she will assume that I will stay here and follow my mother's advice and not attempt to run. Either way, she doesn't mention it and neither do I, and I certainly don't want to bring up what happened with Leon. The flashbacks are bad enough.

I could've killed him. I would've.

In that moment, as I beat him with the broom handle, I'd become a monster. I wanted to hurt him. I needed to see him in pain. It was destructive, violent, fucked-up, and the kiss that followed… I don't even know what that was. Stupidity? Lust? Empathy?

Now all I can cling on to is the hope of escape. I just have to keep my emotions and feelings in check until tomorrow night, then whilst the Numbers perform and The Masks entertain, I'll make my escape or die trying.

"Come on then, open it!" Nala says excitedly, drawing me out of my thoughts.

"What is it?" I ask, not really caring what's inside, but humouring her anyway.

Nala shrugs. "I've no idea. That's why I want you to open it!"

"You didn't take a peek on your way up here?"

"No way. I'm not about to upset Jakub any more than he already is," Nala replies.

"Why is he upset?" I ask, narrowing my eyes at Thirteen who shakes her head.

Can I really believe that Thirteen wouldn't share our conversation or the contents of the letter with them? It's doubtful, but the look she gives me tells me that she hasn't. She asked me to trust her, my mother asked the same of me, but I don't even trust myself right now.

"I've no idea, but I'm sure you'll cheer him up," Nala says, and I can't help but scowl at her exuberance. "You need to put that on and be ready in thirty minutes. I'm to escort you to the terrace gardens. It's warm out. We don't get too many evenings like this. I guess they want to make the most of it before autumn is over and winter sets in."

"Fine. I'll be ready in fifteen," I say, taking the key from Thirteen and striding into the bathroom. It's not as if I can say no. Look what happened the last time I did. Besides, I can't afford any more punishments. Getting locked up in the dungeon with The Masks will completely ruin any plans of escape, so I have to play by the rules, for now.

"She could already be dead..."

The echo of Beast's voice penetrates my thoughts as I stare at my reflection in the bathroom mirror. I'm very aware that this plan of mine could all be for nothing, that tomorrow night The Masks' patience with me could finally wear thin enough for them to let go of their restraint, that they will get their ultimate revenge and kill me. It could happen this evening at dinner, or next week sometime if my plan of escape fails. Fate is the only one who knows what's going to happen, and right now she's not allowing me to see my future. Well, screw her and her games. Tomorrow night, I'm taking matters into my own hands.

Twenty minutes later after I've showered and dressed, Nala is knocking on the bathroom door. "How're you doing? Need any help?"

"I *can* dress myself," I say, opening the bathroom door and stepping into the bedroom.

"Whoa!" Nala exclaims, her eyes popping wide. "You look really, really beautiful! That dress is stunning!"

She's right, it truly is beautiful and in a different world where I wasn't kidnapped and forced to eat with my enemies, I might've enjoyed dressing up like this for the man I loved. As it is, I'm wearing a chastity belt beneath this beautiful dress to prevent three men from taking my virginity without my consent.

It sickens my stomach.

But what's worse...? The fact that on different occasions I've succumbed to their twisted ways. I've come alive beneath their touch, even if it was under duress and fueled by the instinct to survive. I've kissed them back. My clit has throbbed in their presence, desperate for their attention. I've come, loudly, unapologetically.

And I've given up a piece of myself each time.

"Thank you," I reply emotionlessly, running my palms over the floaty skirt that skims my ankles as I walk. The dress is a deep teal, with a scalloped neckline, low back, and straps that hang off my shoulder in a swathe of material. The bodice itself is made from layers of lace that's intricately woven with tiny iridescent pearls.

"Oh, I almost forgot!" Nala says, pulling out a jewelry box from the pocket in the front of her apron. "Jakub wanted to make sure you wore these too."

Handing the necklace with the key to my chastity belt back to Thirteen, I take the box from Nala and open it. Nestled inside the blue silk-lined jewellery box is the necklace Twelve had stolen from Jakub's room of curiosities. Resting on the side are the matching earrings. I look up at Nala in shock, and even Thirteen has moved closer to take a look. Her eyes widening with as much surprise as mine.

"He wants me to wear these?" I repeat.

"Yes," Nala grins. "Put them on then."

"No, I can't," I say, shaking my head. This is too personal. They belonged to his mother. Twelve stole the necklace, wearing it to get The Masks' attention, and look what happened to her.

I can't wear them. I won't. They're tainted in Twelve's misery, her blood.

Nala's face drops. "He thought you might say that. He said if you refuse then he'll make sure Leon finishes what he started down in the dungeon with Konrad, and that this time he'll be taking the key from Thirteen and joining in too."

"But I—"

Thirteen reaches for the necklace, plucking it from the box and stepping behind me and fixing it in place before I can protest further. Then taking one of the earrings, she hands it to me.

"Looks like Thirteen thinks you should wear them too," Nala comments.

Sighing, I take the earrings from Thirteen, putting them on. "There, happy now?" I ask, feeling as though I'm wearing a ball and chain, not a beautiful necklace with years of history embedded in it.

The weight of it sits heavily on my chest. What does this even mean? Knowing Jakub, it's just more mind games. More ways to get into my head and fuck me over. I don't want to wear something personal to him. I don't want to be blackmailed into attending a dinner with three men who've done nothing but constantly hurt me. I don't want to be here. My eyes well with tears and I blink them away, hating myself for another moment of weakness. Thirteen notices and pulls me in for a hug, crushing me against her chest. When she finally lets me go, her eyes tell me everything she can't say with words.

I'm sorry. For everything.

～

"GOOD EVENING, NOTHING," Jakub says, getting to his feet as I step out onto the sunlit terrace, the afternoon's rays surprisingly warm on my skin. Leon and Konrad both rise too, watching me approach, the intensity of their gaze making my skin prickle with fear. I look down, unable to maintain eye contact, but not before noticing what masks they're wearing.

Plain black masks.

The very same masks they wore the day they stopped being children and became the men they are today. Goosebumps scatter over my skin as I approach the table. Even Nala has lost her childish excitement and has become sombre as she takes up her position beside her grandfather, Renard, who is standing next to a trolley stacked with plates of food ready to be served. I've not seen him since the night I was stripped bare in the Grand Hall. He looks older. Tired. I can't help but notice how Nala slides her hand into his and squeezes gently. What's going on there?

"Take a seat, Zero," Konrad says, pulling my attention away from the pair and back to him. I make the fatal mistake of looking up. He gives me a dazzling, welcoming smile, but his eyes tell a story of darkness and lust, blood and pain. I know what he's thinking, wanting, *craving...*

Me, bleeding and cut, whipped and bruised so he can ease his conscience with whispered words of affection and care. It's all lies.

Gritting my jaw, I snap my gaze away and take a seat, focusing on the pretty bunch of wildflowers that make up the low table centrepiece, their perfume reminding me of the open fields near my cottage back home.

Home.

Refusing to let my thoughts wander to that dangerous place, I mentally prepare myself for what I know will be a difficult few hours. If The Masks have taught me anything, it's not to expect the unexpected but to expect the *fucked-up*.

"Renard, Nala, serve up the starter then leave. We have things to discuss and can manage the rest on our own," Jakub says tersely, his voice tight.

"Yes, Sir," Renard responds, briefly looking at me. I can see the concern he has for me, and whilst I should probably feel more afraid because of it, all I can see is opportunity. Perhaps he's the person who'll help me get word to Kate? I put a pin in that thought, resolving to approach him later.

If I get a later, that is.

"You're very thoughtful, *Nought*," Leon says, emphasising his chosen name for me as he takes a sip of his drink, watching me over the rim of the glass.

"No more than usual, *Leon*," I reply tersely, clasping my hands tightly in my lap as I remember how he'd cut me, spread my blood over his cock, came over my back, then called me *Christy*.

"And on form tonight, I see. Are you looking for more punishment?" He taps the table with his finger. "Or perhaps you're the type who likes dishing it out, hmm?"

It's warm, and the sun's rays are pleasant on my skin, but it doesn't stop the goosebumps rising at the memory of what I did to him. "No. I'm nothing like *you*."

Leon smiles, winking. "Oh, I don't know, it's always the quiet ones you have to watch out for..."

We fall silent as Renard and Nala begin to serve the food, quietly moving around us. Renard fills each of our long-stemmed glasses with white wine, but his hands shake so much that the wine spills and Nala takes over for him. I see the look that passes between The Masks, but can't seem to interpret it as Nala finishes pouring the wine then places a plate of oysters before each of us.

"You may leave," Jakub says curtly, with a wave of his hand.

"Sir, *Ma'am*," Renard says, dipping his head to me.

All three men stiffen at his respectful gesture, but Renard doesn't apologise for it. He simply nods, places his hand on the centre of Nala's back and walks away. She glances at me over her shoulder, a warm smile on her face.

I know she believes in The Masks.

She sees three handsome, mysterious men, dressed up in fine black suits sitting beside a woman wearing a pretty dress, and envisions a fairy tale, not the grim truth. She's blind to the stitches on my back, the cuts, to the chastity belt digging into my skin, causing red welts from where it's rubbed too hard. She refuses to notice the lingering darkness in their gaze. She doesn't see the cage that surrounds me, or the way these men play with my life like I'm a toy, a puppet on a string. She doesn't understand how twisted up I am by them.

"Nala is a fine maid. Renard has trained her well," Jakub comments, noticing my attention on her. "Has she been fulfilling all her duties to your satisfaction?"

"*My* satisfaction?"

"Yes, who else's? She's your maid, after all."

"I've no need for a maid. I don't want one." *I don't want to be here.*

"You don't like the company?" Konrad asks, genuinely interested.

"It's not that I don't like the company. Nala is sweet, but she doesn't understand the way of the world…" My voice trails off as I feel the weight of their stare. The truth is, she's been a breath of fresh air, and I've needed her more than I care to admit. "She wishes for things that *cannot* come true."

"What things?" Jakub asks, resting his elbows on the table and steepling his fingers beneath his chin.

"The things all girls who've yet to be damaged by life want... *happily ever afters*. She doesn't understand that they don't exist."

Leon scoffs. "You think you're so fucking insightful, don't you? You've no idea what Nala has lived through. None."

"Leon," Konrad warns, fearing that he's about to spill a truth they don't wish me to hear. What they don't realise is that I already know so much. Growing up here in this castle Nala's been sheltered from the world. Her start in life isn't one I'd wish on my worst enemy, but she's not suffered the traumas that I have, that these men so clearly have at the hands of their father.

She's been cared for, protected, loved, and whilst I've experienced those things too, I've also experienced unimaginable pain just like The Masks.

"Perhaps I don't know everything she's been through," I reply. "But I recognise when a person has grown up without experiencing trauma. Or at least remembering it enough to be affected by it consciously."

Jakub shifts in his seat. "What has she told you?" His voice is even, level, but there's no denying the caution in it. *Shit.*

"Don't blame her. She was just trying to make me feel secure. *Safe.*" I laugh bitterly, shaking my head.

"What did she tell you?" Jakub insists.

"Nala told me you found her in the forest as a baby. She told me the three of you took care of her until Renard stepped in. She told me you were good once."

Silence descends. Oppressive, heavy, weighted with ghosts of the past.

"We were foolish. *Weak.* We're not good anymore," Leon says, his voice frosty, clipped.

I can't argue with him there. They are unapologetically bad, but it doesn't stop me from trying to get inside their heads, just like they've got inside of mine.

"So you were weak because you sheltered a baby, foolish because you wanted to help Nala? That's called empathy, *kindness*. Why is that so wrong?" I press. "What happened to you all?"

"We grew the fuck up," Leon replies tightly. "We became men. We became strong."

"Being an adult doesn't mean you have to lose any of that. A real man isn't afraid of kindness, empathy, *love*. Christ, he really fucked you up, didn't he?"

"You've no idea what you're talking about. The Collector *made* us," Leon counters. "Kindness, love, empathy, it's bullshit. It's weakness."

"No. It's *strength*," I insist.

Leon sneers at me, then grabs his glass of wine and takes a sip. Opposite us, Jakub watches our exchange in silence. He's thoughtful, quiet, on edge. Konrad, however, is grinning from ear-to-ear.

"Christ! You two arguing makes me hard as fuck!" He laughs, shaking his head, like we're all friends here and Leon isn't looking at me like he wants to rip me limb from limb.

"Enough. Eat," Jakub says, picking up an oyster and swallowing it.

"I know what I'd like to eat," Konrad says in a low voice as he leans over and grabs the sliced lemon off my plate, squeezing it over the oysters in front of me. "I find the taste is so much better with a dash of lemon. They're quite the aphrodisiac, just like the taste of you. What I would do to fuck your pussy with my tongue. I bet you taste sweet, Zero."

"I wouldn't know, you'd have to ask Jakub that," I snap.

Konrad stiffens, Leon slams the glass he's holding onto the table. Both of them glare at Jakub who leans back slowly in his seat.

"Count yourself lucky that I didn't take her virginity too," he says without preamble, then turns to face me, his gaze smouldering. "And yes, I can confirm Nothing tastes sweet."

"Well fuck, Brother, anything else we should know about?" Konrad asks before picking up a lemon-drizzled oyster from my plate and holding it out to me.

Jakub doesn't deign to answer him.

"What's this all about?" I ask, looking between the three men and ignoring the proffered oyster. Frankly, I don't trust it not to be poisoned. I don't know why I'm here having a meal like we're equals.

I don't know why Jakub wanted me to wear his mother's jewellery and I certainly don't know why I feel like this meal is about to change everything between us. My gut is telling me to be cautious, my back is prickling with knowing and my heart is racing.

"We've never had a chance to sit and talk. I thought it would be nice to do that," Konrad explains, placing the oyster shell against his lips and tipping his head back to swallow it. I watch his Adam's apple bob up and down as he swallows.

"You thought it would be *nice*? I'm not sure you understand the meaning of the word," I counter, trying to keep a lid on my emotions.

"Careful, Nought, the night is still young," Leon warns. "We've plenty of time to show you how *nasty* we can truly be. You've just scratched the surface."

"Oh, of course!" I roll my eyes, feigning calm when I'm anything but. "I could end up tied to that cross again, drugged and naked so you can both get your kicks."

"I didn't see you complaining. In fact, I distinctly remember you coming so hard you passed out," Leon counters, just like the bastard that he is.

"Screw you. I passed out from blood loss, from sheer fucking terror. I allowed myself a moment of weakness because, really, what alternative did I have, huh? Just because I came doesn't mean I wanted to, you fucking arsehole!" I seethe, my chest heaving, my hand reaching for the blunt knife on the table. Even as I say the words, I'm internally cursing myself. I need to calm down.

I need to play them at their own game, but by God, they make it hard.

Leon grins, and Konrad gives me a look that a parent might give to a child who has pleasantly surprised them with their tenacity. Neither seem in the slightest bit bothered that I'm holding a knife.

"Put it down, Nothing," Jakub says, his voice firm.

I turn my attention to him, still clutching the knife, knowing that any one of them would be able to disarm me without difficulty, but feeling minutely safer for it. "You promised you'd keep them away," I say, sounding heartbroken, feeling heartbroken. I know it was stupid of me to expect better of him, but the tiniest part of me thought that perhaps he would live up to his word.

I was stupid. So, so stupid.

"No, I didn't. I said they wouldn't touch you... I guess I lied."

"You *pig*!" I launch myself at Jakub, knife held aloft, only to be pulled back by Konrad.

Jakub doesn't flinch. He simply takes a sip of wine, his long fingers wrapping around the delicate glass as Konrad rips the knife from my hand, shoves me back into my seat and kisses the top of my head, his fingers lingering in my hair as he says; "You really are fucking beautiful when you're angry."

"Screw you!" I snarl.

"Now now, Zero, didn't anyone tell you it's rude to tease?" Konrad shakes his head, smiling still but his fingers tighten in my hair painfully. Yanking my head back, he lifts the knife to my throat and smirks as he runs the blunt edge against the column of my neck. My nostrils flare but I don't move as he stares down at me, his black hair flopping forward over his mask. Pressing his mouth against my ear he says, "If you try to kill my brother again, I will take this knife and fuck your cunt with the handle before slitting your throat." Letting me go with a shove, he smiles warmly again, morphing back into the softer version of the demon he clearly is. "Of course, I'll make you come first."

"Well, fuck!" Leon whistles. "I didn't think you'd be able to do it, Nought."

"Do what?" I ask, clasping my hands in my lap so none of them can see how badly they're shaking.

"Get Konrad to reveal his true self." He raises his glass and taps the edge of mine, saluting me with it before taking another swig.

Konrad draws in a deep breath, then blows it out slowly. "I tolerate many things, but threatening my brothers? It's my biggest trigger."

"I shouldn't worry, Kon, all you need to do is tell Nought what she wants to hear and she's putty in your hands. Right, Jakub? Promise to protect her from us and get her to give you a blowjob, is that how it really went down?"

"Fuck you!" I retort, gritting my jaw and turning my head away. I can't believe I kissed Leon, that for a moment my need to soothe his pain had overridden everything that he'd done.

How foolish of me. Maybe Leon's right, maybe kindness *is* weakness.

"My brothers and I share everything," Jakub says randomly, interrupting the moment and taking a knife to the tension, slicing right through it. "That includes moments of pleasure, pain and everything in between. I indulged my desires when I shouldn't have. I set this path in motion. I acted selfishly but now that my brothers have had their fill, we're even," he says, picking up a shell and plucking the oyster out with a fork, chewing on it. "Perhaps we can move on, yes?"

"*Even*? This isn't tit-for-tat. No one gets to take from me to even up a score between you all," I protest, still arguing despite the danger I'm in. "Getting even is what got us into this shit in the first place! Just let it go. Let. Me. Go, and this will all end. I'll make sure of it. There'll be no repercussions. I swear to you."

"Do you want to spell it out for her, or should I?" Leon asks with a grin that I want to slap off his face. When no one answers, he continues. "You don't get a say in the decisions we make. You don't get a say in what we do or don't take. You're our *toy*, our *plaything*, a form of *revenge*, that's it. That's *all* you are. You're Nothing. Zero. Nought."

The venom coming from his mouth has me flinching, but it doesn't deter me from saying what I do next. Drawing in a deep breath, I pick up an oyster and tip it down my throat. After swiping the back of my hand over my mouth, I fix my gaze on Leon.

"Funny, because I'm pretty sure I became more than that when you kissed me like a drowning man in your gym, when you called me *Christy* in Konrad's dungeon... Tell me why you have those tattoos, Leon. Is it to remind you of the little girl you saved that day, huh? Is it to remind you that you were good, that you weren't always a fucking monster?"

Konrad stiffens in his seat. "What the fuck is she talking about, Leon?"

"You don't know anything," he argues, baring his teeth at me and ignoring his brother.

"I know a scared man when I see one, he's not so different from that teenage boy who rescued a little girl from a burning building. You can pretend all you want, but I *see* you. I see the angel buried deep inside your chest and the next time I hold up that mirror, you will too."

Their silence is deafening.

The aftermath, explosive.

I don't know who moves first, Leon, Konrad or Jakub.

Either way, the table gets turned over as Leon tries to reach for me, incoherent words pouring from strained lips. I stand, stumbling backwards, my chair falling over. Glasses and plates smash, and oysters and wildflowers go flying. Leon has murder in his eyes. Pain too.

So much pain.

It's the pain which makes me pause and not turn around and run.

He's *hurting*.

I should be glad about that, shouldn't I? Yet... I'm not. It doesn't feel good to see him in distress. It doesn't.

Before he's able to grip me around the throat, Konrad and Jakub wrestle him to the ground, pinning him to the floor beneath them both. Konrad straddles his chest, Jakub his legs.

"Bitch!" Leon snarls, bucking like a wild animal caught in a trap, willing to gnaw off his own leg than stay trapped. Despite the size and weight of both Konrad and Jakub, he seems to have inhuman strength as they both struggle to keep him contained. His rage is like a living, breathing entity. Like it has the power to reach out and throttle me to death. My throat dries out, my heart rate kicking into overdrive as I watch Leon unravel before my very eyes.

"Brother! No!" Konrad shouts, gripping his wrists and pinning them above his head.

"Get her the fuck out of here!" he roars, the veins in his neck pushing against his skin as he fights.

"Easy now," Jakub adds, trying his best to calm his brother.

"I'm going to fucking kill her!" Leon shouts, but it comes out broken, as though deep down he doesn't want to, like it hurts him to even say those words. "I'm going to take her throat in my hands and squeeze the fucking lies from it."

"What she said doesn't mean a damn thing," Konrad says, lowering his voice, straining to keep him in place. "Just breathe, okay? Listen to my voice. It's okay, Brother. It's okay."

"It's not okay," I whisper, the guilt and sorrow building inside my chest taking form. "Nothing about this is okay."

Leon thrashes, his mask falling away. His face is red, an angry vein pulses in his forehead, but it's his eyes that unhinge me. They're made startlingly bright by the tears that brim in them.

I should run. I don't.

Jakub notices. "Back the fuck off!" he warns, locking eyes with me over his shoulder.

"I just—" One hand covers my mouth as a tear rolls from Leon's eye. A fucking tear.

He's *crying*.

We lock gazes and the shame I see in him upends me.

"FUUUCCKKKKK!" Leon roars. "GET HER AWAY FROM ME!"

My teeth chatter and my whole body begins to tremble, but for some unfathomable reason I can't move. It's like my feet are fixed to the stone, and my heart... It thrashes inside my chest, beating wildly for a man I should hate. That I *do* hate. Except right now, at his most dangerous, all I feel is a deep sense of sadness for everything he's lost, and I know that if I don't leave right now, this will be the end of me. This, right here, is my death. I will die at the hands of a man who is crying, raging, violent, because I made him *feel*.

Because I held up the mirror and made him see.

"Get. The. Fuck. Away," Jakub says through gritted teeth.

"He's hurting," I reply, my hand reaching up to his mother's necklace. "I want to help him." I don't know why at that moment, as I rest my fingertips against the cool metal, I decide to say those specific words, but I do. They feel both right and wholly wrong. He doesn't deserve my empathy, but he gets it regardless.

I should be gleeful. I should be *happy* Leon's in pain.

But I'm not.

Right at this moment *I'm not*.

Jakub winces as he stares at me. "Go! Now!"

"But—"

"If you want to help my brother, then get the fuck away from here. RIGHT NOW!" Konrad yells, his gaze cutting into my chest, ripping out my damn empathy, and smearing it all over the pretty dress I'm wearing, making me filthy with it. We lock gazes and I see the love he has for his brother as plain as day. "*Please*," he adds through gritted teeth.

With one firm nod of my head, I turn on my heel and walk away.

Like the confused, fucked-up woman I've become, I don't use this as an opportunity to run. I simply walk back through the castle, past countless rooms, down several corridors and up two flights of stone steps until I reach Thirteen's room. I'm on autopilot.

My mother's letter. Leon's pain. Konrad and Jakub's love. My empathy. Fate's fucking decree. It all pinwheels inside my head. Fucking me up.

"Thirteen, please, let me in," I whisper, my forehead pressed against the wood.

After the third knock, she opens the door, takes one look at my face, and sits me down on the edge of the bed. Removing the jewellery carefully, she places them back in the box, then helps me out of the prettiest dress I've ever worn and hands me a loose, pale grey smock dress and a glass of water. I pull on the dress, and drink the water absently, feeling out of sorts. Strange. Unhinged from reality in a way. All I can feel is Leon's pain, and Jakub's and Konrad's *love*.

It was deep, fierce. It was a… surprise.

All of it was so intense, so overwhelming that instead of using the moment to run, all I could do was return to this room.

All I could do was stay.

Picking up her pad and pencil, Thirteen writes something then hands it to me, tapping the pad so that I stop staring off into the distance and read the words settled on my lap.

You feel it, don't you? You feel their brokenness and their need. Their love for one another.

I look at her and nod. "Yes, I felt it."

She nods, writing more words.

That's why I stay. That's why you must stay. I cracked open the floodgates. That was my job.

"Because of my mother's letter?"

Partly, she writes.

"And the other part?"

That's not important. What's important is that you see. Everything you've said about them is right. They are dark men. But there is hope for them now that you're here. You have a job to do, Christy.

"And what exactly is my job?" I ask softly, already knowing but needing her to say it out loud.

You're the one who will push the gates wide open. You're the one who's strong enough to withstand the flood, who'll survive it. You're the only one who can.

"But what if I don't want to? What then?"

Then all of this was for nothing. Don't you get it? Your mother was right. You can't fight what's written in the stars. You're the only one who'll love The Masks the way they need to be loved. You're theirs. Understand?

With that, Thirteen gently presses a kiss against my cheek, then leaves me to my thoughts.

I lay back on the bed, my mind whirring, my lungs expanding and contracting as I try to gasp for air. Thirteen has echoed Fate's decree, hammering the final nail in the coffin of my future with her words. I feel like I'm suffocating, drowning, sinking beneath an ocean of responsibility.

The weight of this truth sits heavy on my soul.

But how can I be responsible for such a monumental task? These men aren't good, they're not kind, thoughtful. They don't care about me, not in a healthy way, not in *any* way.

They don't want me, not for the right reasons anyway. They mean me *harm*.

They want to hurt, debase, degrade, *use*. They want my screams, my fear, my tears, my heartbreak, my submission. They want their revenge.

Leon wants to draw out the darkest parts of me with pain and fear. Konrad wants to break me then fix me up like some china doll he can smash to pieces then glue back together, over and over again... And Jakub, I'm not certain what he wants other than revenge for his father's death.

What had Thirteen, *Cyn*, said?

You're the one who'll love them the way they need to be loved. You're theirs. Understand?

How can I even contemplate such a task? How can I sit here and even give the idea a fraction of a thought? How can I give up myself like that?

"This is crazy," I mumble, covering my face with my hands.

But it isn't, not really.

It's *fate*.

And I fucking hate it.

Thirteen never said The Masks would love me back, and that's because she knows, like I do, that they're incapable. The only love they have left is for each other. It's a twisted, dark, complicated kind of love but it doesn't extend past the three of them. I know that. I sense that.

How can I ever love *them*?

The truth is, I can't.

I won't sacrifice who I am, what I need to be happy, to save three men who don't deserve to be saved.

Thirteen is wrong. My mother is wrong.

I'm *not* strong enough to do this.

I have to leave.

Tomorrow night, during the show, I will.

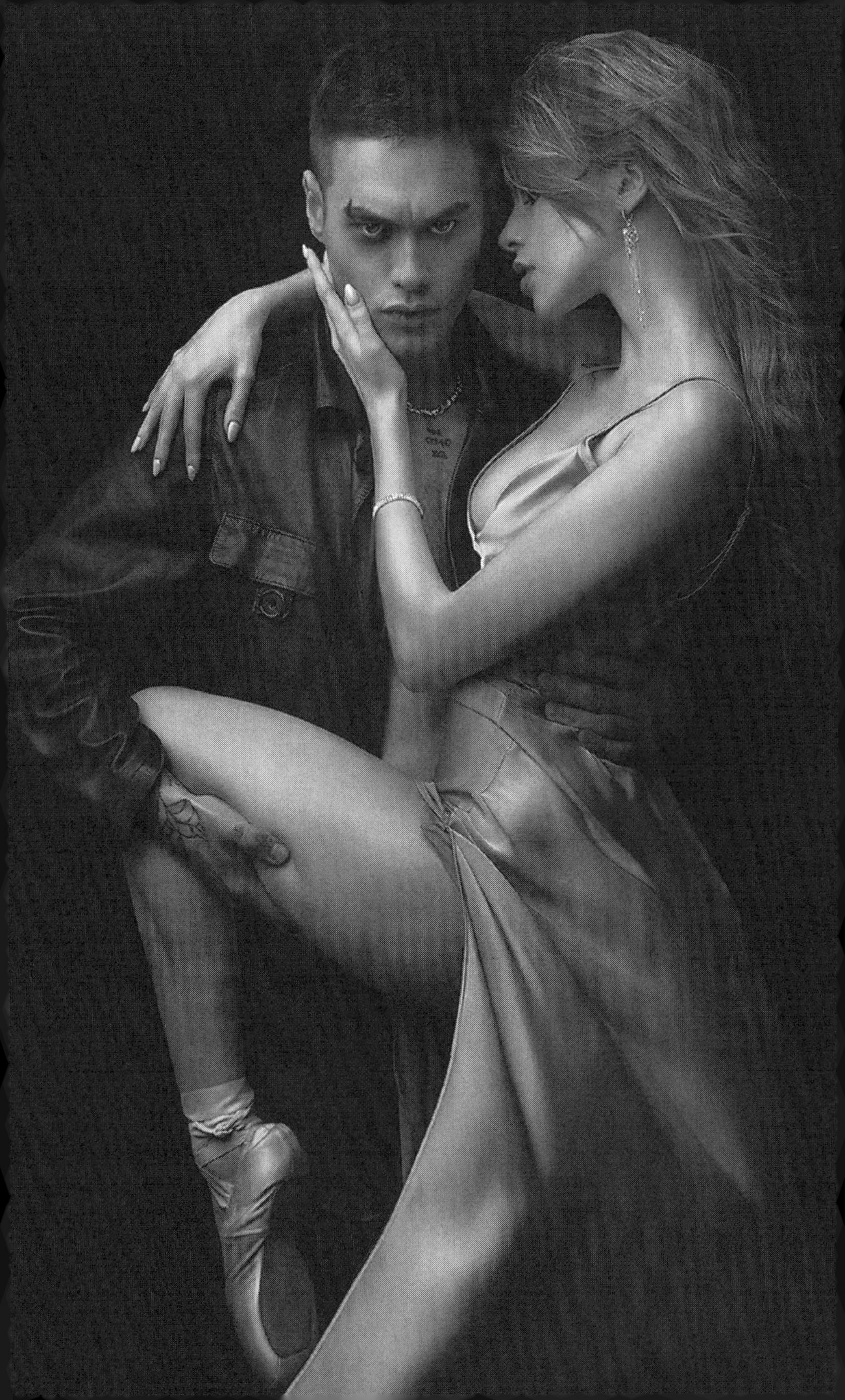

CHAPTER 32

CHRISTY

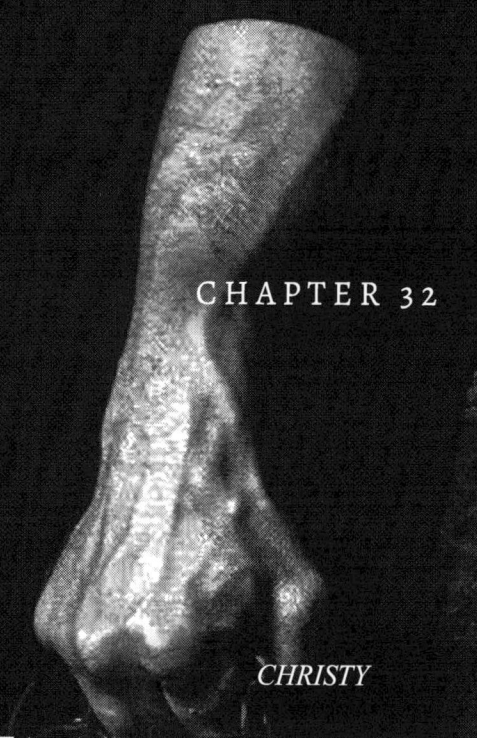

The air thrums with heat, it's thick and cloying. The scent of cigarette smoke lingering, a blanket of silvery-grey clouds hangs above us. The theatre we're performing in is small, intimate and situated on the southern side of the castle where the guests are to remain this evening. The theatre seats a maximum of twenty-one people around three round tables.

Every seat is filled.

Faceless men and women sit in the audience wearing gowns, dark suits and masks. Konrad, Leon and Jakub are seated amongst them, one at each table. They talk in low voices, laughing and entertaining their guests as wine and food are served by the castle staff. Tiny candles flicker on each table, and high above them Two is perched on a swing, gently swaying back and forth in the darkness, waiting for her moment to perform. Right now it's the break between acts. Half of the numbers have already performed, the rest will do so after my solo dance.

In less than two minutes I will step onto the stage and dance for these men and women, for The Masks. I will show them a glimpse of my soul. A piece *I* choose to share, not something they've ripped from me.

I will make The Masks see what they've enslaved, trapped.

I will prove to them that I'm more than a number, more than a toy, more than a puppet.

By the end of this performance I will become Christy the girl.

I will become *human*.

At least that's what I'm hoping for.

Then I will escape as the girl they brought here, not the number they reduced me to.

"Are you sure about this?" Three asks as she ties the ends of two long lengths of string around each of my wrists and hands me the small pair of scissors I requested.

"I am."

"One won't be pleased, she hasn't approved this."

"I don't care."

"And the dress… I thought Konrad told you to wear something else?"

"He did. I'm not."

"You'll be punished," she says gently, her voice wracked with concern.

"I don't care."

Three sighs. "Okay. Then are you ready?"

"Yes," I say firmly, nodding my head, feeling claustrophobic beneath the mask I've been given to wear. Ironically, it's the same shade of pale pink as the dress I wasn't supposed to wear and covers my whole face, not revealing even a glimmer of flesh. Of all the Numbers, I'm the only one wearing a mask, a last minute addition that I've been ordered to wear. I guess this is The Masks' way of claiming me as theirs, of letting their clients know subtly that I belong to them, despite me performing in The Menagerie.

"It's time to get on stage," she says, hugging me before stepping back into the shadows of the backstage area with the rest of the Numbers who aren't performing.

Breathing in deeply to settle my nerves, I step onto the stage. One begins to play the grand piano, a spotlight switching on and covering her in a soft white light that makes her seem impossibly beautiful. The chatter in the audience dies down as they listen to her play. She's naked except for a sheer black kimono that hangs off her shoulders and flows over the stool she's sitting on, revealing her pert breasts and perfectly toned body. The grand piano itself is made of white lacquered wood, contrasting her dark hair, dress, and soul perfectly.

Despite it all, I get a rush of adrenaline as I take up my starting position, still steeped in darkness, and watch her delicate fingers move over the piano keys. As she plays, another spotlight flicks on revealing Six and Seven as they stand to the right of the stage. Six is wearing an emerald green bustier with heeled black pumps, showcasing her curvaceous hips and legs. Next to her Seven stands with his chin tilted up and his chest bare. He wears sheer red trousers, his cock and neatly trimmed pubic hair on display. They're both stunning.

A shiver cascades down my spine as I watch Seven draw in a deep breath. When he opens his mouth, that first exquisite note passing his lips, my whole body shudders. This song, *Dancing After Death* by Matt Maeson is utterly perfect for the way I'm feeling. There's a morbidity to the song, a gentle sway of secrecy, *sorcery*, that fits this night and the darkness in this room perfectly.

Seven's voice rings out around the theatre, a perfect accompaniment to One's piano playing. The beauty of his voice is haunting, emotional, eerie. When Six joins in, harmonising, it becomes goddamn orgasmic.

I'm wet just listening to them sing.

They're both sin and virtue. Celestial and fiendish.

They're exquisite, rare, utterly irreplaceable.

I understand now why The Collector acquired them, why they're so attractive. It isn't just their looks, it's their ability to lift your soul, to make your skin cover in goosebumps, to take you to another place with their voice, their talent. The way they sing, it isn't just about a series of sounds that's pleasant to the ear.

Six and Seven make you *crave* pleasure. They make you want the darkness. Revel in it.

After the first verse, a spotlight appears before me. This is my cue to begin. This is my time.

With one final shuddering breath, I grasp the scissors tightly in my hands then step into the spotlight and dance.

I let go.

My body becomes a vessel for the lyrics and the music. I've practised this dance over and over again these past few days, but those practised steps become perfect now as I move across the stage, the length of string pulled taught from above.

I've become their puppet.

Ignoring the dull ache from the blisters on my feet and refusing to acknowledge the sharp pain as my stitches pull free once again, I dance with every fibre of my being, fully aware that this could well be the last time.

It's not safe here. I'm not safe here.

But like the song suggests, I dance in the face of danger. I dance as though I'm already dead. As though I'm a ghost. There's freedom in that. A lightness. A purity.

The skin on my back tingles. It's a portent, an omen, warning me that I'm close to the truth.

But it doesn't deter me. It gives me the strength to really let go, to free myself from the chains these men have inflicted on my soul. If death is close, then I shall live in this moment.

It won't stop me from running. I'm not scared to flee.

But I will give them something to remember me by.

I will dance as though death is merely a gateway to somewhere better, somewhere far away from here, where I'm free in all the ways that count. Free to dance, free to love the people I want to love, free to live, free to be who I am, scars and all.

So that's what I do.

Lifting onto my pointes, I dance like I've never danced before. Teasing the floor with my silk pointes, I open my arms wide, twisting and turning, then unravelling the ropes that hold my arms aloft. My hair flows out behind me, around me as I move. My dress is a ripple of material that does nothing to hide my flaws, but highlights them.

The audience takes a collective breath as I lose myself to the incredible music. I pitch low, dragging my fingers over the dusty floorboards, then lift up high, leaping into the air in an entrechat, my feet crossing several times before landing in the fifth position. Kicking out, I spin in a pirouette, moving across the stage with a deftness, a lightness that I haven't felt, well... *ever*.

It's a contradiction in itself because surrounding me are people with darkness in their hearts. It sits heavily around us, like an eclipse that devours the sunlight, *any* light.

It's oppressive, frightening. It's the heavy beat of danger just waiting to pounce.

There are three men in this room who've claimed me. Who wish me harm. Fate has given me over to them, and in a small way so have I. I've given up pieces of myself in order to save my life, my sanity whilst imprisoned here.

I've felt empathy for them. Hated them. Lusted after them.

I've been twisted up, abused, used, tortured.

I've been beaten and I've fought back.

But the one thing I will not do is love them.

As the music comes to an end, and the last notes spill from Six and Seven's lips, all I'm left with is the final instrumental verse. Right now, I'm supposed to dance my way over to One. Instead, I walk en-pointe to the centre of the stage, lift my hands to my mask, and remove it, revealing my face. Dropping the mask to the floor, I take the scissors and snip the string, releasing me.

It's my final fuck you to The Masks.

They want to keep me hidden. They want to claim me as theirs. They want to keep me as their toy, their *puppet*.

Screw that. Only I have the power to give myself up to them and I won't. Not ever.

The audience erupts, clapping and cheering as I curtsey, dipping low.

"Encore!" the crowd shouts.

I just stand, breathing heavily, shocked by the audience's reaction, until eventually the lights go out and I run from the stage.

Straight into a hard chest.

"Where do you think you're going?"

No.

"Jakub?" I ask, peering up at him in the dim half light as he grabs hold of my upper arm tightly. "What are you doing back here?"

"You've caused quite a stir, Nothing. Disobeying us like this. Do you want to be punished?"

"Let me go!" I demand, but Jakub shakes his head.

"It seems that you've caught the eye of the Baron. He has a thing for redheads. Apparently you remind him of his daughter."

"What?" I say, swallowing hard as Jakub backs me into a darkened alcove, the rest of the Numbers getting ready for the next portion of the show behind us. My back hits the wall and Jakub presses his chest against mine, resting his forearm beside my head. He's wearing his black mask again, accompanied with a black suit and shirt. He's every inch the shadowed man of my visions.

A predator.

A monster.

A Mask.

"He's willing to pay a very, very handsome amount of money for you. Enough to make me question just how much you really are ours. Money makes the world go round, after all."

"You're not suggesting…" My throat dries out, my pulse thumping erratically.

"Yes, I am. The Baron wants to fuck you because he can't fuck his own daughter. The question is, am I willing to let him?"

"No! Don't you dare!" I push against Jakub's chest but he just grasps my wrists and pins them above my head, leaning in closer so that his whisky breath feathers over my skin.

"Why shouldn't I? You tried to kill me yesterday, you *beat* Leon. You disobey us at every fucking turn. You're a problem."

"It's no more than you deserve!"

"You're a liability."

"And you're a monster!"

"I don't deny it. I never have. So what do you think? Should I let the Baron take your virginity? Should I let him fuck you whilst he thinks about his child as he does it?"

"I would rather die first," I hiss.

"I thought you might say that. Which is why I'm giving you a choice, Nothing." Gripping both wrists with one hand, Jakub reaches into his jacket pocket and brings out two tiny vials.

"What are they?" I ask, staring at the two bottles, one labelled A, the other B.

"They're elixirs. Two of Thirteen's most potent. One will render your body useless, unfeeling, whilst your mind stays intact. If you choose this option you won't feel a thing, but you will remember every minute detail. The other elixir will shut your mind down completely, you won't remember anything, but your body will remain awake. It will bear the marks of your ordeal and you'll be tormented with the knowledge that you'll never know what happened."

"That isn't a choice."

"It is the only one you have."

"And the Baron? How does choosing one of these bottles have anything to do with him?"

"Oh it doesn't. When we say you are ours, we mean it. He won't touch you."

"So what then? What's the purpose of all of this?"

He shrugs, brushing his lips against my birthmark before whispering in my ear. "To have a little fun, of course, and to show you that no matter what you think, *we* are in control. Always. That show of defiance you just performed has done nothing but bind you to us further. You'll never be free of us."

"I hate you!"

"Hate me or don't. This is how it is. If you choose the elixir that shuts down your mind, you will be taken to Thirteen's room and allowed to sleep it off. No one will touch you, not even us. Not tonight, anyway."

"And if I choose the other?" I ask, blinking back my tears, refusing to give him the satisfaction of knowing how terrified I am.

"Then we will deliver you to the *Room of Fantasies* alongside the other Numbers. You will watch everything that happens there, but your body will remain useless, unfeeling. You'll be a living breathing *corpse*, for want of a better word. You'll just have to hope that no one oversteps the mark because you sure as fuck won't be able to get away if they do."

I look from him to the two tiny bottles, wishing I'd run sooner. I'm so *so* stupid.

"I choose B," I say quickly, not wanting to think too hard about it.

Jakub drops the bottle labelled B back into his pocket, then pops the cork out of bottle A and smiles. "Then you'll drink A," he says with an evil grin.

"Wait, no!" I protest, but before I'm able to fight him off, Leon and Konrad step out of the shadows.

"Good evening, Zero. You danced beautifully tonight," Konrad says, pressing a gentle kiss against my temple, before wrapping his arms around me whilst Leon grips my jaw and pinches my nose, cutting off my air supply.

I try to shake off Leon's hold, but he just grips me tighter, his green eyes sharp and unyielding. "This is your punishment, take it like the good little puppet that you are."

In my head I'm screaming every obscenity I can think of so that I can hold my breath for as long as possible. Of course I'm only delaying the inevitable.

It's useless.

No matter how much I want to keep my mouth shut, the instinct to survive takes over, and the second I open my mouth, gasping for air, Jakub tips the elixir onto my tongue and Leon forces my jaw shut.

"Now be a good little puppet and swallow it down, *Nought*," Leon demands as he tips my head back. All I can do is swallow so I don't choke.

Within seconds my limbs lose all sensation, but my mind...

My mind stays intact.

CHAPTER 33

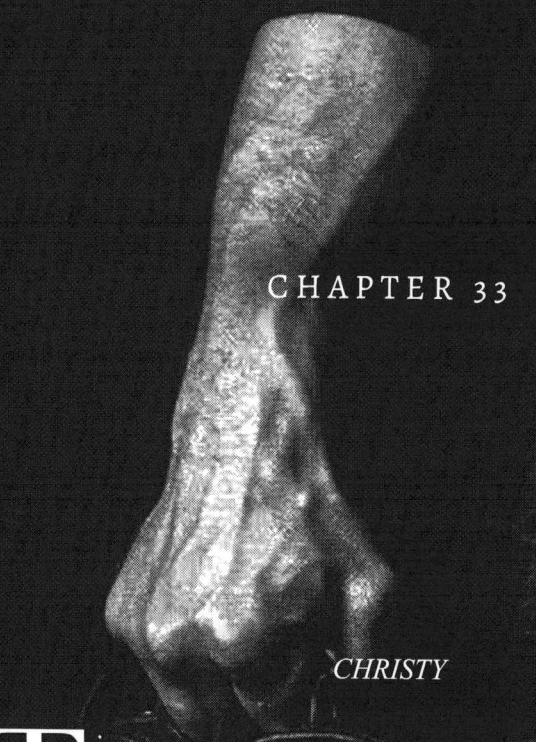

CHRISTY

Time passes.
One moment I'm being carried in Konrad's arms, the next I'm strapped to a wooden frame, my wrists, ankles and forehead fixed in place with leather cuffs.

I can't feel my body.

I try to wriggle my fingers and toes, but no matter how hard I try, I can't move a muscle.

I can't even cry.

Jakub fed me the elixir that numbs my body but keeps my mind awake.

I'm in the *Room of Fantasies*.

Internally I scream, I fight, I rage, but externally I'm a puppet waiting for the puppet masters to bring her back to life.

Trying not to panic, I take in my surroundings, thankful that at least I can move my eyes. As far as I can tell in the dim light, I'm in a room with vaulted ceilings, hundreds of candles casting shadows around the room. I sense people moving within the shadows, beyond them.

Even though I can hear, see and smell, I don't feel a thing. This isn't The Quickening, I'm not turned on by the slightest touch, a whisper of air, or the heady thrum of lustful moans surrounding me.

I'm a shell. *Empty.*

Hollowed out.

Unfeeling.

All I can do is watch. I'm wide-eyed and staring into shadows. I'm unable to fight, unable to move as the room comes alive before me. Slowly, one by one, five gilded birdcages are lit from above, revealing the sweat-slicked, moaning, writhing bodies within.

My senses are flooded, overwhelmed with scents and sounds, moans and movement.

Naked bodies. Entwined. Contorted.

Fucking.

A female voice sings. Not Six this time. This voice is higher, lighter. A soprano. It's beautiful, angelic. Twelve steps into the dim light cast by the sputtering candles placed around the room. She looks sad, empty, but sings with such broken beauty that I wished I could set her free from this unrequited love she's trapped herself within.

She sings like an angel as sin unfolds around us.

In one gilded cage I see the flash of a red lipsticked mouth around a cock. At first I can't tell who it is, but then I notice the long dark hair and see the tears streaming down One's face as a man holds her head in place and fucks her mouth roughly. But she takes it, deep throating him with the ease of a woman who has experienced such a thing before and enjoyed it. Below her spread legs is a woman I don't recognise, her face buried in One's pussy. I watch as One chokes and gags but is pleasured at the same time.

In the next cage Four and Eight are wrapped around each other, kissing passionately, feeling each other's breasts, both getting fucked from behind by two masked men, their bodies pushed together with every punishing thrust.

The cage alongside that holds Seven and Three. He fucks her from behind, her body pressed up against the golden bars, his fingers buried inside her pussy, his hand around her throat as he's whipped by a man wearing black leather chaps, a cowboy hat, a leather studded mask and a hard on.

Next to that, in the fourth cage, Six is on her hands and knees, a gag in her mouth and a chain around her throat as she's fucked by a woman wearing a strap-on and a pretty, red mask, her pendulous breasts swaying as she moves.

Further along in the next cage, the triplets are all tied up in rope, contorted into different positions to allow easy penetration. One man is fucking Nine's mouth as she hangs horizontally from the arched roof, her arms pinned to her side, her legs lifted off the floor. He holds onto her shoulders, using the momentum as she swings to deepthroat her mouth. Beside her, Ten is bent over in half, moaning in pleasure as her chest is pressed against her legs, the rope keeping her in position as she's fucked in the arse. On the floor of the cage, Eleven has her legs spread wide with rope as another man fucks her missionary style, whilst his meaty hands grasp her tiny breasts.

Swinging high above them all is Two. She's naked, her blonde hair flowing free as she fucks one of the guests, their bodies glistening with sweat, his mouth around her nipple, her hand around his throat.

And standing outside each cage are several men and women all in various states of undress, touching themselves, each other, as they walk from cage to cage, drinking champagne, snorting coke from silver trays laid out on tables around the room, watching everything unfold.

When one person finishes with a Number, another person steps inside the cage and it all starts over again. They all moan, groan, scream in pleasure, and the air around us fills with the musky scent of sex, choking the air with lust and sin. Every single person getting high on it.

It's an orgy. A painting of sin and debauchery.

It's wild and raw.

It's frightening and erotic.

It's sinful.

And strapped to a wooden frame on the far side of the room is me.

Vulnerable.

Alone...

Until I'm not.

Until a man old enough to be my father steps away from the group of people watching Six get fucked, and turns his attention to me, cock in hand, obsession in his eyes.

The Baron.

I know it without needing to be introduced. This is the man who wants to fuck me because I look like his daughter.

Inside I scream loudly trying to wake up my body, to force life into my limbs. But it's no use.

I'm cast adrift. My body cannot respond to my commands.

I'm sleeping beauty... and this man approaching isn't a beast but a monster.

A different kind to The Masks.

But no less a monster.

Looking about the room, the man checks to see if anyone's watching him. When he realises no one is, his greedy fingers creep over my skin as he squeezes and gropes.

Inside I'm screaming, my lungs are bruised, my heart bleeding.

"Why are you still dressed? I want to see you bare, my darling petal," he says, pressing his spittle-covered lips against my neck. "Let me see you."

He reaches up to the neck of my dress and tears the material. It splits down the front, baring my breasts for him. He grabs hold of them, licking his lips hungrily. "Pretty pink buds," he says. When I don't react he grins, smiling widely. "You can't move, can you? Oh, how glorious!"

When his fingers reach my crotch, he yanks at the lock then hisses, but that doesn't seem to phase him. Instead he fists his cock then crouches low, his lips hovering over my breast. "I bet you taste just like the dirty little whore that you are, petal. I'm going to enjoy this."

I can't even close my eyes on what's about to happen. All I can do is look into the distance and take his abuse as he lowers his mouth to my nipple and sucks.

Get off me! I shout, willing my body to come alive.

He makes these disgusting slurping noises, and even though I can't feel what he's doing, I can hear him, see him and it makes me want to simultaneously rip his head off and curl up into a ball.

How could they do this? How could The Masks leave me vulnerable like this? I thought I was theirs? My blood boils with anger, with frustration, with hate, with *disappointment.*

I shouldn't have expected any less. They've never lied to me. They've never given me any reason to believe that they care, that I mean more to them than a possession, an object, a toy.

I should've expected this. I should've run earlier. I should've killed Leon when I had the chance. I should've... should've... should've...

"Oh yes," the Baron moans, jacking off as he sucks on me, moving from one nipple to the other.

Both of us are too caught up in this moment, me in a nightmare, the Baron living out his sick fantasy, that we don't see what's about to happen.

Cold air rushes over my skin, and half a beat later, the Baron grunts, slamming into me. He lets out a scream of shock, pushing off me and stumbling backwards, the handle of a knife sticking out of his left shoulder, the blade buried deep into his flesh.

He howls, eyes widening, blood draining from his face, his cock going flaccid.

Everyone in the room stills.

The fucking stops.

Cocks pull out of pussies, bodies untangle. The guests turn and stare as the Baron backs up, away from the knife-thrower. Away from Five.

"There's no need to be rash," he says, fear rippling across his face as Five moves towards him, her fingers resting on another knife that's strapped to her chest.

"What do you want me to do with him?" Five asks, and I realise then that she's not acting alone. Behind her The Masks step out of the shadows.

"You touched what belongs to us," Leon says, his voice cold, rigid with anger as he approaches the terrified man, his cock all but shrivelled up, lost beneath his overhanging belly.

"I'm s—sorry," he says, stumbling over his apology and holding his hands up in surrender. "Everyone out!" Jakub shouts.

The Numbers look from one to the other, then to me and The Masks.

"Take them to the banquet hall," Konrad instructs, looking directly at One who nods, ushering everyone out.

"Five," Leon says, jerking his chin towards Nine, Ten and Eleven who are still tied up in rope.

Five deftly cuts the rope, freeing them. They leave like all the rest, taking Twelve with them, until it's just me, the Baron, and The Masks.

"Surely we can resolve this. I have money. I shall pay for what I took," the Baron says, his hands shaking.

Leon shakes his head, a slow smile creeping up beneath his half-mask. "Oh, you'll pay."

"It was a misunderstanding…"

"Did you fall and trip onto her breast, huh? Is that what you're saying?"

"I—" The man backs up towards the opposite wall, the knife sticking out of his shoulder, blood trickling from the wound. Fear widening his eyes. He's right to be afraid. Tonight, death has come for him in the form of three men dressed head to toe in black. Monsters dressed like the Grim Reaper.

"She was just strapped there and I thought—"

"You thought you could touch what isn't yours?" Konrad asks.

"Please, have mercy. It was a mistake!"

Jakub shakes his head. "There is no mercy. Especially not when it comes to what belongs to us."

"You knew the rules. We said *no*," Leon says.

One minute he's standing by Jakub's side, the next he's striding towards the Baron and pulling the blade from his shoulder. The Baron screams in pain, blood spurting from the wound and colouring the wall behind him in splashes of scarlet blood. "She's ours!"

"No, please—"

But the Baron's cry is cut short as Leon slashes the knife across his throat in a flash of silver and parted flesh. His knees give way as he collapses to the floor, a crimson river of blood flooding his neck and chest. Leon passes the knife to Konrad, who takes it and slams it into the Baron's gut, slicing him open. The Baron's eyes widen, but he can't scream.

"You piece of shit," Konrad snarls, passing the knife to Jakub who takes it and pries the Baron's mouth open, cutting out his tongue.

"That's for your daughter, you sick fuck."

But the Baron doesn't hear him. He's already dead.

Internally, I let out a bloodcurdling scream, thankful at least that I can't draw attention to myself, not when death lingers in the air and violence runs through The Masks' veins. It makes no difference though. Screaming or total silence, The Masks still turn to face me. I'm alone with three twisted, fucked-up men with no way to protect myself. I don't even have any words, my voice is as useless as my body.

I'm at their mercy.

"The eyes really are the window to the soul," Jakub remarks as the three of them move towards me. "You're more afraid than you've ever been. Your courage, it's gone. Stripped away."

He's right, it has. Being mute, unable to move can do that to a person. Every step towards me is purposeful, every look full of meaning. They are the hunters and I am their prey.

"He touched you," Konrad says, standing before me.

Of course he touched me, I think. Scream, actually. *Don't throw a piece of meat to a wolf and expect it not to take a bite.*

Konrad tips his head to the side. "You have so much to say. I can almost hear you shouting, Zero. For now, however, you're going to listen."

God damn these men!

Reaching for me, Konrad presses his hand against my cheek, cupping my face. "When I saw what he was doing to you… Fuck, Zero, I wanted to burn the whole fucking world down."

"I needed to be certain," Jakub says, reaching for me too. He slides his hand over the centre of my chest, resting it above my beating heart.

Certain of what? I silently ask, questions ghosting over my face.

"You were right to check, Brother," Leon adds, dusting his

knuckles over my clavicle as he buries his face in my hair and breathes me in.

My pulse thrums, my heart kicking up a notch. Its beat is erratic, afraid, and *alive* as they stroke me. Their fingers are made of ink and twilight, velvet and charcoal. Their concern is felt, not communicated as they touch my body, searching for bruises and marks, checking that I'm okay.

"You're a problem, Nothing," Jakub whispers against my ear, his words soft, laced with confusion and pain.

"You remind us of things we wish to forget," Leon adds, his fingers rising up my neck and pressing against my lips.

"You're a witch who's cast a spell over us," Konrad says, his hands smoothing over my ribcage, skirting the underside of my breasts.

"You don't belong here," Jakub continues, running his lips over my birthmark, burying his face in my hair.

Leon pushes his fingers inside my mouth. "You fuck with our heads."

Konrad crouches before me and slides his hands over my lower belly. "You make us wish for things we cannot have...."

I take shallow breaths, afraid of them.

Afraid of how I *feel* around them; both terrified for my life and more alive than I've ever felt before. I'm a quivering mess of emotions as they continue to touch me softly, kiss me gently, stroke me languidly.

They soothe me with their apology.

Calm me with their touch.

Break me with their sorrow.

Scar me with their darkness.

And just for a moment I'm the centre of their universe; a beating, fleshy heart.

Alive, unharmed, cared for, *revered.*

Until I'm not.

"You're a danger to everything we've built here," Jakub says, stepping away abruptly. It's only then I notice a cut over his eyebrow, it trickles with blood. "You've made us question our loyalty to one another."

Konrad bites my hip bone, standing suddenly, backing up. He too has a bruise forming on his cheek. "You're our enemy's sister."

"You're my mirror," Leon accuses, his lip split and bleeding as he moves to stand in front of me.

I see my reflection in his eyes. I see my fear, but also something else... *sadness*. I hurt for them, for me, for us. Leon searches my face, watching me closely as he presses his lips against mine in a kiss so tender that I can almost feel it. Almost.

My skin covers in goosebumps. My back prickles in warning. My heart batters against my ribcage wanting out. My soul cries for help, for mercy.

"We can't allow you to live," Jakub says. Cold, hard, unflinching.

"Time's up, Nought," Leon whispers against my lips.

Then he wraps his hands around my throat, finishing what he started all those years ago.

THE END, *for now*...

TO CONTINUE ON...

The Masks and The Dancer,
book two of Their Obsession is currently on pre-order.
You can grab your copy here!
https://books2read.com/TheirObsession2

If you enjoyed this book and want to find out more about this world and all the characters in it, might I suggest you check out my Academy of Stardom series where you will find out the back story behind why The Masks kidnapped Christy.

Keep scrolling for a sneak preview of **Freestyle** *book one in the* **Academy of Stardom** *series.*

SNEAK PEEK

Keep scrolling for a sneak preview of **Freestyle** *book one in the* **Academy of Stardom** *series.*

PROLOGUE

ZAYN

We're the Breakers.
We're friends. A crew. A fucking team.
Me, York, Xeno, Dax.
Inseparable.
We all loved the same girl.
See a Penny, pick it up, all day long you'll have good luck.
She was ours. Our Pen. Our shiny gold coin, and aside from dance, the only other bright thing in the pile of stinking shit that was our lives.
She was our first, our last, our everything.
Not anymore.
It's been three years. Three years since we've seen her, talked to her, laughed with her, danced with her, fucking touched her.
Now we're back.
Forgiveness is a luxury we can't afford.
Too much has happened.
She believes we betrayed *her*. The truth is it was Pen who betrayed *us*.

We can't let that go.
We won't.

CHAPTER 1

Present Day

"I can do this. I can do this. I *can* fucking do this," I repeat under my breath, over and over again as I enter the main lobby of the Academy.

The air is thick with nervous excitement as I stand in the long queue leading to the harassed looking receptionist. Around me chatter and laughter lifts into the air and floats up high into the glass domed roof. There are girls in leotards and expensive dance gear talking in groups with boys who are just as well turned out. They all look like they've walked out of an Abercrombie and Fitch ad, but I refuse to feel inferior. Just because they look the part doesn't mean they can actually dance. I glance down at my beat-up Nike trainers, baggy sweatpants, and thin black t-shirt that I've tied up around my waist and blow out a steady breath.

You can do this, Pen.

A group to my left starts laughing loudly and my body flushes with heat under their scrutiny.

"I didn't realise the academy was opening the doors to the local chavs," one particular snooty bitch remarks. I meet her disgusted gaze with a steely one of my own.

"Chav?" I bark out a laugh. "*Bitch*, I'm a street kid and we learnt from a young age that words have zero power. My fists, however, *they* pack a punch," I retort through a gritted smile. Her pretty mouth drops open and her cheeks flush a crimson red. I don't suppose she expected me to respond.

Well, fuck her.

In my world, bitches get stitches. She's lucky I'm here to make a good impression or her pretty white teeth would be scattered across the parquet flooring by now. I refuse to let anyone make me feel small. I deserve to be here. This is my last chance to get a dance scholarship. It's a one-year, intensive course that should I be lucky enough to win, would open more doors for me than hoping to get spotted dancing at nightclubs. I'm twenty and fully aware that the older I get the harder it will be for me to have a career in dance.

"Ignore her, she's an arsehole," the girl in front says as she turns to face me. She gives me a lopsided smile then swipes a strand of curly, orange hair off her face before holding her hand out for me to shake. I look at it hovering between us. "I'm Clancy," she explains.

"Clancy?"

"That's right, it means *red-headed warrior*."

"Because of the hair?" I ask, ignoring her hand, which she drops back to her side.

"No, because my mum once loved the Clancy Brothers…"

"Who the fuck are the Clancy Brothers?"

She snorts with laughter, and shakes her head. "Never mind. *Yes*, because of the hair."

"Got it," I note.

"Aren't you going to tell me your name?" She cocks her head and gives me an amused look, not put off by my scowl.

"I'm Pen," I answer after too long a silence.

"Nice to meet you, Pen. Is this a call-back or your first audition?"

"My first audition."

"Me too." She glances across the room to the stuck-up, haughty cow who dared to belittle me, and pulls a face. "That's Tiffany. First class bitch of epic proportions."

"You know her?" I ask as we move forward, the queue slowly moving up. I'm eight places from the front and getting more and more nervous with every passing minute, though I do a good job of hiding it. I just want to grab my registration documents and get to the audition.

"Know her? Yeah, I know her. That's my sister. She's auditioning here today as well. Specializes in ballet, tap *and* modern," Clancy explains, puffing out a breath and rolling her eyes for good measure.

"She's your *sister*?" I look between them both. They're nothing alike. In fact they're complete opposites. Clancy is petite like me, with pale skin and bright red, curly hair, freckles, and pale green eyes. Pretty. Quirky. Tiffany, however, is classically beautiful, modelesque. She's tall, slim, with dark hair and olive skin. She's got no tits to speak of, but is beautiful in a cat-like way. Though I'm betting she'd sooner scratch your eyes out than rub against your leg, and has the attitude that only the privileged carry around with them like an expensive Louis Vuitton bag. You know the kind of people I'm talking about, right? The ones that shop at Fortnum and Mason, who drive the latest Audi, wear Givenchy and drip with jewels. Money keeps people like Tiffany on a pedestal, except for days like today, when raw talent counts for something and money can't always buy happiness or a future in dance. Well, that's what I tell myself anyway.

"That bitch is your sister?" I repeat, trying to correlate the two.

"My *step*sister," Clancy clarifies.

I pull a face. "Shit outta luck there. What a piece of work."

"Don't worry, we hate each other. You can call her all the names you like. I really don't care. She's made my life hell for the last five years since her mum married my dad. You're currently looking at Cinder-fucking-rella. I kid you not, she more than makes up for the lack of a second ugly stepsister, the least she deserves is a bit of her own medicine."

"Fuck, that sucks."

"Yeah, it really, *really* does." Clancy grins and I give her a begrudging smile. She seems alright and nowhere near as stuck up as her catty stepsister.

"Is she already a student?" I ask.

"No, she's auditioning as well today for a scholarship."

"A scholarship?" I scrunch up my nose. "Then why is Tiffany acting like she's one of the rich kids that go here."

"Because she *was* a rich kid before her mum left her dad and married mine for love. Her dad was an abusive twat and cut them off in spite, so Tiffany has to rely on my father to support her. We're not poor, but he can't afford the fees for the two of us. So here we are."

I nod, making a mental note. There's nothing worse than a stuck-up posh nob than an ex stuck-up posh nob pretending they're still rich. We fall back into silence mainly because I'm not great at making friends. Actually, that's not strictly true. Once upon a time I made four best friends, but then it all went to shit.

Pushing thoughts of the *Breakers* firmly out of my head, I focus on the receptionist in front of me now that I've finally reached the front of the queue. Out of the corner of my eye I see Clancy hovering by the end of the desk. She's chewing on a nail and when I glance at her she gives me a rueful smile.

"Thought I'd wait for you," she shrugs, unperturbed by my lack of social skills and standoffishness.

"Whatever you want," I mutter.

"Name," the woman behind the desk snaps, raising her perfectly plucked eyebrows.

"Pen Scott."

"Pen Scott?" the woman repeats, running her finger over the long list in front of her. She looks up at me with her murky brown eyes. "Not on the list. Move aside," she snaps.

"Wait, what?!" I look at her in shock whilst the boy who's standing behind me tries to elbow me out of the way. "Back the fuck off!" I growl at him under my breath before addressing the receptionist once more. "I received an invitation to audition. Check again."

"Listen, you're not on the list. If you're not on the list there's no audition, got it?"

"Got it?" the boy repeats, staring down his nose at me and giving me the same shitty look as everyone else in this goddamn place. Everyone bar Clancy, who's currently looking at me with pity.

"This is bullshit. I've got a letter of invitation! Here," I growl, pulling out the crumpled audition letter and slamming it on the counter.

The receptionist sighs, taking it from me. "So you do. But you're not on the list and I have very strict instructions from the principal not to let anyone audition unless they're on the list..."

I'm close to throwing a fit right here in the middle of the prestigious Stardom Academy atrium when Clancy steps up beside me and rests her hand on my arm.

"There must be a clerical error. Pen has the letter of invitation to audition. I'm sure Madam Tuillard would hate it if a potential student was turned away because someone hadn't done their job properly."

Clancy gives my arm a squeeze and I get the feeling she's willing me not to go apeshit. I take a deep breath and in the calmest voice possible, ask the receptionist to check again.

She looks down her list of names one last time. "Oh, wait," she eventually says, "There's a Penelope *Sott* right here on the list..."

"That's it. Must've been a typo." Clancy smiles sweetly at the receptionist who nods her head and gives me a tight smile.

"Yes, must be. Studio 14, second floor, third door on the right." With that she dismisses us both without an apology. Fucking old hag.

～

"You're all here today to audition for a scholarship at Stardom Academy. We have just thirty places open and over two hundred dancers auditioning today. You lucky few have myself and my business partner as judges. Make this count, because another opportunity like this won't come around again," a tall, elegant looking woman announces to the room. There must be about thirty dancers in here, though I'm not paying much attention to them, honestly. I need to focus.

"Who's that?" I ask under my breath.

"You're kidding, right?"

I pull a face. "Should I know her?"

Clancy shakes her head, eyeing the graceful ballerina who is currently talking to a guy who looks like a cross between Ne-Yo and Usher. He's hot and vaguely familiar, though I can't seem to place why. The pair together are polar opposites. Elegance and grace versus edgy and street. I like that.

"She's Madame Tuillard, founder of the academy and the principal."

"I thought Madame Tuillard was ancient?"

"Nope, not exactly ancient, she's forty. Set this place up five years ago. She was a prima ballerina for some of the most famous ballet companies in the world. Danced with the greatest. Have you ever heard of Luka Petrin, he stopped dancing when his wife committed suicide? Rumour has it that she killed herself because he was such a manwhore. Madame Tuillard danced with him too, perhaps they shagged…"

"Awesome," I cut in, not particularly interested in ballet and even less so in some famous dancers' sex lives. Don't get me wrong, I do appreciate ballet and its place in the world of dance, but it's just so… *controlled*. Every step has to be perfectly executed. A ballet dancer has to have perfect toes, perfect hands, perfect legs, perfect posture, perfect face, perfect body, perfect *everything*.

Perfect, perfect, perfect.

I like to move my body in a different way. I like the imperfection of hip-hop, of break dance, even contemporary allows for it. I like the freedom those dances allow me, and the fact I can improvise in those dances without pissing off someone like Madame Tuillard who epitomises perfection with her willowy figure and coiffed hair. I like the way I can express myself through those dances.

"And the guy?"

"Ah, that's Duncan Neath, or D-Neath to the dance world at large."

"*He's* D-Neath? Fuck!" I glance back over at the guy and a thread of nervous energy lashes through my stomach. That explains why he's vaguely familiar. I can't believe I'm about to audition in front of *the* D-Neath.

"You've heard of him then?"

"Heard of him? He's a bit of a legend where I come from. He grew up not far from where I live. The guy's known in all the illegal underground dance clubs. Believe me, his reputation precedes him, and it isn't all about dance either."

"So I've heard…"

"You have?"

"Yup. My dad's a lawyer in a big law firm in London. They represented him. Got his sentence down from fourteen years to just five for drug racketeering."

"How come he's here then?"

"He was released a year ago. Apparently they're fucking…" Clancy explains, her eyes widening with glee as she looks between D-Neath and Tuillard.

"Shut-up! Those two?"

"Opposites attract and all that…" Clancy's voice trails off as Madame Tuillard coughs, her pretty grey eyes falling on us both. She arches a brow and we both shift uncomfortably under her stare.

"Let's get started, shall we?" she says, glaring down her nose at both of us.

Nervous energy ripples beneath my skin as she picks up a clipboard and runs her fingers over the list of names before her. Around us, the chatter dies down and everyone holds a collective breath as they wait to be called.

"First up is *Zayn Bernard*," she says, looking up from her clipboard and towards the back of the studio.

"What the *fuck*?" I whisper-shout, my whole body going rigid. Next to me Clancy flinches, my abject horror startling her.

No.

Fucking.

Way.

"What is it?" she hisses, but I can't answer her. All I can do is shift my gaze to where Madame Tuillard is staring.

"Why? How?" I grind out, my mouth drying up as I watch the boy I once loved unfurling from his spot in the furthest corner of the room. I hadn't noticed him when I entered, too distracted with my residual anger at the receptionist and that stuck up bitch Tiffany, but by the look on his face, he sure as fuck noticed me. He's scowling, a sneer pulling up his lip as he stares directly at me and unzips his black hoodie. Shaking it off, it falls to the studio floor at his feet, and all I can do is stare open-mouthed at his muscled physique and tight black t-shirt. Both his arms are covered in multicoloured tattoos that work their way up from the crook of his elbows to his shoulders, disappearing beneath the material. The last time I'd seen him he didn't have any tattoos. None. He wasn't as broad or as tall either. He was a boy on the cusp of manhood. All four of them were.

Zayn, Xeno, Dax and York were my Breakers and I was their girl.

Was being the operative word.

Now Zayn's a man. A man who's looking at me like I'm an enemy, not a long-lost friend.

A shiver tracks down my spine as my stomach curdles with anxiety and long held pain.

"Do you know him?" Clancy presses.

Out of the corner of my eye, I can see her check him out. In fact, every damn female in the room is unable to take their eyes off him, Madame Tuillard included. He knows it too. He's always had this kind of magnetism, and he oozes confidence. I'd admired that once. Now I can barely look at him without wanting to sprint from the studio and throw away my chance of a future in dance. It takes every ounce of strength to remain seated.

"Yeah. We've met before," I say vaguely, not willing to elaborate further. I can't. It hurts too much. Looking at him hurts. His hair is the same shade of dark brown, his eyes still a deep black and his mouth just as plump and as kissable as it was three years ago when I last saw him and the others...

Stop it.

"He's *hot*," she states, matter-of-factly. "But can he *dance?*"

"He can dance," I confirm with a whisper, wrapping my arms around my legs and hugging myself tightly as I watch him move out into the empty space. "He can most definitely dance…"

As if he heard me, Zayn meets my gaze and winks, reminding me of the first time we met six years ago. Except this time his wink isn't followed by a warm smile and the possibility of friendship.

Now there's nothing but hate in his eyes.

AUTHOR NOTE

Well phew, can I take a breath now?

I'm telling you, The Masks have been my single most difficult characters to write so far. Their story was always going to be dark. I knew it the moment they were mentioned back in Lyrical, book two of the Academy of Stardom series. Way back then they begged for my attention, but I couldn't give them what they needed until I'd finished writing that series and even though The Dancer and The Masks was one of the toughest books I've ever written, I'm so glad that I persevered.

As you might have guessed, this is a dark romance. It's been a while since I've been able to indulge the darker side of my writing, and this book really took me through a whole gamut of emotions. I'm not going to lie, some scenes were hard for me to write, but none were written just to be provocative. Every scene, every dark act by The Masks needed to be told in order to really unveil who they are. I don't write those kinds of scenes lightly and I always knew that Christy wouldn't be the type of character to accept her fate or just roll over.

She was always going to fight back, she was always going to take ownership of what was happening to her and she was never going to let

AUTHOR NOTE

The Masks forget that their behaviour was unacceptable. That was really important to me as a writer and a woman. I think she is a remarkable character.

In book two, ***The Masks and The Dancer*** I will be delving even deeper into their relationship, it will be just as twisted, just as dark and you will be seeing some familiar faces (Grim and Beast and a couple of misfits *nudge, nudge, wink, wink) and further introduced to some characters that I know many of you can't wait to read about... The Deana-Dhe *cough, cough. It will also be cathartic. There will be redemption, healing and of course, eventually, a hard won HEA.

∼

If this is the first book you've read by me, then you're in luck! All of my contemporary books so far are set in the same world and characters often cross over from one series to the next. If you want to get lost in the world of Bea Paige, here is my recommended reading order:

The Brothers Freed trilogy - start with Avalanche of Desire
Academy of Misfits trilogy - start with Delinquent
Beyond The Horizon standalone
Academy of Stardom series - start with Freestyle
Finding Their Muse series - start with Steps
The Dancer and The Masks duet

Before I go, I'd like to thank my beta readers, Janet, Gina, Jennifer, Lisa and of course, last but by no means least, my gorgeous PA and friend Courtney. You ladies rock! Without your unwavering support I wouldn't be able to do this. Thank you. Thank you. Thank you.

Special thanks to Katie Friend for coming up with The Menagerie! It was absolutely perfect.

Of course without you, dear reader, none of this would be possible. I get to write every day bringing these worlds and characters to life because you continue to have faith in me and read my book babies. I am eternally grateful! Thank you for picking up my books and for giving this indie author a chance.

Lastly, I hope you enjoyed this book and trust me to give you all a satisfying happy ending when The Masks and The Dancer releases in a few months time. Until then, make sure you come on over to my Facebook Group, Queen Bea's Hive, to keep up with new releases, teasers, book news and more.

Much love, Bea Paige.

ABOUT BEA PAIGE

Bea Paige lives a very secretive life in London… She likes red wine and Haribo sweets (preferably together) and occasionally swings around poles when the mood takes her.

Bea loves to write about love and all the different facets of such a powerful emotion. When she's not writing about love and passion, you'll find her reading about it and ugly crying.

Bea is always writing, and new ideas seem to appear at the most unlikely time, like in the shower or when driving her car.

She has lots more books planned,
so be sure to subscribe to her newsletter:
beapaige.co.uk/newsletter-sign-up

Check Be a out on TikTok:
https://www.tiktok.com/@beapaigeauthor

facebook.com/BeaPaigeAuthor
instagram.com/beapaigeauthor
pinterest.com/beapaigeauthor
bookbub.com/authors/bea-paige

ALSO BY BEA PAIGE

THEIR OBSESSION DUET

The Dancer and The Masks

The Masks and The Dancer

ACADEMY OF STARDOM

(ACADEMY REVERSE HAREM ROMANCE)

#1 Freestyle

#2 Lyrical

#3 Breakers

#4 Finale

ACADEMY OF MISFITS

(ACADEMY REVERSE HAREM ROMANCE)

#1 Delinquent

#2 Reject

#3 Family

FINDING THEIR MUSE

(DARK CONTEMPORARY ROMANCE / REVERSE HAREM)

#1 Steps

#2 Strokes

#3 Strings

#4 Symphony

#5 Finding Their Muse boxset

THE BROTHERS FREED SERIES

(CONTEMPORARY ROMANCE / REVERSE HAREM)

#1 Avalanche of Desire

#2 Storm of Seduction

#3 Dawn of Love

#4 Brothers Freed Boxset

CONTEMPORARY STANDALONES

Beyond the Horizon

THE INFERNAL DESCENT TRILOGY

(CO-WRITTEN WITH SKYE MACKINNON)

#1 Hell's Calling

#2 Hell's Weeping

#3 Hell's Burning

#4 Infernal Descent boxset

Printed in Great Britain
by Amazon